# Some Sunday

## MARGARET
## JOHNSON-HODGE

KENSINGTON PUBLISHING CORP.

DAFINA BOOKS are published by

Kensington Publishing Corp.
850 Third Avenue
New York, NY 10022

ISBN 1-57566-916-1

This book is dedicated to Elizabeth Ray Goodrow,
the smartest woman I know.

# *Acknowledgments*

I said I wasn't going to do this anymore. I said I wasn't going to put another acknowledgment into another book of mine, but with so many people who have been so wonderful to me, there is no way I can not *not* thank them, so here goes:

First, I have to give all praises to the Creator of All Things, whose love is endless, blessings have been countless, and lessons given to me have shown me all of my strengths. *Is God good?* All the time and through Him, all things are possible. I want to continue to thank my husband, Terence A. Hodge, for your never-ending support and love. Thank you for believing in me, for loving me, and still making me laugh. Do you know how much I love you? Like that Stevie Wonder song—it's for "Always."

I want to say thank you to my mother, Alma H. Johnson, for loving me strong and raising me right. Mom, you were the first to own my heart, a first love that is still going strong.

I want to give a big o' hug to my writerbrotherfriend Timmothy McCann. Timm, your kindness, wisdom, generosity, and caring heart has made so many writing blue days so much brighter that I couldn't count them even if I wanted to. You are my bud, for sure, and an incredible writer to boot.

I want to thank my writersisterfriends Brenda Connor-Bey and Carmen Green. I love you both deeply. Bren, Carm, you are the wind beneath my wings, for real.

I want to give a heartfelt thanks to my agent, Claudia Menza. Claudia, you believed in me, shared my vision, and you made it happen.

And last, but not least, I want to thank my editor, Karen Thomas, who took my hand and led me from the forest so that I could see *all* the trees.

May God Bless and keep you all.

Some Sunday, I'm going to awake and the
world's going to be all right again . . .

# Chapter 1

The house on 112th Avenue in the middle of Hollis, Queens, New York, was not particularly grand, new, or specific. It mirrored the one before it, the one after it, and the dozen across the street. Tight and studious, it held the same three bedrooms, one bath, two stories with a basement; the same shingles that adorned it in the fifties were still going strong in 1994.

To a passer by it was just a speck in the landscape of closely placed homes and century-old oaks. But to the woman who dwelled inside it, it was a refuge, which these days she had no desire to leave.

Life wasn't fair and it had been especially unfair to Sandy Hutchinson Burton, but it did go on. It went on despite the death of her husband. Went on even though all she wanted was for it to stop. Life went on even though it had denied her much and with that continuum came responsibilities, like the one she was facing now.

Sandy thought about not going.

She found herself on the verge of just saying no. She didn't want to get up, get dressed, take the short drive less than two miles away, but life no longer gave her that option.

Every six months like clockwork, Sandy had to be tested for the various strains of HIV. Her dead husband Adrian had made it so. He had died of it and she had to make certain she was free of it, the deadly disease appearing six weeks before their wedding day.

On September 21, they had said I do. Less than two months later he was dead and buried. Death of a spouse was what any married couple eventually faced, but its arrival came too soon.

At thirty-four Sandy Hutchinson had found the love of her life; at thirty-six that love was gone. There was a cheating in that deliverance, a denial as detrimental as a land mine. It had obliterated everything important to her, all that she held dear. In the aftermath she struggled to make a way for herself; rebuild a new life.

Adrian had been married to Gennifer before he met Sandy. Infidelity on Gennifer's part had caused them to separate. They got back together and decided to make a fresh start. But when a standard medical test revealed that Gennifer was HIV positive, their separation became final.

Out of that relation for two years when he met Sandy, Adrian had been testing negative all along. The love between them flourished into plans for a wedding, and by the time he tested positive, Sandy was too deep in love to walk away.

Adrian had elevated her as a woman, made all her desires come true. He had wiped away years of self-doubt and placed no one above her. Through the good times and the bad, his love remained steadfast and true. A yin to her yang, leaving him was an option she could not use.

People often wondered how Sandy had stayed with him. Her answer was both simple and profound: Adrian had been a dream come true, the one she had wanted forever, and there was no way she could walk away from that.

The handshake was warm and firm. The crinkle about the brown eyes, kind and open. "You've been okay, Mrs. Burton?"

"Been okay, Doctor."

He indicated the chair. She took a seat.

"Are you taking those vitamins I suggested?" he asked as he wrapped the pressure cuff around her forearm. Sandy nodded, winced as the band filled, constricting her blood flow.

"Pressure's good," Dr. Mathias said, reaching for a tongue depressor. "Say ahh." He looked into her mouth, made notes on her chart, then continued his exam, probing the glands of her throat with gentleness.

Dr. Mathias retrieved a pair of rubber gloves, tied a piece of white tubing around Sandy's forearm, and ran an alcohol swab along the crook. "Deep breath," he warned, sliding the needle in so easy Sandy didn't even feel a pinch.

"We'll know in a few days," he said softly, the concern in his voice, full. But if Dr. Mathias was worried, Sandy was not. God had plans for her. It wasn't her time to go. If she knew nothing else, she knew this much: she'd be earthbound for a while.

Get with it.

Sandy was trying but it was hard. She wasn't up to company but her friends were on their way. She knew what they wanted—for her to find that new day. But she wasn't up to the challenge and could not control her sorrow.

She'd known it, and owned for so long now, it was a familiar comfort. Anesthetically balming, she was in need of it. It numbed her, allowing the next second of her life to go on.

Sandy had looked after a dying husband when neither her love nor all the medicine in the world could save him. She had bathed him, cooked for him, cleaned up his vomit and feces, and never once stopped loving him. She had watched his once muscular body degenerate to skin and bones and the beautiful butterscotch skin turn black and moldy with sores.

The cloak of sorrow suited her. It was her reprieve and she just wanted to be left alone. She did not want to entertain, pretend she was on her way to recovery, but the ringing doorbell dismantled the option. Her friends had arrived.

With a smile too brittle to be real, Sandy opened her door. Janice was leading the pack, Britney and her baby in the middle, with Martha bringing up the rear. These had been her allies during the hard times, her close friends who had rallied around her in force. They loved her, cared about her, but Sandy just wanted them to go away.

"Hey," Janice said carefully, opening her arms wide.

"Hey yourself," Sandy answered quickly, returning the hug. Janice was not the brightest of the four women, but there was no doubt she was the most beautiful. A pretty shade of brown, soft short glossy curls and legs to die for, Janice won the beauty contest hands down.

But beauty did not equal wisdom and Sandy often thought Janice had gotten too much of one and not enough of another. When Janice loved, she loved hard, deep, and often for the wrong reason. It wasn't until she got together with Sandy's brother Clifford that she reached a true balance of giving love and receiving it.

The two of them had been best friends since high school, and the familiarity often bred contempt. A time had come where their friendship had been nearly done in over a man that Janice had chosen but was no good for her. A major rift, it had been healed through Martha's intervention. Water under the bridge now, the two women were going strong.

Janice headed for the living room, Britney coming up behind her. Voted the one less likely to find that happily ever after, Britney had surprised everyone and done just that. What had once been a lonely, single, timid, overweight, financially challenged woman had blossomed into a stay at home mom with a husband who worshipped her and a five bedroom, two bath home to prove it.

She had had a baby a few months ago, completing the picture. It was the baby that drew Sandy's attention as she reached out and took up Bereace, juggling her a few times to test the baby's weight. "My goodness, Bereace, what have you been eating?" Her eyes found Britney. "What you been feeding this child?"

"She doesn't eat that much, believe it or not. Probably genetics. You know me and Maurice ain't little." It was a statement that was true, one Sandy saw for herself as Britney made her way into the living room. Carmel brown, with a mane of thick long hair, before Sandy was the wider-than-wide buttocks and the round robust hips, trademarks Britney always owned.

"How's it going, Sandy?" Martha asked, pulling the door closed behind her. The bright red wool jacket set off Martha's rich mocha hue, giving additional sophistication to her short pixie hairstyle and inquisitive dark eyes. The tallest of the group, Martha looked fashion perfect in black denim jeans and the red turtleneck that matched shade for shade the sanguine in her jacket. As an assistant district attorney, she considered wardrobe to be an important part of her life.

"Red," Sandy said, touching the edge of Martha's sleeve.

"It's a cloudy day," Martha offered. "Figured I brighten things up."

They were all different women, bringing something special to the well of friendship. Martha was the wisest, Janice the cutest, Britney the friendliest, and Sandy, in that moment, the most sorrowful. "I bought strawberry shortcake," she called out, making her way toward her living room. "And Chinese food. Figured we could use something different."

No one disagreed.

If losing a husband had been hard, witnessing a good friend's sorrow was just as brutal. It had taken months just to get Sandy to agree to the get-together. During that time each woman had borne the yoke of her pain, fitting squarely upon their shoulders. They were all looking forward to different times, better times, the defining moment that said Sandy would heal. And as always, they carried the hope that today would bring forth that revelation.

They sat around the living room, munching on spring rolls, pu pu sticks, and fried dumplings, Bereace on the floor before them, chewing on a brightly colored teething ring.

"She's cutting teeth already?" Sandy asked, dumbstruck by the swiftness of Britney's baby's growth.

"Isn't that something? Seemed like just yesterday I was having her, now here she is cutting teeth."

Martha cut her eyes at Britney. "Only you would go into labor on Sandy's wedding day."

"It wasn't like I had a choice," Britney shot back. "Babies come when they're ready."

"One thing I regret," Sandy offered, her voice fragile under the weight of her words.

"What's that?" Martha asked, already knowing.

"Not having his baby."

These were the moments that were risky—a word, a phrase could send Sandy into the deepest of depressions. Every day life became daunting, full of reminders of what would never be. Her friends tried to tread carefully, but there were always pitfalls.

"You're young, Sandy, you still have time," Janice offered softly.

Yes, time was a commodity she still owned. But there was no comfort in that predicament, nothing in it that could undo the pain. *I won't cry,* eyes blinking, lassoing loose tears. *I won't,* she insisted to herself, almost there, sadness nearly tamed, when Martha's voice came, disturbing her determination.

"Let it go, Sandy. Don't try and hold it back. Just let it go."

A sob flew from her lips like brittle confetti, falling on her friends with impact.

Janice was up in a flash, but Martha warned her back. "Leave her . . . she'll be okay."

They all looked away, offering as much privacy as their close contact could allow, checking fingernails, the walls, as Sandy let loose her sorrow. But even through the pain she could feel their hearts, ethereal and warm.

It had been a while since she had done this, broken down without restraint, but the release was sweet, sweeter with each new tear. Sadness flowed fully, let up a bit. Shifted to a lessening, then faded away. Sandy sniffled, took up a napkin. Blew her nose noisily. Wiped the dampness about her face.

With wet eyes she looked around the room, settled on Martha. Sandy never thought the day would arrive when she would feel so connected to her, Martha's attitude in both speech and deed, abrupt and brash. But Martha had come and emotionally rescued her when she herself didn't even know she needed saving. For that Sandy was forever grateful.

"Thank you, thank you for understanding."

Martha smiled. "That's what we're here for, Sandy."

Janice looked at her gently. "We know how hard it is."

Britney flipped her wrist. "Oh, girl, tears are a good thing."

"One day I'm going to be okay," Sandy said with a careful smile. "Just don't know when."

"It's only been four months," Martha warned. "None of us are expecting miracles. We know what you went through, looking after Adrian like you did. It takes time."

Time, that word again. Time, a cornucopia of all that Sandy didn't want, needed. Her life back, that's what she really desired, the life she had had with Adrian, but that was no longer possible. *Will such a life ever be?* Sandy wondered as Janice moved them beyond the moment.

"Hey, did anybody catch that movie on HBO the other night?"

\* \* \*

Like solitude, sleep had also become a refuge. Monday through Friday Sandy arose bright and early, but weekends caught her sleeping as late as her body could stand. She would rise, dehydrated and near punch drunk, hours coming and going before her body could correct itself.

But the black void, where nothing existed—not her pain, nor her sorrow, nor Adrian's absence—was appealing. It demanded nothing of her and in it she found a true respite. The Sunday after her friends' visit was no different.

Sandy woke that next afternoon, fuzzy headed and a bit numb. She lay there, staring at the ceiling, mindful of the tight clean cool space beside her. She reached her hand out, ran fingers along the surface, longing for that warm body to fill it.

She wanted more than her own presence to occupy the three-bedroom, one-bathroom house. Missed the completeness that a simple late-night conversation could bring. Sandy would have given a king's ransom just to have Adrian's leg block access to the middle of the bed just one more time; witness his smiling face across from her at the kitchen table.

She was tired of meals becoming leftovers she didn't want to eat, the dirty clothes hamper that took too long to fill. She was in need of helping hands to bring groceries from the car. Wanted just once to dash to the bathroom and find it occupied.

It was these little things that drew life together, little things that made it complete, but she was cleaved in half, incapable of a healing. Locked away in a tiny cell, she couldn't find the key.

So she lay there, immobile, filled with longing. She would have gone on that way had not the doorbell rang. Forcing herself from her bed, she grabbed her robe and made her way down the steps, fingers moving across her uncombed hair.

She peeked out the windowpane, thought, *Not Adrian.* But in her eyes it could have been. Adrian's brother Winston looked every bit like him. Managing a smile, she let him in.

Winston never called, just showed up, and sometimes Sandy would turn him away.

There were moments when she was glad to see him, other times when she couldn't bear the sight. Being in his presence, it was difficult discerning him from her husband, and moments came when she became confused. They would be in the middle of a conversation and suddenly it would be Adrian before her, Sandy finding herself touching him in ways that went beyond appropriate.

She would pull back, mind her station. Tell herself a thousand times that it was not her husband, just the brother who looked like him. Now here he was before her again.

"Sleeping?" he asked, seeing the clutched robe, the wild hair.

"Resting," she offered, closing the door.

Before her was the same wavy dark brown hair, the caramel skin. Before her were the eyes like honey, the same expanse of lips. Winston's voice was Adrian's, the shape of fingers, duplicate too. Even the way he looked at her sometimes was a conjuring of the man she had loved with everything she owned. *Except he's dead.*

"How's your folks?" she found herself asking.

"Just fine."

"And Rachel?"

Winston nodded. "She's doing good . . . what about you, you doing okay?"

"As okay as I can be, I guess." She took a deep breath, remembered her state of dress. "I'm just going to run upstairs to put on some clothes."

Winston nodded. "Go ahead. I'll be here."

Sandy sat, lights off, the setting sun blazing full in the room about her. She sat in a sea of brilliant gold; Winston lost somewhere in the shadows.

She picked up her wine, took a sip. Her third glass, she was beyond counting.

In the corner, away from her, Winston watched. That she was beautiful had never been a question. That he was sitting witnessing it, his heart drinking her in with every beat, was.

He had been there awhile and the brilliant low sun was telling just how long. Winston never planned to stay long, but more and more he'd found his visits extending themselves. She had been through so much and he just wanted to ease her pain. He knew it would take some time for her to get through it and just wanted to help her get there.

He flipped his wrist, pushed the button on his watch, saw the hour, and tried to ready himself for departure. If coming unannounced like he did was hard, leaving her was always harder.

Being with Sandy gave him peace.

Sometimes they would sit so close he could see the fine hairs along her earlobes. Other times they were like they were now, he in one corner, she in another, it was always Sandy's choice.

"I'm still dreaming him." Her voice caught him off guard, the blaze of light about her blinding.

"Me too."

"Does he talk to you?"

"No."

"He does to me."

"What does he say?"

She shrugged, a careless gesture unsure of its importance. "That he loves me, always with me, that kind of thing."

"He does love you, Sandy."

But it was a love she could not touch.

Sometimes they would talk of Adrian and the sharing would be a comfort, but this time around it wasn't. Though Winston could not see it, he could feel the sadness that had come over her. Powerless to change it, he was in no mood to bear witness. "Better be on my way," he decided, standing. "Walk me to the door?"

If letting Winston in was sometimes hard, seeing him go was harder. Having him there made the empty spaces of her life less empty and a void would arrive the moment he left. But she was grateful that he had come and would not prevent him from leaving.

Sandy shivered as she stood in her foyer, the cold air sneaking its way around the windowsills and jam. She was reaching for the doorknob when his voice found her, surprising her with its directness, a real need to know.

"When was the last time you've been anywhere?"

She did not expect the question though she had felt it often. Life had been on hold from the moment Adrian had gotten sick. Was still stagnant now that he was dead. Sandy could not remember the last time she had been anywhere, but nowadays, it was just how her life was going.

"Can't even remember, Wint."

"How about next weekend?"

Her eyes moved to his, uncertain. "Next weekend?"

"Yeah. Get out the house. I think it's time, Sandy."

"For?"

His voice was gentle. "To start living again."

"I know that," and a part of her did, but the rules were changed. It was new shoes she was walking in and she wasn't certain of the fit. The next step toward betterment was due, but she couldn't place a bet on when.

"Well, now that you know, do something about it . . . Next Saturday, we'll get out and about."

"Next Saturday," she repeated as if he had just requested the moon.

"Yeah." He leaned over, kissed her forehead. "Next Saturday, out of this house. I'll see you then."

Winston left and she closed the door behind him, the idea of getting "out and about" unsettling. She would have to, she knew that, but the time didn't feel like now. It was still winter, and she hated cold weather. Perhaps in the spring.

She'd call him tomorrow, tell him that she changed her mind. Set some faraway date for the outing. But by the time Monday came, the idea was no longer so scary; not a yes, but the firm no had vanished.

By Wednesday, it felt like a plan. Friday she was gung ho. Saturday morning when Winston called telling her to "get up and get dressed" because he would be there in an hour, something inside her sparked.

It took a while to get a handle on it. A couple of seconds to determine all that it was. You hold on to what you need, let go of what you don't. What Sandy was feeling had left her long ago. Now it had returned.

Its name, anticipation.


Sandy slid into Winston's Camry, asking for the seventh time since he had arrived, "Where are we going?"

"Out," was all he would say.

"No, seriously, where are we going?"

"Out and about."

"I know we're going 'out' but it would be nice to know where."

"You bring your gloves?" Winston asked.

"Why?"

"Got some strolling to do, that's all."

"Like in walking?"

"Yeah, something like that."

"I left them home."

"You can use mine," Winston offered.

"What are you going to use?"

"Pockets," he answered, the Camry racing along the pot-holed parkway.

Sandy knew exactly where they were headed four blocks before they got there. Knew what sights she would see, the sounds she would witness, a part of her missing it.

The area of Flatbush and Nostrand Avenue in Brooklyn was a mecca for the transplanted Caribbean population who had settled in New York City and its surrounding boroughs. Offering island staples not available in the local Keyfood Supermarket or A&P, Flatbush and Nostrand was a magnet for people who called places like St. Lucia and Jamaica, West Indies, home.

Offering fresh meats, homeland spices, various fruits and vegetables, the area was a world unto itself, rich with the patois of a dozen Caribbean Islands. On Saturdays business was brisk, the atmosphere always lively and foot traffic always thick.

The first time Sandy had come had been with Adrian.

She had felt like she had stepped into a whole different world. She couldn't understand the various dialects, the sidewalks had been jam-packed, and it had been the first time she heard Adrian speak *that* way.

Until that moment Adrian had just been a gorgeous man she'd met who had parents who came from Trinidad. Until that moment Sandy had assumed he talked like she talked all the time. But when she heard the Trinidadian patois flow from his mouth, it was like she hadn't known him at all.

*"O'oh I be,"* he had told her, *"wedder I tawk like dis, or I talk like this."* Eventually Sandy came to realize who he was with determined how he spoke. With her, it was business as usual. Around his folks, his patois was like breathing—automatic. No doubt Winston would let loose too.

"I know where we're going . . . Flatbush . . . food shopping right?"

"Yeah," Winston answered, turning a left under the elevated train tracks. "Pick up a few things . . . figure the fresh air."

"Cold air," she tossed back. Outside the weather was near freezing.

"Cold, fresh, whatever. It will all do you some good."

"Since when does cold air do anybody good?"

"Fresh air. Cooped up in your house all the time, it's time for one good long clean breath."

"Oh yeah?" she asked with a raise of her brow.

"Oh yeah," he answered, closed lips taming his smile.

Parking was difficult.

Winston circled a five-block area five times before he found a legal place to put the Camry. Sandy stepped out of the car, the cold air finding every bit of exposed flesh she owned.

"You need the gloves," Winston decided, going into his glove compartment to retrieve a lumpy black leather pair. "They're kinda beat up, but they're lined."

Sandy took them, slipped them on, glad for the rabbit fur that engulfed her fingers. Too big, they were warm, and in that moment it was all she cared about. "Which way?"

"This way," nudging his head left. The two of them heading down the street.

They heard it before they saw it. Music, as forceful as a hurricane, barreling down on them. Two speakers, five feet tall, planted outside of a record store, were its source. Full of bass and lyrics Sandy could not understand, the music claimed her quick. She and Adrian used to always go dancing. Winston made it their first stop.

Together and apart they searched the bins of CDs, Sandy looking for nothing in particular, Winston in search of Beenie Man. "You ever listen to him?" he asked.

"Beenie Man?"

"Yeah. Ya eber hear him?"

And there it was, the switch, Winston moving into his accent *like breathing* she thought, unable to contain her smile. "I think."

"Me play it for you soon. Show ya what good music is." He headed for the register, Sandy behind him, noting the hat on top of the clerk's head. Knitted in red, green, and yellow acrylic, it was as tall as a stove piper. Sandy would bet a week's pay that there was a mountain of dreads beneath it.

CD bought, the two of them headed back out onto the street. The next stop was a fish market where Winston bought two whole blue fish. "Ya stuff dis, den ya bake it. Jus incredible," he told her.

Then it was on to the vegetable stand where he picked up bread fruit. "Ya make a kinda breakfast wit it." He selected plantains in both green and yellow. "Ya boil these green ones. Taste a little like potato."

It took a little while for Sandy to understand that Winston was schooling her; that he was continuing a tradition Adrian had started—educating her in the ways of Caribbean life. She asked a question of her own. "Cod fish. Why do they dry it with so much salt?"

"Preservative."

"But why go through all that fuss? Why not just get fresh cod?"

Winston laughed, head back, mouth open. Found her eyes as the laughter faded. "It's differant in da islands. Ya go fishing and den you got all dis fish. Ya wanta to keep some for later. For a long time we didn't have frigerator and ting. So we use what we got."

"Salt."

"Right."

The last item on his list was tamarind candy. "Ya eber try dis?" In truth Sandy hadn't. "Good good treat. Jus lubbed it as a kid." Items on the counter, Winston waited for his total, paid, and back on the streets they went.

An abstract memory filled her: spice, hot meat, flaky crust. Sandy began looking around, the strip familiar. She continued to search and found what she was looking for on the other side of Flatbush. "Over there," she insisted, taking his arm.

Drivers blew their horns at their middle-of-the-road crossing, but Sandy paid it no mind. She went up to the Plexiglas window, rapped twice.

"Two beef patties," she uttered. Turned toward Winston. "Ginger beer?"

He smiled, nodded, pleased, surprised.

"And a ginger beer." She found her money, paid, handed the pattie and the drink to Winston, took her change, her meat-filled pastry. "Careful it's hot," she warned, a smile wider than the harvest moon filling her.

"Well now, da Yankee don found new roots."

"No, I just know a good hot beef pattie when I see one." She slipped off the borrowed gloves and shoved them into her pocket.

Winston watched her take a bite, mouth opening against the intense heat, fingers waving across her mouth. Happy, joyful. He wondered if she knew.

                                    *   *   *

Groceries in the trunk, Sandy and Winston sat in the idling car finishing off the rest of the tamarind candy.

"What amazes me is the things people in the Caribbean came up with. Take this candy, for instance," she said, holding it aloft. "It's basically a fruit that's more seed than fruit and at first bite you'd never think it could be a candy, 'cause it's hot and kind of salty, but voilà, it's a candy."

More discoveries. She had had many with Adrian.

In that moment the thought of him didn't hurt so much. Sandy found she could put the pain in a box even if she couldn't close the lid. Suddenly she wasn't certain if that was a good thing or a bad. Wasn't certain if there was some required time she had to spend in limbo before she could reclaim her life; if the slight pleasure she was feeling from this outing was even due her.

"Ready?" Winston asked, sensing her receding joy.

She nodded, looked out of the window, the last bit of tamarind both bitter and sweet inside her mouth.

# Chapter 2

Once upon a time, music had been her ally, a soft companion in Sandy's downtime, giving her soul time to stretch, her mind a chance to lift the clutter. But it had been a while since she had indulged in that pleasure; months since she'd played more than the radio.

So much had been taken from her that she'd come to accept denial as the norm. In mourning, simple pleasures didn't fit into the niche, a large part of her unwilling to attempt them.

She had had her favorite songs, ones she would play over and over, but the one that made her most complete had been "Harpo's Blues."

Recorded in the seventies, Sandy had never heard of the song, or the singer, Phoebe Snow, until she'd met Adrian. He had played it on the ride home from their first date, and from that moment it became a part of her.

After his death, it was all she wanted to hear, but soon, like footprints, time faded the impression, making the lyrics less compelling, the melody less haunting until it became just another song she had loved too long and too hard. She fell out of favor with it.

But here she was, standing at her turntable, laying the needle to the vinyl, readying her soul for the first rift. Here Sandy stood, emotionally struggling with locks and chains of the past, trying to gain entry to a time long gone.

*"I wish I was a willow."*

Pain engulfed her. Her hand reached out and snatched the stylus. *Not now.* She wasn't certain when but knew it would not be soon. Still the need for music, for rhythm, beats, notes along the scale, remained.

She dropped down to the floor and began going through the albums. When that search yielded her nothing, she went through the CDs. Found one of Adrian's. Slipped it into the CD player.

Closed her eyes and began to dance to the reggae beat.

It was Adrian who she danced with. Adrian who she whined her hips for. Adrian who grinned mischievously at the way she moved for him.

Eyes closed, soul open, body loose, it was Adrian who urged her on. Adrian who kept her body moving in between the songs, Adrian who murmured, *Yes, das right. Dance, Sandy, dance.* But it was no one when she opened her eyes. No one as sweat gathered along her scalp, trickled down her spine, just the silence she had once come to long for and now felt like a void bent on suffocating.

It was a silence as flat and infinite as a sea of glass, absent of noise, movement. Life. Like gargoyles perched in the corners, it seemed to be waiting for her demise. Waiting for her to give up, give in. Draw the last breath.

Some part of her was ready. Ready to abandon the life that had shattered into a thousand pieces. Ready to join Adrian, her sweet sweet Adrian.

She tightened her lips, refused another breath. Her vision blurred. Her heart pitted out an irregular rhythm. Sandy closed her eyes, waited for death to come, a sweet peace finding her as she willed death to her door.

It had been a secret wish, a surefire end to her misery. She had never dared it, never felt powerful enough to induce it, but in that moment she felt she could. No more pain. No more sorrow, just her and Adrian together for an eternity.

Her heart skipped a beat, her lungs began to burn. The world around her grew fuzzy as she struggled to bring an end to her being. But survival was an instinctive thing and her body rebelled. The breath she'd held released itself, lips parting, clamoring for air.

Tears rolled down her face. The walls pressed in on her. She looked about her, knowing she was on the brink of madness, that she could not stay there, had to get out.

Sandy grabbed her jacket, her keys and moved through the front door. Past seven in the evening, the sky was dark and the air was cold. But it was a coldness she couldn't feel, a darkness that held no impact. She felt nothing, was nothing as she moved along 112th Avenue, a soul lost in limbo, autonomous and without direction.

By the time she reached Farmers Boulevard, her head felt clearer. She became aware of the chill around her fingers, the exposed flesh of her neck. Huddling down into the jacket, her hands sought the warmth of the flannel-lined pockets, the numbness that had found her, fading away.

She came back to herself, chilled by the impossible feat she had tried to commit. Did she really think she could stop her life; that she had the power to die at will? In the aftermath the truth was as glaring as the streetlights above her. She could not go on like this.

But forward wasn't a clear path. There was nothing on her horizon, not a sign post, a road map, or even a speck of graveled road. It was as blank as a blackboard scrubbed clean. Sandy scanned the familiar main strip, in search of guidance, the next step.

A neon-lit Budweiser Beer sign caught her attention. An ad—six generic cans of soda for a dollar—became a lure. Sandy entered the brightly lit grocery store, no specific want in mind. Gazing upon the food stuffs stacked floor to ceiling, it felt all brand new.

"You need something?" the man behind the counter asked.

Yes, but she wasn't certain what. A nervous laugh left her. "Trying to decide," eyes continuing their search. The candy bars piled high and pushed against the wall of Plexiglas caught her attention. "I'll have a Baby Ruth."

Sandy was unwrapping it by the time the store door closed behind her. Took fast bites as she waited to cross the street. It had all but vanished by the time she'd reached 112th Avenue, her tongue devouring the chocolate smears clinging to her fingers.

Just confection and nuts, it appeased a hunger, one she didn't even know she owned. Something was moving through her, about her, urging her forward. Sandy didn't question or struggle, just went with the flow.

\* \* \*

Good sleep found her.

Not because she was exhausted, or was going through the weariness that had no name, but an uplifting had nestled into her soul, spreading its warmth through bone and marrow, soothing the body that had been desensitized for too long.

It took a moment for Sandy to understand that this morning was different, a moment to recognize how much better she felt. She found herself examining how life used to be, things that she used to enjoy. Recalled her solo act the evening before and wanted to nourish that part of her.

Reggae, clubbing, and all the vague boundaries in between had been a major part of her life at one time.

She wanted to baptize her soul in the music, give birth to a different self through dance. It was something she was capable of doing, well within her power. All she needed was someone to go with.

She called Winston.

"Hi, it's me. Do you know that club in Queens Village, Bumpers?"

"Yeah . . . why?"

"Can we go there?"

Her words halted Winston's tongue. "You mean like dancing go there?"

"Yeah. I used to go there all the time with Adrian . . . feel like going back." Adrian was dead, but she wasn't. Life had gone on without her for long enough.

"Sure. We can do that."

"Great . . . Saturday?"

"Saturday's fine . . . good for you Sandy," he said after a while.

"Yeah, good for me."

But if Winston thought it was a good thing, Winston's mother didn't. He had mentioned it to her in passing, switching the subject immediately after, but Alice Burton did not let her son slide.

"Sandy. You're taking her dancing."

It was not a question and Winston knew she did not mean for it to be one. Still he found himself fumbling with a response as she washed up dinner dishes. "She ask me. Me told her yeah."

Alice Burton had witnessed the great love that had happened between her firstborn son Adrian and Sandy. At first she had been reserved but as time passed she'd had no choice but to respect the power of it.

She had also seen how her second-born had stepped into her dead son's shoes. Told herself it was because Winston and Adrian had been close, that Sandy needed to depend on someone.

But a deeper truth had gleaned itself, a truth now shining brightly in her son's eyes. "She's your brother's wife."

For as long as Winston could remember, his mother had the ability to melt him to the core with just a gaze. Now felt no different as he struggled to hold her stare. He couldn't, looked away, his guilt manifesting in the breach. "Dead brudder, an me and San-dee jus friends."

"Related. You two are related," Winston's mother warned. She sighed, switching intent. "I know how you feel about her, Winston. But that doesn't make it right. Dead or not, she is still Adrian's wife."

"So what me suppose to do den? Tell meself me don't feel what me feel?"

"And what about Sandy? Does she even know?"

His shook his head no.

"All I'm saying, Winston, is this: Two people look at the same situation and each are going to see different things. You can't always control how you feel, but you certainly have control over what you do, and don't."

Saturday night Winston stood in his mirror, checking the closeness of his shave and the lay of his untucked shirt. He picked up his hair brush, brushed down his close-cropped hair, and ran the bristly edges over his eyebrows.

Next he picked up his cologne and poured it into his open palm. He was rubbing them together when his doorbell rang. Splashing it against his face as he moved, he looked out the peephole and saw his younger brother staring back.

"Wha tup?" Junie asked, taking in the silky shirt, the loose baggy pants. Shoes made of real alligator.

"Me on me way out, das all."

"A date? Ya got a date? Who?"

Winston turned away, glad that his mother had granted him privacy. Glad that she had not spilled his secret, one that he had been harboring from the moment he and Sandy had met. First look, his heart had raced at the sight of her. First look, Winston had wanted her.

He hadn't known who she was, only that she had stood on the other side of his brother's door one day and that his heart opened like a flower, blooming, before both her role and unavailability could be discovered.

Seconds later Adrian had appeared, his arm going around Sandy easy. ". . . this is my little brother Winston. Winston, Sandy." In that moment everything changed.

Winston hadn't known about the betrayal Adrian's wife Gennifer had committed, only that Adrian had left her and had obviously started seeing Sandy. As quickly as his heart had opened to her, it slammed shut. Adrian was still married. Sandy was dating him. Morally it was wrong and hating her came easy.

But truth cannot stay buried forever and eventually the whole of it was revealed. Gennifer had stepped outside of the marriage. Gennifer had had the affair. Gennifer had gotten AIDS as a result of it, giving both herself and Adrian a death sentence. Sandy had been the innocent.

"Who ya gowen wit?" Junie asked.

"A friend. All ya need to know."

"When ya meet dis friend 'cause me don't remember ya having a friend in a long time?"

Winston stood in front of the bathroom mirror. Recapped the bottle of cologne. Craned his neck to get a look at both sides of his face, turned, moved past his brother.

"She a secret or sumting?"

Winston didn't answer. His mother was right on one point: Two people could look at the same situation and see two different things. No sense in stirring up the pot if nothing was to come of the night but a dance or two.

The bottle of foundation fell into the sink and shattered into half a dozen pieces. Sandy looked at the mess, glanced back at her face, and went to get some paper towels.

She knew it was going to be something. Getting a run in her panty hose, her dress not ready in time at the cleaners. She knew in all likelihood her hair wouldn't hold its curls, that she'd smear her newly applied nail polish.

Sandy knew the evening would not go without some hitch, but as she scrapped up pieces of mocha-covered glass, she hadn't planned on it being her twenty-dollar bottle of foundation. It was a brand-new bottle. Money was money. Finances, once a foe, had become a cautious ally.

She remembered the days when she hadn't had enough of it, where her life had been a system of robbing Peter to pay Paul. Now she had a financial advisor and mutual fund accounts. But there was blood on that money.

Gennifer's blood, Adrian's blood, a killing field of economic security. When Gennifer had died, Adrian received the insurance benefits. When Adrian died, all that he had became Sandy's. Having money made her wiser when it came to spending, and no matter how she cut it, she had just dropped twenty bucks down the drain.

*Because I'm scared.*

For the first time since she'd met Adrian, she was about to step out with another man. For the first since Adrian, the heels she wore, the perfume she'd put on, the bright red lipstick she applied was for someone else. *Someone who looks so much like Adrian it's hard to keep them apart.*

This was her biggest fear.

Yes, she'd decided to grab life by the horns again and going out with Winston had, at first glance, seemed innocent enough, but now Sandy was afraid she was about to cross a line, go where she'd caught herself on the edge of before. Sandy was afraid that she was going to make the leap, cross the boundary, go there.

A part of her wanted to do just that.

Something had been returned to her, basic need flaring like solar flares about the sun. Beyond food, beyond shelter, being clothed, an old want had emerged, dismissing what was, for what would be.

The door bell rang.

The sight on the other side made her heart miss a beat. Winston was a handsome man but tonight he seemed to be glowing like a night sky full of super novas, casting her in its light. "Wow," the word leaving her like a first breath.

"Well, wow back," Winston offered, Sandy a vision of smoky dark skin and red velvet; the dress clinging to the swell of her breasts, falling away to mid-thigh length.

He forced himself not to stare, force down the need to take a five-day cruise with his eyes. Resisted the siren song of jet-black curls, sumptuous cleavage, legs curvy and prominent above the sexy black high heels. "You look fantastic."

"Thank you," she managed. "Just got to get my coat."

"I'll be outside."

They turned, brother-in-law and sister-in-law, off in different directions; the evening ahead, a mystery nuzzling inside of them both.

Winston took her arm as they entered the club, the contact surprising, electric, intense. It was a defining moment for both of them, one they both felt but would never share. For there beneath the fancy clothes, coifed hair, bodies splashed in cologne and perfume, their titles hung; a tangible wall between them.

*You're related,* all Winston could think as he pulled out Sandy's chair, asked what she wanted to drink. *He's my brother-in-law,* not only did Sandy think but felt as she couldn't even look at him when she told him a rum and Coke.

By the time Winston returned, it was all she knew. The innocence of this undertaking, a chance to get out and dance, vanished beneath butterscotch skin and honey-dipped eyes; disappeared beneath Winston's cologne riding every breath she took.

*Adrian told me to live my life when he was gone,* but he had never specified with whom. In that moment, the who had become Winston.

Sandy had been resisting it for a while, had stepped back from the line a dozen times, putting distance between them, resisting hard. But the parameters had shifted when she'd made that call, and in this moment, she wanted him.

It was not a forever want. Wasn't a rest-of-her-life want, but there was no denying its existence. Months since she had been held, made love to, touched that way, the want was now a wild horse she could not tame.

He had shown her kindness, consideration, and concern, always at the ready to do her bidding. Would he grant her this one wish? Would Adrian understand that that part of her she had shut down had now returned?

After months of looking after her dying husband; months passing where she had not even considered it, wasn't it due her?

For one night it could be like being with Adrian again. For one night, she could pretend he hadn't died, was still there for. This night the magic could return, bringing all its wonder and grace. This night the cleaving her soul took could be re-mended.

These were the thoughts that were roaming around her head when Winston caught her eye. "Whatcha tinking about?"

"Adrian," all she could admit to, the man before her looking so much like her husband she ached.

Winston nodded, sipped his Stout, his thoughts in the same direction.

Sandy had asked for this evening and he had been only too happy to oblige, but now he wasn't sure it was a good move, if his mother had been right.

They were related, not by blood, but by marriage. A marriage witnessed by God, before friends and family alike; a union no man was supposed to tear asunder. But Adrian had; had broken God's convent and, in the end, left them in the precarious situation.

A situation where all he could think about was her. A situation where he had to be careful of every move he made, nearly every word he uttered. Where his heart was placed under lock and key.

But she was there and he was there. *Too late now,* Winston decided. He put down his beer. Got up from the chair. "Come, let's dance." Waited for her to get up too.

Careful and conservative was how Sandy was dancing, as if she had pebbles in her shoes or her knees hurt. It suited Winston, made the dance easier as he kept his eyes beyond her face, the ruby red of her lips.

Winston danced as if he were doing it solo, keeping both a physical and an emotional distance from the woman he loved. He was determined not to tempt her, engage her, try and draw her near. Would be respectable. Prove his mother wrong. Show that he was capable of taking Sandy dancing and keep his distance.

But Sandy changed the rules.

Changed them quick and abrupt. She closed her eyes, leaned back her head, unrestricted her body. Her pelvis tilted forward, warm hands latching on to his waist. Before he could react, pull away, she pressed against him, her pelvis a rolling frolicking river, smoothing away the rough edges of his soul.

\* \* \*

"Whoo," she let out hours later as she got into Winston's Camry, nudging the shoes off her aching feet. "Did we dance tonight, or did we dance?"

"We danced," Winston said, unable to hold back his joy. "We danced so much I don't think I'll be able to walk tomorrow."

Her hand landed on his arm. Stayed as his eyes found hers. She said nothing and he returned the favor. Slowly he looked away, started the engine. Pulled away from the curb. Seventeen minutes later they were in front of her house, engine idling, the hour late. Her voice came, sweet and timbre, grateful, tender. "I had a good time tonight."

Winston nodded, throat gone dry.

"Walk me to my door?"

It was neither necessary nor required but Winston told her yes. They left the car, the sounds of doors slamming in the late hour echoing around them. Sandy shivered, cold, hurried up the walkway, Winston two paces behind her.

She found her key, put it in the lock. Turned it, swinging open her door. Her eyes found him, unable to hide their want, her voice precarious, near edgy. "Want to come in for a minute?"

For a hot second Winston nearly said no. For a hot minute, he was mindful of his mother's warning, the can of worms no doubt about to be opened. But he had waited for this moment for over two years. He let his heart lead.

They stepped inside, Sandy closed the door, her arms doing what she knew they would do. They latched around his neck, her lips moved to his, felt no resistance as her tongue soloed in need of a partner.

They went on that way, kissing, holding each other through the bulk of heavy woolen coats, a cool fire growing hotter with each beat of their hearts. A stab of sensibility claimed Winston and he tried to pull back, but Sandy refused to release him.

Up the stairs they went, without words only direct intent. She didn't turn on the bedroom lamp, allowing them the shelter of the near darkness. Backs to one another they undressed, Sandy doing a quick search of her night stand, retrieving condoms.

It was the first thing he put on before he came to her. The first step of what just yesterday seemed unobtainable. But here she was before him, naked *and* wanting. *Wanting me,* Winston realized with a deep swallow, his hand lifting to touch a shoulder soft as satin, dark as onyx, the sight of her taking his breath.

His touch made her tremble. His touch made everything she owned quiver. Her whole body felt consumed by fire, a fire that she knew, this night, he would quench. Right or wrong. Moral and unjust, Sandy had stopped caring the moment she'd decided it would be Winston.

Winston.

But in the shadows it became Adrian. In the shadows it was her husband's arm extended, her husband's fingers gliding down her goose-pimpled arm. In the shadows it was his voice, "I want you so much," the flash of teeth, the sparkle of eyes sprinkled with desire that she witnessed.

It was Adrian's hand that trailed along her waist, drew circles across her belly, *his* body drawing her like a siren song. It was Adrian waiting and all she had to do was reach out and take hold.

She did.

Sandy moved toward the man lost in shadows. Was nearly there when he stepped into a shaft of light coming from the street lamp outside her window. *No, not Adrian,* she realized with a swallow. But her soul had already crossed the line.

She pressed herself to him. Winston's arms found the fit of her waist, inhaled the sweat and pomade of her hair. Pulled her close, a lifetime coming and going before he was able to let her go.

She held on to him for dear life. Held on to him like she never wanted to let him go. She was being made love to like she hadn't in nearly six months; knew without a doubt the caramel body over her, the hot thickness inside of her, all of it familiar as her own name.

She came with an intensity that birthed the cosmos, felt Winston come too. He was pulling out and away from her, when her need pulled him back. He broke away long ago for a new condom, then succumbed to her passion, lingering in the temporal space of utter possibility, that world that neither recognized nor respected yesterday, or the weight of tomorrow.

It was dark, late, the street lamp making strips of ochre through the not quite closed blinds. Rays, like railroad tracks, lay across Sandy's face as Winston looked down at her, resisting the urge to kiss her. Wake her one last time.

He was not certain how he felt, could not assemble the questions and emotions churning through him. Could only slip his arm free from her, free from his brother's wife.

*Dead brother.* But in that moment, the notion held no merit; dead or alive having no worth. Winston had slept with his sister-in-law, the true heart of the matter, and the implications threatened to crush him.

He had loved Sandy from the moment they met. But he sensed what he and Sandy had just done hadn't been about love at all. It had been about Adrian and the sorrow his death had brought. Sandy was in need of comforting, had reached out to the first person she saw.

Nothing more, nothing less.

This was the thought that arrived and stayed as Winston silently got dressed. The thought that kept him company as he got behind the wheel of his car, headed home, her essence filling him with every breath he took.

Sandy awoke early.

Earlier than her normal Sunday morning routine allowed. But the need for that deep endless sleep had abandoned her. In its place was a redefining of what she'd needed and didn't. She'd needed Winston last night but was grateful that he hadn't stayed the whole night. She was not up to a "morning after," the particulars trying to bring down shame.

She understood what she had done and why. Could not deny the groundedness she felt in the aftermath. She would not let regret in, no matter what the consequences. Hoped Winston understood.

It had not been about him, but about her, what she'd needed to kick start her soul. She didn't feel she had used him. He had had plenty opportunity to say no.

For months Sandy Hutchinson-Burton had put her own needs on hold, tucked them away in a basement where nobody lived. This time around she'd put self first, going after what she needed, taking after months of giving every single bit of her self.

*My time,* she decided fiercely, *mine.*

\* \* \*

But life was a fragile thing. Certainties vanished under scrutiny and final decisions became sheets in the wind.

Sunday morning Sandy had awakened determined there'd be no regret, but by Sunday evening her determined stance began to give way to responsibility, her thoughts turning to Winston and how her decision affected him.

The more she thought, the less certain things became; the whole of it becoming a pebble in her belly she could not shift. She would have to call him, talk about it. Share her truth. Explain why it happened, clarify who they were to each other.

That much she owed, that much he deserved.

# Chapter 3

Winston was waiting. Waiting for the phone call, for the confessional, the denial. He was waiting for Sandy to call him, speak about it, give her take. He needed to hear her thoughts in the aftermath. He needed clarification.

Winston needed to know for certain if what they'd done was just a passing fancy. Winston needed to know for sure if it had just been about her loneliness or if his heart could finally be set free.

The wait wasn't too long.

Monday evening, a little after eight, the phone rang, Sandy on the other end. "We have to talk," she began.

"Yeah, I think we do."

"Is it too late for you to come over?"

In truth Winston was tired. He had had a long day exasperated by waiting to hear from her, but the thought of waking tomorrow with the questions still unanswered forced his tongue. "No, it's not too late."

"Okay. I'll see you soon."

Forty minutes later she let him in, heading toward the kitchen where she was warming up some leftovers. "Just yesterday's dinner, but you're more than welcome to some," she said, checking the meat loaf and mashed potatoes revolving in the microwave.

"No, I'm good."

She went to the refrigerator, grabbed the ketchup. "You know that night wasn't really about you," her words hard to speak, Winston's hypothesis, *not about love,* becoming fact. He nodded, face set. Allowed her to continue. "And I hope you understand what it was about."

"I have an idea," a hurt in him deep.

"It's no secret I miss your brother. No secret that you look just like him. Add two and two . . ."

"And you get four."

"Right." She turned and faced him. "I don't want you to think it could have been anybody . . . I feel a closeness to you. You've been there for me like nobody else has, but that night . . ." She swallowed, hard. "I just needed to be held, touched, y'know. Maybe even before that night, but I wasn't trying to take advantage. It was just that, it was what I needed, and I know that may sound selfish, but God, Wint, you know what I've been through."

He nodded. "I know, Sandy." He looked away, gathering his thoughts. In all likelihood it was the last thing she wanted to know. But he could not leave without telling her. "You know, all my life I looked up to Adrian. Always admired the things he had in life."

Something about how he said his words, the sense of burden and guilt within them, found her. Sandy felt it, half-hesitant to have it confirmed. "Women included?"

"Women included."

"Like me?"

He looked away. "I guess you could say that."

But it was hard to swallow. Certainly they had gotten closer since Adrian's death, but there had been those times before. "Since when," all she wanted to know, " because I remember the days you hated me."

"I never hated you, Sandy."

"What do you call it? I was there, remember? You looking like you wanted to spit in my eye, beat me down."

"Never."

"Never?"

"Never."

She was seeing him in a new light, amazed at the secret he had kept so close to his heart. "How long?"

"How long what?"

"You've been checking me out."

He swallowed. "Since forever."

"You never said anything."

"How could I? You were my brother's girlfriend, then his wife." Winston sighed, unburdening his soul. "I acted the way I acted for a lot of reasons but not because I hated you."

"Because Adrian was still married."

"That too . . . but mostly because two seconds after meeting you, I found out you were with Adrian"—he looked off—"and it was a double shock," found her eyes again, a concern she could touch filling his. "Look, I didn't plan on making this a long visit, but I wanted to get the air cleared. I'm not expecting anything from you but I just had to get things straight."

"So, we're cool?" she asked, relieved.

"We're cool. Better be on my way."

He left soon after, Sandy saddled with new thoughts. For over two years Winston had been attracted to her, and unwittingly she had given him the one thing he no doubt wanted. He would ask nothing of her, make no demands, but what about his heart?

No doubt sleeping with her had changed the depth of his emotions. No doubt, for a few minutes, the possibility of them taking it further went through his head. But from where she was standing, it wasn't a consideration. She liked Winston, but a committed relationship with him wasn't on her agenda.

Her phone rang. "Hello?"

"Sandy, it's me, Martha. How's it going?"

"Hey. It's going all right."

"You're sounding better."

"Am I?"

"A whole lot. What's been going on?"

"Nothing."

"I was thinking that maybe it's time."

"For?"

"Start going places and doing things."

Sandy didn't mean to laugh, but it felt downright bizarre that both Martha and Winston had come to the same conclusion. "Really."

"Yeah. This weekend. We could all get together and go to Club Enchant."

Club Enchant. It was where she'd first met Adrian. "I don't know, Martha."

"Well, it's too late. It's all been planned. Everyone's coming, you included."

"Really?"

"Absolutely. Me and Calvin will swing by and pick you up around eleven." Martha paused. "I know it's hard, Sandy, but life stays hard until you push yourself to that next step. And if I have to be the one who does the pushing, so be it."

*Too late, somebody already has*—words Sandy didn't even think about saying out loud.

Janice had had her eye on Sandy's brother Clifford from the moment she met him in Sandy's kitchen twenty-one years ago. She remembered the day clearly, she and Sandy eating ice pops, Cliff coming into the house, sweaty, funky. Fine.

Sweat marks had ringed the armpits of his T-shirt, glistened at the crown of his eight-inch sandy Afro. Sweat danced on his top lip that showed a hint of mustache, and he had a basketball tight up under one arm.

He didn't seem to notice his sister Sandy or Janice. Cliff went straight to the refrigerator and drank half the glass bottle of ice water without benefit of a cup.

He was closing the refrigerator, wiping moisture off his mouth with his forearm, when he noticed he was not alone. He didn't say a word, just gave a quick nod in their direction, white hi-top Converse sneakers disappearing up the hall.

"Who's that?" was all Janice had wanted to know, her heart locked down with the sight of him.

"That?" Sandy's chocolate brown face slipped into a frown. "That ain't nobody but my stupid brother Cliff . . . he just a fool."

"But he's *fine*," Janice had whispered, nails digging into Sandy's arm.

"And conceited," Sandy sang back, removing fingers from her flesh. She took a moment to examine the marks. Dabbed at it with a spit-laden finger. "Forget it. He's way out of your league."

But Janice never did.

As the years turned her from a fourteen-year-old with a mad crush to a thirty-something woman whose heart still flushed at the sight of him, she never forgot that day. And while in the past Cliff had never given her more than a nod or a few words at best, something happened over a year ago that changed everything for them.

They got together.

Cliff had been in search of a hit it and quit it, Janice, in need of forever, the end result surprising everybody. Marriage was on their horizon, the wedding just a few months away, but for Janice it felt like the good times had vanished under familiarity.

That she was even thinking back to the first time, that she was drifting through the good old days, told her the present days weren't that great. It was a thought that clung to her as she put the tender, perfectly seasoned London broil away.

It was the second night this week Cliff had missed dinner, his job demanding more of his time. And maybe if life hadn't been so cruel to her in the past, it would not have mattered, but there was a worry in her heart she could not rid herself of.

Janice could not point back to one relationship she had had that did not offer its variants of trouble times. Even with Cliff they had hit the rocks, but when he asked her to marry him, she considered herself saved. Saved from the heartaches, saved from the indiscretions, saved from worry and mistrust. He loved her, wanted her to be with him forever, all that Janice was certain that she needed.

Two missed meals were not a lot, even though she had put great effort into tonight's dinner. The meat was done up just the way he liked it, juicy with just a little pink. There were string beans fresh from the farm, which she had picked up at the Farmers' Market, and new russet potatoes she had spent time selecting, washing, and sautéing in real butter.

Janice had bought a key lime pie even though it was not her favorite, had laid out the good plates, dinner candles, and had Boney James on the CD player. It was supposed to be an evening of ease, of kicking back and enjoying their life. But the phone rang at quarter to seven, putting everything on hold.

She waited till seven-forty before she carved the meat. By eight-ten, she had to blow out the lit tapers. Eight-fifteen she made herself a plate, still hopeful that by nine he would get home soon.

Now as she scrubbed the platter, she wondered if she had real reason to be concerned or if she was just being silly.

It was hard to tell. Janice had had so many bad relationships she

could no longer distinguish a real hunch from foolish unease. She
was about to call his office when that familiar sound of a key turning
a lock reached her ears. *Thank God.*

He came through the door, tie askew, weariness about his eyes, but
fire caught them when he saw her standing there. "Hey, babe." Cliff
took in the snuffed tapers. " Sorry I'm late."

Moments like these made her weak, weepy, and oh so grateful.
Made his apology so unneeded she told him so. "It's all right. I just
put it away. Want me to heat it up for you?"

But food was the last thing on his mind. There before him were
those Tina Turner legs in the short shorts, the sleeveless T-shirt over
her luscious breasts. Even from where he stood, he could make out
the rosebud nipples, round and high, making his heart beat fast.

He smiled slowly, near dreamy, head shaking to and fro. "All I want
right now is you. Come on over here."

His words were the right ones, even the way he pressed his body
against hers seemed correct, but Janice felt something not quite right
though she could not put a finger on it. She was still trying to get a
reading when his hands tried to work themselves up under the tight
fit of her shorts. Found herself accommodating him, undoing the
snap and laying open the zipper.

Then his hands were over her behind, warm, rough, yet tender.
Being foolish, she decided as his finger found her honey spot, the
tremble in her body complete.

But her euphoria was short-lived and by the next day Janice was
plagued with doubt. "Am I crazy?" she was asking Sandy on the
phone, both of them taking a work break.

"No Janice, you're not crazy, but I know for a fact that Cliff is working real hard these days."

"I was always the last to know. I don't want to be in that position
anymore."

"You have to learn to trust."

"It's so hard, Sandy. You know what I've been through. I can't stop
myself from thinking something will go wrong."

"I think my brother's on the up and up. You're the first woman he
ever asked to marry him."

"Yeah, but still . . . I swear this is going to be the longest eight months
of my life."

"Doesn't have to be."

"My heart knows that, but my head? . . . I don't want to be one of those women who goes off 'cause their husband is five minutes late. I don't want to have to snoop in his wallet, check every entry on the credit card bill."

"So don't. Now I know it's hard accepting that after all these years you've got a good man and you know I try not to take up for my brother, creton that he is, but I really don't think you have to worry about him."

"I hope you're right," she said after a while. "So what's been doing with you?"

Sandy would tell her friend one day, but now was not the time. "Nothing much."

"Martha says we're going out this weekend."

"Yeah, she was saying something about that."

"You're not going to chicken out, are you?"

"She wants to go to Club Enchant."

"It's where we always go."

"The memories, Janice."

"Are just that. You're not going to ever go to the movie theater you and Adrian went to, the McDonald's, are you?"

"It's not the same."

"Yeah it is. There's going to be so much that reminds you of him that sometimes you will probably feel like you are on overload, but you can't go about life avoiding the places you two went. You've got to deal with it, Sandy."

"Look who's giving advice."

Janice laughed. " 'Bout time, don't you think?"

Tired and queasy.

For Britney that was not a good sign at all.

She sat on the edge of her bed, flipped open her pocket calendar, and looked at the month of January. She saw the date circled in black and counted off twenty-eight days. February 7th. It was now February 17th.

*Ten days late.*

She closed the calendar, pitched it back into her bag, and fell back against the bed. Stared up at the ceiling, closed her eyes.

A life she had never dreamed of she now owned. A life she never thought entitled to was now hers. But there was no joy from that realization, just a slippery sensation of the grass being so much greener on the other side.

As a pudgy child Britney had watched with envy as her friends snuck kisses behind the handball courts and exchanged love notes in the hallways of Benjamin Schlesinger Junior High School. In high school while her pals were getting ready for some party on a Saturday night, Britney had been holed up in her room feasting on junk food as if it were going out of style.

College had started out lonely until Martha noticed her one day and took her under her wing. She introduced her to Janice and Sandy, and for the first time in a while Britney felt a part of things again. She eventually started meeting guys but none seemed interested in any long haul. Britney had nearly resigned herself to being alone when Maurice entered her life.

He wasn't the finest, the cutest, or the smartest man she ever met. He was tall, big, dark brown, and had jowls instead of a jaw. He possessed a big wide butt, love handles, and could fit a 34B cup easily. He was too loud at times, drank too much on occasion, and had never attended a college class in his life.

But he loved her. Loved her like no man ever had and it showed in everything he did.

He bought her a house before they got married. Renovated it before they moved in. Would tell anybody who listened that he did it because he loved her and she deserved the best, but it was hard seeing the best now as *ten days late* roamed around her head.

Across the room Bereace sat chewing on her father's belt, its maroon surface stained dark with spitty drool. That her child preferred leather to the half-dozen teething rings was no longer a surprise— there wasn't much about her child that was.

Bereace had been nothing like Britney thought a baby to be—that cute little bundle of pure joy never materializing. What Britney received was a fast-growing, inquisitive, colicky little busy body that was into everything all the time, including the toilet bowl and the toilet paper.

Bereace had yet to sleep through the night, preferred the space between her mother and father to her own crib, and favored the cabinet under the sinks. She had eaten hair grease, attempted to slurp down Draino, and her favorite playtime was between the hours of midnight and three in the morning.

While Britney loved her daughter, she couldn't even think about having another one so soon. But dates didn't lie and she was nearly two weeks late. *And feeling awfully queasy.*

She knew when she got pregnant and had hoped at the time that God would forgive her for not taking precautions. But Bereace had taken one of those rare afternoon naps and she had just stepped out of the shower and Maurice had been standing there, with that look in his eye, and for the first time in months she wanted it too.

So right there in the bathroom, with no diaphragm, no condom, nothing but the two of them wedged up against the sink, they had had a fast encounter with Maurice promising to pull out. But when the moment came, the last thing either one of them wanted to do was separate.

Afterward Maurice had gotten that look and Britney had gotten that look and worried about it for a good half a minute before she had assured both him and herself that it would be okay. She convinced them both that it had been a "safe time," even if she was almost certain it hadn't been.

They had gone on with their lives, other trysts taking place in the bathroom but with birth control. Britney had been certain God had forgiven her that one oversight and, a week before her period was due, felt all the premenstrual signals. There was the lower back pain, a tender swelling in her pelvis, and a craving for anything chocolate.

Then when her due date came and went, she made it unimportant, convinced that God would not give her another so soon. She convinced herself nobody knew her life better and He saw the time she was having with Bereace. Was certain He knew she could not even entertain the idea of another, that one baby was more than enough.

While she and Maurice had joked about having a whole tribe, it was her body took the brunt of that responsibility. She had just reached her prebaby weight with another ten pounds lost for good measure and had promised herself a body she would not be ashamed to wear a bathing suit in by summer.

The ringing phone brought her out of her stupor, moving her sluggishly toward the cordless on the night stand.

"Hello?"

"Brit."

"Oh, what's up, Martha?"

"Not you. You sound beat, girl."

"I am."

"Are you sick or something?"

Or something. "No, just a little tired. What's doing?"

"This Saturday."

"What about it?"

"We're going to hang at Club Enchant."

"We?"

"Yeah, all of us. Me, Calvin, Janice, Cliff, you, Maurice . . . Sandy."

"I don't know, Martha. Maurice has been working a lot of overtime and Bereace is a handful."

"You two haven't been anywhere or done anything since she was born. You have to get out sometimes, besides, it'll be good for Sandy. The more of us, the less lonely she'll feel."

"I have to check with Maurice."

"Well, hit me back as soon as you can."

"I will."

But Britney already knew she wouldn't if she didn't have to.


It was strange being back to the place she and Adrian had first met. Strange to be among the thick crowd, thumping music and couples.

"Hey!"

Sandy looked up, saw Calvin smiling at her. He had come into her friend Martha's life and wiped away all the cobwebs. Made eight years of useless relationships vanish for Sandy's good friend.

"What, Calvin?" she said with a reluctant smile.

"You owe me a dance, so come on let's do it."

But Sandy wasn't in the mood. Just wanted to be left alone. "Later."

"Not later. Now." Calvin saw her hesitancy. "I lift trash cans that weigh more than you. Don't make me have to drag you to that dance floor."

"Go ahead, Sandy," Martha urged. "You came to party, not to warm that seat."

But sitting was just what she wanted to do, at home and alone. Still she got up when Calvin did.

The dance floor was crowded, barely space to breathe, but Sandy managed a two-feet shuffle in time with the beat. She gazed upon the man that had brought her friend Martha so much joy and could do nothing about the envy.

"Stop thinking and dance," Calvin scolded. "Come on, give a brother a show." It was hard to resist, hard to tune his cheering out, and Sandy let the music take her. Four songs later they headed back to their table, Sandy finishing her drink before her brother Cliff had her back on the dance floor.

She didn't have the best of times, but it hadn't been the worst. Just somewhere in the middle, which suited her fine.

# Chapter 4

When Adrian had come into Sandy's life, he had done more than open his heart, he opened up his world. But the most eye-opening journey had been to East New York, Brooklyn, the place where he grew up.

Though it had been many years since Adrian called Belmont Avenue home, his parents still did. Before Adrian came into her life, East New York had been fifteen-second sound bites about drugs and murder. He showed her different.

Everyone wasn't starting a church or trying to be the latest drug kingpin. There was a whole between world where everyday people were trying to live everyday lives.

People like Mr. Burton, Adrian's father.

He had come to this country from Trinidad in the fifties, finding work with his hands to put food in his children's stomachs and a dry roof over his children's heads. Mrs. Burton, American-born, had worked in a department store, neither job making them rich, but it was enough to raise four children and get them through college.

Law-abiding and respectful, they represented a large segment of the Brooklyn neighborhood. And though it was not the safest place to be, it was still a community that cared, filled with hardworking people trying to do the right thing.

Sandy pulled the Camry behind Winston's car, hit the remote alarm, contented as the horn honked and the lights flashed. She made her way through the link gate, making sure to latch it behind her, and went up the slight brick steps. Ringing the bell, she gazed up at the two-story building, blunt and square before her.

During the industrial revolution as the tired masses washed up on the shore of Ellis Island in search of a new dream, builders began looking east to supply the hordes with housing. With Lower Manhattan bursting at the seems and upper Manhattan too far away, sights were set on Brooklyn and Queens, the boroughs across the water.

Farmland became multidwellings, elegant brownstones sprung up along the Brooklyn-Manhattan shore. But as more and more people moved into the cosmopolitan oasis, cornices, mahogany trim, and crown moldings were replaced with flat-faced walk-ups, offering the basic necessities but not much else.

Adrian's parents' home was no exception, its façade offering not a hint of grace. But inside waited a cornucopia of love and that was what really mattered.

"Sandy," Mrs. Burton said. "Good to see you. Come on in. Dinner's just about ready."

Sandy hugged her, feeling a kinship that words could not explain. Moving down the dark tight hall, she headed toward the glow at the end, the kitchen door open, issuing good food smells.

"Junie and Wint are here. Rachel's on her way. Mr. Burton's in the living room watching TV." Mrs. Burton watched her daughter-in-law enter the kitchen, happy that there had been no more talk of her from her son.

Yes, Winston had taken her dancing, but they hadn't had another date since. He had only dropped by once afterward, to remind her of this day's meal, he had told his mother evenly. Mrs. Burton had looked into her son's eyes and saw it for herself. Whatever hopes Winston possessed had been dashed, of which she was grateful.

Sandy passed the two bedrooms affixed at the back, made her way past the dining room and into the living room. She spotted Winston but Mr. Burton spotted her first. He tossed aside his newspaper and got up to greet her.

"Ah, dere she is. Jusa fine and sweet and nice. How ya been, Sandy?" he asked, pulling back from his embrace. "Been good nuh?"

"Been just fine, Mr. Burton."

Junie came to her next, wrapping his lanky body about her. "Good to see ya, San-dee," he uttered, drawing back from her quickly. She had never quite figured Junie out. The youngest of the family, Sandy could never determine if he approved of her or not. She put it off to youth, a certain wariness within his soul. At twenty-five, life was still unsettled, friends and foes yet to be defined.

*"Ah, dere she is. Jusa fine and sweet and nice,"* Winston mimicked, his accent Mr. Burton perfect. He was teasing her, they both knew, and despite herself she smiled. She looked forward to the hug he gave, at ease with him.

Then the doorbell was ringing and Adrian's sister Rachel was entering the room, her voice quick, chiding. "What dis? Ya beat me here. Life must be getting real good."

Sandy pulled Rachel to her, gave her a hug and a kiss.

Everyone gathered at the table, bowed their heads, and said grace. Then talk grew lively as bowls of stewed chicken, dumplings, and salad vanished quickly off their plates.

It was hard to believe that Mr. Burton had once hated Sandy, been rude to her, had spoken sharp bitter words. Hard to believe any of that had been a part of their life as he hugged her goodbye at the door.

She was used to the long hard embraces, as if Adrian were living inside her bones. Was used to the way his voice grew choppy as words of praise fell off his lips. It felt good to be accepted in a way she had never been accepted before. Was a nice realization that she had two real families, Adrian's and her own.

Sandy said good night, Winston by her side. Together they headed down the steps and out the front yard, lingered by her car.

"I had a good time," she offered.

"Well, we're glad you did."

She studied him a moment, looked away.

"Stop thinking about it," he warned.

"Thinking about what?"

"I'm okay with it, Sandy. You need to be too."

She was glad they were able to have such an exchange. Glad that the situation hadn't grown too uncomfortable, but it was hard not to think about it. Winston had wanted her for so long. "Not often a man comes to me and tells me he's been scoping me for nearly two years. A man who's my brother-in-law no less."

She wasn't trying to hurt him, but saw a flicker of it in his eyes. Found herself apologizing, "Sorry," a word he would not accept.

"For what? Not your fault. Just how things go . . . better get on home." He eased off her car and headed to his, was inside in no time flat. Winston sat, letting his car warm as Sandy pulled off from behind him, his heart fastened in her passenger seat.

The evening had been hard but he was grateful it was behind him. Every time he looked up, there she'd been, smiling, animated. Happy.

*Without me.*

Something had happened that night, transforming her in a way he had not seen since before Adrian died. Winston had helped to get her there, but she'd left him by the roadside.

It wouldn't have been so hard if she wasn't all he wanted. Would have been easier if there were another woman to distract him. But there wasn't. Love had not been kind to him. Winston had never really found the connection, the tuning-fork clarity he felt for Sandy, but still he would respect her choice.

Turning on his car lights, he put his car in drive and eased away from the curb, wanting.

It was still winter but spring weather made an early arrival, sending temperatures into the fifties with lots of warm sunshine. After a near brutal season, it was a welcome change, one that signaled the exodus of clothes. Sandy went through her closet, took out the heavy wools, the cashmeres, and the blends. She lined them neatly into the plastic bag and headed to the basement for storage.

Her spring clothes were in the bag just as she'd left them, near the wall where boxes were stored. It was the smell she noticed first, the fuzzy black mold second as she opened the bag, not wanting to believe her eyes.

She didn't have to dig, shift, or anything to know that the spoils included her lime linen jacket, her favorite Donna Karan slacks. Sandy was pissed by the time she shook out the contents, finding silk shells, linen skirts, and cotton sun dresses supporting a new life form.

She had known her basement was not the driest place but assumed the plastic bag would protect them. The fuzzy black, gray, and green mold told her different. Out to the garbage they went.

When she had first moved into her home, getting the basement renovated had been on her list, but the notion had slid by the wayside, and she was hardly down there anyway. But ruined clothes turned it into a priority and she set about finding a carpenter.

She combed the yellow pages. Thought about it and dropped the idea. As a woman alone, she was the perfect candidate to be ripped off. Sandy called her father instead.

He told her of a neighbor who had just had some work done. He'd get the name and number and call her back.

Britney watched her husband sit on the edge of the bed, taking the last bit of energy he possessed to remove his work shoes. She preferred that he left them at the front door—the City of New York toss-offs had a tendency to cling to their bottoms—but knew enough not to complain.

Her husband was putting in seventy-hour weeks and the last thing he wanted was her nagging. He probably didn't want to be a father again either and in that case he was in good company.

Life had changed a whole lot since their daughter had been born. Maurice told Britney she didn't have to work, but the purse strings were growing tighter each day. A big man with big dreams, Maurice liked to live over the top. A hoopty for the few errands she ran would have been fine, but Maurice insisted on a brand new Celica.

The whole house had been painted and carpeted right before they moved in, but four months later, Maurice had the painters and carpenters back to make the nursery more child-friendly.

He insisted Britney go to the hairdresser once a week, and she had more clothes than she would ever need, but he was always taking her to the mall to buy more.

Such living didn't come cheap and the price was there on her husband's tired face. He had dropped thirty pounds with all his hard laboring, and while it looked good on him, he'd take a full night sleep over the loss any day of the week.

But the news had been confirmed a week ago and Britney had been trying to find the right time to say it. Now or never she realized as he stripped down to his Jockey's. She waited until he was in their bed. Took another second as he fixed the pillow beneath his head.

"Mo?"

"Huh."

The weariness in his voice made her heart ache. "I'm pregnant."

The thirteen-hour day Maurice had just worked vanished. He sat up, searching her face, wide eyes and terrified.

"You sure, baby, you sure?"

"Two tests, one at home. One at the doctor. I haven't had a period since the beginning of January."

"Damn . . ."

In that moment Britney knew Maurice was scared too. Felt a deep comfort.


When Sandy had called the number her father had given her and set the appointment, she expected an old callused gray hair man in overalls and a conductor's cap to be ringing her bell, not the young, fine, kind of tall, warm brown, thirty-ish man who did.

"Yes?"

"Sandy Burton?"

"Yes."

"I'm Randall. Randall Hoakes. The carpenter?"

The carpenter. Where were his overalls? His tool belt? His rheumy eyes and arthritic fingers? The man standing on her top stoop had on a leather jacket, dark jeans, and Timberlands.

"May I come in?" he asked, smile pleasant. It took Sandy a minute to decide. She was a woman alone and anything could happen and did.

"My father said three," he went on to offer.

Yes, that's right, she had agreed to that time because she had a hair appointment at four and Mr. Hoakes had assured her that it would only take him a few minutes to do an inspection and give an estimate. But the Mr. Hoakes she had talked to on the phone sounded old. The man before her was young.

"Did he get the time wrong? If he did, then I apologize."

"Your father," she stated, needing confirming.

"Yes. He takes the calls, I go out and do the work. Retired, gives him something to do."

"Well, he should tell people to expect his son. I was looking for an old man," Sandy said, opening her screen door, the man moving past her anything but.

\* \* \*

He was quick and assiduous with his work, fingering the crumbling masonry, inspecting exposed light fixtures, jotting things down on a legal pad.

"I'd say nothing has been done down here since the house was built."

You didn't need to be a professional to make that assessment and Sandy wasn't impressed. But her old neighbor Mr. Clarkston had said he'd done an excellent job. So she said nothing, just followed behind him closely, looking at everything he did.

She did not invite him to her kitchen table, but Randall sat himself down to it anyway. Motioned for her to come join him.

"Masonry's crumbling so I suggest you have the foundation tested for leaks. It's an expertise I'm not licensed in, so I can either recommend someone or you can find someone on your own."

Sandy nodded.

"I can reseal the foundation walls, paint, sheet rock, panel, or whatever you prefer. I'm a licensed electrician so doing the rewiring won't be a problem."

"Rewiring?"

"If you want new lights. Those wires are very old. Need to be replaced."

Sandy frowned. She had money but didn't want to blow it all on the basement. "How much is that going to cost?"

His smile was gentle, professionally corralling. "Let me explain what needs to be done and then you can decide what you want done, all right?"

She nodded, having no other choice.

"Now with regards to the floor, you have a couple of choices. If you plan to be down there often, I can install a floor heating system, which literally brings heat up through the floor. If that's not the route you want to go, I can install a small hot air unit, do carpeting or vinyl right over the cement.

"Now the storage room you mentioned will be a raised room. I can make it twenty by twenty, twenty by ten, whatever you think will be adequate."

"Why raised?"

"Your sewer overflow is down there. One good backup and you can easily get an inch of sewage, if not more."

"Oh." She hadn't realized that.

"I recommend replacing the windows with newer thermal ones. And since the ceiling is sort of low, I wouldn't recommend a drop."

"Drop?" She was feeling downright ignorant.

He lifted both hands, lowering one a foot. "You know, where panels hang a foot below the true ceiling. The good thing about a drop is it allows easy access to the ceiling pipes. The bad thing is ..." He smiled, studying her left hand, her wedding band telling stories that were far from the truth. "If your husband's, like, six four, well, he might have to duck."

"I'm a widow," she managed softly, as if it were a something to be shamed of.

He frowned a bit. "Sorry to hear that." Moved on, pulling out a calculator. "You've heard what needs to be done. What is it you had in mind?"

"Well, my main concern is the storage room. I want to be able to put my clothes in there and not have to worry about new life forms."

"Cedar is an excellent wood and I can install a dehumidifier. Make sure the moths don't get in and your things stay dry."

"Sounds good, but how much?"

"Well, Mrs. Burton, do you want the whole caboose or just enough to keep your clothes dry?"

"The whole caboose."

Randall worked some numbers, wrote one down, and pushed it toward her.

Sandy sighed with relief. "That's all?"

"I'm cheap and I'm good."

Sandy extended her hand his way, the contact warm as summer. "We've got a deal."

It was rare that Britney invited her friends over, motherhood giving her enough to do, but when she summoned her girlfriends on a Friday night, they all sensed it was important.

The first surprise was the way she looked, run-down and hollowed out. The second surprise was the missing smell of food that normally drifted from her kitchen when they came. There was some soda on the coffee table but the bottle wasn't even full. She had laid out cheese and crackers but it wasn't much of that either.

"No chicken?' Martha asked, taking up a cracker, a wedge of cheese. Coming straight from work, she was famished.

"We got crackers, we got cheese, that's all we got. You can eat it or don't."

Britney had become brassier in the time since she met Maurice, but this new attitude was thick. Martha found herself studying her friend hard, trying to determine its source. As an assistant district attorney, it was her job to read people. When she sensed what was going on with Britney, her mouth fell open.

"Yeah, I am. I was going to wait until Sandy and Janice got here, but it's just like you to beat me to the punch."

Martha's surprise turned to joy. "Isn't that a kick in the head."

"Oh, you think so? I can hardly handle Bereace. What makes you think I want another one?"

"What's not to want?"

"Easy for you to say, Miss Career Woman. Raising one baby isn't no joke."

"I never said it was, Brit, but can't you see what you have in front of you? You have a husband who loves you, a nice home. You don't have to work. How many women do you know have it like that?"

It was a fair assessment but it did not take into account that raising children was work. That unlike a paying job, there were no sick days, no tidy forty-hour weeks, no vacations or that personal day.

"I work more now than when I was working, so don't be trying to tell me how easy I got it," Britney insisted, her voice cracking.

It was the first time Martha had ever seen Britney break down. She'd tear up in a minute, but big wet blubbery boo-hoos had never happened. Yet there Britney was sobbing, hands to her face.

Martha put an arm around her, understood when Britney gently pulled away. She was feeling overwhelmed, and a friendly arm wasn't going to lighten that burden. Martha let her be.

Britney had gone off to blow her nose when the doorbell rang.

Martha answered, letting Janice and Sandy in. "Britney has some news."

"Give a leg to be in her place," Sandy was saying as Janice drove her home. But beneath that assessment lay a darker truth, one that reared its head from time to time. From the moment Britney had been pregnant with her first child, jealousy found Sandy and stayed.

She had been engaged to Adrian at the time, and though he was still testing negative, a total of ten years would have to pass with him testing negative before they could even think about having children.

Sandy had looked upon Britney, who in her eyes had gained all that she couldn't, and a green-eyed monster emerged. *Why not me?* she'd asked herself long ago. *Why can't I have the same fair shake?*

Before Maurice, Britney couldn't buy a man. Now she was living her dream life with another baby on the way. Envy found Sandy all over again. "I don't know how she did it."

"Did what?" Janice asked.

"Get all that she got. Remember how it was before? We'd go out and she'd sit there all night, nobody paying her any mind. Her hair would be all jacked up. She'd wear those funny old cheap dresses, hardly opening her mouth. Now look at her. She got a good man, a house, babies. Don't have to work. How did she manage that?"

"Some people get breaks."

"And she has the nerve to be unhappy about it."

"You know how people are, never knowing what they really have. And to Britney, another baby is too soon."

Sandy let her anger go. Considered her friend. "What about you? Are you going to wait?"

"A hot second, yeah, but I'm too close to forty to wait too long."

"We're only thirty-six."

"And before you know it, we'll be thirty-seven. Then we'll blink and we'll be looking at the big four-o."

"How come age doesn't get big until you hit thirty? Suddenly we have the big three-o, then the big four-o. How come there's no big two-o?"

Janice laughed. "Because twenty doesn't count. You're hardly legal, still smelling yourself, trying to figure out what adulthood is."

"Guess you're right." Sandy paused for a moment. "Isn't it funny how Britney's hitting all those milestones before us?"

"I think how she was living before Maurice is the reason she's living this way now. She'd been alone for so long and I think the universe is correcting itself or something."

Deep, but Janice had become just that in the past few months. She was making more sense than she ever had before.

"Go on, Gandhi," Sandy said with a laugh. But it did not quite touch a new sadness in the face of lost dreams.

Sandy stood looking at her boss, determined not to give in to his peeved expression. "A week?" he asked again as if she had requested the moon inside her pocket.

"Yes, Reginald, a week."

"You just got back," which was a half-truth. Yes, she had taken time to look after Adrian when he got sick and she had taken grieving time when he passed away, but she had been steadily back on the job since December. It was now the beginning of March.

Her work was not that extensive—any of the other seven admins could handle his correspondence, appointments, and phones for five working days. "I'm having work done and I have to be there inside my house. I need a week off, Reginald."

She was not backing down. It was too important. She was getting her basement fixed and she would be there supervising every step of the way.

"One week and not a day more."

Sandy nodded, then left his office. She looked forward to the work to begin.

Where was his helper?

Randall had begun bringing in supplies when she realized it would be just him alone. "You're going to do the whole thing by yourself?"

"Sure am. This way I can ensure the job is done right."

She hung around as he began loosening the crumbling masonry, watched with curiosity as he mixed cement, water, and sand. Stirring it up to the right consistency, he began applying it to the wire-scraped walls, moving the spade with deftness and ease.

"You make it look easy," Sandy found herself saying.

"Been doing it awhile."

"I was going to put on some coffee. Would you like a cup?"

He looked up at her for the first time. "That would be great."

He took three minutes to drink it, and immediately got back to work. Sensing that her basement was in good hands, Sandy went upstairs to watch a little television.

She was enjoying a first-run episode of *Sally* when he came up to announce he had to shut the power off. "I'm about to start the rewiring. It'll be off for a little while."

TV was abandoned for a book.

By lunch time he had finished the electrical work and declined Sandy's offer to share some leftovers. "I bring my own meals from home, it's cheaper and quicker," he explained, pointing to his lunch pail on the sill.

That he carried one came off as both antiquated and frugal—a merit badge as far as Sandy was concerned. Carpentry was not a steady profession, and it took determination to carve out a living from it. But there was nothing desperate about Randall at all.

Sawdust and machinery were a realm that welcomed him; Sandy could tell his work was both a comfort and a joy. He was about his business, which was a good thing, even though she wished he had joined her for lunch.

She liked his presence, the muscularity of his demeanor. With the exception of her father and Winston, her house had not held it. It felt good to have it back. She enjoyed having someone else moving around her space, chipping at the emptiness her house sometimes offered.

He left around three that afternoon. Said he would return early to-morrow. The basement didn't look much better than when he started, but Sandy knew it was just a matter of time.

When he arrived early the next morning, Sandy had the coffee ready and mugs out. She insisted that he sit and join her.

She found he had things important to talk about, had a quiet passion for life. Found herself relaxed, at ease, conversing with him. But as soon as the groove between them started to really get good, he abandoned his coffee and headed down the stairs.

He began applying sealant, the mixture sticky and black. The sound of the buzz saw came an hour and a half later. Then sharp *pa-tows!* began filling the air. Curiosity drew her down, the noise deadly and full of impact.

"What is that?" she shouted from the top of the stairs.

He shifted the safety glasses from his face, weapon aloft. "Nail gun. Didn't scare you, did it?"

"Yes," Sandy admitted with a laugh, taking all of him in. He was construction man calendar perfect, nail gun up and legs spread wide. Sweat danced on his brow, colored the arm pits of his navy blue T-shirt. Bits of sawdust clung to the swells that were his muscles.

It took a moment to realize she was staring, that she was drinking him like she'd been parched for weeks.

Sandy turned and made her way upstairs, wondering with whom did he lay his head.

"Mrs. Burton?"

The name was still weird to her. Sandy hadn't spent much time being in that role. She never got the chance to flaunt what God had brought together. On her job she still went by Ms. Hutchinson.

She got up off the couch. "Yeah?"

"I'm starting your storage closet . . . laid out some lines. I need you to check it before I do the two by fours."

She moved down the steps behind him, saw the markings on the floor, and stepped into the space. Moving about, she imagined white wire shelving, boxes stacked neatly. Nodded and stepped out of the square. "Yeah, I'd say it would work."

He pointed toward the walls. "Sealant's dry, should be able to sheet rock tomorrow. Have you decided on a paint?"

"Semigloss in that soft yellow. Be bright and cheerful, don't you think?"

Randall.

Moving around her house as if he were a real part of it, entering doorways, going up and down steps. Day three found Sandy at sweet peace in his musings.

It took that long to realize what was happening to her. That long to connect the dots, add two and two. She was becoming attracted to him, in bits and in infinite measures. When she first realized it, she told herself she wasn't, that she was just lonely and he was a man. But as time went on, her heart began to speak a different wonder and soon her head was listening.

Sometimes she would go down to the basement and they would converse. With wide-eyed charm he would express himself, the world still a curious and fascinating place. She found herself looking forward to their talks, knowing they would soon come to an end.

In a few days her basement would be all finished and Randall would be off to another job. The present always moved too swiftly. Sandy learned to take her fill while she could.

# Chapter 5

"You digging him?" They were schoolgirl close, walking through the mall. Janice, who was up on Sandy's shoulder, got shoved away.

"No . . . not like that."

"Sounds like it to me, the way you're talking. Randall this and Randall that."

"He's a nice guy."

"Your father's a 'nice guy.' There's definitely more . . . tell me about the nail gun again."

"Get away from me," Sandy insisted, half mad but mostly tickled.

"You know you love me."

"Says who?"

Janice smiled. "You. Remember? You told me. Said, 'You know I love you, girl.' " Her face grew serious. "And it's been a diamond I've been carrying around in my heart ever since."

Sandy looked at her, emotions plucked. "I'm not crying today, Janice."

"Of course not. You can't," her own voice choked, "can't be going home red eyed, especially with Mr. Randall waiting . . . doesn't it strike you just a little bit funny that a job he swore would take five days is now on number seven?"

"He's very good, takes his time."

"Are we talking about your basement or something else?"

"Oh, shut up."

On many fronts Janice was right.

It had begun when she first witnessed the magic he created with wood and plaster, how his love for what he did spoke of a caring soul. Then there was that tenderness that came into his eyes sometimes, a softness so gentle she just wanted to take pieces of it.

It was the hard honest skillful living he made, the way he went about his work with dedication. It was the joy she felt just from talking with him, a completeness filling her every time she was in his space.

More and more she felt her heart opening to him even though her husband had barely been in the ground five months. Even though she knew it was what Adrian would want, she had no idea if Randall had even considered it, or would.

More than a respectable mourning period, the widow role she had donned, her husband had died of HIV. What man wouldn't be afraid?

*Winston hadn't.*

But Winston had been the exception. No doubt Randall would be the rule.


"Can you believe it?" Martha was asking over African peanut soup and flat bread.

Calvin broke off a piece. "Believe what?" Dipped it into the mix. They were at a Nigerian restaurant not too far from her job off of Montague Street; a newfound cuisine they both enjoyed.

"Britney. Pregnant again." She shook her head. "Some women have all the luck."

His glance was casual, barely caressing her face. "Never thought you were the type."

"What type?" But Martha knew. A different need had found her. It was one she had never entertained until recently and no doubt it was showing on her face.

"The type who wanted children." His look was careful. "Your job keeps you awfully busy."

"But it's just that, a job. Not my whole life."

"Since when?"

Since you, Martha wanted to say but didn't. She simply shrugged and looked away.

"You catching the fever?"

"What fever?"

"The 'my-friend-got-that-so-I-want-it-too' fever."

"No." But there was little conviction in her voice.

The City of New York Department of Sanitation's locker room on the outskirts of Jamaica Bay was a rumble of voices, laughter, and metal slamming into metal. With care, Maurice removed his pants and his shirt, and with the same care placed them on the hanger.

Next to him Calvin was donning the work uniform, a strange near deep green. The garbage trucks would be rolling out in twenty minutes and the men took the time offered to talk.

"Your dick has got me in hot water, Mo."

"What?"

"I said your dick has got me into trouble . . . your Johnson. Your Jimmy. Your Mr. Sweet Black. You've knocked Britney up *again* and now Martha's looking to be knocked up too."

Maurice was basically a levelheaded fellow, slow to be roused, hardly surprised. But Calvin's words sent his jaws wide open, showing old fillings, pink gums, a pasty-looking tongue. "What?"

"Close your mouth, man."

"Hit me again?"

"Yo dick," Calvin indicated with his finger, "done got—"

"No, I got that part. Tell me again about Martha wanting a *baby?*"

"You surprised? How you think I'm feeling?"

"So what are you going to do?"

"Buy my own condoms and make sure there's no holes poked through."

"No, seriously, man, what are you going to do?"

"I'm not even thinking that far," Calvin answered, concerned.

"You want kids?"

"What man doesn't. But I'm old-fashioned, you know. Marriage, then the babies . . . but on the other hand, you know that's a route I don't want to travel."

"One bad apple don't spoil the whole bunch."

"Easy for you to say, yours is working."

"So you tell her it's not even in your language."

Calvin paused from tying his boot. "That's the thing. Don't know how."

"You've never been at a loss for words before."

"Never known Martha."

When Maurice had come to him those many months back and told him about a friend of his girlfriend's, Calvin had been hesitant, was certain it wouldn't work out, but had gone to the club to meet Martha anyway.

He tasted her sassiness halfway across the room, knew without touching her she'd be sweet chocolate in his arms. He knew she was an assistant district attorney and didn't take no mess, that dating a garbage man had never been part of her agenda. She'd be on the lookout for flaws.

So Calvin had come correctly from the moment he entered her space, taking her hand, kissing the back, ordering her drink within the first minute they met. He made a slight show of his money, spoke with all the upbringing his mother instilled in him, proceeded carefully. Got Martha interested.

That simple night became the first of many, and soon a few weeks became months. He cooked for her, something no woman could resist, and often she'd come in from a hard day's work, a fresh-cooked meal on the table.

He understood her fierceness, her need to protect herself. He opened himself up to her in a way he hadn't with any woman in a long time. He never thought her the marriage type, was certain she was gung-ho on her career. Felt safe in that assessment, certain that consideration was years away.

It allowed them to carve out a nice niche, but that next step had grabbed Martha by surprise. He was feeling her, even understanding it, just wasn't certain if he would be snatched up too.

The yellow gave the whole room a soft, gentle glow. The recessed lighting made it supper club chic. The faux marble tiles in the pale cream set off the silk ficus sitting six feet high in the corner.

"Looks better than my upstairs," Sandy said, happy with the results.

"I think it came out good," Randall offered, moving to the window. "Tilts for easy cleaning," he demonstrated for her. Then it was off to the storage room, floor to ceiling in cedar. There were rows of rack shelving, sliding drawers of various sizes. "You don't need a bag or anything. Just hang them or slip them in the drawer."

Sandy walked through barefoot and wide-eyed. "Smells like a forest."

"Part of its charm. Expensive, but worth it. You made the right choice." Randall laughed. "No more new life forms growing on your clothes."

That he remembered pleased her, made her next request easier on her lips. "Can you stay for dinner?"

"Love to, but as you know, I ran late on this job. Which means now I'm running late on the next. Have to shoot over to Home Depot to pick up my supplies. Big job. Got to start early."

But Home Depot was open until nine. It was just a little after five. There was more than enough time to break bread, converse a little, stay. She just wasn't ready to see him go.

"Won't take but a minute," she said carefully. ". . . truth is I'm going to miss having you around. All that banging and knocking, it's gonna get real quiet. A few minutes, what do you say?"

Randall looked into her eyes, saw the loneliness. Recalled his father's warning those many years back. *"You going to meet a lot of women, lonely women who ain't had a man in their house in years. You're a fine young man and they gonna be drawn to that, so you got to keep the business about the business."*

But Sandy was different. Attractive, tender. Had rich dark brown skin he was certain would be like silk, round black eyes simple to get lost in. She was curvy with enough caboose to send him into more than one daydream.

Her smile, when it came, was like heaven opened, lighting up everything it touched. It was trembling now, uncertain whether to hold back or set itself free.

"Sure. I got a few minutes," Randall found himself saying. "What's on the menu?" he asked, looking up the stairs.

The truth of the matter was Sandy didn't have a clue, her invite totally unplanned. She shrugged. "Let's go see."

She knew what was inside her refrigerator but was hoping something had been overlooked. She hadn't been big on dinner and beyond half a baked chicken and a wrinkled baked yam, there wasn't much else to serve.

"Something wrong?"

She looked up over the door, smiled, embarrassed beyond belief. "I guess I should have checked my frig or gone shopping before I invited you. There's nothing here much."

Randall was beside her in a flash, peering into the Arctic bareness. "You got carrots or potatoes?"

"Maybe canned."

"Flour and Crisco?" She nodded, curiosity piqued. "Celery flakes?" She was certain she did. "Rolling pin?" That she didn't have.

"Two-liter soda bottle then," he decided, pulling out the chicken and placing it on the counter.

"Full or empty?"

"Full if you got. If not, cool water can do the trick." Randall looked down at his hands, looked back at her. "Mind if I wash up first?"

"Yeah sure, this way . . . what are you going to make?"

His smile hit her like a rainbow, the first sun break on what had been almost half a year's worth of gloomy days. "You'll know soon enough . . . can I use your bathroom?" he asked, pointing up the stairs.

"Be my guest."

Chicken potpie.

Done so quickly, so efficiently, and so deftly that in a little over an hour they were sitting down to its flaky tenderness.

"Didn't even think to make one," Sandy said, taking up a forkful.

"That's because it's just you. I learned how to stretch and make do from my mother. Six of us, times could get lean."

"How many brothers?"

"Four, including me."

"No sisters?"

Randall shook his head no. "My father says the next generation is going to be nothing but girls. Says that nature is going to perform a balancing act."

"Balancing act?"

"Definitely. Nature is always correcting itself. If it didn't, we'd be in chaos."

"Well, I wish it would realize I need some balancing."

He stopped eating. Laid his fork aside. Studied her before he asked his question, the one dancing on his tongue for a while. "How long?"

Sandy didn't have to ask "what." "Almost six months."

Randall nodded, chewed. Contemplated. "Must be hard."

"Very," her eyes tearing up, she reached for a napkin. "Got to stop this crying," she insisted, dabbing at her eyes, feeling annoyed. She felt his hand on hers for the first time, a gentleness so profound she trembled.

She allowed him to take the napkin. Held her face still, his touch gentle as he dabbed the corner of her eyes.

"Don't ever deny yourself the sadness, Sandy . . . you have every right . . ." His voice mirrored his eyes, soft and understanding. Sandy looked away, turned a bit, blowing her nose. She balled the paper up and took it to the trash.

When she sat back down, the chicken potpie no longer held her interest. She felt his eyes on her and risked a look. Meeting his in the unfettered space between them, she got back up and asked if he wanted something to drink.

"Sure."

Then she was back in her seat, a glass of Sprite in her hand. Absent sips she took, her heart a land mine.

"Great guy?"

It was his voice, not so much the question that pulled her back into the present. A smile unstoppable spreading across her face. "Yes, he was. My butterscotch dream."

"Butterscotch?"

Her fingers moved over her wrist. "Kinda caramel skin." Shrugged. "I always thought of him as butterscotch . . . my butterscotch dream."

"Married long?"

"No."

"What, a few years?"

Her smile began to fade. It would be gone by the time her sentence was through. "Two months and then he was dead." She found herself looking at him, waiting for the bomb to drop.

"Two months?" Puzzlement. Confusion. "What happened?"

"A heart attack," Sandy answered quickly, forgiving herself the lie. She would tell him one day if it came to that, but for now it was case closed.

"My uncle died of a heart attack. So did three of my grandparents." Randall looked off. "I guess it runs in our family or something. Me, I want to go the old-fashion way."

"In your sleep?"

"You got it. Just take my ninety-six-year-old behind to bed and never wake up. No pain, no agony. Just that final sleep."

Sandy found herself surprised that she could talk about death, that the notion no longer hurt her. "I had a great uncle who died in a chair. He was going to the store with his wife and she told him to go put on his shoes. When it took too long for him to come back, she went to see what was wrong. And there he was, feet still bare, sitting in the chair dead." Her head shook. "We laugh about it now," a smile coming back into her, "but it wasn't funny then. Can you imagine?"

"No, can't say I can. I can say that I have to get going. Normally when I cook," his eyes took in the flour-covered counter, the assemble of dirty dishes, "I clean up. Maybe next time."

There was no doubting the intent of his gaze or how his words were a door opened to her. For a second Sandy debated walking through it. At the last minute, she took the step.

"Next time you can cook again. The potpie was slamming."

"I'm very good, probably the best," he boasted, "like a four-star chef when I really start to burn." He took his plate to the garbage can, scraped off the remainders. Took it to the sink and rinsed it before setting it down.

"I'm off," he said.

"Let me walk you to the door."

He allowed her to lead and didn't even try to stop himself from taking in the back of her. Sweet and juicy, like a plum waiting to be plucked, the perusing seemed too short.

There was nothing accidental in the way he bumped into the back of her, no accident in how he was slow to move away. There was no accident in the fire that jumped her soul, or the way he was looking at her as things became set in stone.

"Dinner then?" she asked, mouth dry.

"Definitely. I'll call you."

He moved closer and her whole world shifted into a betterment she could taste. She saw his fingers rise and was certain she knew their destination: the slope of her cheek, the underside of her chin. But impact came at the corner of her mouth, one callused finger grazing the surface. "Got a little crust on your face," he said, teasing her. It took a second to realize he was.

He wasn't going to kiss her, just leave behind a little something. A token she would not soon forget, whispering a promise she was ready to hear.

The phone call came sooner than she thought it would.

Less than two hours after he had left her house, he was on her phone inviting her to his place for dinner. "You seemed to like my chicken, so I figured I do a lemon pepper."

*That was quick,* was what she thought. "Sounds good," was what she said.

"Tomorrow, after work?"

"Sure. Love to. Just need to know where you live."

Sayres Avenue.

Sandy had seen the quaint attached Tudor-style homes for as long as she could remember. She'd wondered who had decided that European-style clusters would fit so nicely and so complacently in an area surrounded by single-family homes and a commercial strip.

Now as she passed through his block a third time, with not a single parking space in sight, she knew she'd have to find a pay phone and let him know. "I can't find any place to park."

"Swing back around. I'll meet you out front."

Sandy did just that, Randall hopping into the passenger seat. He directed her around the corner, the apparent absence of garages not hitting her until they turned into the alley behind his house. Such sites were common in California but in the county of Queens it was nearly unheard of. "Different, but it works," he told her as they slowly drifted by garages that filled both sides.

"Stop," he instructed, aiming his remote. The doublewide garage door rolled up, revealing a vintage navy blue Mercedes 450 SL. There was space on the other side but it didn't seem wide enough to accommodate another car. "Can you do it?"

"Not sure." The last thing she wanted was to scrape that car.

"Then let me."

They exchanged seats, Randall handling her car with ease. "Only thing is I'm going to have to get out on your side," which Sandy understood. The two cars were so close, using the driver's door was not an option.

They left her car, headed toward the back, a garden door their destination. He unlocked it, held it open, and she stepped through.

She'd never imagined what lay behind his house would hold such wonder.

It was country English quaint with wild flowers and stone gnomes. In the moonlight she could see the flag stone walkway and the wooden gazebo barely big enough to hold two. "Always wanted one," he offered, "even though the yard's not that big."

Up the back steps they went, he unlocking the door. The aroma of dinner surrounded her—roasted meat, fresh vegetables; something yeasty like baked bread. The kitchen was small, barely big enough for the table. Stone dishwear and pretty crystal glasses were placed on top, awaiting hungry guests.

"Just have to carve the chicken and reheat the broccoli. Come on in the living room and relax." She followed him, taking in the rough-hewn beams that ran along the ceiling, genteel against the eggshell-colored walls.

There was a fireplace and inside roared a fire. Drawn to it, Sandy stood watching the dance of orange flames. "Oh, this is nice," she said, slipping off her jacket, easing her pocketbook off her shoulder, the room cozy, near rural, and warm.

Randall was eating, eyes to his plate, but he could feel Sandy across from him like a caress. He was trying to figure out what lay beyond dinner. Was trying to assimilate all the things running through his heart. He knew Sandy was recently widowed, and wondered if her loneliness had brought her here.

It had been a while since he had been involved with anyone, his job keeping him busy, leaving little room for affairs of the heart. His last involvement had ended last Thanksgiving over turkey, stuffing, and cranberry sauce.

Randall had always known that Yvette liked him more than he liked her. Made it unimportant as time went on. They had been proceeding nicely until that fall when work began cutting into their time.

He'd tried to explain it best he could, that it was his job, his lifeblood, how he made his living. But Yvette had grown tired of the middle-of-the-night phone calls about broken water heaters and houses with no heat.

Randall had missed the Thanksgiving meal altogether, showing up at her house long after the last guest had left. He apologized, the job taking long, but for Yvette it was the last straw. She told him just that.

Randall remembered being hungry, his first meal of the day on his plate. Remembered how the candied yams were singing a siren song he could not resist. So he nodded at her assessment, picked up his fork, and started to eat, wanting to fill the emptiness in his belly before he left for the last time.

Yvette had taken it as a sign of utmost inconsideration. Had stood up and snatched his plate away. "Get out," she had told him, dumping the fine meal into the trash. "Get out and don't even think about coming back."

Randall left without an argument, the hunger in his belly no less pronounced. It was Thanksgiving and not even Burger King was open. He ended up at his parents' home. Over leftovers and in the late quiet, he sat in his parents' kitchen eating the remains of the holiday meal, his father tempered and watchful across from him.

In between bites he had shared his breakup with Yvette, knowing his father would offer his take. "You never loved that girl anyway. Consider yourself lucky."

Randall knew his pops was right, but his ego still took a bruising. He began thrusting himself back into his work and eventually the whole incident became unimportant.

The day Randall knocked on Sandy's door, he didn't think of it as being anything more than another job he would complete, but now that she was sitting before him, he understood just how wrong he had been.

"What are you thinking on so hard?"

Randall looked up. Wagered truth from fiction and risked the truth. "My last relationship . . . and the day I came to your house."

"Which was?"

"Just another job to do."

"No, your last relationship." The word *last* had her captive, sounded good on her tongue. Last meant over, long ago, and done with. It meant Randall was free.

"Thanksgiving."

"Thanksgiving?"

Randall nodded.

"Like sitting at the table eating Thanksgiving, or the meal's over and you're on your way home Thanksgiving."

"At the table," Randall said with a smile, curious to see her reaction.

"Just you and her, or family?"

"Just me and her."

"What happened?"

"Let's just say we realized we weren't a match made in heaven."

"The both of you decided?"

Randall thought about it for a second. "Yeah, I guess you can say that."

"And since then?"

"No one."

Why did she feel like the world had just been handed to her on a silver platter? Sandy could not contain the joy running through her heart.

She looked down at her plate. Felt the gladness moving through her. "That was absolutely wonderful."

"It's been a while since I've done this, but I think I did okay."

Humble. She liked that in a man. Sandy sighed, looked about. "You know I'm sitting over here trying not to ask for seconds."

"More than welcome, I have plenty left."

"No, I'm gonna hold out for dessert."

"Ready?" he asked, getting up from the table.

"Was gonna wait for you."

"No, go ahead. I'm a slow eater." He went to the stove and slipped on the mittens, opened the oven, and took out the pie.

"Tell me you made it from scratch," Sandy said, taking in the crispy bubbling surface.

"No, Mrs. Smith."

He laid the pie on a burner and went to the cabinet. Retrieved a dessert plate and got the ice cream. "You have to tell me how much," he said, reaching for a knife. Sandy got up and joined him.

Drawing closer than courtesy allowed, she could not stop herself from entering his space. She just wanted to be near him. Randall didn't seem to mind.

Without thought, her hand slipped over his as he placed the knife into the crust. Slowly they pulled it out and he allowed her the second cut. "Not too much," she warned, the blade dancing across the top. A three-inch slice, what she decided on.

He laid it carefully on the plate, telling her where the ice cream scooper was. She found it, took the lid off the Breyer's, got a big scoop, ice cream melting on impact. Randall got her a fork, put the ice cream back. Together they headed back to the table.

"Put a fork in me," she was saying a few minutes later. "Because I'm so full I'm just done."

"Well, I'm glad you enjoyed it."

"It's been a while . . . since a man has cooked for me, I mean."

"Did your husband cook?"

Her smile came easy, unexpectant. Full. "Did he cook? Adrian was a master. Oxtail peas, and rice. Goat head soup," the last item nibbling at the joy. Goat head soup had been the first meal Adrian ever made for her.

"West Indian?" he asked carefully, surprised.

"Yeah. Born here but his people were from Trinidad."

Silence came, the past intruding on the present. Randall finished his dinner, Sandy watching. Then there was no more food in front of either of them and Randall got up, taking the empties with him. He placed them in the sink, reached for the wine. "More?"

Sandy shook her head. There wasn't a drop of space in her stomach for anything.

"You ever checked out Pat Metheny?"

"Heard the name. Jazz, right?"

"Kinda. A strange mix of jazz, confusion, and a little Midwestern tossed in. Come on, I'll play some for you."

They headed toward the living room, Sandy to the couch. Randall went to the entertainment unit. A deep glossy red wood, she wondered out loud if he had made it.

"Had to. The stuff they sell in the stores is poorly made and outrageously expensive. It took me a while, but it was worth it."

Then music was filling the air, a delicate samba of a synthesized guitar, soft licks of the snare, and smooth drumbeats. It took up Sandy's heart, pushing her toward some anticipated place.

She turned toward him quickly. "What's that called?"

"'Are You Going with Me?'"

"Really?"

Randall nodded, picked up his wine, sat on the floor against the bottom of the sofa, her leg six inches from his shoulder. "Lean back . . . close your eyes. It's quite a journey." Never were truer words spoken.

Desperation and need filling rifts of soft simple hope, that's what the music felt like. Sandy found herself riding, perilously and blindly toward a sweetness that was climactic.

As the song ended, it was all she could do to catch her breath, soul wide open, exposed and flayed. She remembered the first time she had heard "Harpo's Blues." Thought no song could touch her more deeply.

Understood Randall had just proved that theory wrong.

Seven minutes after eight in the evening wasn't that late but Sandy found herself preparing to go. "Work tomorrow," she told him, getting up.

She might not have made the announcement had Randall not remained on the floor at her feet, sipping his wine till it was all gone, saying few words as the CD played on.

Maybe if he had turned and glanced at her more, had gently pulled her hand, indicating for her to join him on the floor, share more than space, the music, the roaring fire, she would have not uttered it. But he had remained where he was and she wasn't brave enough to join him without a real invitation.

"Let me get your things."

He returned with them, easing her jacket upon her back, handing over her pocketbook.

Sandy fixed the collar, buttoned buttons, glanced around out of habit, and was about to head toward the kitchen when the hand she had waited to find her, did.

He was looking at her carefully, eyes a little red, a bit glassy. The wine, she thought as she waited for his smile to appear. Her own face danced about one, unsure of what he was thinking, feeling, as he continued to ponder her depths.

"Much as I want to, I won't," he said carefully. "I prefer to be friends first, then lovers."

Sandy nodded, even if his words felt old-fashioned and put-offish. She made a move to step beyond him when his hand lassoed her wrist again. "It doesn't mean I'm not interested, I'm very much interested, but I can't trust myself in this moment."

It would have been better if she didn't sense a distress in his words, a sadness that danced in his eyes. "Friends then," Sandy said, wanting to move beyond the disappointment. "Hey, it works for me."

He was slow to let go, his hand holding on for as long as it could. Then Sandy was moving through the kitchen and toward the back

door. Through the moonlit garden she went, the heels of her shoes
hitting the flagstone with tiny taps. Into the garage they ventured, the
two cars sleek and shiny beneath the fluorescent light.

"I'll take her out," he offered, extending his hands for the keys.
Soon she and her car were out in the alley.

She stood by the driver's door. Waited for him to get out. "Good
night," she offered, eyes away from his, when a brush of his lips found
hers. Startled, she nearly pulled back, confused, mixed signaled. But
hands easing around her back, the soft tongue making acquaintance
with her own, made the perplexity fall away.

They stood there, pressed close, lips and tongue doing a soft tango,
her winter coat bunching and in the way.

Sandy pulled away first, her head spinning. Looked at him, wondering if he had it all planned. "Friends first?" she wanted confirming, her last bit of breath returning. "Some kiss for just friends."

"If I'd done it in the house, probably wouldn't have let you go . . .
out here seemed the safer bet. Just want to take it slow, get to know
each other." It made sense and she gave him credit. "I'm going to be
busy for the next seven days. I'll call but I don't know when. So don't
think I'm playing games or changing my mind."

"That's fine." And it was.

# Chapter 6

Winston was halfway to Sandy's house when he made a U-turn. He exited at 150th Street near JFK International Airport and took the overpass, heading back the way he came. He had hoped that she would still accept his unannounced visits, hoped that that part of their lives would not change, but as he drew closer to his destination, he faced the fact. It had.

Life was full of risks; no one knew it more than Winston did. He knew it had been a risk to sleep with Sandy, an even greater risk to expose his heart. Had sensed she wouldn't do much with the knowledge, and thus far his hunch had been right.

She was not the first woman he had longed for. In all likelihood she would not be the last. Still it was more than loneliness that caused that night to happen. There had been more to the moment than brother- and sister-in-law doing the unthinkable. Winston had no doubt.

In hindsight, it had been in the way she clung to him, the way she had moaned his name. It was in the way her body had taken him in as if he were the alpha and the omega, all she would ever need. He had felt her love in that moment, a love that was still with him, seemingly incapable of going away.

*Except she doesn't know it, or want to know,* which was the crushing truth and there was no way to make her.

To the outside world, Winston was a fine specimen, handsome, pretty-boy attractive. But inside lived a man who saw his physical attributes as a handicap, a hindrance that got in the way. Often women were unable to see beyond the butterscotch complexion, the "good" hair, the eyes of honey, making him uncomfortable in his own skin.

It made him uncertain of a woman's attraction. Had him asking himself if it were Winston the cutie or the man beneath that drew their eye.

He had watched his oldest brother Adrian in awe and envy, saw how easily he had accepted what God had bestowed on him. Wondered privately of Adrian's innate ability to separate real intent from casual curiosity.

It was one of the things that made leaving Sandy alone so hard.

She knew the man behind the face. Knew and liked him, knew and opened her world up to him; one she now seemed bent on closing.

Like all things, Winston knew he had to deal with it in the same way he had done in the past. Knew he had to suppress all he felt, forget about that night. Problem was he just didn't know how.

How do you approach a subject that you once considered for so long unapproachable? How do you tuck away old experiences, push away pessimism, and reach for something you weren't certain could be yours?

This was Martha's dilemma as she sat across from Calvin, his eyes flipping through her law review magazine, the dinner he had prepared growing cold.

"Damn . . ." he muttered, hitting the flossy page with a tap of his fingers.

"What?"

He looked up at Martha absently, shook his head. "Nothing." But in his eyes she could see it was everything.

When Britney first talked about Martha meeting Calvin, Martha had had great reservations. He wasn't white collar, didn't have a Ph.D. after his name, and of all things, hauled trash for a living.

He was so below her standards, so far away from the man she thought she wanted, it had taken everything she owned to agree to meet him. But when she did, when their eyes met, he had spoken, taking her hand, smiling warmly in her direction, she decided to at least give him a chance.

When she discovered that he not only knew a little about the law but had a deep interest and respect for it, Martha felt that God was giving her that chance she never got with her ex, Leon. They would embark on lively discussions about her court cases, he a feisty knowledgeable opponent.

She had come to look forward to such moments, but that joy had ended with a particularly heated debate a few weeks back. Caught up, both of them let go of words that should have never been spoken.

Calvin had, in so many words, told her that he would have made a better prosecutor than she ever would.

Martha had blinked, stunned. Took a look at her $45,000-a-year garbage man and went off. *"Just because you took some classes at John Jay doesn't even bring you close to what I can and can't do,"* she had insisted. *"You're nothing but a San Man, remember? Last time I heard, nobody was passing out law degrees at the city dump."*

In the heat of the argument she had meant every word, but ten seconds later she was sorry.

Calvin didn't say a thing, didn't try to hurt her back with words, didn't stomp out of her apartment. He had kept his cool, nodded at her assessment, and continued sipping his cappuccino like it was a talent.

Martha spent the better part of the evening trying to apologize, and Calvin allowed her her words but never spoke about law, attorneys, the cases she worked as an assistant district attorney ever again.

He still read her professional magazines, but kept his comments to himself. It hurt, especially now as she tried to gather up the nerve to ask what a year ago would have never come out of her mouth.

"Ever think about settling down?" She didn't mean for her voice to get so whispery and fragile, but it was the scariest thing she'd ever uttered and there was no way to curtail her fears.

"Been there, done that," he offered, his eyes fast on the magazine, one hand reaching for a fork.

"What do you mean?"

"Just like I said," he commented, bringing a plump saucy shrimp to his mouth. "Been there, done that."

"You're saying you've been married before?"

Calvin chewed, nodded.

"When?"

His eyes met hers. "Long before I met you, all right?"

But it wasn't all right. She had been seeing Calvin for some time. It was the first time she even got hint that there had been a Missus before her.

"No, it's not all right. How are you going to try and suggest it is?"

He reached out, placed his hand on her wrist. "I was but now I'm not. Court adjourned." Calvin closed the magazine, picked up his plate. Took it to the living room and turned on ESPN.

He wasn't going to talk about it. Martha knew what she had to do. In her line of work, access to court records was a given.

But did she really want to know?

*What difference would it make if he was married one year or ten, he's not anymore. Why do you want to dig up something you may not want to find out?*

Because it was her nature to uncover the truth. Her nature to know it all. It was her heart taking her places and she needed to make sure that road would be free to travel. Needed to know that Calvin was open to the idea and that his first marriage would not cloud up the possibility of a second.

She was thirty-six years old, her baby-making days coming to a fast end. For a long time she didn't think it was possible but now life was saying it was: a husband, some kids. A real family.

"Finished?"

His voice caught her off guard. Last thing she remembered, he had been eating his dinner in the living room. Now he was standing in the doorway of the kitchen, empty plate in hand.

Martha looked down at her own plate, several spoonfuls of rice, shrimp, and snow peas before her. "Still eating," she managed.

"Talking about seconds, you want any more?"

She took in the man who had claimed her heart, who had stripped her of loneliness and gave her back her worth. Tried to reason why any woman would ever walk away from him.

*Who left who,* she found herself thinking. *How come you and her didn't work out?*

Adrian had had a first wife too, something Sandy didn't even know until later. Had had a wife he was still legally married to but had separated from because she had had an affair, came down with AIDS, and eventually died.

Was that Calvin's story? Had his wife cheated on him? Were they even divorced?

"Do you?" Calvin went on to ask, things dancing in his eyes, this first breach in an otherwise smooth relationship catching them both off guard.

Martha's stomach was so full of knots she doubted she could even finish what was on her plate, less any seconds. She shook her head, pulled her eyes from his. "No, I'm done."

Martha looked at the brown folder lying on the metal table before her. She had been sitting there a good three minutes staring at the cover.

*Do I really want to know?*

It had been easy enough to track down the county. Easier still to flash her ADA badge, request the file, take off her coat, and sit in the hard padded chair.

It had been simple to ease her attaché between her feet, take a deep breath, but that was as far as she got. *Stepping out of bounds here.*

While public information was public information, there was nothing public about what she was about to do. She could never tell Calvin. She would have to read the file, gather up the information, and keep quiet.

*But what if it's something I don't want to know? Something that needs to be addressed? What if it was spousal abuse? He had beaten her?*

The glare of the overhead fluorescence lights seemed to brighten as she placed her hand on the edge of the folder and slowly opened the file.

Rasheyla Lewis Boden versus Calvin Eugene Boden. *So she had started the proceedings.* Martha tried to picture what a Rasheyla looked liked. Was she pretty? Tall? Smart? The name was unusual. Martha wondered about her roots.

Nowadays Rasheyla went along with Moesha, Shatoya, and Mustapha. But back in the late fifties? What kind of parents named their children that?

Martha remembered as a child there had been a middle-aged man who lived on her block with his wife and children. One day they were known as the Smiths, and the next, their last name became X.

It had caused quite a stir, she recalled. Her own parents stopped being friendly, and Martha had been told to stay away from their house. *Radicals, the whole lot of them,* her mother had warned. It wasn't until decades after the fact did Martha realize they had joined the Nation of Islam.

Had Rasheyla been a Muslim? Had that caused the rift in her marriage to Calvin? Had it been him wanting ham hocks and Rasheyla unable to touch pork?

Martha sat back and rubbed her eyes, tired and no less settled. While she discovered the grounds had been for irreconcilable differences, it didn't indicate just what those differences were.

She found a copy of the marriage certificate, calculated dates and came up with ages. Calvin had been twenty, Rasheyla, nineteen. *Young love or a bun in the oven,* either way it was heavy with implication.

She closed the file, got up, picked up her coat and her briefcase, and headed toward the clerk's window. She handed back the file and made her way up out of the basement of the Queens County Court House, rush hour traffic heavy on Queens Boulevard.

Her eyes dusted the tiny windows of the Criminal Courthouse across the way, passed a newly married couple taking pictures in the square and envied their ignorance.

*Fools in love,* she thought bitterly, old wounds manifesting with every step she took.

# Chapter 7

*Who named me Guru,* was all Britney wanted to know as Martha sat across from her, more troubled than Britney could ever recall her being.

"Am I crazy?" she kept on asking Britney as if motherhood and wifedom had crowned her the Grand Pooh-bah of relationships.

"Of course not, Martha. I already told you you weren't. There is nothing wrong with wanting to get married, have some kids."

"If Calvin finds out what I did . . ." Her head shook, all resemblance of the powerful prosecutor vanishing under the burdens of her heart.

"Well, he's not, not unless you tell him."

"I still can't believe I did that. That's so not like me."

"Because there was never a Calvin in your life, that's why. And he's changed everything for you, mostly good. A good man will do that. Just look at me."

"I guess you're right. But something has changed between us."

"It happens in all relationships. You grow closer or farther apart but nothing stays the same."

"It feels like farther apart."

"Well, just because you feel it doesn't make it so."

But that was little comfort. So tiny, Martha couldn't even include it anywhere inside herself. Just made her up more confession. "He wasn't there."

"Wasn't where?"

"Home, when I got there. He's always there, unless he calls and says he won't be. No dinner, no Calvin. No nothing."

Britney's brow went up. "He cooks?"

"Every day when I come home, there's Calvin, there's food. Not today though."

Britney had no wisdom for that.

Calvin took in the silence of his apartment and tried to find the peace he was looking for. He had come home to chill, not contend with the remnants of what had once been a happy-go-lucky relationship. But it was plaguing his mind and there was no escaping.

Every time he looked at Martha, all he saw was the "M" word. Like a great big brand, it seemed to encompass her from head to toe. She hadn't uttered another word about it, but it was in the very air she breathed, lingering.

A few days ago when the hour struck five and there was no Martha closing the front door, he had found himself thinking about where she could be. If she were staying late, or had to do something after work, she always called him to let him know.

That day there had been no phone call.

Concern turned to worry. Worry turned to fear. Calvin had called her job and got no answer. Keeping his eye on the clock, he waited for her arrival. As he waited, he thought. Tried to figure out where she could be and why. He found himself traversing through their current state of affairs and things began to fall into place.

He knew Martha well enough to know that his decision not to talk about his first marriage would not be enough for her. That she would not leave it alone, would not let it rest. As an assistant district attorney, her profession was uncovering all truths, even his.

The more he thought about it, the more things began to add up, a snowball of thoughts crashing into a final destination. He had confessed to a first marriage but had not supplied the facts; she was late coming home, but had not called.

By nature she possessed a deep need to know; by profession she had access to part of the truth. A hunch claimed him and would not let him go: she had gone to the court house and pulled his divorce file.

Calvin had had no proof, just a very bad feeling. But when she walked through the door forty-three minutes late, talking about an accident on the Brooklyn-Queens Expressway that had slowed the traffic to a standstill, there for the first time he saw the lies dancing in her eyes, swirling in the ugly colors of guilt and deceit.

Martha had always been truthful, up front, honest. But she had stood there, bearing false witness, confirming his hunch and that had hurt him to his soul.

Calvin didn't even know it had until he felt a sting that started in his heart then worked its way up to his eyes. He was not a man who cried, but felt, for the first time in decades, he could do just that, the trust he demanded and she had always given, out the window.

They didn't say much to each other the rest of the evening. She washing up dishes after dinner, he talking about getting an early start. They hugged goodbye, but didn't kiss. Then Calvin was in his car, heading to the apartment he hardly saw.

Initially he had found comfort in the familiar, and the next day after his shift he decided to go to his apartment. But the peace was fleeting. They hadn't spoken in days.

He missed her.

Martha left Britney's house of diapers, spit-up, and teething rings. She left the world of pediatric appointments, studio portraits, and little shoes set in bronze. She left there, her heart wanting to take all of it with her in one swoop.

Her soul was so heavy with need by the time she opened her apartment door in Jamaica Estates she felt as if she would explode from it. She went to her answering machine, saw the light blinking, grew hopeful.

But as she picked up, heard her mother's voice and nothing after that, the hope died.

It didn't seem right, didn't seem fair that just last week she and Calvin were going along so well she just knew God had given her that second chance she had been too scared and too proud to ask for.

Just last week they were happy, loving, enjoying. *Blessed.* Martha wasn't certain where that notion had come from, she a lapsed Catholic since the age of fourteen. But the idea came, and stayed, reverberated through her deeply.

*I had been blessed, hadn't I?* The more she thought about it, the deeper the hurt came, and before she could even stop to think, she was in her kitchen cabinet pulling out the Bacardi.

It had been a while since she took a drink for no reason other than to soothe her nerves. Now seemed as good a time as any.

Where was the message?

A day and a half had passed, nearly two days since they'd talked, and Martha had been certain while she sat in the courtroom that, upon her return to her office, Calvin would have left one.

But when she inquired with Kelly, there wasn't a single note for her. All Martha could do was stand there.

"You want something?" Kelly asked.

"No messages?"

"I didn't take any. Mary Ann was on the desk when I went to lunch, but I'm almost certain," Kelly began, shifting through the piles of pink papers, "there wasn't any for you."

Suddenly Martha felt thirsty, nearly parched for a drink. She thought about Brendt's, the bar right off Montague. Swallowed, said "Okay, thanks," fighting the idea. She would have gone on with her battle had she not run smack into Miles.

"Hey, chief, you okay?"

She looked up, surprised. She hadn't even seen him coming. "Miles."

"Martha . . . you look a little spaced. Everything all right?" His arm moved around her shoulder. Martha found comfort in it being there. She remembered the time she had almost slept with him, her last-minute change of heart. Since then they had managed themselves back to good coworkers and Martha felt a need to bare her soul. "No, not really. Can I get a hug?"

Miles felt her sadness. Drew her near.

She held on to Miles for no other reason than his arms held a strength her own heart did not possess. She held on to him, nose pressed against his dreads that smelled of sweat and flowers, the scent comforting. She held on to him to assure herself that the world was not as ugly as it once had been for her and she had come a long long way. That there were better things than alcohol to soothe the soul, like arms of someone who cared.

She let him go, smiled at him warmly. "Thanks, guy."

"Anytime, my sister, anytime." With that, Miles continued on his way and Martha, hers.

But the comfort was short-lived, and by the time she had pulled into her reserved parking space at 170-01 Hightower Drive, a couple of glasses of Bacardi was all she could consider. She didn't even stop to check her mail. Just wanted the numbness alcohol could bring.

Wanted to drown her sorrows the same way her own mother had been drowning hers since Martha was a child. Wanted inebriation to take over, rule her world. Free her from responsibility.

Her mind's eyes had her already in the cabinet, reaching for the bottle as she put the key into the lock. So deep was her intent it took a minute to realize that *Hiroshima* was playing from the living room and food smells were coming from the kitchen.

So startled her hand went to her heart. "Calvin?"

"Dawn," he answered, coming from the kitchen.

"What?" the unexpected surprise still with her. Martha wasn't sure if she wanted a drink, wanted Calvin gone or anything. Didn't understand what he meant by dawn, why he was there or if he would stay.

"I said dawn. I know you're ready to shoot me. Figured dawn was the best time."

It took a second to understand he was doing a few things: teasing her and waving a white flag. It took another three seconds before she accepted it. "You almost gave me a heart attack."

"Last thing I wanted to do."

Martha thought about how close she'd come to the edge of things, how not seconds ago she was ready to toss in the towel on life and become a full-fledged drunk. But mostly she considered how the sight of Calvin standing in the kitchen doorway, their favorite music in the background, cooking smells from the kitchen, had obliterated that choice.

"God, I missed you," she found herself saying, moving toward him, feet planted firmly on the ground for the first time in days.

"Only been gone two days," he offered, snaking his arms around her, holding her tight. Egyptian Musk. It was drifting from her in waves. So heavy was it in his nose, Calvin pulled back. "Since when do you wear Egyptian Musk?"

Martha seemed just as surprised. "Since never, why?"

"You smell like it."

"Miles," the word out of her mouth without thought, or consequence.

One brow raised. "Miles?"

"Yeah, you know? The dread-headed guy from my job. You met him."

In fact Calvin had, and had immediately noticed a slight reservation from the brother the moment Martha had introduced him. Initially Calvin had thought it was because he hauled garbage, didn't have that Ph.D. after his name. But another instinct took over and he concluded it was because Calvin had what Mr. Dread Headed wanted—Martha.

Calvin never mentioned it, kept the bit of news to himself. But here Martha was coming home smelling like she'd taken a bath in him. The issue bubbled up in his throat.

"Why are you smelling like Miles?"

At first Martha couldn't even believe he was asking. Her heart was so far from Miles it was too ridiculous to entertain. "He hugged me."

"Hugged you?"

"Yeah."

"Why?"

It was the first sample of jealousy Calvin had shown. It touched her, but it also tickled. "You don't think—"

"Don't know what I think, Martha. All I know I'm gone from your life for two days and you come home smelling like Mr. Dreadful." It was an old hurt she was dancing on but Martha didn't know that.

"Number one, his name is Miles, and he was a friend long before I met you. Number two, it's not even that kind of party, Calvin. I was feeling kind of low today at work. Asked him for a hug, that's all."

"Low about what?"

"You."

She turned away from him, the tickle gone. Wanted out of her work clothes and headed for the bedroom. She was sitting on the bed, rubbing one tired foot when Calvin entered.

"Me?"

"Yeah. You. You, me, us. All of that."

He sat down next to her. "What about us?"

Martha searched his face, settled on his eyes. "For the first time in a long time I'm thinking about things, about life, where it can take me, and I'm scared, Calvin. Not even in my nature to be, but I am, just scared silly."

"Scared of what?"

"Of wanting something you don't."

"Marriage." It wasn't a question.

"Yes. Marriage. White gown, morning sickness, a dozen little nappy-headed kids getting on my last nerve." It was truth-telling time. Martha went with it. "I needed to know about your marriage. Needed to know what type of husband you made. Went to the courthouse. Pulled the records."

He looked away, his head shaking, hurt with him. "You could have asked me, Martha. You didn't have to go that route."

"I tried but you told me, 'Case closed.' "

"No, you asked me if I was married before, not the type of husband I was."

Stare-down time. Two pair of eyes, hearts fixed on opposite sides of the spectrum. Martha pushed her envelope. "What type of husband did you make?"

"Obviously not a very good one if I got divorced."

"Why?"

He looked at her a long time, eyes piercing her soul. "I really don't know. Only that I tried it and failed."

"Was it because she was a Muslim?"

He frowned. "Rayshela?"

"Yeah."

"No. Just a regular old go-to-church-sometimes Baptist."

"But her name?"

"Was just something her mother made up. Her father was named Ray. Her mother's name was Sheila. Get it, Rayshela?"

*Like Britney and Maurice coming up with "Bereace."* Martha the prosecutor moved in, determined to confiscate all she could from this moment. "She started the proceedings, am I right?"

Calvin nodded, pain in his eyes.

"What was it, did you cheat on her? Beat her? What?"

"I did nothing but loved her." Calvin got up from the bed, old sorrow shifting into new.

Martha reached out, placed a hand on his. "I'm sorry, Calvin." When he did not answer, she took her hand away.

From the moment Martha had become a prosecutor, she had adhered to the belief that the truth will set you free, but as she got into bed, and rolled on to her side, behind her a different truth was speaking and it had not set her free.

It hadn't liberated Calvin either.

She could feel him breathing. Could feel a tension in him taut as a spring wound. Felt he had things to say. She wished he would say them; longed to hear him speak.

Martha wanted to shatter the silence, dismantle the wall that was growing thick and full. But she had forced too much from him already. Knew better than to try and get more.

There was only one thing she could really do in the moment, something she wanted even if she wasn't certain he did. She sat up, slipped the nightgown off her back, turned, scooted close, and pressed her nipples against his back. Felt like she was waging war as she forced her hand then her arm up under his side.

That he did not shift nor move to allow access told her much, but she was determined to get them past the moment and what better way than making love? He was death-still as her hand landed on his stomach. No slight contraction, no reaction could she sense. With her other hand, she reached over him and slid her palm into his underwear, his body telling her things he wouldn't.

Half-hard, Calvin's penis swelled and elongated. She felt the heat in his skin, knew his breath was growing heavy, but the rest of him didn't move an inch. No accommodation, giving in to her caresses. Calvin remained statue still.

She ceased. Pulled her arm away, anger and hurt too deep to let a tear even think about falling.

Calvin's mind was racing.

Though he hadn't been certain just when he would give in to the hot warm musings of the woman he loved, he had been certain that the point would come. That he would roll toward her, kiss her deep, find condoms. Venture back into the tender part of her soul.

But he knew Martha. Knew he had hurt her and she would play hard ball to get back at him. So he forgot about the healing, shifted a little, sleep far far away.

\* \* \*

Sandy ran the soapy cloth around the burners on her stove. Dug a finger to loosen a hard rice grain. She looked at the phone and it stared back at her. Two days since she'd heard from Randall, she knew today would be the day.

So certain, joy found her as her phone begun to ring. But when she said hello, heard the voice, it fell away.

"Winston."

"Yeah. Just calling to remind you of Saturday after next."

"Saturday?"

"Adrian's birthday. We're going to the cemetery."

How could she had forgotten? "Oh . . . yeah. Right. Saturday." Confusion still had her. "We're meeting here, right?" she asked, rubbing her forehead, eyes scrunched.

"Yeah. Around two. My mom and sister are cooking, so you don't have to make anything."

"The cake."

"Mom's making black cake."

"Yeah, right."

"You okay?"

She had been up until ten seconds ago when she realized she had forgotten her own husband's birthday, plans to visit his grave, and her mother-in-law was making black cake.

Black cake, a rich heady combination of flour, molasses, eggs, chopped fruits and nuts, and a nice soaking of 100 proof rum; a confection so heady that small slices were the wisest choice. Black cake, the staple of any West Indian celebration, be it a wedding or a dead son's birthday, forgotten in the arrival of a new man. Guilt found her.

"Sandy?"

"Yeah, I'm here."

"So it's set then?"

"Yeah, it's set."

Silence. She could feel Winston on the other end, sensing all that he would not say. She felt a need to explain but wasn't certain what the explanation would be. *You were a good fuck, but that's all. Besides, there's a new man in my life . . . ?*

Sandy knew she should say something. Knew Winston was waiting for words of comfort from her, even if it was just "How have you been?" But she felt no real desire to know, that part of her life over and done with.

"So I guess I'll see you then," she offered.

"Guess you will."

"Take care." Sandy hung up the phone. Found herself leaning against the wall, rooted, thinking for a long time.

She picked up the phone again. Looked at the piece of paper with the phone number she nearly knew by heart. Listened to it ring. Got no answer. Heard the answering machine come on. Didn't leave a message, finished up her kitchen chores.

When she had left Randall's house, she had been riding a high so swift, so clear, so welcomed, she barely recognized the sorrowed widowed weepy woman she had been just weeks before.

It was a high that had sustained her straight through the next day, lessening as early Tuesday evening became late night. Yes, he had told her he would be busy. But she was certain he'd find the time to pick up the phone.

But it was Wednesday now and there was no call from him. *I'll give him one more day. One more to call me. Get beyond it if he doesn't,* a lie her heart refused to hear even as her head insisted so.

Randall promised himself that after he soaked in his claw foot tub, dried off, and had a bite to eat, he would call Sandy. He had made the same promise to himself yesterday and the day before, but hadn't. Three long hard days, all of them starting at eight in the morning and not ending until ten o'clock at night, he was just beaten down and wrung out.

He had been so behind in his schedule that he forced himself to work until he was exhausted, until every muscle ached and it hurt just to walk. By the time he put his key in his door this night, he had to resist the urge just to lie on the floor and not move.

He forced himself upstairs, ran the tub full of hot water and epson salts, then stripped. Got into the tub and closed his eyes. When he awoke, it was past midnight, and the water was cold. *Too late to call Sandy now.*

He'd make it up to her tomorrow, last thoughts as he crawled naked into the bed.

# Chapter 8

While most residents of Queens took mass transit to work, Sandy drove into Manhattan five days a week. What she spent on gas, tolls, and parking equaled a car note and she had to leave extra early to get there on time, but she had needed the solitude her car offered after she'd returned to work.

In her car she didn't have to have strangers witness her crying spells. In her car she could cry, sing, sometimes address the husband who was no longer there. In her car she could play her music loud, soft, or drink in the air-tight silence; the Camry was a nurturing womb getting her from Point A to Point B.

But as Sandy made her way home, she realized it had been a while since she'd cried, months since she'd had one-way conversations with her dead husband. She realized that even on the coldest days she sometimes cracked the window, letting the noisy exhaust-laden rush-hour traffic air in.

*I'm better, aren't I?* A question that did not require an answer as she pulled up to her street and saw the white van parked out front.

The white van had sat, from time to time, in front of her house and so the sight wasn't unusual. What was unusual was it had not been parked there in nearly a week, when Randall had finished the basement.

But there it was, engine idling.

Sandy pulled up behind him, counted to five, and then with a deep breath, grabbed her pocketbook, her tote, and got out of her car.

Her words were ready with a scolding that never left as he appeared out of nowhere, kissing her like there was nothing else he wanted to do.

Sandy broke away, his smile curing her blues. His words, "Work. Not because I didn't want to see you," balmy, soft. "By the time I got in, it was so late and I was so tired. Today I quit early."

"I understand," and she did, the kiss still with her, hope dancing in his eyes that she could only consider to be real. "Just glad you came. Feel like cooking?"

In truth, Randall didn't. He just wanted to sit in her presence, discover more bits and pieces about her. "These last days have been so rough, I don't think I have enough strength to lift a pot."

They entered her house, Sandy turning on lights. "Well, as usual there's not much in my frig. We could order out."

"Sounds like a plan." He looked down at his work boots. "Mind if I take these off? I was doing a fence today, the backyard was muddy. I wouldn't want to track dirt all over your floors."

"No, go ahead."

He eased out of his Timberlands, edged them neatly against the wall. It was a simple sight, but the image touched her heart. Made her smile, a joy she kept secret as she turned away.

"Pizza? Chinese? What?" Sandy asked.

"You choose."

"Pizza?"

Randall nodded. "Pizza it is."

Randall sat in her living room, gazed around him. "Nineteen thirties," he decided.

"Nineteen thirties what?"

"This house. I'm guessing its age. They built the best houses back then."

"Have you always been into building?"

He smiled. "My father was a tinkerer. He had a workshop in the garage. On Saturdays I'd spend time with him there, fascinated by what he did with wood."

"So it's like a generational thing?"

"I guess you can say that. I always appreciated the beauty of a good piece of wood. Loved how you can take a piece of timber and craft it into something special."

Sandy looked around her. "I was thinking about making a small library in that corner. I have all these books in boxes, with no place to put them."

"That's simple enough to do. What kind of wood?" Sandy shrugged. She had no idea. "Different woods are good for different things. With a book shelf you should use a hard wood. After a time those books start to bear down on it, can cause it to buckle in the middle."

"I never realized that." But there were many things Sandy hadn't realized until she'd met Randall. Each discovery was like a drop of honey on her tongue. "How much would it cost?"

"Book shelves? Again, it would depend on the type of wood, how high you wanted them, and how you wanted them finished." Randall went to the corner. Lifted a hand level to his chest. "What, about this high?"

"Higher."

He lifted his hand to his forehead. "Like this?"

"Six feet always sounded like a good height to me."

"Well, I'm five-eleven, so that would be about"—his hand moved an inch above his head—"here."

"Yeah, that's about right."

He nodded. "Consider it done."

"You'd do it for me?"

He took a moment to look at her before he answered, a kind of wonder coming into his face. "I can't think of a single reason why I wouldn't."

There it was. The bridge, sturdy over raging waters, Eden on the other side. They were poised at the beginning, feet barely touching its graceful edge. The first step taken, the world of new acquaintances, left behind.

She looked away, afraid her eyes would reveal too much. Reminded herself that they had to take things slow. "Time . . . money, there are reasons."

"Time?" Randall said, coming to sit back beside her. "Don't have a lot of that. Ditto money. But sometimes you manage to get what you need."

Yes, he was with her, right there beside her. She felt it in the tempered space between, his words a link holding them tight. In that moment, she felt him. Felt him as he was, under her skin, drifting along every beat of her heart. The look in his eyes said he was feeling her too.

The doorbell rang. "Pizza," she exclaimed, getting up, clumsy on her own feet. Sandy took the twenty off the sofa table, went to the door. Came back less than a minute later, a large white box in her hand. "Smells good," simple words as she headed to the kitchen, Randall a few paces behind her.

Randall helped himself to three slices, half of one leaning off the plate. Sandy took hers one at a time. She folded the crispy crust until it bent in the middle, held the slice three inches from her plate. Waited for the gooey mixture of tomato sauce and melted mozzarella to descend into a thick plump drop before she scooped it up with her fingers and popped it into her mouth.

"You too?" Randall asked.

"Me too what?"

"Separating the sauce and cheese from the crust. My brother does that. Used to drive me crazy."

"It's the only way to eat it. Eat that part first, then eat the crust."

"In that case, you should just order a baked crust with some sauce and cheese on the side."

"Can't," she offered, biting into the crunchy near-burnt bottom. For all the Pizza Huts, Dominoes, and Little Ceasar's of the world, not one of them could beat a real authentic New York slice. Extra-large by standard slices, most were baked in real brick ovens until the bottoms were so toasty they were blackened in spots. The sauce was richer and sweeter and the cheese was heaven.

"Why not?"

"Because the sauce has to cook on the crust and the cheese has to cook on the sauce. It's a real science, don't you know?" Sandy offered, taking another bite.

"Do now." To test her method, Randall bent the crust on his next slice, waited for the soft plop to his plate, grabbing it with his thumb and middle finger. He slipped it into his mouth, chewed, face indecisive as to whether it was good, bad, or worth the energy. "It's okay," he decided, finishing it off with a bite of crust.

"One of the reasons why I don't think I could ever live anywhere else. Been a couple of places in my lifetime and nobody does pizza like New York."

"What about Jersey?"

"Haven't had Jersey pizza, but I had New Orleans, California, and even the supposedly world-famous Chicago . . . not."

He seemed nonplussed. "Not . . . I haven't heard that expression in a long time."

Sandy flicked her wrist. "Oh please, I was the original 'not' girl. Used to say it so much made my own self sick of the word."

"You?"

"Yeah, me."

Silence came as Randall picked up a napkin, cleaned his fingers, dabbed his mouth, determined not to think about tomorrow, the extra work he had to put in because of this extravagance.

He had put the last support post into the soft mushy earth of Mr. Hataway's backyard, estimating that he would be able to lay in the parallel two by fours before the sky grew too dark when he decided to stop. That he had to come and see Sandy.

Some women saw Randall as picky. Randall saw himself as having a clear eye about what did and didn't work for him in a relationship. Too strong a woman turned him off. He wanted to be the one changing the lightbulbs, putting up the shelves.

By nature he fixed what had been broken, restored what had been worn away. This was part of Sandy's charm.

Beyond her smoky beauty and the smile that could light the world, there was a sorrow in her that needed healing. A sorrow he felt drawn to. A sorrow he wanted to mend.

Now here he was across from her and there was no other place he wanted to be.

"Just what are you thinking on so hard?" she wanted to know.

"You," his eyes never leaving her face. "I was thinking about you and how little things could come to mean so much."

"Like?"

"Like you and that pizza. When my brother did it, it turned my gut. But when you do it, it's cute."

"Cute?"

"Yeah, cute, as in pretty, sweet, touching."

"Eating pizza," she wanted confirmed.

"*You* eat pizza, yeah."

"Oh, you are too much," she decided, waggling a finger at him.

"And then some," Randall answered, picking up his Sprite and taking a long chug.

Randall ate four slices, Sandy had two, and the rest of the pie was slipped into freezer bags and placed into her refrigerator. "Put them into the oven later and they're as good as fresh," she told him.

Sandy washed up the few dishes, refused his offer to dry. Swept the floor, wiped off the counters, and took one look around her. *Slow,* she thought as she made her way back to the living room, Randall in the darkness behind her. *Slow,* she repeated in her head as she picked up the remote, clicked on the television, channel surfing to find something they could watch.

"I just think they have too much money, that's the reason none of them can stay together," Sandy was saying as *Entertainment Tonight* went to a commercial, the story of another Hollywood couple breaking up fading from the screen. "Don't you think so?" she asked, turning toward Randall.

Head back, mouth open, there was no doubt he was fast asleep. Her hand went to shake him, her mouth ready to call his name, but she stopped herself.

As beautiful as a toddler in the midst of an afternoon nap, that's how angelic he looked. All defense gone, lost to the nether world, every line in his face had vanished, leaving the surface smooth, soft.

Sandy felt a deep need to place her lips upon the rise of his forehead, the slope of his nose. A cheekbone, that closed eyelid.

She looked down at his hands, saw her own close to them, realizing for the first time that there wasn't much different in skin tone, another second coming before she understood that for the first time since she was a child, a man who wasn't light-skinned, high yellow, *butterscotch* now placed a bid on her heart.

She had always been the different one, different from both her mother and her brother. She didn't have the light skin, the wavy hair, eyes that changed color depending on the weather like they had. *Just black everywhere.*

When she was a youngster, strangers would ask her mother whose child was she. Her brother Cliff used to call her names like Smoky and Midnight. Sandy's parents whipped him but he kept it up. She was her father's child, her Grandma Tee used to say.

Near blue-black, Sandy had taken on all her father's genes and not a single one from her mother. As a result, her skin tone became a hindrance for her, one that magnified when she started dating.

Her father always found issue with the regular brown-skinned boys she brought home, but the brighter, damn near white ones, were a whole different matter—Samuel Hutchinson could not say enough about them.

Sandy loved her father; his wisdom and guidance, golden. Wanting to please him and trusting his opinions, after a while light-skinned boys were all she'd come to want for herself.

Until now.

Her eyes raced to Randall's face, marveling at the man who had changed so much. In that moment she understood that she had sought out light-skinned men to complete her, make her whole. That she had searched them out with her father's blessings, to compensate for what he perceived was a hindrance—her own dark skin.

Hadn't her father done the same thing? Hadn't he found the lightest woman he could and married her? No doubt Sandy coming out as dark as himself was a disappointment, one he tried to correct by steering her toward the opposite end of her own complexion.

She had never thought about it until now. Had never tried to figure out why. While she never understood why her father never saw the same worth in a man who was black like him, she had never allowed herself to take that thought to the next step. But now she did.

Her father was trying to lighten up his color line.

Somehow Sandy had missed that gene pool, but Samuel Hutchinson was going to make sure her children and his grandchildren didn't. And if biasing her against whom she saw in the mirror, his own blackberry face was the price, then so be it.

The world's treatment of you was still based on color. Light-skinned blacks were considered smarter, worthier, more attractive, something Sandy realized that her father had undoubtedly learned early.

Yet in that moment, sitting next to Randall, it no longer mattered. In that moment who she was, *smoky, blackie, midnight,* became okay; that how she looked was just fine.

Randall had returned a worth to her. He had allowed her to be comfortable inside her skin. Had opened up the heart that had been shut closed. Randall, doing so much for her, fast asleep on her couch.

She found herself hoping that it would always remain so as she touched his shoulder gently, his name, prayer-soft "Randall, Randall, wake up," leaving her lips.

His eyes shot open, red tinged and wearied. He blinked, rubbed them with callused fingers, sat up straighter. Looked at her apologetic. "Fell asleep?"

She nodded, smiled. Knew there was only one place he needed to be. "Come on, time to get you home."

"I'm just bushed."

"I know. And I appreciate you taking time to come and see me."

Randall stood, stretched, made a noise like a lion as he yawned. Shook his shoulders. Rubbed his face again. "Can you get my jacket?" he asked as he headed for his boots.

Sandy went to the coat closet, pulled it out. She could not stop herself from pressing her nose to the lining. Woodsy, strong, Randall's scent filled her nose.

"I'm going to be busy for the next few days, but I'm always home no later than eleven. Is that too late?"

"For?"

"To call you."

"No, that's fine. Even if I'm sleep, I won't mind waking up."

"You sure?"

"Positive." She opened her arms to hug him, but Randall had other plans. His lips pressed to hers, all that they were meeting in the joining.

It was Randall who broke away. "Really," he said, putting her at arm's length, "I got to go."

Sandy nodded. "Get home safe." Watched as he bounded down her steps and made his way to his van, vanishing behind it; her heart tender in the aftermath.

She could tell it now.

Sandy could get on the phone with her friends and share the Randall story. She called Janice first.

"Second date?" Janice asked. "You never even told me about the first."

"Because I wasn't sure if anything would come from it."

"So it's a good thing?"

"Oh my God yes, a very good thing."

"You two didn't."

"No. Later, much later."

"Well, I am happy for you."

"Happy for myself," Sandy admitted.

"When do I get a peek?"

"Sometime later."

"Well, you sound happier than I've heard you sound in a long time."

"'Bout time, don't you think? But you have to do me a favor. I want to be the one to tell my folks. So don't tell Cliff, or them."

"Because Adrian hasn't been dead long?"

"Yeah." But there was more.

Randall didn't fit the mold her father saw for her. *Isn't light-skinned enough,* and then there was that truth Sandy still had to tell him. She wasn't certain if she and Randall would survive it, could not predict that outcome. Saw no sense in telling her parents about someone who may or may not be around.

Sandy got off the phone with Janice and called Martha, who was happy to hear the news, then she called Britney, who was just as glad. She wasn't certain what the future would bring, but in that moment hope had returned.

Winston stood in his living room, the golden-framed eight-by-ten picture in his hands. He stared upon the photograph, one finger dragging itself over the hard shiny glass. It glided over his brother's image, over Sandy's, his own.

Taken at the Queens Botanical Gardens, the wedding photo gave no suggestion of the cold gray wet gloomy day that had been September 21st. It gave no hint of the heartbreaking surrender his heart had felt from the moment Sandy and Adrian had said I do.

The picture did not reveal how much he had both loved and hated his brother as they stood in tuxedos, smiling for the photographer, looking more like twins than they'd ever looked before. And Sandy, a vision in white lace and satin and pearls, happy, so very happy.

Even in the still-life photo, Winston could see her love for Adrian. Could feel it. Paper, chemicals, and glass unable to contain it, flatten it, or hold it back.

It had not been his choice to fall for Sandy, but he had. Had not been his choice to share that special night with her, but his heart could not say no. And in the aftermath he was lonelier than he ever had been. Wanting her more than he had ever wanted her.

He had not seen her since that Sunday dinner. Had not sat in her presence, been witness to her beauty. Winston wanted to go ring her bell every waking minute, but knew he couldn't. Could only hope that she would reach out to him, reconnect. Take them back to at least where they were before they became lovers. Half of something, better than nothing at all.

It was a crazy day at work.

So much so Sandy had not been able to go out for lunch, but had to order in. In the half hour it took for it to arrive, all she wanted to do was dig in. She had managed to eat all of her potato salad and half of the sandwich in between typing up her boss's letters, but she really wanted to take two minutes to finish the other half; down the going-flat can of Sprite.

She looked at her half a roast beef on rye, fingers busy along the keys, eager to finish the sentence she was typing. She entered the period key, took her hands off the keyboard, and was reaching for the rest of her lunch when her phone rang.

"Malgovy, Connor and Dalton, Sandy Hutchinson speaking."

"Well, hello, Ms. Malgovy, Connor and Dalton Sandy Hutchinson speaking."

"Randall," more sigh than question.

"Sandy," he volleyed back to her. "Running late."

"Oh."

"Yeah, looks like I'm going to be here till about nine or so."

"Oh." The disappointment was in her thick. They were supposed to be going to the nine o'clock show at the Fresh Meadows Cinaplex.

"I know we were supposed to go to the movie, but I was wondering if you mind if we stay in. You could maybe pick something up, go to my house. Wait for me. I can swing by on my break, leave a key under the doormat, or something."

Or something. The implication was heavy. But that's how things were moving for them, heavy, full, racing toward a final destination, one that Sandy had been trying to put the breaks on. "Like let myself in?"

"Yeah."

The key to his house, the key to more. Sandy swallowed. "You don't mind?"

He laughed, relieving a quick tension that whispered along the phone line. "You plan on robbing me?"

"Course not."

"Then I don't mind."

Sandy tried to be casual about it. Tried to not be too obvious in slipping her hand under the doormat and retrieving the key. Tried to keep her cool as she fit the key into the lock and gave the heavy wooden door a push.

She tried not to feel like she was going through Randall's underwear drawer as she let herself in, hand moving across the nubby glossy wall in search of a light switch. Found one. Shadows became a couch, a side table, the fireplace now cold and gray with spent ashes.

Shadows became the entertainment center Randall himself had crafted. Became the copy of Richard Wright's *Native Son* lying on the coffee table.

She closed the door and the silence pressed around her quick. With care, she took off her coat, hung it in his closet, which was heavy with the scent of him: sawdust, sweat, adhesives, cologne.

A good smell.

Sandy made her way through the dining room and took the bags of food to the kitchen. She turned on the light, saw not even a dirty dish in the sink, the stove sparkling clean. She looked down at her hands, decided to wash them.

She had never used his bathroom so she had no idea where it was. She opened one door and found stairs leading to the basement. Another, the food pantry. That only left one place—upstairs. She wasn't sure she wanted to go up there.

Upstairs was where his bedroom was. Upstairs was a private domain, and though she had no intentions of snooping, she wasn't ready to see that place she may or may not get the chance to rest her head.

Sandy didn't want to know if he slept on a king-size bed or a queen. If his bed was four-poster, or sleigh-style. She didn't want to know if his comforter was big and fluffy or how many pillows adorned it.

She did not want to know a thing about his bedroom or his bed unless she was certain one day she would share it with him. That one Sunday morning the rising sun would find her nestled in its confines.

There was the kitchen sink, but her mother had instilled in her a long time ago that dirty hands had no business being washed in the same place you washed dishes. *"You don't bring the outside world's dirt to the kitchen sink. Use the bathroom,"* her mother used to say.

She had to go upstairs.

She looked up into the dark landing and paused. Clicked on the light and made her way up, saw the bathroom off to the right, the other doors closed. Relieved she went inside, turned on more lights, and washed her hands.

Coming back downstairs, she turned the television on for company, and went back to the kitchen to eat.

She was on the couch dozing when the sound of the key turning in the lock awoke her. Sandy hadn't even been certain when she'd fallen asleep, only that she found herself coming to as Randall came in.

She had never seen him look so weary.

"Hey," she called out, getting up off the sofa.

"Took a whole lot longer than I thought," the evidence of his hard work all over him. There was sheet rock powder in his hair, dusting the side of his face. His hands looked ashy and swollen, his eyes hollowed and exhausted. His pants were spattered with drops of white.

She went to hug him, but he gently urged her back. "I'm a mess. No sense in you becoming a mess too . . . gonna go upstairs, run a bath, be down in a while."

Sandy heard the sound of footsteps above her, the opening and closing of doors, the rush of water filling a tub. Then twenty-three minutes passed and not a sound could be heard. She debated with herself to go up or not.

Went up.

Sandy knocked on the closed bathroom door. "Hey, you okay in there?" Got no answer. She knocked again, and again, calling his name. Stared at the doorknob handle, debated. Reached for it, gave it a twist, her eyes cautiously moving around the slightly cracked door.

"Randall?"

The claw foot tub was filled near the brim with water, Randall's naked body stretched out in it, knees slightly bent. Head back, mouth open, Sandy knew the position. He was fast asleep.

She forced her eyes no farther than his shoulders as she moved toward him, touched one, water splashing her feet as he came awake, disoriented.

"Damn," he muttered, sitting up, water racing over the hardest, tightest, tauntest chest and upper stomach she'd ever seen; the sight like electricity, charging her.

She turned away, embarrassed, hot, bothered; things in her going retro to the first time. Her body, ready, willing, hardening, softening, pulsing.

Sandy turned away, was nearly gone when she heard the sound of rushing waters, felt a strong hand on her wrist, the pull back toward him.

She turned, looking away, afraid to look, want. *Have.* But her eyes disobeyed her as she took in his body.

Randall, naked, dripping wet. Water dancing, glistening on the muscles of his long sculptured arms, the grooves that nestled downward about his stomach, the wet pubic hair, the penis stirring.

Randall, wanting her.

Sandy swallowed, fought with herself hard. Stepped back, gave a tense laugh, eyes fixed on the sink. "You're all wet." She snatched a towel off the rack. Tossed it at his chest, turning, leaving the bathroom, fleeing away from desire and need.

His. Her own.

Randall came downstairs a few minutes later, sweat pants and a white undershirt on but *not a single thing underneath them.* Sandy could tell by the slight lump that shifted as he made his way. She could feel his fire, his desire before he hit the bottom step.

He clapped his hands together, rubbed them. "What's on the menu?"

"Rib Shack?" she said, nervous, unable to hold his eyes. "Chopped barbecue, cold slaw. Fries, sure they're cold now."

"You going to join me?"

"Watch you eat? Yeah, why not." The table would be between them. Keep them apart for a little while at least.

He devoured his food, fast, insidious, like he hadn't had a bite in weeks. Randall ate like Sandy never saw him eat before, quick and swift. She knew why.

*Because food isn't on his mind.*

It seemed they had just sat down to the table before he was rising, dumping the empty container into the garbage, downing the last bit of soda from the can. "That was good," his eyes saying what he wanted for dessert.

"Yeah, they make good food."

He lifted his arms to her, beckoning her with every cell in his body. But Sandy was rooted to the floor, could not move, could not breathe, could only think, *Tell him, tell him now.* But now still seemed too soon. Now seemed too risky. Now held no promise.

Even though Randall wanted her, even though they had made it to the first step, where they were more than just acquaintances, beyond just friends, she wasn't certain if his like of her was deep enough, vested enough, intense enough to stand the truth.

So she lied. "We can hug, but that's all." He looked puzzled. "Wrong time," she managed.

"Oh," his arms dropped a little.

"Yeah, oh. So you still want me over there?"

"Hug will work."

So Sandy went, moving against the body that wanted her, that she wanted. Felt all of Randy like she had never felt him before. Wondered if she would get the chance to know him that way.

"You feel good," he murmured.

"You too."

"Spend the night."

"We can't."

"I know that. Just want to wake up next to you, that too much to ask?"

"Even though?"

"It's a period, Sandy, not the plague."

She pulled away. "You're gonna behave?"

"I'll behave."

"Okay."

They turned off the lights, the television, made their way upstairs. Randall swung the bedroom door open, a four-poster bed, rich and imposing before her. "Don't tell me you made this too?"

He looked sheepish. "Sometimes I go for weeks without work. Got to do something."

She ran her hand over the pineapple-shaped edge. "How did you do this?"

"With a turning wheel. I have it in my basement. You set it to the cuts you want and push the button." He moved toward his dresser drawer. "Will a T-shirt do?"

"How big?"

"Oh, I see what you mean." He closed the drawer, opened another. "Got a football jersey. Kind of beat-up, but it will come to your knees."

"That'll work."

Sandy took it, went to the bathroom. Stared at herself in the mirror, full of thoughts. She pulled away, got undressed. Left her bra on for safe measure. Folded her clothes into a neat pile. When she got back to the bedroom, Randall was already in bed. Sandy was glad it was a king-size.

She moved to her side, two pillows, fresh, barely used, awaiting her head. "I say my prayers, hope you don't mind."

"No, not at all."

Sandy dropped down to her knees, brought her hands together, bowed her head. Made her pleas quick, rose. Pulled back the covers. Got in, the cold sheets making her shiver.

"Cold?"

"A little."

He scooted over, slipped his arms around her, pulled her back to his chest. His heat took away every bit of chill her body knew, sleep a million miles away.

"This is not going to work," Sandy confessed. "Why don't you go on your side and I'll stay over here."

"Can we hold hands?"

"Hands are good."

He shifted, took her hand. Held it. Two minutes later he was fast asleep, leaving Sandy to study unfamiliar shadows dusting his bedroom. Leaving her wide awake, wanting, and full of lies.

Something was drawing her to consciousness.

Slowly she opened her eyes, morning light soft in the room, Randall's face half a foot from her own. It took a moment to realize he had been watching her sleeping. Her smile came easy. "Morning," she whispered.

"Morning. You sleep okay?"

"Yeah, pretty good."

"I have to get going. You can stay if you like. The doors are self-locking."

Sandy sat up. "No, I better get home. It's Saturday. Have a house to clean, laundry. That kind of stuff."

"You're a sight to behold, you know that?"

Her hand went to her hair. "I can imagine."

He urged it away. "No, not like that, Sandy. You're beautiful. One of the most beautiful women I've ever seen."

She looked away, embarrassed.

"You have to have known that."

She looked back at him. "There's so much I didn't know."

"Like?"

Her hand touched his face. "You for one. That day you rang my doorbell I never thought we'd end up here."

"Where's here?"

Her eyes moved from his. "Here. In your house, in your bed, together."

"Technically speaking we are just in the bed, we're not in bed *together.*"

"You know what I mean. Never thought it could be like this ever again for me."

"You loved him a lot, didn't you?"

"With everything I owned, and when he died, a big part of me died too. But now," her head shook, tears filling the corner of her eyes.

He reached for her, drew her near. "Ditto," he said softly in her ear.

They left together. Back on his work schedule, he told her he wouldn't be free until the middle of next week. "I have Thursday off, maybe we can go see that movie."

"Looking forward to it," she told him back.

# Chapter 9

When the clock struck seven-fifteen in the evening and Cliff hadn't come home yet, it should have been old hat for Janice. Lately Cliff wasn't getting home before eight.

Janice had stopped waiting for him before she had her supper and got in the habit of putting his helping into a Tupperware dish, making it easy to heat up. But this evening felt different.

This evening, *Where is he really?* had slipped into her mind and refused to leave. This evening Janice remembered the times Cliff used to get home no later than seven and now he was coming in past eight.

This evening the whys arrived.

*Why all of a sudden? Why doesn't he seem to mind it much? Why doesn't he ask for more help? Why hasn't he called to say he's going to be late?*

Janice had a bunch of whys and not a single answer, except one. *Because he's up to something.* The more she thought about it, the more possible it became. Hundreds of women flowed in and out of his office building every day. Hundreds passing by Cliff on a near daily basis.

The temptation was strong and the old Cliff would have succumbed *in a heartbeat,* Janice thought bitterly.

*He told me himself. Told me about how much of a Playa he used to be and how love hadn't even been a part of his vocabulary.* Until he'd met Janice, he had gone on to say, but she wasn't remembering that part. Could not remember how she had changed not only his head, but his heart.

In that moment all Janice knew was Cliff was coming home late on a regular basis, that once upon a time messing around had been his forte and the opportunity to cheat presented itself every time he walked into his office.

In that moment, despite assurances from both Cliff and Sandy, Janice was near certain that Cliff was doing the buck wild with someone else while she sat waiting at home. Men had been getting over her ever since she could remember. Why should now be any different?

So real was the revelation, so deep did it penetrate her heart, that Janice called his office. When it took him five rings to answer, slightly out of breath, she knew she had been right.

But Janice hadn't been right.

Cliff had been returning from the men's room when his phone began to ring. He knew who it was and made a mad dash to answer it. He had meant to call Janice, but in truth he just wanted to get his work done. Cliff had decided to call her when he was leaving instead.

He snatched up the receiver, catching his breath. "Hello?" heard nothing. "Hello?" No answer, then the click of the dial tone. "Damn." He hung up, knowing he was in the doghouse again.

Cliff had to decide whether to take his punishment now—by calling home—or just get it later when he walked through the front door. He looked at the work he had yet to finish and knew the longer it took to get home, the worse it would be.

He left his office and headed home.

He spent the train and bus ride home deciding how he could explain, once again, that he had been at work. Cliff spent the commute trying to conjure up new unused words that would, once and for all, put her unfounded suspicions to rest.

He had tried them all.

Cliff had humored her, cajoled her, promised her, made the sweetest love to her. He had given her tiny tokens of appreciation, called her office throughout the day and once, had even marched her to the bathroom mirror, made her look at her own reflection, while he insisted that *that* face was the only one he loved, wanted.

Now as the F train surged toward the 179th Street Station, he found he was out of new explanations. He hoped that her anger wouldn't last all night. He was tired and all he really wanted was a good night's rest.

"Nine-thirty?" her first words to him. "Since when you come home at nine-thirty?"

Another question was burning in her eyes and Cliff wished she'd just come out and ask him. He wished she would just ask him so he could tell her once and for all, *no, I'm not cheating on you.* But he knew Janice. Knew she'd never speak it. Would dance around it, insinuate the hell out of it, but would never ask.

"I didn't leave till after eight."

"And why's that, Cliff?" Her eyebrows were scrunched, her face hard and edgy. Her mouth was so pinched it could cut paper.

"Because I had that much work Janice, that's why . . . you know I was there. You called, didn't you?"

She told her lie and didn't even blink. "No. I didn't call your office."

Cliff was in no mood to argue. He just wanted her to have her say, whatever it was this time around so he could change his clothes and eat his dinner. "Fine. You didn't."

"You didn't even call me to say you were going to be late."

"I was going to call when I left."

"But you didn't, did you?" With that she left the living room, Cliff only too happy to see her go.

Cliff was fast asleep. Janice, wide awake. She waited until his snores began before she slipped out of bed.

She went to the bathroom and pulled out his undershirt and dress shirt. She checked for lipstick, sniffed both for the slightest hint of perfume. Found none. Not a stray hair, not a whiff of another body. Just Cliff's cologne and the faint odor of deodorant. No sweat, no funk. Nothing.

If Cliff had engaged in some illicit activity, an aroma would have been on his clothes. There wasn't.

Janice stood in their bathroom, Cliff's dirty clothes in her hand, and felt downright foolish. How did she even get such a thought? She didn't know, only that she loved him and *he loves me.*

Putting the clothes back, she made her way to bed. Nestled close to him, disturbing his sleep. Sex was the last thing on Cliff's mind. All he really wanted was to sleep, but he knew enough not to rock the boat, that he loved her. Wanted peace. So he gave Janice what she wanted.

Sandy got in from work that following Thursday, tired from her commute but determined to perk up for her movie date with Randall. Two minutes after closing the door behind her, the doorbell rang.

"Just got in," she told Randall, taking off her shoes. "What time is the show?"

"Eight."

"Good, gives me time to change. Be back in a minute." Sandy went up the stairs, Randall took a seat on the sofa, looked around him. Saw the wedding album tucked under a lamp table. Curiosity made him pull it out.

The sight of Sandy in a wedding gown standing next to her dead husband jolted him a bit. Randall knew the photos would do that, but seeing the man Sandy had been married to—a man in which the only similarities between them were they were both African-American and both around the same height—was a comfort. Her attraction to him was honest.

He had wondered if he resembled Sandy's husband, was pleased that he didn't, but another man did. A man who looked so much like the groom it was scary. Twins? Sandy had never mentioned her husband having a twin brother.

He flipped to the end of the book, was returning it to its resting place when Sandy came down the stairs.

"My wedding album?"

"Yeah. Hope you don't mind."

Some part of her did. Some part of her viewed that as a life long gone. But another part of her was relieved that he had seen who had been in her life before.

She took the book from him, ready to slip it back down beneath the lamp table, but for reasons she could not explain, opened it up to the first page. Saw herself and Adrian happy, newly married. "Sometimes it feels like I dreamed the whole thing. Other times, it's like all I know."

"Now?"

"Now? Rock and a hard place?" she answered with a careful smile, one that trembled, lost its joy. Sorrow coming back with the next beat of her heart.

Sandy blinked back tears, mad at herself but unable to stop the flow. Randall was beside her in a heartbeat, holding her. "Go ahead and cry, it's okay."

But it wasn't okay. She was supposed to be beyond it all, on to her new life. But the agony she'd gone through would not go away, just went on tearing her heart into bits so she clung to Randall while she mourned Adrian. Cried a river in his arms until she was certain she was all cried out.

When her moans became whimpers, when her sniffles arrived, Randall pulled back from her, his hands wiping away her tears. "You okay now?"

She nodded, not trusting a single word from her mouth.

"You sure?"

She nodded again, attempted a smile.

He kissed her. He kissed her long, slow, passionate, and gentle. Sandy found herself kissing him back, hands free range over his back, the slopes of his shoulders. Hands feeling a freedom to travel with no restrictions, no restraint; Randall's hands doing the same.

His skilled fingers traveled over her round plump behind, testing the firmness, the softness, the warmness.

Her body became a part of him, her pelvis flushed to his as his hands dipped down into the tight fit of her jeans, satin panties making the glide easier. Big warm callused hands over the rise of her buttocks, across the slopes of her waist, on a quest for her center like a heat-seeking missile.

His fingers slipping under her panties, thumbs moving forward, contact making her buck. She couldn't turn away from the sensation if she wanted to, despite the warning of *slow*, moving through her head.

*I'll go blindly and foolishly,* she decided as they made their way to her bedroom upstairs. *I won't think, just feel,* she decided as they entered it.

In a heartbeat they were near naked, on her bed, underwear the only modesty. Randall's eyes drinking in the swell of her breasts, the inny of navel, the beginning of fine black silky hair peaking over the edge of her bikini underwear.

Sandy knew that he would take her nipple into his mouth, perhaps move his tongue to lower wetter warmer places, and that notion made her sit up, half spin until her feet were touching the floor. The reality of the unwise decision she'd made bringing it all to a halt. "We're supposed to be friends first," she managed. "That's what you said, friends."

"I know what I said. I can't always predict the future . . . I want you now." He reached for her, but she pulled away.

"Randall."

"Yeah."

Guilt weighed heavy on her. "I have something to say." *Should have told him long before this point.* But she hadn't and would face the consequences. "I think we need to get dressed before I do."

It was a decision he would appreciate later even if in that moment he had no clue. No need for him to be looking upon her near naked body for signs of a disease she didn't have. No need to be staring at the one thing he wanted now but would probably fear later.

Better to give them decency and him a quick exit when her last word arrived. Better to save them the embarrassment of finding clothes and getting into them quickly before he went racing out of her life forever.

She made them go downstairs to the living room, turning on side table lamps to offer just enough illumination without the spotlight feel of the ceiling fixture. He had tried to sit close to her, but she requested distance.

"Don't really know where to start, but I guess I should start at the beginning."

Randall didn't know what she was going to tell him. Had no idea what was so important that it had pulled them from the magic that had begun upstairs. His only hope was it wouldn't take too long, need for her still in him like a fever.

"The day you came here, the last thing on my mind was this," her hands shifted through space. "You were cute and all, but I was still a widow, in mourning. Wasn't thinking about you or any other man."

*She still loves her husband,* Randall thought, which was okay. He didn't expect her to just forget him because he had arrived on the scene. Randall almost smiled. Out of respect, the seriousness on her face, he didn't.

"But then as time went on, I felt things. Next thing I know you're cooking in my kitchen, making me meals in yours. When you said you wanted to be friends first, a part of me was relieved. I wanted you to get to know me as a person first too." She looked away for the first time. "Didn't think we'd arrive here so quickly. Didn't think I'd have to stop in the middle of it to have this talk. Was hoping it would come at a different time, but it's not. So, I just have to say it."

"I understand, Sandy."

"You do? How?"

"I know you loved your husband and I'm not trying to replace that love. I know it takes time."

Her head nodded. "Yes, it does. But that's not it." She swallowed, swallowed some more, not wanting to confess, tell it. She didn't want him to be away from her forever. Didn't want her truth to steal their hope, end what had so innocently begun.

Sandy found herself looking at him deeply, missing him already. Took another deep breath, dimly wondering how her life had arrived at this moment. That after all she'd gone through, watching her husband die, the nightmare was still far from over. That she still carried the scars that would always bring doubt. "He died of AIDS."

"Who?" But Randall sensed the answer. Made himself sit still, awaiting confirmation.

"My husband."

It seemed the last syllable of the last word was barely out of her mouth before Randall was standing. Standing and staring, standing and wide-eyed. Standing and scared. "AIDS?"

Sandy nodded, forced herself to watch, witness the truth inside his eyes, painful as it was.

"Your husband had AIDS." Randall felt his legs grow weak. Did not try to fight it, plumped back down in the chair. His mind was racing, trying to assimilate tossed-off facts that he had read about, seen on the TV. But even as he searched out a conclusion, fear filled the room like fog.

"I'm negative," Sandy went on to say. "I've had every test known to mankind. I'm okay."

But his expression suggested she had just announced she was Jesus Christ, that's how much doubt lay there. "What difference does that make? You've been exposed." He found it hard to breathe, to think, to settle a fast-rising anger. Could not believe he had been caught like this, snared in her sticky widowed trap. Could not believe such tenderness and kindness harbored such a conniving soul.

"We always practiced safe sex."

"From jump street," Randall countered.

"Yes, from day one. He insisted on it."

"You slept with him knowing he had the disease?"

"He was my husband. I loved him. How could I not?"

"How? The man had AIDS." That he even had to explain it made him doubt Sandy's state of mind. He decided she was crazy; a fact he had somehow missed. "Because you loved him? That don't even make sense."

But to her it made all the sense in the world, and she found a need to defend what in that moment seemed indefensible. Too late she realized her mistake. She should have told it differently, revealing the whole of it from A to Z.

Sandy realized that she should have shared the real beginning, how when she met Adrian, he had been testing negative, right up until six weeks before their wedding. She should have stated that by the time she found out, her heart had been too invested. That there had been no way she could have walked away.

She was about to but saw it was too late. Randall was horrified and angry. "You should have told me from the beginning. Should have told me the truth." He took four steps, then turned quick and abrupt. "How could you put me at risk?"

"I didn't."

"Weren't we just upstairs near naked . . . kissing? Body fluids. I know about body fluids," words spit out like venom. "Your tongue in my mouth. My damn dick up against your wet panties . . ." He looked at her with eyes she didn't recognize. "I can't believe you did this." Then he was walking away and out of the front door, which slammed so hard Sandy was afraid it would fall off of its hinges.

She felt no surprise, no outrage. Randall's reaction was exactly how she'd always suspected it would be, though it wasn't the one she'd hoped for. Sandy had walked in his shoes. Had tasted the fear. Knew it all too well.

*Was this how it was for you, Adrian? When I got too scared to be with you and my fear sent me running out the door? Was this how it felt, like no one would ever love you again?*

In that moment Sandy understood the ramifications of having AIDS even though she didn't have it. *But my husband did,* and as far as the world was concerned, what went for the goose would go for the gander.

Her phone rang.

She was in no mood to pick it up. She just wanted to sit, feel sorry for herself but the phone would not cease. Just kept on ringing until she answered.

"Hello?"

"Sandy?"

"Yeah."

"It's Wint . . . thinking about you. Decided to give you a call."

She wiped her eye. Tried to clear the frog from her throat. "Hey."

"What's wrong?"

No lies. "Everything."

Somehow he knew that. Had sensed it, making him pick up the phone. Check on her. Now that he knew, his next words were automatic. "I'm coming over."

"No, you don't have to," but in truth she was glad he was.

Winston wasn't certain what would happen when he arrived, but knew enough to play it by ear. There was no doubt she was hurting again. It was all in her voice. The same hurt shown in her eyes when she opened the door and let him in.

He just wanted to hold her but smiled a bit instead. "Wah? Da world come to an end?"

"No, just feels like it."

They settled in her living room, sharing the couch, Sandy asking the question she thought she never would. "How come you're not afraid?"

"Of what?"

Her voice broke. "Me."

Winston could not retain his arms. Could not retain the need to soothe her. He opened them, uttered, "Come," and waited as she settled against his chest. He soothed her with his hand, slow palm over the spine, tense and tight. He kissed the top of her head with near-fatherly intent, his answer coming slowly. "I know what you've been through. How could I burden you with fear?"

"But were you?"

"Afraid?" Winston shook his head. "No. I don't think God would do that. Adrian and Gen were enough."

Her voice was tiny, small. "And that you love me, right?"

He had never come out and said it. Somehow considered it a secret. But she already knew. Had no choice but to confess. "Yeah, Sandy, I do."

"But other people are afraid."

"That's on them."

She nestled against the warmth of his chest, the muffled thumps of his heart. "Thank you, Winston."

"For?"

"For not being afraid." Because if nothing else, he had given her the one thing that possibly no other man ever would again—physical love. Possessed both the willingness and the heart to offer up the emotional as well.

Sandy grew quiet, allowing Winston to hold her, taking comfort in that measure, a true dictum that she wasn't alone.

Winston waited for the embrace to become more, for her head to lift, seek out his lips. But the moment never arrived as she pulled away, smiled wearily in his direction, and asked if he was hungry. "Haven't had dinner yet and I'm starved," she confessed.

It was not the type of sharing he was looking for, but Winston knew, that for the moment, he would take whatever she was willing to give.

"You okay, son?"

It was the second time that morning that his father had asked him that question. Randall wished he would quit. He just wanted to enjoy the early morning breakfast with his father, and that second cup of coffee, before heading off.

He didn't want to talk about what was gnawing at his belly. How fear, like new pennies, bittered the inside of his mouth. Randall saw no need to disclose the Sandy drama, the whole of it still tough and obtrusive, a spiky ache he could not will away.

"Just fine, Dad."

"Look worried."

"I'm not."

"Ronnie asked about you."

Veronica "Ronnie" James had known Randall since the age of ten. As children, they had been playmates, as adults, quick lovers. And though it had been a while since their encounters went beyond "Hey, how you doing," that sense of longing remained in her eye.

By nature Randall liked to proceed slow. By nature he liked the somewhat cautious route. But Ronnie had had them married with children before the last throb of orgasm had left her body. Had them old and gray sitting in rockers on her front porch before he pulled out.

"Told her you were doing all right," his father added, drinking up the last little bit of coffee. Considered his son with careful eyes. "How long before you finish the Wheaton job?"

"A day or two. Then it's on to the Harrisons."

"Got a roof over on a Hundred and Forty-eighth Street and some windows on a Hundred and Eighth. Going to be busy for a while, far as I can see," which suited Randall just fine.

The gently rolling plains, brown with winter and trees supporting dead leaves that forgot to let go last fall, were a stark reality to what the day was about. With a heavy heart, Sandy left the confines of her Camry, Rachel beside her, Junie easing his body out of the back.

Sandy stood on the paved road that separated the cemetery plots straight through the middle and waited for her father-in-law, mother-in-law, and Winston to join her. It had been a cold October day when they had buried Adrian and this day seemed just as bleak. Though spring was but weeks away, distinguishing the two were difficult.

The sunshine was full but it felt like an ironic reminder that life still existed beyond the stone walls of Richwood Cemetery.

"You okay?"

She did not see Winston until his arm slipped around her shoulder. Looked up at him and nodded. Sandy headed across the lawn still caught in winter's clutches. Took the kneeling pad from Junie, placed it at the tombstone, and dropped to her knees.

It was as much ceremony as it was heartfelt necessity that she ran the cloth over its smooth glossy surface. Over the *A,* the *d,* the *r* her hand moved, taking care to wipe away the dust-filled crevices.

Mr. Burton came, resting gnarly fingers on the edge, eyes off and far far away. Mrs. Burton joined Sandy; an old pillow beneath her knees as she lowered her head, whispered words, shed tears over her eldest son's final resting place.

Sandy reached for the flowers Junie held, inhaled briefly the spray of tulips, orchids, and baby's breath. Carefully laying them against the bottom of the headstone, she lowered her head, thought words private and deep.

Whispering "Happy birthday," she pressed two kissed fingers against his name, rose, and allowed others access.

She stood there, wishing for more than the stone could ever give. Sandy was in need of those times when life had been certain, when her love had existed in a place she could touch. Sandy needed Adrian to tell her it was okay, that he was at peace. That he would love her forever.

She needed his warm embrace like she had never needed anything else. Knew the headstone and plot of dead earth below could not give it.

Winston moved forward. Hands folded, head lowered, he stood there a long time, mute, huddled in thought. "Happy birthday, Bro," he managed, his voice soft, near breaking, turning and moving away.

Junie came next, Rachel last, each taking time to remember the oldest brother that had always been there for them. It was not enough and it placed an emptiness inside them all as they turned and headed back toward their cars.

But the emptiness faded away to loud voices, people in motion, and Sandy's dining room overflowing with food. Heavy Trinidadian accents filled the air as Mr. Burton and Winston engaged in debates, Rachel adding her two cents and Junie occasionally getting into the fray.

Mrs. Burton looked upon it all; the joy filling the room, the animation of her loved ones' faces and smiled, thankful for the gladness. She had been keeping a watchful eye on Sandy, her son Winston, looking for interaction that said something had changed between them.

While moments came when she thought maybe it had, over all Mrs. Burton had not seen enough to cause her to worry. She caught Sandy's eye. "We're planning a trip home. Would love for you to join us."

"Home?"

"Trinidad. Have you ever been?"

Sandy shook her head no.

"Then you must try and make it. In June. Two weeks. It would do you good. Get a chance to meet some more of the family."

The family.

Just a few weeks ago they had felt that way to her, but who they were had changed because of Randall. Everything had changed because of Randall. Long gone, running like a thief in the night, his brief passage had done more harm than good.

"Oh, you have to come, San-dee," Rachel insisted.

"Be nice. Have a good time," Junie added. "Ya swim, ya eat, ya part-tee. Jus kick back, relax."

"I'll think about it," all she could commit to, life unsettled once more.

Randall felt conspicuous calling from the pay phone, giving a phony first name, pocket full of quarters. On borrowed time, he was supposed to have been back on the job twenty minutes ago, but Randall had to get some information and he needed it now.

He had never felt more ignorant in his life, more put on the spot, feeling as if every passerby knew why he was on the phone. One Hundred and Fiftieth Street and Liberty Avenue was an extremely busy intersection, the noise of the auto parts place on both sides of the street filled the air around him. Even with one finger in his ear he could barely hear the counselor's voice.

"If the person practiced safe sex, yes, it is highly possible the virus was not passed on."

"What about kissing?"

"If there are no lesions or cuts in the mouth, then it is rare for the virus to be transported through saliva."

"Rare, but not impossible."

"Unfortunately in 1994 we are still learning about the disease every day, and while we can not state that it's one hundred percent certain, the study seems to indicate it is extremely rare."

Randall swallowed, the next question hard. "If I wanted to take the test . . ."

"You can check with your local medical provider. If they aren't able to do it directly, they can recommend someone who can."

The peace of mind he was hoping for did not arrive. Randall knew it was not coming. Yes, he had the "facts" now, as many facts as he could get, but they did nothing to quell his fears. Did not allow Sandy to become a "go." Halted his tongue.

"Sir, are you there?"

"Yeah, I'm here . . . thanks anyway." Randall hung up the phone, looked at his watch. With a heavy heart, he headed for his van.

# Chapter 10

Exactness.

All of her life Martha had hungered for it, preferring the assertion of black and white with no gray area. Even though she knew it was not how life worked, she still longed for it. Wanted it to be so for herself and Calvin.

He had been so complete and so full in her life that she never even considered the day that he would no longer be. But the past two days had shown her different. The past two days he had been gone.

It wasn't like she didn't know where he was. Just yesterday she had called and found him at home. When she asked if he was okay, he had told her he was just fine. When she asked what was he doing, he answered watching TV.

The third question would not come out. It just got jammed in her throat, forcing her to move on to a fourth not even considered until that moment. "So am I seeing you tomorrow?"

"Probably not."

She hadn't been able to ask him why. Just answered okay, she'd talk with him later, uncertain as to when or even where.

It left a huge hole in her, a hole she had spent years trying to mend. A hole that had only taken Calvin a little over a month to repair. The hole in her had a voice and it told her constantly that she had blown it. That she had blown the best chance in her life to be happy, something Martha refused to believe.

No one had that kind of power over her, she insisted to herself. *No one except Calvin* came the protest.

She knew exactly how this mess had started but wasn't certain of how it would end. Only that she wanted to take it all back, forget about marriage and babies and just be with him again.

Martha knew that she didn't want to drink away her sorrows, call on the counsel of friends. Didn't want the apartment to be empty when she got home either, but the silence made it so.

She didn't want to eat leftovers, remember how times used to be. Wanted the phone to ring, the intercom to sound. Wanted lively debates about law with the man whom she had come to love.

Lastly, Martha didn't want to call Britney and bare her soul, but it was too heavy inside of her not to share.

Britney had never seen her husband so tired.

Could not recall Maurice looking so whipped and so beat the bags under his eyes looked etched with a black marker.

She knew he just wanted to get into bed and get nine hours of undisturbed sleep. The last thing she wanted was to deny him that simple pleasure. But she had promised Martha.

"Mo?"

He mumbled a response, his head having found the perfect spot in the fancy pillows that sprang back to life every morning.

"Mo? You up?" She knew he wasn't, or didn't want to be. "Are you?"

"Am now," he answered, opening his eyes and finding Britney looking at him, something on her mind. "What's up?"

"Calvin," Britney said with a near suck of her teeth. "What's the story with him?"

Maurice frowned. "What do you mean?"

"He's been away from Martha for three days and she needs to know if he's going to make it permanent."

"He didn't say anything to me," Maurice said, his lie careful, near smooth. But he knew his wife would want more than that, that she would insist on all the details even if he didn't know them.

"Could you ask him?"

"Ask him what?"

Britney sighed. "You know, ask him."

Maurice didn't want to. Wasn't his business far as he was concerned, but he gave the answer that would allow him peace. "Do it tomorrow." He stared at her, his annoyance prevalent. "Anything else?"

Britney shook her head, turned off the lamp by the bed. Lay awake waiting for the shaking of the crib bars, the high-pitched squeal. Bereace seemed downright psychic with her need to deprive her mother of a good night's sleep. She would be quiet as a church mouse until Britney settled into bed, and then she began shaking those bars, whining at the top of her lungs until her mother rounded the door.

But the next thing Britney knew it was morning and Maurice was kissing her goodbye. With a start she got up and raced to her baby's room. Found Bereace fast asleep, bottom up. Realized with awe and delight that for the first time ever, Bereace had slept through the whole night in her own room, all by her lonesome.

Prayed it was the beginning of that forever.

"I know it ain't my business, man," Maurice began, watching Calvin out the corner of his eye as they suited up for another day of trash hauling.

"Yeah, you're right, it's not. But don't tell me. Britney put you up to it, right?"

Maurice chuckled, relieved. "Yeah, you know women."

"And she wants me to tell you so you can tell her so she can tell Martha what I'm up to, right?"

"Bingo."

"And if I don't tell you something, Britney's going to rag you until I do."

Maurice sighed, not wanting to be a part of it. He was certain Calvin had his reasons and a man was entitled to that. "Right again."

"Just pulling back, that's all."

"Pulling back or pulling out?" Maurice found himself asking. "Because if your intentions aren't about Martha anymore, she deserves to know."

"Back . . . not out. Not yet. Just need to give my head some breathing room, y'know? I mean I dig the hell out of Martha but I'm not sure I want to go where she wants to go."

"Are you talking about marriage?"

"Yeah."

"Swore you never would again."

"Exactly. But Martha is the first good thing that has happened to me in years and I'm not trying to lose that. None of us are spring chickens. I'm looking at thirty-eight this fall."

"So it's not completely out of the question then."

"No, not completely, but not fully in it either. I need to think this out. Being around her don't allow me that."

"Why?"

Calvin laughed. "Man, you ain't that dense. You know what it's like. You with her and all you know and all you can feel and breathe is what she wants, what makes her happy. Could be something so far from your view can't even see the sign post, but that don't even matter. Then when you away from her, you be scratching your head saying to yourself 'Man, what was I thinking?' "

"That deep?"

"Yeah, that deep. Today's day four. And it's like I'm counting every second of every minute I haven't been with her. That shits hard, man. Real hard. But on the other hand, my head needs a breather."

"You tell her?"

"Hell, no. You know women. You talk about breathing room and all they hear is you leaving them."

"She needs to know what it's about."

"Figured it would just make it worse."

"Staying away ain't gonna make it better." Maurice considered him. Parted with some personal knowledge. "Martha may be a lot of things, but she ain't no fool. She's not like most women. The door on her heart? Will close in a heartbeat. You play your hand wrong and she's gone."

"But what am I supposed to tell her?"

"What you just told me."

Calvin buttoned the last button on his shirt. Reached for his utility jacket. Paused, considered the conversation. Leaned in close. "This is on the down low, right?"

"And you know that. Just 'cause Brit's my wife don't mean she know everything."

\* \* \*

Calvin called Martha. He waited until after four when court was over and called her at work. The sound of her voice said she had been expecting a call. Just not from him.

"Hey," he began.

"Hey," she answered back.

"Can we meet at your place? Some things I need to explain."

"That's fine."

"Not in the mood for cooking. I'll pick something up."

"Works for me."

"Okay. I'll see you later."

There had been a time in Martha's life when she wouldn't even have thought about giving any man a second go-round. You wronged her once, there was no second chance. She had never been a desperate ninny, never took the drama and foolishness like it was okay. She made up her mind on the way home she wasn't about to.

Decided she was going to be strong in her stance, wouldn't beg for a second chance and certainly not grovel. Martha decided if Calvin wanted out, then so be it. But as she put her key into her apartment door, she heard strains of Hiroshima and smelled Chinese take-out. As she felt Calvin's presence filling her apartment, every inch of her heart before she even got the door open, she knew better.

Knew that this was what it meant to have him in her life, him there like a loving spouse, offering her a sweet end to her too hard, too long day. This was what she, not seconds ago, had been willing to forsake. What had been missing for the past few days.

"Hey," she said softly, her eyes finding his.

"Hey back," he returned, standing in the doorway of her kitchen.

That they had reached this impasse at all had taken them both by surprise. Fundamentally there was permanence to them, and though they had never spoken about it, each had felt it.

Until the marriage thing.

*Me with my big ideas,* Martha thought, laying her briefcase against the wall. *I should have just kept my mouth shut and let life just lead us.*

Suddenly a need to apologize filled her. "I'm sorry. I was wrong, I should never have done what I did. I should have never tried to push you into something you didn't want to get into."

"And I was wrong," he countered. "I should have told you what I was up to even if I didn't think you would like it."

"Which was?"

"Time. A little space. Some breathing room." His head shook. "You've taken me places I didn't think I ever wanted to go . . . made me run for cover."

"Got scared?"

"Yeah."

"So are you still scared?"

Calvin's smile was careful. "Guess not. I'm here, right?"

"What about your space? Your breathing room?"

"What we want isn't always what we need."

"So what is it that you want?"

"To be happy."

"What do you need?"

"You." He did not lift his arms to her, but they both felt how much he wanted to. Not quite there yet, there were additional conclusions that needed exploring, additional revelations from the soul.

"Forever? Will you need me that long? . . . I can't do temporary, Calvin. It's not how I go."

"I'm supposed to predict the future?"

"No, but you can define the probability."

"What if I told you I can't?"

"Can't or won't? There aren't any guarantees, I know that. But we have to be clear on where we are going, and where we're not."

"Sounds like square one," Calvin uttered, disillusioned. He had been certain they were going to be all right, make it okay. Calvin had been certain by the look on her face, how his heart felt; the apologies that flowed the moment she walked through the door.

But that deferment was fading fast, as anger mottled her face. "Square one?" Martha asked with a raise of her brow. "Maybe we never left."

"Don't say that," he countered, trying to reel her in, stop things before they got beyond their control.

But once again Martha had reached a milestone he never wanted to consider. "Why not? Has anything really changed? Has my heart, your mind? If you can't even entertain the notion of marriage, then I need to know that."

"Why?"

"So I can decide what happens next."

Calvin found himself right there with her, stirring up discontent, nestling in the bitterness. "Is that you talking or someone else?"

"I'm the only one standing here."

"But all your girls have either taken that stroll down the aisle or are about to."

"So the fuck what? Don't I have the right to want that too?"

Calvin sighed, beat down by her inability to consider anything other than herself. "You got the right to want anything your heart desires. Me? I have the same rights. And I don't know yet. Now you can accept that, or don't."

Martha understood then that she could go on with him like they were and forget about marriage, hoping that one day it would be a part of his vocabulary. Or she could just say forget it, go on without him, and try and find another.

Problem was there was no other. Calvin was the original. There was no replacing him. To keep him meant abandoning her hopes, letting go of what she wanted. "I can't accept it, Calvin."

Her announcement surprised him. She could tell by how his eyes widened, then narrowed. All of it became just a memory by the time he nodded his head. Spoke. "If you can't, you can't." He looked away from her, turning toward the kitchen. Indicated the large brown paper bag sitting on the white countertop. "Spare ribs and pork fried rice."

But to Martha, he was speaking Greek. "What?"

"Dinner. In the kitchen. What I picked up." His eyes drifted about her, settled a few inches above her head. "Well, guess I'll be on my way." He went to the closet and got his jacket, stopped at the coffee table, and picked up his keys.

Martha, eyes kind of wide, heart beating too fast, felt as if she were about to shut down. The first man she had loved since Leon, the first man in eight years to bring her real joy, was going away forever. Why? Because he wouldn't even consider the "M" word, something she hadn't even been thinking about herself until a few weeks ago.

Calvin held the keys aloft, took one off. Carefully he laid it on the Queen Anne table.

They had had such good times. He was smart, worked hard, made money, and now he was giving back her apartment key. No more music and home-cooked meals when she got home. No more laughter and hot debates. No more Calvin.

He reached for the lock, turned it.

Was she really going to let him just walk away? Was she really going to hold fast to some stupid dream that may or may not even be her own and let him just go?

The door swung open.

All she had to say was "Okay." Say "Okay, I can accept that." Just say it and stop him. Say it and keep him. Stop him from walking out.

"Take care, Martha." Calvin went through the door. Pulled it closed, the door nearly to the threshold when her voice came.

"Calvin . . . wait." The door shut with ease.

Martha ran to it, wrenched it open. Saw him by the elevator, unreadable things on his face. "Wait, Calvin," her voice part pleading, part annoyance. But she must have whispered it or said it in some language he didn't understand because he pushed the call button.

"Did you hear me? I said wait," the prosecutor tone rising as she moved out into the hallway, the apartment door banging behind her. "Calvin," she called again, the elevator arriving and he stepping inside. "Wait," she insisted as she slipped inside as the doors began to close, moving in front of him, his eyes making her air.

"I've changed my mind," she said, frantic. She touched his face. Tried to shift his gaze, but his eyes refused to find hers. She released him. Stood back, understanding fully. "Oh, it's like that? You don't want to hear anything I have to say, right?"

The lobby came into view through the elevator window. Calvin moved toward the door. It glided open. He stepped out.

"Well, fine, leave, go right ahead. But you remember—I was willing to try." She was shouting, her voice echoing through the shiny gleaming empty lobby like thunder. "You hear me? I was willing to try," as Calvin opened the door and disappeared into the start of evening, glowing soft with dusk.

How could he tell her all he was feeling? How could he share his fear, old truths, still tender wounds? How could he reveal how naive he had once been, how juvenile and idealistic his outlook had once gleaned?

Calvin couldn't.

He couldn't tell her about Rayshela, his first love, the little girl/not quite grown nineteen-year-old he had married soon after they had graduated from high school. He could not tell Martha how love that had seemed unbreakable crumbled under a young man's ideals and newlywed reality.

Calvin wasn't ready to disclose how keeping a roof over their heads, food in their stomachs, and clothes on their back had undone what neither ever thought would be undoable. But that was just what had happened.

Back in 1977 Calvin had been new to Sanitation, a rookie working rookie hours and making rookie money. When he was working, Rayshela was at home, and when he was home, Rayshela was working.

Their ages didn't help, not during the "party till you drop" seventies, where clubbing was a seven-day-a-week affair, no longer limited to the weekends. All of Rayshela's girlfriends had been hanging out and hanging tough while she played housewife, waiting for her husband to come home from another hard smelly shift.

Rayshela realized that there was more to life than working nine to five, cooking dinner, and keeping the apartment clean. That life should offer more than being awakened at ungodly hours in the morning for a little loving before she had to get up and go to work herself.

Rayshela realized that her husband had dreams that took lots of money, and all his effort was going into making some, period, the end. That he wanted the best for both of them and went the extra mile to secure it, even if it meant there was no time for themselves.

Rayshela got tired of sitting home all the time. She began heeding her friends' advice that at nineteen she should be out enjoying life and not waiting for a husband who had no time for her. That this club was happening, that club was slamming, and she really needed to get dressed and go with them.

She did. Cautiously, she began going, keeping her associations with men limited to just a dance. But soon just a dance turned into just one drink. And just one drink turned into secret dates. And secret dates turned into infidelity, and infidelity turned into love for a man who was not her husband.

A man who took her places and did things with her. A man who's rap was so strong, so powerful, so full of what she felt her life should be about that she asked Calvin for a divorce. Being the person Calvin was, he granted her wish, broken heart and all.

At twenty he had married the girl of his dreams. At twenty-two she was gone.

This was the story he had no desire to tell Martha, ego and old pain still having the ability to brew itself up inside him. And while he knew Martha and Rayshela were two separate people and Martha would never do anything like that, it was still hard for him to even consider taking the chance.

He had tested the waters of matrimony once and nearly drowned. He wasn't ready to take another dip.

It sounded good in his head as he eased his Infiniti out of the parking space. Sounded good and perfect and right. But his heart was saying wrong move. His heart was weepy with regret.

Martha stood at her apartment door as if she could will it open with her mind. She tried the handle for the ninth time and got nothing for her effort. She could not believe she could not get in, that just beyond the slab of wood and metal lay her apartment keys and a phone. That her haste to chase down Calvin caused her to be locked out of her apartment.

She twisted the knob one more time, banged a good hard fist against the door, and turned. She considered neighbors she hardly knew, hardly spoke to. Wondered if they would recognize her from the fishbowl view of their peephole, or would they just consider her a black woman who had somehow gotten into their apartment building and was out to commit a crime.

When Martha was looking for a suitable apartment building, she knew before she even scanned the real estate section where she didn't want to live. She loved black people, was one herself, but she knew that in most cases, no matter how nice and neat dwellings started out, eventually they could give into the mandates of decline.

It would start with simple things.

Someone peeing in the elevator. A scrawl of graffiti in the basement laundry room. A broken lobby door, the elevator temporarily going out of service. It would move onto the landscape outside the building being less cared for, a couple of roaches in the kitchen, the sidewalks not being swept daily, more pee stains in the stairwells.

The up and coming would begin moving out, the less desirables would begin moving in. Teenagers would begin to congregate outside the building, graffiti would become more evident. More of the up and coming would move out, more of the less desirables would move in. The janitor would get fired and the maintenance man would be responsible for cleanup, repairs, and landscaping. Since all those duties couldn't be handled by one person, the decline would come on slow and steady.

This was the reason Martha set her visions elsewhere, decided to go where she would be a real minority. It was the reason why she chose the Manor Apartments in Jamaica Estates because she knew white folks with a little money would not allow such travesties.

But for the upside, there was a down. As only one of a handful of blacks living in the building, she was often viewed as suspect, even with her ADA badge hanging around her neck. Sometimes her neighbors would stare at it and stare at her, unable to believe that she had not only passed the bar, but was nearly on the same level as Richard Brown, the DA for the county of Queens. That she had that much power.

But Martha wasn't feeling very powerful now as she took a tally of who and who wasn't behind the ten closed doors lining the hallway.

To her left lived an old woman by the name of Freidmann. And though she spoke to Martha, it always came off as if someone were twisting the old woman's arm. To her right lived Chad and Pepper Godfrey, a thirty-something white couple who had married last year. Pepper had knocked on her door one day, but just to ask her to lower her music.

Beyond the Godfreys lived Albert Steinbacher, an old man who kept to himself and was known for muttering. He smelled of cat dander and sour milk and his teeth had a yellow cast so deep they seemed dyed. He had never spoken to Martha in all the time they had been neighbors.

On the right two doors down was Christof, a gay forty-something man who was friendly but he was away on vacation and Martha had been dutifully collecting his mail for him. Beyond those borders Martha wasn't sure who lived where.

She moved to her right, lifted her finger, and set her face to something less angry. She didn't tempt a smile, but she let the furrow in her brow go as she heard the slip of metal over the peephole lift, and felt eyes giving her a full inspection. Three seconds later the door cracked open a bit.

"Yes?"

Not, "Hi," "Why, hello," but just 'Yes?" as if she had no right ringing the bell.

"Pepper, right?"

The hand went to the white throat in a heartbeat. "Yes." Dark brown eyes blinked at her, telling tales about the blond hair.

"I'm Martha, live next door?"

"Yes, I know who you are."

Martha swallowed. "I seem to have locked myself out and was wondering if I could use your phone."

The dark eyes did a slow careful sweep, starting at Martha's La-Roche shoes up to the strand of fresh water pearls around her neck. Martha tried not to take it personal. Tried to remember that time she went to visit a cousin in Canton, Georgia, and how different it was, in all places, the South.

Beyond a wonderful elegant two-story home with two fireplaces, three and a half baths, and a deck that offered a breathtaking view of the mountains, her cousin's neighbors had been both white and friendly, which had really tripped her out.

At first Martha had thought they were just being kind, but when her cousin had told of how they all got together at least once a month, hosting cookouts and taking trips to the summer music series at Chastain Park, Martha knew that it was as real as real got.

She found herself wondering whether if she and Pepper had been right now in Canton, Georgia, would she be feeling like a suspect, or would Pepper have invited her in and served iced tea as they chilled on the outdoor deck until the locksmith came.

Martha found herself wondering whether if they had been in Canton, Georgia, where the confederate flag still waved under the guise of the state symbol, would Pepper be holding on to her neck as if Martha had a razor and was about to slash it.

"My phone?"

"Yes, you know." She put a pinkie to her mouth, a thumb to her ear. "Phone."

Pepper blinked again, the both of them hearing, "Who is it?" followed by the appearance of Chad. "Yes?" he went on to ask too.

Pepper turned, seeking her husband's face. "She's locked out. Wants to use our phone?" It was not a statement. It was a question, poised to the man of the house, the defender of Pepper's life. If Chad said okay, then Martha could. If Chad said no, then Martha was back to square one.

Chad, too, looked her over carefully, searching no doubt for signs of weapons, intents of harm. "Wait here."

He left, came back. Handed Martha the phone. She looked at it, looked at Chad. "I don't know a number offhand. Do you have a yellow pages?"

Chad and Pepper looked at each other, disappointment and something else in their eyes. It seemed forever before they opened the door to let her in.

They confined her to the chair in the hallway by the front door, Chad keeping sentry as he leaned against the wall, Pepper serving as backup as she took a chair in the living room keeping Martha in her line of sight.

So on the spot, so under the microscope did Martha feel, she started talking, about herself. She was determined to reveal who she wasn't, but mostly who she was.

"Did you read about the Minelli case?"

At first her words went nowhere, simply hung in the air. Chad continued to watch her, while Pepper sat quietly in the rear.

"You know William Minelli, the man found with a head stuffed in his freezer?"

Chad looked back at Pepper, Morse code between husband and wife. Let go of a "Yeah" cautiously and all too late Martha saw her mistake.

She should have picked a less grisly case. Something neat and clean like that drug bust she had two weeks before. "I'm the ADA for it."

"ADA," Chad countered, disbelief full in his voice.

"Yes." Martha patted her jacket pocket. The one on her skirt. Realized she had put her ID in her pocketbook. "Don't have my badge, it's locked in my apartment, but I work in Brooklyn." Her head shook. "Some case, I tell you."

"ADA, that's what?" Pepper asked from the living room.

"Assistant District Attorney," Martha said, feeling shamed, realizing that she was trying to defend her honor. It took another two seconds before she got angry. Another three before she stood. "You know what. I'm going to wait downstairs. Locksmith should be here soon."

She reached for the door. Opened it. Heard Pepper say, "Are you really an Assistant District Attorney?" Didn't answer. Just headed out like she didn't hear a thing.

She had the power to make people invisible too.

*   *   *

Beaten down, that's how Martha felt as she watched the locksmith leave, her seventy-five-dollar check in his pocket, her apartment open and accessible to her. Now that the heat of the drama was beyond her, she felt sapped of everything, had little hope for anything. Sat on the sofa, thinking.

No tears. Crying wasn't an easy feat for her anyway. But inside, the sorrow was raining buckets, and she felt as if she would choke if she didn't let it out.

A drink.

Two drinks. She lost count after four, the night vanishing in a haze of inebriation as morning found her hungover, her head unable to leave her pillow even as she stared at the clock that read quarter after nine. Reality was slow to move into the mix and it took a while for her to accept that she was supposed to have been at her desk forty-five minutes ago.

The phone began to ring, the sound of the electronic chimes like a sledgehammer against the side of her head. She didn't have to be psychic to know who it was but she needed more strength than she possessed to answer it.

Martha let the answering machine take over, the sound of her boss's voice filling her bedroom.

She closed her eyes, willing the nausea in her belly to settle, the hopelessness to leave her, a battle she did not win. She was clutching the cool porcelain of her toilet bowl when the phone began to ring again. In the middle of an upchuck, she couldn't answer if she wanted to.

Hardworking, a skillful prosecutor, it was money in the bank. But Martha found herself making a huge withdrawal twenty minutes later, phone pressed to her ear, listening to her boss tell her things she already knew.

She found herself nodding, saying few words, as Dominic let off steam. Frothy, near irate, there was little she could utter except that she had overslept.

"So why didn't you call?"

She had no real answer for that and tried her best to dance around it. Besides her boss didn't want to know the real truth; did not want to hear about her twisted life and the bottle of Bacardi Dark that had been almost full last night but didn't even hold a corner this morning.

She was certain Dominic did not want to know about how weak she had become, the real person she was—scared of wanting, scared of needing. After all, she was known as Masterful Martha around the office and it was the only person her boss really wanted to witness.

But Dominic Gant had not moved up in the ranks without keen insight and a nose for the truth. He knew enough that something had happened, and even if Martha made it to work today, it would not be very productive.

"Take the day off," he told her. "But you make sure you get your butt in here first thing tomorrow."

"Thanks, Dom." There was no surprise when he didn't say she was welcome.

# Chapter 11

The silence had arrived over a week ago, came through Sandy's front door, plunked itself down, and made itself at home. An unwelcomed guest beyond its stay, it was there when she opened her eyes in the morning and closed them at night.

There had been a time when she had longed for it, craved it like a fiend, but those days had vanished with Randall.

She was hungry for life again, stagnation no longer suiting her. Sandy tried to fill the emptiness with phone calls to her friends and impromptu visits to her parents, but the void had only deepened.

She had one life line, that much she knew, but she had been resisting the urge to use it. Felt that Randall would come back, at the very least, call her. Reopen that door he had so quickly closed.

But Randall hadn't come back, hadn't called, and now destitution was in her thick. This was the reason she picked up the phone, dialed the number she rarely dialed. It was the reason her voice came from her weak and uncertain, heart beating so fast she just knew it was going to leave her chest.

But there was no denying the relief when he answered. No denying the feeling that somebody somewhere cared for her when he asked what she was up to and if she wanted company. There was no denying that in this moment she needed him, Winston, like she never thought she would need him again.

The brown bag was the first thing she noticed.

Even through the layer of laminated cardboard and sturdy paper she could smell the contents. Was glad that he thought enough to bring food along.

"This place in Flatbush," Winston told her as he moved toward her kitchen and set the bag on the countertop. "They make the best oxtail, outside of my mother, of course."

"How'd you know?" she found herself asking as she removed the paper lid and inhaled the oxtail, peas, and rice, and plantain.

"How I know what?"

"That I hadn't felt up to cooking?"

He looked at her, merriment in his eyes. "Sandy, you're about a lot of things, but I don't think cooking is one of them."

There in his voice was the same tone, the same concern, the same love she had heard inside of Adrian's. There across from her was the near-to-same face she had fallen in love with despite the difficulties.

He was right, of course. Adrian had done most of the cooking, and after he died, her meals had become catch as catch can. "Guess you're right," her voice fading, new emotions coming into the mix.

Things had changed between them; a new polar axis rooting up under their feet. She understood the power of love and how much Winston loved her. Found herself feeling out the possibility of being more than friends, no longer wanting to be alone.

She didn't feel about Winston the way he felt about her. Knew his emotions ran much deeper. But maybe it was enough to try, make an attempt; a thought that moved her to confession.

"You look just like him, you know that, don't you?"

Winston nodded, eyes to his food. "Yeah, I know."

"And it makes things difficult for me sometimes."

"I know that too."

"It's not about not wanting to be loved Winston. It's about you looking so much like Adrian and trying to separate the two."

"You're talking to the converted. You don't have to explain it to me. But I didn't come here to talk about me and you or Adrian. I came here to sit here, eat this food and just enjoy being with you. No strings."

She wasn't aware she needed to hear those words until he spoke them. Did not know the impact it would have until she felt it. "How come nobody has claimed you?" she found herself asking.

Honey eyes found her. "Somebody has."

It was one of those moments that could go away or remain forever. She wasn't certain which she preferred. Sandy drew back from the edge. Decided she would allow time to reveal all that would and would not be between them.

She changed the subject. "How's your family?" she begin, forking up peas and rice.

"They're fine. And yours?"

"Doing okay. I got the basement finished."

"Oh yeah?"

"Yeah. Take you down when we finish."


"Looks bran spankin' new," Winston was saying a little while later, taking in the new ceiling, the new floor, the soft yellowy walls. "I can't believe it. Are you sure this is the same place?"

"Positive. My clothes were molding and it just smelled bad, and I decided to have it done."

"You have to give a party."

"A what?"

His hands raised above his head, brushing the ceiling. "A party. You know. Dance, drink, music." He wiggled his hips. "Party."

"What reason?"

"Since when do you need a reason to have a good time?"

Sandy thought about it. Envisioned her house full of people, music, and laughter. "You're right. I don't need a reason at all." She wasn't aware of how she was looking at him, was oblivious to the appreciation dancing in her eyes. But Winston was.

"Haven't seen that look in a while."

"What look?"

"The one you have now. The one that says you're glad I'm here. Nice to see it back."

She looked away, her head shifting a few inches. "Being with you ain't always easy."

"I know."

"You know how I felt about your brother." But he didn't know about Randall and it was double jeopardy for her now; two men she'd wanted and could no longer have. "You've been here for me like nobody else. I know how you feel about me. I just have to decide how I really feel about you."

"I'm not rushing you, Sandy."

"I know that, and it's stuff like that that makes it hard. You are so understanding, Winston, and I think, how come I don't know. I look at you and women would give their right arm to have you."

"Like I said, that's fine. I'm not going to pressure you about anything, except maybe the party."

"Yes, the party," but her mind was elsewhere.

"If you think too hard, your brain will explode."

"Hard not to think about things when you're around."

"Like?" She looked away. "I need to know, Sandy."

"That night."

"What about it?"

"Sometimes it makes me embarrassed."

"We've been through that before. It was something that just happened."

"But now it seems like for the wrong reasons."

"It was what you needed, isn't that what you said?"

"Yeah, that's what I said, but you're my brother-in-law."

"Was. Who we were changed the day Adrian died."

"He's still my husband."

"But you are no longer his wife."

The words hit Sandy like a sledgehammer, the truth of it hitting home hard. She could love Adrian to the end of time but they would never be man and wife again. "He's really gone, isn't he?" she asked softly.

"Yes, Sandy, he is."

"I loved him, Winston. Loved him like I never loved anybody else." She had never said those words out loud. Had felt them, but had never allowed them to leave her mouth, fearing the power of it, the unchangeable truth of it.

The confession encompassed all that would never be, stripping her soul to the marrow. The greatest love of her life was gone. She would never know that wonder, experience such joy. That hurt.

Sandy looked about her, regrouping, blinking back wetness. She took a breath, then another. Released it, Winston before her. Winston who loved her, who was ready to go where Randall wouldn't, Adrian couldn't. Winston who knew her history and was not afraid.

"A party, right?" she asked in need of affirmation.

"Yep. A stone cold, throw down, dance till the rooster's crow party."

"Ain't no roosters in Hollis."

Winston laughed. "Right, I'm thinking of home."

"Trinidad?"

"Yeah."

"You were born here, right?"

"Yeah, but Trinidad will always be home."

"Indian?" she asked, curious in a way she never had been before.

"What?"

"Your roots. You have Indian roots, right? It would explain the wavy hair, the butterscotch skin, the eyes of golden honey."

"Part of the bunch. We got it all. East Indian, African, European. But a white man see me? I'm black like everyone else."

"I know what you mean."

"Your mother is light," which was an understatement. Sandy's mother had skin so fair you could see the blue veins beneath the surface.

"Who you telling? Her and my brother. Standing side by side, we look like strangers."

"Same thing with my mother. My father's genes just took the ball and ran with it."

Sandy nodded. "All of you look just like him."

"Some genes are stronger than others."

She looked at him. *Alone or not alone?* In that moment it didn't even seem like an option. "Come on," she said, heading for the steps. "Let's go look at the calendar. We got a party to plan."

Winston liked the "we" very much.

Every day that Cliff walked through the front door, Janice hoped he would look a little less tired, a little less wearied. Hoped that he would make it to the table before the food grew cold, would be able to sit across from her to eat.

Janice tossed the *Essence* magazine aside as she heard the familiar turn of locks coming from her front door. Took her feet off the sofa and placed them on the floor as the door swung open. She could not discourage the worry across her brow as she took in the love of her life's face. At that moment, she just wanted to soothe away the weariness with a stroke of her hand.

"Hey," she said, standing.

"Hey back," Cliff answered, glad to see she was in a good mood. "Your sister called."

"Oh yeah?"

"Yeah. She's having a party. Can you believe it?"

It was a good piece of news in an otherwise hard day. Raised his spirits. "She is?"

"Yep. Called a little while ago. Two Saturdays from now. You know she got the basement finished."

"Yeah, I remember you were telling me. Been meaning to get over there . . . just been so tired." Nobody knew that better than Janice.

"Want me to heat up dinner?"

Cliff kissed her lips lightly, plopped into a chair. "No, I picked something up."

It was such a tiny thing, so incidental in their life that it should not have bothered her, much less hurt. But Janice had taken on her upcoming wifely duties early and one of them was making a good hot meal for her soon-to-be husband every night. Him not wanting to eat it became a tiny burr in her side, sticking to old suspicion she had been trying hard to push down.

"You knew I was cooking."

"I know, Janice, but at six o clock I was still at my desk and I was starved. Couldn't wait."

Couldn't or didn't want to, all she could consider as the idea that roast chicken, new potatoes, and green beans would become leftovers.

He extended his hand to her, fending off another disagreement. "Come here."

But the anger she was feeling felt good. She was reluctant to let it go.

"Come on, babe, don't be like this . . . you gonna leave me hanging?"

No man had wanted her like Cliff had wanted her. No man had ever been so evident and full with his need of her. No man had ever begged for her touch, implored himself to have her by his side, gave up the goods like he had.

The goods.

The problem was Janice wasn't used to it. She had spent the last twenty years of her relationship life steeped in drama; an endless roller coaster ride of extreme highs, deep lows, and little in between time. Being with Cliff was between time all the time. She missed that even if she didn't realize it.

"Third time this week," she admonished.

Work, he wanted to tell her. He sensed that defending himself would only make it worse. He just wanted to make it better. He searched his brain for a resolution. "I know. Tell you what. Tomorrow's Friday. What say you meet me at the office and we'll go to that restaurant down in Soho, you know the one where we had my office party?"

It took a moment to realize she was debating his offer, that she was looking her gift horse in the mouth.

"And afterwards we can go to the Bottom Line, catch some jazz," Cliff offered, hoping to reel her in; appease her. Calm her brewing sea.

"Okay," she said, going toward the body that, though wearied, welcomed her full and strong.

"A party."

There was such unexpectancy in Martha's voice that for a moment Sandy wasn't sure it was Martha on the other end of the phone. Sandy had been certain her decision would be met with great praise, with a "there you go, girl," or at least an "about time." But the woman on the phone sounded empty, near hollow. Sorrowed.

"You okay?"

"Just fine." But there was no doubt Martha wasn't just fine. No doubt something had happened, and though she had not shared it, she was smack dab in the middle of it.

It was out of Sandy's mouth in a heartbeat. "I'm coming over."

Martha didn't try to argue.

She was in need of Sandy. In need of somebody to unburden with, share. Care about her. It had been a while since she'd felt so alone, so forgotten. So abandoned. Her only recourse was the bottle and she had been fighting the urge.

The unopened bottle was centered on her dining room table, where she had placed it hours ago. Martha had been sitting there staring and wanting when the phone rang. She had been in the midst of her test of wills when Sandy called.

Martha was happy that Sandy was coming over. She was ready to talk.

Sandy had never seen Martha bawl.

She had seen her eyes misty enough when Adrian had gotten sick and after he died, but she had never seen Martha so weepy, so moaned infused before. But that was how she was the moment Sandy sat down.

She reached out and held her, Martha's tears wetting her shoulder. "Everything's just over," she muttered, comfortable with letting go; safe inside her friend's embrace.

"What is it, Martha?"

"Calvin . . . he's gone."

It was a sucker-punching moment. The last thing Sandy expected to hear. *Calvin? Gone? How? When?* came into her head, forcing her tongue, easing Martha back. "What happened?"

Martha sighed, slumped a little. "I had to push the damn envelope." She grabbed a tissue. Blew her nose. "Marriage . . . I want it."

"Marriage?"

"Yeah . . . I asked him about it. Turned out he was married before. He wouldn't tell me the details so I went down to the courthouse. I dug up the records." Her head shook. "I didn't find out much except her name. How old she was. That she started the proceedings."

"Calvin know?"

"Yeah, I told him, but that's not what did it . . . he doesn't know if he wants to go there again and it's all I can know. I can't find the compromise. No middle ground. We're through."

But Sandy was stuck at the beginning of the confession. "Marriage, Martha?"

"Why do you say it like I can't or wouldn't want to?"

"Well, because, just that . . . after Leon."

Leon . . . a name Sandy hadn't uttered in years. Leon, the man who had asked Martha to marry her at the age of twenty-five and changed his mind three weeks before the wedding. The last man who had loved Martha until Calvin.

"Because I didn't know I wanted it myself *until* Calvin . . . I looked at you, Brit, Janice, and suddenly I wanted it too." Martha felt raw inside, raw and exposed. Gave out all her secrets. "See that bottle over there."

"Yeah."

"I've been sitting there since I got home. I was just sitting here and looking at it when you called. I want it but know I shouldn't have it . . . got tore up the other night. Overslept. Hung over. I missed work. Thank God I wasn't due in court."

"Just throw the damn bottle out."

"It's not that simple."

Sandy knew it wasn't. Knew about the incidents Martha had had with booze in the past. Martha and drinking, not a new issue. Sandy thought those days were over for her. Now she knew different.

"Maybe you need to address it."

News flash, that's how the word traveled about Martha and Calvin. Sandy called Janice and Britney respectively. Janice was surprised. Britney wasn't.

"I knew about their troubles," she confessed.

"Since when?"

"A while ago. Martha came over and told me about it."

"And you didn't tell nobody?"

"I was trying to give her some privacy."

"Sound like keeping secrets."

"We going there again?" They had traveled down that road before, accusations about cutting each other off, holding back information, explosive.

"No. We're not . . . can't believe it, though. He was so right for her."

"Nobody's perfect."

"Yeah, but for Martha, Calvin sure came close." Sandy switched gears. "So you think you're going to be able to make it?"

"If I have to drag myself there, yeah, I'm coming. I need a break from motherhood and pregnant or not, I'm going."

An idea came to her. "Think I should invite Calvin?"

"As much as I would like to say yeah, that's not our business."

But Sandy wasn't listening. It was too important. "I'll just call and invite him. He's my friend too."

# Chapter 12

"She's drinking."

Maurice didn't say good morning, what's up, chief, or any of the regular salutations. Just offered his news and waited for it to sink in. He was relieved when concern danced inside of Calvin's eyes.

"Drinking?"

"Brit said Sandy said—"

Calvin raised a hand. "Wait, hold up. This one of those he said she said things?"

"Like I said, Sandy said Martha told her she got so drunk one night she couldn't make it to work the next day."

"You sure?"

"You think I got the time or the energy to make up some nonsense about somebody else's life?"

Calvin looked away. Looked back at Maurice. "Ain't my fault."

"Never said it was, Bro. All I'm saying is Martha's drinking."

In many ways Calvin had been looking for an "in," some reason to go back, stand in her presence. He missed her like he hadn't missed anyone in a long time. But he hadn't expected the cause to be so immediate, so troubling. Hadn't expected such a gut-shaking revelation to be a pathway.

He had seen Martha drink, but had never seen her drunk. Knew her favorite was Bacardi neat, but had never witnessed her inebriated. Didn't think she possessed such a weakness, her strong will and strength, admirable. He was surprised to hear about it. Knew somehow he had been the cause.

"Drinking?" he asked, wanting confirmed.

Maurice raised an invisible glass to his mouth, worked his Adam's apple like he was chugga-lugging. Stumbled sleepy-eyed. Straightened, then held Calvin's eyes. Didn't blink, didn't speak, just waited for the knowledge to hit home.

It did.

"There has to be some compromise."

When Martha got to her apartment building, the last person she expected to see was Calvin leaned up against brick face. And the last thing she expected to hear were those words. "'Cause this is the stupidest thing either one of us has done. Got to be some way to fix it."

For a moment she couldn't speak, shame finding her, her eyes drifting from his. No doubt the news had reached him. No doubt it was the reason he was there.

"Who told?"

"Your sister-friend grapevine." He pitched his head toward the lobby. "Can we go in?"

Martha nodded her head, opened the lobby door, the two of them taking the elevator up. Soon they were inside her apartment.

"It only happened once," she defended. "I don't know why everybody's carrying on so." She wasn't an alcoholic. Nobody could make her say she was. "One time. No big deal."

"There's always a first time right before the second, the third." Something Martha knew to be true. Hadn't she wanted to do it again, get pissy drunk? Only her will disallowed it, a determination that was getting stronger with every second Calvin stood there.

"The last time was my last time."

He knew he could debate it, but there were other more pressing issues that needed to be addressed. So he nodded, conceded to her declaration, understanding the depth to which he had missed her. "Got to be a compromise," he insisted.

"How can there be? I want marriage, you don't."

"More than what I don't want, Martha, is what I do. And being away from you is no longer it."

She stood there, feeling him, missing him. Wanting him. Could not stop herself from hugging him, stop the whisperyness of her voice, or the ache that shifted through her soul. "I don't want you away from me either."

"So we gonna do this?" he uttered past the shoulder fitted under his chin.

"Yeah, we are."

"And marriage?"

"If and when you're ready."

Magic words that allowed them enough faith to pull away, smiles fragile toward each other. Uncertainty dancing with certainty, less of one, more of the other, but it was enough to move them toward Go.

Sandy's plan was simple, almost childish, but there was something she needed if it was going to work. She needed Calvin home. Needed him home to answer his phone. She couldn't leave a message like his machine requested. Sandy had to speak to him personally, convince him that coming to her party would be a good thing.

But three days of trying turned him up MIA. She thought to call Martha but that would ruin the plan. Sandy wondered where he could be. Unable to find him, she settled for the next best thing. Britney.

"Hey, girl. It's me. Sandy. How you doing?"

"Well, the good news is I no longer have morning sickness. The bad news is my whole body is filled with fluid and all I want to do is sleep, but I'm coming to that party."

"Been trying to call Calvin for three days now. No answer."

"Calvin?"

"Yeah. You know. I want to invite him."

There was a slight pause. "Martha didn't tell you?"

"Tell me what?"

"Girl, hold on a minute. Let me turn down the fire under my rice."

Sandy knew it was going to be news. Just wasn't certain if it would be good or bad.

It was not her nature nor had it ever been to get jealous of the connection between Martha and Britney. Sandy had long ago seen the foolishness of it; had Martha's own words that she was her best friend; that Martha and Britney's lives put together couldn't hold a candle to how Martha felt about her.

But times had changed, evidence everywhere Sandy looked, especially with Britney spilling a whole kettle of beans that Martha hadn't even thought to share. Major beans, milestone beans, like how she and Calvin were back together.

Before Sandy jumped the gun. Before she made the phone call to Martha to blast her for her secrecy, Sandy called Janice to see if somehow Martha had skipped her, but told everyone else. When Janice was as surprised as Sandy, Sandy knew.

Found herself burning. Burning and dialing, simmering when Martha picked up the phone. The lashing, ready on her tongue, faded as she heard the joy in Martha's voice, the kind that had been gone from her just days ago.

"Hello?" It was a whole symphony jammed inside of one word. A whole musical arrangement flowing through two syllables, telling anyone listening that her world was just fine again. Telling Sandy that having an attitude in this moment wasn't the best thing.

"It's me. Sandy."

"I've been meaning to call you."

But Martha's words became a confession of guilt and the fire Sandy had dashed, returned. "Oh really. What were you going to call me about? That you and Calvin are back together?"

"Don't tell me you're mad?"

"Mad? No, I ain't mad. Disappointed, yeah, but I ain't mad."

"I was going to call you Sandy, I swear." Her voice had dropped to a whisper, which translated Martha was not alone.

"He there?"

"Yeah." Dreamy. Martha's voice was downright dreamy.

"You know I'm dying for details."

"I can't tell you now."

"Well, when?"

"Tomorrow. At work. I promise."

"You better," Sandy warned. "All right, go on back to your man. I'll talk with you later." Sandy sat back against the couch, looking off and seeing nothing.

She was inside Martha's shoes now, feeling the power of reconciliation, remembering those days when she had it for herself. Sandy sat there, lost in her past, dismissive of her present. Great times, she found herself thinking, when love regained was like heaven opened.

Would she ever know that sensation again?

Would it ever be hers to claim? Would she and Winston ever dance on that edge, surviving it, pulling them closer? She wasn't sure. Understood the foolishness in even wanting such an adventure.

But Sandy could not stop the long-ago flavor of it, the bitterness and the sweet. Could not help but hold close such moments when the power of love overcame any and everything.

Camry.

Civic. Maxima. Escort. Camry. Camry.

Randall had never before noticed how many Camrys there were on the road. Never paid it any mind until now, suddenly Toyotas everywhere he looked.

He didn't even realize he was looking. Didn't even understand that he was searching until he heard himself mutter, "There goes another one," like there was somebody else in his beat-up van. But there wasn't. Randall was alone.

Had been for weeks. Thrusting himself into work wasn't doing it anymore. Putting in long hours and coming home exhausted was no longer an elixir. Physically he had never been so fit, but emotionally he was running from himself.

He had called up Ronnie. Called her up last Friday night and taken her to a movie, not realizing how desperate that move had been until he woke up Saturday morning, lying next to a woman he swore he'd never tangle with again.

Then he started seeing Camrys. All styles and colors. Some were in the style Sandy drove, but most weren't.

He began making more stops to the pay phone, calling home to check his messages. Found himself listening to "Are You Going with Me" all the time. Her smile was with him, the sound of her laughter, a constant in his ear. He didn't have to close his eyes to see her face beyond the glow of lit candles, experience that heaven they'd almost reached.

But the flip side of the coin was the risk, one that seemed too deep to wager. She said she was negative, but so had a lot of people who were now six feet under. What made her different?

It was a question his heart answered before the thought was through.

Jeanne Hutchinson looked upon the daughter who had been through what no child of hers should have ever gone through and could not stop the joy that filled her heart. Sitting before her at the kitchen table was the child she had raised and knew, full of vigor, full of life. Anticipative.

"A party? Oh, Sandy, that's wonderful."

Sandy nodded, lips fast over her smile. She wasn't sure if the next bit of her news would be so well received but she knew she would have to share it before her mother found out on her own.

"I'm kinda seeing Winston." She waited for the sky to fall, for her mother's face to do a transformation. But the reaction to her announcement was light-years from it.

"Kinda? . . . Since Adrian died, Sandy," her mother said with a soft smile.

"What do you mean?"

"I saw how much you leaned on him. How much he liked being leaned on. Figured it was just a matter of time."

"It wasn't even like that."

"Oh no? You think not. It was, but you were just too deep into things to know it. Your Grandma Tee called it after the funeral. Said he would be the next one."

"She didn't say anything to me."

"Does your grandmother say anything to anybody straight out?" Her mother looked away for a moment. "You know that day you brought Adrian home, I was so happy for you, because he was a good man." Her eyes found her daughter's. "Didn't hurt that he was cute. Then he was gone and my heart broke for you. Like somebody took a knife and kept on stabbing me. Winston? No, he's not Adrian, but from what I see, it's just that apple falling from the tree. And I'm happy for you, Sandy, really I am."

"Even though we're related?"

"There's no blood between you and it's not as rare as you think. You know your Aunt Edna? Her sister Imogene ended up marrying her brother-in-law after her husband died." She placed her hands on

Sandy's shoulders. "Life's too short to be denying yourself happiness."

Sandy looked up into her mother's light brown eyes, danced over the long brown hair. "Think Daddy will mind?"

"Your father?" Jeanne Hutchinson sucked her teeth. "The sun and the moon fell on Adrian as far as he was concerned. How could he mind?"

But things weren't so calm about it over at the Burton household. Mrs. Burton thought it was wrong. Mr. Burton was delighted. He had seen Winston struggle in his relationships with women, and for one reason or another they never lasted. He had tried to deny one son his happiness and regretted that decision every day of his life. Mr. Burton wasn't about to make the same mistake, and besides, he had come to adore Sandy.

Junie wasn't certain it would last, Rachel had some reservation as well, but they gave their blessings and hoped for the best.

Once the families were informed, the time came for Sandy to tell her friends.

Martha stood at Sandy's doorway, eyes dancing over her carefully. "You got some."

Sandy shoved her lightly, shaking her head, unable to contain her smile. "Is there anything you don't know?"

"It's all over your face. Hard not to know." Martha stepped inside, leaned in close. "Randall?"

"Who?" But Sandy knew who.

"Randall, the carpenter."

"No."

Martha pulled back, studying her friend more closely. Was still trying to determine things when the doorbell rang. Britney arrived, looking a little like death warmed over, but Sandy was just glad she had made it.

She made them wait.

Changed the subject a dozen times until Janice got there, apologizing the moment she stepped inside. "Got caught up at the catering hall. I swear, if I never eat another canapé, it will be too soon."

"Sandy's got a man," Martha announced.

"Is that true?"

Sandy nodded, eyes evasive.

"Who?"

"Not Randall," Martha offered, matter-of-fact.

Janice turned and looked at her. "The carpenter, right?"

It was in that moment that Sandy realized her breakup with Randall had come and gone without a word to her friends. She debated with herself to tell or not. Decided on the not. "It's Winston."

Mouths fell open. Eyes blinked in rapid surprise. Weariness left Britney quick. "As in Adrian's brother Winston?"

Sandy nodded. Watched her friends' faces. Was surprised to see the absence of happiness on most of them. Only Martha seemed pleased.

"Well, damn, girl, why not? Best of both worlds, far as I'm seeing." She raised her glass of soda.

Janice sat there blinking. "What happened with the carpenter?"

Which annoyed Sandy to no end. Couldn't Janice see that was a dead issue? "Nothing happened."

"But I thought, I mean it sounded like—"

"I know what it sounded 'like,' but it wasn't at all."

"Is that legal?" Britney's question.

Martha sucked her teeth. "Pregnancy making you dense? What kind of question is that?"

"Well, just that Winston and Sandy are related. In-laws, I mean."

"There's no blood between them." Martha shook her head. "I swear, only you."

Janice raised a finger. "No, she's not the only one. I was just thinking the same thing."

"Why are you all trying to rain on Sandy's parade? Can't you see how happy she is, how much better she's feeling? What should you care who it is, as long as he's decent and treats her good." She turned toward Sandy. "Don't pay these fools no mind. You go, girl."

Sandy went.

The discussion did not end at 112th Avenue. It continued the moment Britney and Janice arrived home, each carrying the news like a rabbit caught in a sack, squirming and struggling to be freed.

"You aren't going to believe who your sister is seeing," Janice began the moment she closed the door.

"Who?"

"Winston." Janice waited for the disgust to find him, eager for a slanderfest against her best friend's choice, but Cliff was delighted.

"Well, all right."

"What you mean all right? They are, like, related."

Cliff had gotten to see the various "Janices" over their time together. The fact that she saw only wrong in something good did not surprise him. "They're not related."

"Yes, they are."

"Says who?"

Which forced Janice to think about it. Even Martha who knew the law said they weren't, but there were other principles involved, like morality. Just seemed creepy to her. "Me . . . and Brit."

Cliff looked at her a hot minute, then shook his head. "Then you're both crazy." With that said, he left the room.

Britney got the same argument from Maurice.

"Who are you to say who Sandy can be with? She's happy, right?"

"So you're saying if something happened to you, you wouldn't mind me seeing your brother Melvin?"

Maurice's face screwed up. "Hell no. He's a bum."

"But if he wasn't a bum. Had a good job and stuff, is that what you want for me?"

"Baby, if for some reason I couldn't be here for you, all I'd want was someone who could be good to you. Treat you the way you need to be treated."

But Britney wasn't convinced. She got on the phone and called Janice, the two of them taking up a whole forty-six minutes about why it was wrong, but mostly why it wouldn't last.

There was no reason for Sandy to be nervous, but she was. Beyond the first party she had given in a long time, the evening ahead would be her first official social function with Winston at her side. And while most hadn't blinked an eye, she could feel the cool reception from two of her closest friends, one being her best.

She looked around her basement, finger foods out, bar stocked. It wasn't quite nine and her guests weren't due until ten. She had to shower, do her makeup, and get dressed. But she found herself rooted, taking in the transformations, the one in her heart and the one that encompassed her world.

Had he really done it?

Had Randall really come into her life, brief as it was, and changed the parameters both physically and emotionally? If he had not made the slow entry/fast exit, would she have even been in a position to give Winston a real try at her heart, have this celebration in her basement?

She did not mean to let him enter her thoughts. Had been successfully pushing his memory away for weeks now. But in the soft renovated silence of her basement, he was everywhere, from the new shiny floor to the pale yellow walls, warm and inviting.

*But he's gone.* She went upstairs, looked at prepared foods lining the kitchen counter, her cake centered on the table. Sandy moved toward it, resisting the urge to taste a wave of whipped cream. The inscription—*Welcome back, Sandy*—making her smile.

She was in the shower when the doorbell rang. Wet, she grabbed her robe, tied it around her tight, and hurried down the steps. She looked through the pane of glass, her heart beating hard at the sight.

*So fine. God, he's so fine.*

There before her was the close-cut hair, the clean-shaved face. The loose silk white shirt falling ceremoniously over the tailored tapered black slacks. She didn't have to open the door to smell his cologne. Did not have to hug him to feel his warmth.

Sandy just had to look at him to feel him. Feeling Winston, not her husband dead and buried.

"Not dressed yet?" Winston asked, looking her over.

"I was in the shower."

"Junie's unloading."

"Better get upstairs." She took two steps, paused, and turned. "I have the table set up in the corner. You'll see it when you get down there."

"Go," he urged with a sweep of his hand. "I got it covered."

It was a tiny thing, so slight, so simple any other time it would not have registered. But it did, becoming proof positive that she now had a significant other. Someone to pick up the slack, handle things. Do what needed to be done. Be her backbone, her backup. That other half.

It felt good, delicious and grounding. Made her thoughts of Randall and all that wasn't vanish, poof, into the air. In that moment being with Winston had become all good.


"We don't have to go," Maurice was saying, watching Britney struggle into panty hose that had gotten too small when she wasn't looking.

Some women had pregnancies that were downright dreamy, gaining no more than twenty pounds the whole term, never sick, never tired, never feeling worn down; just wearing their maternity like a wondrous badge of honor.

Then there was Britney. Just a few months, she was swollen, tired, and miserable.

She looked like the walking dead, Maurice thought, as his wife wrangled the stockings toward her hips. Even he knew that they would never make their destination—her waist. Wondered why Britney didn't.

Despite her struggles, Britney was looking forward to the evening. She and Maurice hadn't been anywhere since Bereace had been born and she was determined to get her panty hose up.

She grunted, she wiggled, sweat breaking out beneath her curls, streaking thin lines along her matte finish.

"Why don't you put on some pants? This way you can do the knee-high thing."

She looked at her husband like she wanted to murder him, continued her wager. But when she felt the run dance from her ankle up to her butt, she gave up the ghost. Britney pulled them down, using her feet to take them off completely. Kicking them into a corner, she went to her sock drawer.

Grabbing a fresh pack of knee-highs, she sat and put them on. Knew before she even reached her closet that her feet were too swollen for her high heels, but tried to put them on anyway.

They felt like bondage, but she took a few steps. Discovered the few steps were painful and knew there was no way she could survive the night. She kicked them off and searched her closet for her little navy blue flats. Couldn't help but sigh against the cool soft comfort they gave her as she put on her pants and the matching jacket.

Before Maurice, she thought she was just too big to be sexy and too poor to be fashionable. Before Maurice, shopping consisted of trips to the super sale days at May's Department Store where polyester was all she would consider, her choices old gray-haired women styles.

Britney had never thought she had any curves to her large body, never thought high heels could be a friend. But when Maurice entered her world, heart and wallet open, she had discovered different.

Specialty shoe stores allowed her the sleekiness of pumps that fit her feet and gave her much-needed support. The Avenue and Ashley Stuart offered her fashions that were both stylish and near tailor made.

Before Bereace was born, Britney had been reinvented into a fashionable size twenty Diva. Discovered makeup and hair styles, a whole new sophistication, but such days had vanished under motherhood.

She still had the clothes but the majority had grown too small. Trips to the beauty parlor were forsaken over motherly duties and that rare afternoon nap. Maurice had offered to take her shopping, but Britney didn't see the point. Pregnant, she only needed maternity clothes, of which she already owned quite a few.

Dressed now, Britney stood before the full-length mirror, giving herself one hard long look. She saw how unflattering her little flat shoes were against the rest of her outfit. Missed her glory days.

*Not going to worry.*

This was Janice's mantra as she slipped into the short tight knit skirt, adjusted the fit of her barely-covering-her-navel silk blouse.

I'm not, she told herself as she finger-styled her short curly hair, put on the brightest, glossiest lipstick she owned.

Legs to die for, breasts naturally perky and high, she looked back at herself in the mirror and saw all the sexiness the world could ever possess. But it didn't seem enough. Gave no bona fide guarantee that Cliff would be content.

Rachel, after all, was a knockout, and not too long ago Rachel and Cliff had had a thing. Janice knew about "things." Had spent a great deal of her life living out the dramas. Knew some things were over before they started, others like a revolving door. The opportunity to pick up where it left off always existing, waiting for reentry.

"Almost ready?" she heard Cliff call out.

"Five more minutes," she responded, keeping her voice light. She took one last look at herself in the mirror. Saw a pretty woman staring back. But no way did it match the beauty that was Rachel, Sandy's sister-in-law, who would be at the party too.

Martha and Calvin were the first to arrive. "I brought you this," Martha said, handing her a bottle of Crystal's. "Figure we can have it when all the rest of the guests are gone."

Sandy looked at her, appreciating her more than she had, at one time, thought was possible. "You know I love you," Sandy said, right before she gave her a hug.

"And I love you too, now let me go. You're messing up my outfit."

"And please don't do that," Calvin offered, opening his arms wide. "Took her ten million years just to decide on which one."

Sandy laughed, pulled away. Took in the both of them, glad for the moment. "Come on down. Winston and Junie are here."

She was nearly to the basement steps when the doorbell rang again. "Be back." It was Mr. and Mrs. Burton and Rachel.

"Come on in," Sandy sung, giving out hugs, feeling like a true hostess.

"Where would you like the patties?"

Sandy looked at the large tin pan, spice drifting from beneath the foil. "You made these? Didn't have too."

"Of course I did. No party's complete without them." But though Mrs. Burton's smile was bright, beneath it was little joy. Sandy recognized the expression. Had seen it long ago the first time she'd met Mrs. Burton. It was a smile offering little warmth, barely concealing condemnation.

In that moment Sandy knew the "disapproval" list had grown to three.

As long as Janice lived, she would never forget that eyebrow, slick as silk, perfectly arched. Janice remembered how it raised an inch higher than the other, permanent and fixed, as if it would never come down.

It had been after the services for Adrian that Rachel had cornered her in the kitchen, telling her things she didn't want to know or hear, but in need of both knowing and hearing.

Janice would always remember that one eyebrow, defiant and high, as Rachel told her that she could no longer hold on to Cliff because Janice loved him more. Could still experience the mixed emotions she felt about that proclamation, curious to know who had made Rachel God.

But later, when Cliff found her, opened himself back to her, Janice understood the unselfish thing Rachel had done. How that decision had returned to her the man she longed for even after she had walked away.

Now as Janice tagged behind Cliff as they moved through the party, she saw that same brow go up. Found herself unable to look away from it, adrenaline moving through her as Cliff made a bee-line Rachel's way.

In the simple unassuming ankle-length floral dress, Rachel was a knockout, filled with a beauty and grace Janice felt she would never possess.

"Well, well, well. If it isn't Miss and Misder Cleef."

Cliff reached for her first, bringing her near, hugging her tight. "Good to see you, girl." He spoke as if he had not seen her in a lifetime and wanted nothing more. "How've you been?"

The eyebrow remained in place. "Good, but not as good as you, me sure." Her eyes drifted to Janice, the eyebrow dropping. "Me hear dears a marriage in da works."

Janice nodded, near embarrassed. "Yeah, October."

"Well, now, dat's a good ting, no? Me happy for the both of ya." But something slipped from Rachel's eye. The joy.

Janice saw it. Wondered if Cliff did as she followed him to the dee-jay table.

"Rude bwoy?" he bellowed to Winston. "What tup, Jun-nee?"

"What tup, Bro," Junie offered, bringing his fist to Cliffs.

Winston gave a smile, "Ya looking good, man. Looking real fine." His eyes fell on Janice, things unreadable in her eyes. "Hey, Janice."

"Wint." Nothing more, nothing less.

"How's it going? How're the wedding plans?"

"Going just fine." She looked around, away, uncomfortable with his new role in her friend's life. Knew if she remained, she would gawk at him. Saw Britney, Martha, Calvin, and Maurice on the opposite side of the room. She chose an alternative. "Going to go say hi." Left.

Cliff looked at Winston. "What can I say, man?"

"Nutten."

"I think it's great news," jabbing at Winston's shoulder. "You know you my boy, just like Adrian was my boy. Got my blessings."

Winston nodded, humbled. "Thanks. Means a lot."

Jumpup.

Fast, insidious, and compelling, The Mighty Sparrow was singing about whining your boom-boom, the lyrics bawdy and quick. Junie was an excellent deejay and Sandy found herself dancing more times than she could count, everyone asking her to the dance floor, she too gracious, too happy, to decline.

"Don't know how," Janice was saying, holding back the arm Cliff was trying to pull.

"What know? Just move to the beat."

"I don't know how to do *that.*"

"Do what? It's dancing. You can dance, can't you?"

She could, but reggae was not her thing and Rachel was on the dance floor doing it better than anyone ever could. Rachel had the tinny, the whinny, and the boom-boom, rolled into a delectable motion that was as flawless as a wave, as rolling as a river.

Like some damn Jamaican whore, Janice was thinking, even though she knew Rachel's roots were in Trinidad and Janice wouldn't know a Jamaican whore if one walked up to her and slapped her. There was no way she was going out there and show her lack of talent. She refused to look foolish.

"Didn't we come here to party?" Cliff asked, annoyed.

"Yeah, and as soon as he plays some American music, we will."

"Well, I'm gonna dance," Cliff decided, ready to get out there and get into the groove.

"Go ahead. I'll be here," Janice balked. "I'm not stopping you." She felt Martha's eyes on her. Looked at her and gave her a hard cold stare. Don't, her eyes warned. But Martha would not take the hint.

She snatched Janice's arm. Janice jerked away. Martha pulled harder. "Come with me." Dragged Janice off to the storage room.

Not giving her a chance to refute, rebuke, or deny a thing, Martha let her have it. "What are you doing?"

"What do you mean, what am I doing?"

"Since when can't you dance?"

"That's between me and Cliff."

"Like hell it is. He's your fiancé, the man you wanted forever and supposed to be marrying asked you to dance with him and you tell him no?"

"I don't like reggae, okay?"

"Not, it's not okay."

Stare-down time. Janice looking hard at Martha. Martha looking hard at Janice. Janice was the first to look away. "Whatever."

"Yeah, right. Whatever. You refuse to dance with him then gonna pitch a fit when he finds somebody else to dance with, don't sound like no 'whatever' to me." Janice's eyes bloomed. "Go ahead, tell me I'm wrong."

"You're wrong." But Martha was so right it stunned.

"The question is why. I already know the answer. Do you?" Janice looked away. "Can't be happy with good times, can you? Got to stir things up, don't you?" Martha sighed, let go her anger. "You have to stop that, Janice. You have to be happy with your happiness. Cliff loves you . . . stop trying to prove he doesn't."

With that, Martha walked out.

Janice stood there, taking it all in. Saw it clear as glass, the truth self-evident. She left the storage room determined to fix it, honor him, but Cliff had already taken her words and made it deed.

"Ah, shake it tup now, gal. Move dat boom-boom," he was saying, watching the sway of Rachel's hips, the gladness that sparkled in her eyes.

"Ya trying to start sumtim, Misder Cleef? Is that what ya trying to do?"

"Just trying to have fun."

"So where's the wife? Where she? She's the one ya should be having fun wit."

His smiled dimmed. "She don't like reggae."

That brow went up. "Don't like raygay? Me never heard of such a thing. Who don't like raygay?"

"Janice."

Rachel nodded, lips pursed. "Ya marrying a girl who don't like this here good music? What else she don't like?" There was a gleam in her eye, so deep, so serious Rachel wasn't even aware it was there. But Cliff was.

He shook his head, getting back into the grove. "Enough talk. Let's just dance."

Forever.

That's what it felt like.

Feet glued to the floor, heart pumping hard, a lifetime passed as she watched her soon-to-be husband dance loose and slow with his ex-fling. Not a girlfriend, not a partner, but a fling. A blink in his lifetime, that in this moment, seemed to be shining bright again.

Just three records, it was the longest three records of Janice's life, especially when the fast beat moved to a slow one, and Cliff reached for Rachel's waist, to draw her close, allow their bodies to touch. Rekindle that flame?

But Rachel smiled, backed away, shook her head, uttered words Janice could not hear. Red-faced and heart beating, all Janice could do was wait for Cliff's return.

"Had fun?" she hissed, even though everything inside her tried to swallow those words.

"Sure did. Did you?" Cliff snapped, angry at the duality she was presenting. "Didn't you tell me to go and dance? Don't be getting pissed because I did." He left her, headed for the bar. Rachel was already there pouring herself a drink.

Destiny or coincidence, Janice wasn't sure. Knew only the laughter that came from their mouths, Cliff and Rachel standing close.

Britney was trying to wait for the cake.

She was trying to hold on long enough to be part of the highlight of the evening, but exhaustion claimed her. She had only managed three dances with her husband and knew there would be no more. She got up from her chair and went to find Sandy.

"You cutting the cake soon?"

Sandy had forgotten about the beautiful confectionery upstairs in her kitchen. Had forgot about the plans for a champagne toast and a few words she would speak. She had been having that much fun.

She looked at her friend closely. Knew without asking, though she did. "Tired?"

"Ain't the word. I'm about to pass out." Britney looked at her watch. "But hey, I did manage to hang on 'til what, ten to one. Not bad."

"No, Brit. Not bad at all. We'll do it now."

Sandy went over to Junie, whispered in his ear. The music faded and a microphone squeaked. Then Sandy's voice was moving through the basement, amplified and joy-filled. "Everybody, we're going to stop the party." Moans issued in unison. "For just a hot minute. We're going upstairs to cut the cake, have some champagne, all right?"

The exodus was slow. The narrow stairs leading to the kitchen admitting only one at a time. Winston poured Taylor's into the plastic champagne cups while Sandy, her mother, and her mother in-law handed them out.

Glass in hand, she stood among the overflowing crowd in her kitchen and raised her glass. Was about to speak when she paused, searching the room. Found Winston's eyes and beckoned him over. Reached out and took his hand, giving it a squeeze.

"I just want to say thank you," Sandy began, voice breaking. "Thank you for supporting me, for loving me, for caring about me. For being with me during the hard times and the good." Her eyes moved across the room, lingering on every face there. "I love you all, from the bottom of my heart I do. Salute."

She clinked her drink with Winston and took a long sip. Applause broke out as they shared a chaste kiss.

Official now, Sandy and Winston were an item.

# Chapter 13

The black garbage bag was already filled to capacity, but Winston was determined to make more room for used paper plates, plastic cups, and crumpled napkins.

"Got more bags," Sandy said from the other side of the room.

"No, I can get these to fit."

Frugality was a quality that Winston possessed. No doubt it came from being one of a family of six and both parents making minimal wage. No doubt in his life he had watched a dollar manipulated to the breaking point, with a little extra something squeezed out of it for good measure.

To herself she called him cheap, to his face she would have called him frugal. Either way, the synonyms belonged to the man now in her life. For the first time all evening Sandy allowed that thought to hit home, sink in. Wasn't as scary as she thought it would be.

For tonight, after the garbage had been placed outside, countertops were wiped, and floors were swept; after she found room in her refrigerator for leftover finger foods and a good-size chunk of her cake, they would ascend together, make a right toward her bedroom. Get undressed and get into her bed.

Then morning would come, a long hushed promise arriving, soft as that new dawn.

Across the room, if she knew nothing else, this much she knew. Her Some Sunday awaited.

She sat on the edge of her bed, slipped off a shoe, rubbed the sole of one foot.

"Tired?"

She nodded, smiled. Found his eyes. "Had a great time, though."

Winston stood in front of the mirror, back to her, face reflected in the mirror. Looked away as he undid the buttons on his shirt. "Me too."

With her dress still upon her back, panty hose to be removed, bra to be freed, night gown retrieved, Sandy felt no need to move, just sit and watch Winston, the slow peep show, as he undressed.

He did not seem to mind. He was neither self-conscious nor explicit as he slipped his shirt off his back, undid the belt of his slacks. Butterscotch skin glowed honey from the bedroom lamp. "Hanger?" he asked, turning slightly, just enough to show a hint of pectoral.

She went to her closet. Pushed hangers. Looked for an empty. Found a wood one, thick and strong. Handed it over and turned away. Slipped the dress off her shoulder, eggshell satin pooling at her feet.

Sandy stepped out of it, bent to retrieve it, sensing him before she felt him, hands around her waist soft. The kiss on her neck, along her spine, the rise of her behind, soul shaking.

She giggled because it tickled. Giggled because he loved her. Giggled because the moment felt that good. Then joy became desire, warm and full as his hands danced across her belly.

"Got to get undressed, Wint," she said playful, yearning. Wanting him.

"We will . . ." His breath came warm along the back of her thighs, a place no man had ventured, seemed to know.

Then he planted kisses on the inside of her thighs, and though there was that place his tongue would not venture, it was more than enough that it teased the parameters.

They found the bed or maybe the bed found them and they were on it, inside it, close. "No fear?" she asked him, studying the eyes alit with love.

"None."

He moved against her, she against him. Skin getting acquainted, the next step lingering. The promise, within the next heartbeat, tremor, not there yet. No seeking of entry, repositioning of limbs, just warm bodies in the midst of a slow sliding tease.

Sandy pulled away. Opened her nightstand drawer. Searched for the condoms. Found none. She sat up, looked over. The "Damn" leaving her with confirmation.

"What?"

"No condoms."

"None?"

"No . . . store?"

"Is one opened?" Not at that hour. "Tomorrow then," he decided, reaching for her. His lips to hers, so deep and so full, she pulled back.

"We can't," she managed, a heartbeat from a gamble.

"*We* can't, but I can." Then he touched her. There in the sticky wet place, he ventured. Stroking her, culling her to the point of no return. Her hand began a mission of its own. With deftness and intensity, they journeyed, wetness coating his fingers, hot drops against and about her hand.

Sandy caught her breath, lay back, looked down, sperm glistening about her wrist. "How many?" she asked, curious.

"How many what?"

"How many little Winstons do you think this has?"

He laughed at her curiosity. Pleased that she would even inquire. Shrugged. "Don't know, twenty-five thou?"

"That many, huh? Lot of mouths to feed."

It was his turn for laughter. "Come on. A shower awaits."

It was late. Traffic along 169th Street, near nonexistent. Martha leaned her head back, tired and just a bit sleepy. But not drunk.

"You did good tonight," Calvin offered, second sighted.

"Did I?"

"Yeah, you did. I watched you. Three drinks in all, the first a Bacardi, the second wine, the third soda."

"I told you it wasn't a problem." But there was defensiveness in her voice as if it was, or could be. Calvin caught it. Let it go.

"Wonder how Sandy does it?"

"Does what?"

"Not get the hell confused," Calvin said, awed. "All night long I kept on seeing Adrian, but it wasn't him. Just Winston." His head shook. "Got to give it to the sister. Couldn't have picked a better candidate."

Martha had been trying not to get into any disagreement about anything. But now he was picking at a business of which he had no part in. He was messing with her friend's choice.

"Candidate?"

He smiled at her, a flash of white teeth in the darkness. "Yeah, Adrian was it. The beginning, the end, and the middle. Left a hell of a legacy. The next man has some mighty big shoes to fill . . . I knew Wint was contemplating. Just didn't know he would do something about it."

"Yeah, well, he has and I'm glad."

"Me too."

"So you agree with me. It's a good thing."

"You see your girl tonight? I haven't seen her that happy since I don't know when. Who wouldn't be happy?" He risked his eyes off the road, did a quick study of Martha's face. "Let me guess . . . Janice."

"Bingo."

"I'm not surprised . . . I know she's your friend and all, but sometimes . . ." Calvin didn't finish. There was no need. Janice was a legacy onto her self.

Cliff was glad for the silence on the car ride home and just as glad it hung around as he and Janice took turns in the bathroom, extra care in getting undressed. The anger around them, inside of them, was dense, knife cutting thick. Cliff felt he could reach out and grab a handful. He was so peeved at Janice as she turned her back to unsnap her bra, he could throw something.

Holding on.

Did she know what that felt like? Did she even have a clue?

Cliff had spent most of his dating life running in and out of women's live. Had never really tried to settle down with anyone, enjoying the playa's groove. But with age and Adrian's death came a wisdom. Life was too short and there was nothing better than being with the one you loved.

So he changed.

Changed quickly and correctly. Changed immediately and directly.

Became the man he never thought he had the ability to be, ready for "till death do us part." It had not been easy to maintain it, women drawn to him like honey to bees. Every time he stepped out the door, there was some temptation, one he had been trying hard to resist.

Bettering one's life sometimes took support from others, someone to cheer on the accomplishments, give a hearty pat on the back. In the last few months Janice seemed to be doing just the opposite. Questions she'd never asked, dancing in her eyes.

Good deeds were accepted with suspicion, innocent delays varnished with mistrust. Cliff understood her history, recognized her pain, but hoped his dedication would clear away all doubt. Yet the harder he tried, the less she seemed to accept it.

Cliff didn't realize just how fractured the situation had become until the party. He could not believe Janice refused to do something as simple as dance with him, knowing just how much he wanted to. But she had, refusing to budge until his threat became deed, he left to dance with someone else, with her blessings.

Maybe he chose Rachel to spite her. Maybe he felt a need to stoke the fires Janice was hell-bent on starting. Cliff wasn't certain. Only that as he and Rachel moved across the dance floor, a clarity came to him, one deep, affable, and unsuspected.

Before him had been the gorgeous, smart, self-confident Rachel, just the type of woman Janice used to be. At their beginning Janice had been relentless in what was and wasn't acceptable. Had taken a stand against future grief and heartbreak.

Unswayed by his good looks, uninduced by his charm, Janice had been firm and insistent, demanding all of his heart in a single stroke. But it seemed that as soon as he had delivered those goods, she flipped the switch, becoming mistrustful, on the lookout for deceit.

The last few months found him walking a line so straight it hurt. All he really wanted was the woman Janice used to be.

Cliff fed on strength, feasted on self-confidence, things Janice no longer owned. He found himself in need of them, uncertain if she would ever regain them. The memory of the one who still did, riding his bones as he got into his side of the bed, Janice into hers.

Crazy. Ca-ray-zee, all that floated through her mind as she got off the E train at 53rd and Lexington and took the long New York city blocks toward First Avenue. Crazy with a capital C-R-A-Z-Y. Knowing

this, thinking this, feeling it, didn't stop her, change her mind, or anything. Did not prevent her from signing in at the lobby and taking the
elevator to the twentieth floor that Monday afternoon.

Nope.

*Done crazier shit. Like driving to Jersey and getting a police escort back over
the bridge. Now that was crayzee.* It no longer hurt to remember that, no
longer made her stomach twinge to recall it. Became an old history
she was certain she'd never have to encounter again, full of things she
would never do again, ever.

But she lied.

It was the only reason she was "dropping" by Cliff's job at five
twenty-one in the afternoon when she should have been halfway
home to Queens. Because things hadn't been right since Sandy's
party. Just wrong and tight and sullen. Janice couldn't take another
day of it.

She couldn't wait until twenty after eight or seven after nine when
he finally came through the door to talk about it. She couldn't stand
the thought of another night of couch watch, waiting for the sound of
his keys in the door, his weary face coming through.

She did not want to spend another morning going through the
laundry, smelling his shirts, and looking for traces of makeup. Didn't
want to count the condoms in the night stand right before she went
to work to make sure he didn't take one with him.

Didn't, but she had done all of it; her deeds pushing her farther
out on a ledge.

"Close the door," Cliff uttered, rising from his cluttered desk, her
visit feeling just as it was—an invasion. He moved around his desk,
but not much farther. Hands eased into his pants pockets as he took
her in. "What's going on?"

That he was asking surprised her. That he was feigning ignorance
didn't. Sunday morning had become a bitter Sunday night, with Cliff
sleeping on the couch and Janice in the bedroom. Few words had
been spoken the next morning when they had left for work and it didn't
seem like any good ones were going to be spoken now.

"That's what I came to find out," Janice answered, hot.

"Memory serves me right, you kicked me out of the bed."

"Yeah, but you went without protest, now didn't you."

Cliff turned away. "I'm now doing this here." In truth Cliff never thought he'd ever have to have such a conversation with Janice. He never saw them coming to a point where she would bogard his office because things between them had become so strained.

But here she was, angry and mad enough to spit fire. *At me,* he realized, knowing why but refusing to take full responsibility. Janice had started it.

After months of trying to convince her that he was on the up and up, bending over backward, going out of his way to appease her, he was tired of it. "I'm not talking about anything here," he insisted.

"Then where?"

"When I get home," he decided, going back to his desk.

"And what time is that going to be?"

*Never,* came the thought, with a sweetness he could taste. The idea of just walking away from it all, walking away from Janice and her madness, soothing.

He looked up, his eyes lasers of animosity. "When I get there."

*When I get there.*

Four little words with powerful effect. Four words possessing change, moving the divide deeper and giving license to a breeding ground of thought. Like, *He ain't never coming home, or if he does, it's going to be so late I'll be out of my mind when he does.*

And, *Everything was fine till she decided it wasn't. She think I'm up to something? Maybe I'll show her just how much.*

But mostly it became: *What in the world is happening to us?*

It was a question Janice asked herself all the way home. Found no answers an hour later as she slipped her key into the door, kicked off her shoes. Knew how the whole mess started, at the party, but wasn't sure how it would end.

There was supposed to be a wedding in a few months, a new chapter in the rest of their lives. But in that moment she could not see it, visualize it, or anything. In that moment that road up ahead had gone away.

Normally Janice watched TV on the couch till Cliff came through the door, but this night she could not stand the idea of him never arriving and chose the bedroom instead. She had heated up leftovers for herself, cleaned the kitchen, and gone into their room. Lying across the bed and turning on the TV, she flicked channels endlessly, nothing held her attention but the clock.

6:49. 6:50. 6:52. She had managed to look away until 6:57, then her clock watch was back on. Seven o'clock rolled around. Eight. Then at six minutes after nine, there came the sound of the key, and for the first time since she got home, she found her breath.

Cliff came into the bedroom, not speaking and changing into sweats. He left her, went to the kitchen, rattlings told her he was making something to eat. He came back to the bedroom, retrieving a pillow from the bed, a comforter from the closet, left out. Soon after, his snores were filling the air from the living room, his promise of a talk, unkept.

Cliff wouldn't talk about it because inside his heart lived dangerous words. Inside his heart was a turning away with no promise of return. Inside Cliff's heart was a fragile balance of *Do I walk or do I stay? Do I give it one more try or just cut my losses now?*

Inside Cliff's heart was a land mine, waiting to explode. One step in the wrong direction and everything would detonate.

Before Janice, Cliff had had no use for love. He couldn't see the merit in being content with just one slice when he could have the whole pie. Because of Janice, he had done a complete 360-degree turn, experiencing for the first time the joys of being with just one person; a joy he still desired but wasn't sure if he wanted to try and have with Janice.

Because the joy Janice had brought him was gone, done away with by her never-ending suspicions and accusation-filled eyes. Done away with forcing him to walk a tight straight line even though he was already on the straight and narrow.

The same love that had liberated him now had him under lock and key. And though new to the game, Cliff knew that, in reality, that wasn't love at all.

Nearly May, the gravy train was over.

The mouth-watering paychecks chock full of overtime from snow removal and street salting were gone. They had vanished into the heart of spring, full of warmer days and lots of sunshine. Maurice knew it, but still it hurt in places he couldn't even register as he looked at his pay stub.

He knew his monthly expenses down to the penny. Knew that the good times were about to become lean. He thought about his promise to Britney that she would never have to work again. Found himself wondering if he would be able to keep that pledge.

The summer vacation on the Big Red Boat would have to be canceled. Ditto plans for a backyard pool. There would be fewer meals out and fewer rentals from Blockbuster. He'd have to hold on to his three-year-old Towne Car a little longer.

He would stop forcing Britney to get that weekly pedicure. Was relieved that she would need maternity clothes for a while. The mutual fund for his daughter's college cost would have to be halted. There would be more brown bags for lunch.

Most of his adult life Maurice had never wanted. Just had it like that. Loved sharing his haves with Britney. Made him feel like a man.

But the gravy train was over, those sweet times gone for a while. In about eight months the snow season would be back again, but it seemed too far away to contemplate.

When she was single, Britney swore that if she was ever able to own a washing machine and a dryer, she wouldn't want for another thing. She had hated going to the laundromat and was certain that if she could do laundry in the comfort of her own home, it would be heaven.

But now that she had just that, she still found the chore no less unpleasant. Even though the basement was finished, complete with good lighting, carpeting, cable TV, and a very comfortable couch, she dreaded it—the endless cycle of loading, unloading, folding, and putting away.

It would take her most of the day and she'd been putting it off. But just that morning Maurice had told her he was down to his last work shirt.

Hoisting Bereace to one hip, she began the trek downward. Mind elsewhere, she had taken two steps before she realized the carpet was soaked. She looked down, startled. Wiggled her toes, saw water ooze up through. Surprised, curious, she began tromping in a widening circle. Realized the carpet was drenched.

Britney headed toward the rec room. Was relieved when the wetness ended and the dry began. Putting Bereace down, she went into the laundry room. Heard *pitter pitter pitter* but could not locate it.

Detective now, she flipped on the light and looked around. Checking the washing machine connections, she saw they were tight and dry. She knew the furnace didn't hold water, but the hot water heater did. She was halfway to it when she saw the leak. A trickle now, no doubt at one time it had been a stream.

The floor was covered in wetness and strange mold formations were starting to bloom. Getting her child, she went back upstairs. Got out the yellow pages. Called two plumbers and jotted down their prices.

Paging Maurice, Britney waited for him to call her back. Gave the figures over the phone. "Too much," he told her. "Try and find that guy Sandy used." In truth, Maurice wasn't certain if the prices were too high or not, but he knew his cards were maxed out and there wasn't a lot of money in the bank. At least with somebody he almost knew, maybe he could work out a pay arrangement. A little something now. A little something later.

"It's at home," Sandy told Britney over the phone.

"You don't have his number in your phone book?"

"No." Truth was at one time Sandy did. But she had since scratched that entry out. The only number she had was the one on the contract, which was in the file cabinet in the second bedroom..

"Well, do you remember the name of his company?" Sandy told her she didn't. "And you won't be home until when?"

"About six-thirty."

"Can't wait that long. Basement is a mess and we don't have any hot water."

Sandy knew Britney was in a bind. "I used to know the number," she found herself saying. Problem was she had erased it from both her heart and mind.

"Can you think of it? I've got stuff growing down there, loads of laundry to do. Bereace has thrown up and we both need a bath."

Sandy thought a minute. "Five, two . . . five, two . . ." Tried to visualize the rest. "Nine? Seven?" Sighed. "Brit, I'm just not sure."

"Well, you know his last name? Where he lives?"

"Hoakes. On Sayres."

"How you spell that?" Sandy told her. "Can you check the white pages for me?"

Could she? Yes, but she didn't want to. "Don't you have a white pages?"

"I can't even think where they are. Doesn't your job have a whole bunch?"

"What about Information," Sandy found herself saying. "You can call Information."

"Yeah, but even if I found it, he won't know me from Adam."

"Just tell him you are a friend of mine."

"You know how I am with people I don't know." Which was true. Britney had an aversion for strangers.

"Yeah, but you need to get that heater fixed now, don't you?" Silence. Guilt rushed Sandy. She swallowed, head nodding. "All right, girl. I'll try and find him. Give you a call back."

"Thank you." But there was no kindness in that consideration.

"Residence. In Jamaica, Queens. First name Randall. Last name Hoakes, on Sayres Avenue."

"Checking for a Randall Hoakes on Sayres Avenue in Jamaica Queens, I have the following number."

Her heart picked up its rhythm, her hand writing fast and sloppy. Each numeral became the piece of a puzzle, fitting neatly into place. So complete was the picture emerging that Sandy jotted down the last digit before the operator spoke it.

"Thank you."

Sandy hung up the phone. Stared at the paper, afraid. She looked at the time. Figured it was a good bet that he was out repairing something. Found herself glad at that notion as she picked up the receiver and dialed.

Randall spooned the last of the Maypo into his mouth, popped in the last bit of buttered toast. Took up his bowl and plate. Headed for the sink. He was in his off season. Would be for another week or two, then the work orders would start rolling in as people remodeled for June weddings and high school graduation parties.

Randall had no immediate plans for the day. Considered working on the hope chest he had started. Maybe take in an afternoon matinee. Worse came to worst, he could go and shoot the breeze with his pops, let his mother fawn over him.

He was mentally working out the rest of his day when the phone rang. "Hello?"

The sound of his voice stole her next breath. "Randall?"

Silence. Then, "Sandy?"

"Yeah. Listen. A friend of mine is in a pinch. Her hot water heater's busted and she needs someone to fix it ASAP."

"This is a surprise."

But Sandy was trying not to go there. Wanted to keep the call about what it was—her friend needing service. "She has a baby with one on the way. Basement's soaked. No hot water. Can you help her?"

"Heater? Yeah, I do heaters."

"Got a pen?"

"Hold on." The phone was put down. It seemed a lifetime before he came back on the line. "You've been good?"

*As opposed to being bad or diseased?* she wondered, nearly out loud. "Just fine . . . Name's Britney Campbell. She's on a Hundred and Thirty-second off of Rockaway. Phone number is—"

"Is she home now?"

"Home and waiting."

"I'll give her a call."

"Great. Thanks." Sandy hung up.

Randall held the receiver to his ear long after she had. Got himself together and called her friend.

Crises often did away with phobias. Crises stripped away self-indulgences and allowed you to interact with a stranger as if you had known them all your life. This was the reason Britney could not stop the smile that rushed her face when she opened her door. The reason why she hugged Randall hard, grateful he had come to her rescue.

"What a nightmare," she said, pulling back, relief still in her.

"Which way to the basement?"

"This way."

Randall followed behind her, taking the moment for all it was worth. No, it was not Sandy, but it was her good friend. Another step closer.

Randall didn't have to go down the steps to sense the damage. It hung in the air, damp and decay-filled. Beyond the heater, he knew the carpet would have to be replaced. There would be baseboards to be refitted and an antifungal agent to apply.

It was not the idea of having work to do that thrilled him. It was the notion that he was in and would be back to the home of Sandy's friend. Maybe she'd come by when he was there, maybe she'd call on the phone. Maybe this Britney would give him a pathway back, one he was unable to create for himself.

"Cracked," Randall was saying seven minutes later. "Definitely has to be replaced. The water damage is not extensive but there are things that need to be replaced, like part of the carpet, the baseboard around the stairs."

"How much?"

"Heater, installed, will run you about five. Carpet, I'll have to check. The baseboards? You won't need much. I could toss that in for free."

Free. Britney liked free. "You take checks?"

"Normally I don't, but since you're a friend of Sandy's, that's not a problem."

"How soon can you start?"

"Leave here, have the hot water unit in a few hours. For the carpet, I'll need to run a sample over to my supply place. Can probably get started on that tomorrow. I'll also need to spray some antifungal agents down there, to kill the mold. I wouldn't suggest you take your little one down there for a few days, but after that you'll be good to go."

Britney went off to get her checkbook.

She was so certain that Maurice would be pleased that she didn't call him back. Just waited for him to come through the front door, a smile on her face, weariness on his. He didn't seem to remember the broken heater, the at-home crisis and how he had left her to find a good deal.

He didn't seem to recall that the basement had been half saturated, for a hot minute there had been no hot water and his last clean shirt was upon his back. All Maurice seemed to know was he had a thirst and half the jug of spring water seemed to quench it as he stood in the kitchen, refrigerator door wide opened, plastic to his lips.

"Mo?"

He waited until the bottle was caving in to answer. "Yeah?" But his eyes were not on her, just about the kitchen that didn't hold a single hot pot of anything.

"Seven hundred and fifty."

Numbers drew his attention. Money, heavy on his mind. "Seven hundred and fifty what?"

"Dollars . . . the whole thing. Heater, baseboards, carpet, some anti-fungal stuff." Britney stood there waiting for praise at being not only smart, but capable. It didn't come. Just a scowl. "That much?"

"That much? Those other people I called wanted just that much to replace the heater."

His eye grew leery. "When do we need the money?"

"Already gave it to him."

"How?"

She didn't know what he meant by "how." "I wrote a check, how else?"

"A check?" He was not yelling, but she could feel it inside him waiting to be let go of. Rarely did her husband get upset, but when he did, sometimes it was like a whole different Maurice inside him.

"Yeah, you know, a check from our checkbook."

In that moment he realized his mistake. Realized his deep dark secret should have been shared two paychecks ago. Anger faded, as a sadness filled him, his voice so tiny, so small, so wounded, it was hard to believe it belonged to him. "We ain't got it."

It took five minutes to break it down to her, three minutes for her to take it in, the knowledge immediate and exact. The extra pack of pork chops she had defrosted for dinner was put back for another day. Britney made extra beans and rice to replace their absence.

She dished out extra helpings of lettuce and tomatoes. Made a cornbread from scratch, and though the meal was filling, every bite told them both of the lean days to come.

She didn't wash Maurice's work shirts separately like she normally did. Tossed in other clothes until the wash tub was full. There was no extra dash of Liquid Tide. One cupful was all she allowed.

Britney cried silently over the washing machine as she remembered the phone call she'd made. It didn't matter that Randall ended up telling her these things happened, that he would finish up the work and they could pay him on time. If anything, his generosity only made her feel worse.

Made her feel incapable, no longer that shining star.

There was no doubt she had been the true winner in the race to secure a good life. While her other girlfriends were getting dinner and a movie, Maurice bought her a house. While they were still waddling their way through the trials and tribulations of relationships, she was walking down the aisle. Britney had been the first to have a child and the first to be a stay-at-home mother.

Her husband indulged her like none of her other friends were, and for the first time in her life she had been riding high above them. Was the Queen Bee. Britney never considered it wouldn't last. Never considered that struggle would revisit her. Never thought that writing a seven-hundred-and-fifty-dollar check would bring it all to an end.

But it had.

Britney got into bed, Maurice silent, his back to her. She knew he wasn't asleep, though he was giving a good performance. She found herself wishing things were different, but they weren't.

There were a lot of questions she could ask in that moment, one being: What happened? But she knew it like she knew her middle name. They had been living beyond their means. That car he'd bought her, the toys and gadgets for the child, the beauty sessions, trips to the mall, more than they could afford.

It was love and pride that fostered the extravagance, but in that moment Britney could only acknowledge the pride. "When were you going to tell me?"

The bed shifted, Maurice turned toward her, more wounded than she had ever seen him. "Didn't think I had to. Thought we'd be all right."

"You thought? Since when do you think about anything?" It was a low cutting blow, but Britney was beyond sensibilities. "We're sitting up here with stuff we don't even need, not a dime in the bank, and a damn bounced check with my friend's friend and for what? Because you didn't think to tell me, 'Brit, we can't afford what we have?' "

"I'm sorry, baby." That soft wounded voice was back, filled with a love that had wanted only the best for her. She could not refuse it or him. Could not refuse the need to reach out and hold him. Soothe him. Place her spin on things. "After the baby is born, I'm going back to work."

She didn't wait for an answer, wasn't even looking for one. Just went on holding him until a peace claimed him, she giving him that much even as her heart trembled at his transgression.

# Chapter 14

A penny wise, a pound wiser.

This was the creed Randall lived by, a creed that had caused that check from Sandy's friend to bounce because he had deposited it into his business account right before he had gone and picked up the hot water heater. This was the same creed that had allowed him to swallow the twenty-eight-dollar insufficient fund fee and then take his own money and buy the supplies he needed to do the repairs.

No matter how tight times became, Randall always operated on a surplus. Sometimes that surplus grew as low as four dollars and twelve cents but he had learned early that it was better to have enough for a Big Mac value meal than to have no money at all.

It wasn't how he liked to do business, but there was no doubt Sandy's friend had been caught off guard. He had seen their house, seen the nice car in the driveway. Had taken in the workmanship that was their basement, truth everywhere he looked.

Then there was the fact that Britney was a lifeline to Sandy. If nothing else, he might be able to find out what she was up to these days, and with whom.

But the gladness Britney had welcomed Randall with that first day had vanished when he arrived early the next. She was polite, cordial even, but beneath her veneer laid a deep restraint. Randall didn't know why and so he went about his work. Took a lunch break in his van, sensing she would not allow him use of her kitchen table.

What Randall didn't know, didn't even suspect, was that Britney was in deep pain.

Hurt found her when she called the bank and was told their checking account balance was four hundred and thirty-six dollars in the red. Hurt dug into her heart because there was no money and wouldn't be for the next two weeks when Maurice got paid again.

Automatic deduction had taken care of the mortgage and the car notes. But that left the utilities and groceries wide open. They had some money in the mutual fund for their daughter's college but they swore that, high or hell water, they would never touch it. Maurice had a few dollars in his credit union, but forty-nine dollars would not do it either.

It became a simple choice. Starve or pawn her fur coat. Britney got herself and Bereace dressed, shouted down the stairs to Randall that she had an errand to run, and then she, her baby, and her fur were heading out the door.

Twenty-seven minutes later Britney was leaving the Pawn Shop on Jamaica Avenue. The coat had cost Maurice twenty-five hundred. The pawnbroker only gave her two hundred. That hurt too. But hurt yielded only self-pity and inability. Britney had no time for either.

On the drive home she remembered the life insurance policies. Knew there was cash value in them. She wasn't certain how much, but would be on the phone when she got home to find out.

Janice had worked through her lunch hour, eating a sandwich at her desk, afraid to leave it for too long. Nothing had been settled between her and her soon-to-be husband and she was hoping that one of the four phone calls she had placed to him at work would be returned.

So when the phone rang at quarter after three, she was full of optimism. But it quickly died when she heard Sandy on the other end.

"You and Cliff got plans after work?"

"No, why?"

"Me and Wint are going to Pillards, thought maybe you wanted to join us."

Janice had heard of Pillards. Had been wanting to go for a while. But Cliff wasn't even talking to her now. Double dating was out of the question. "Can't."

"Why not?"

Tell it. Or don't. "Your brother's putting in overtime. He won't get off till late."

"We'll be there for a while. He can meet us there."

"I'm really tired these days, Sandy."

But to her it sounded like an excuse. Sandy couldn't keep quiet. "He makes me happy, Janice."

"Who?"

"Wint . . . I don't see why you're having such a problem with it."

Yes, she had a problem with Wint, but it didn't even register on her real problem scale. In fact, if she had the opportunity, she would love to go on a double date. At least it would mean Cliff would be forced to talk to her again. "That's not it," she said softly.

And "don't tell" became "tell."

"Why?" Not "Okay, I understand. It's cool." Just *why?* as if Sandy hadn't spent a whole minute explaining that her friend was in trouble and she couldn't go to the club after work because Janice needed her.

It was the first time Sandy saw the difference between Adrian and Winston.

Adrian would have understood even if he didn't want to. Adrian would have sent her off with his blessings, asking that she come by later if she wanted. Adrian would have never asked her why.

"I just told you, Wint. We can go another night."

"I was looking forward to tonight."

"Yeah, so was I. But Janice needs me."

And I don't. Winston didn't speak it. Just thought it. Took a breath, another. Said, "Okay." But he could not do away with the feeling of being cheated. Like a pebble, it lay inside his belly.

When you wanted something for so long and you finally got it, it was hard to share, hard to let it go, if even for a little while. Winston knew about female bonding and how deep those ties went, but sometimes Sandy seemed obsessive with her friends. Sometimes they felt more important than he would ever be.

Like now as he sat back, his planned evening shot, Sandy off to rescue Janice.

At her age, Janice should have been beyond rescuing. She should have been ashamed for even needing it. Winston had never known his sister or his mother to be so weak. Problems came, you handled them on your own. He forced himself to let the anger go. "You'll come by later?"

"Where?" But Sandy knew, smiled.

"My place, after you're done with Janice."

"You sure you want to see me? Just a few seconds ago you were pissed at me."

"Was . . . not anymore."

"Not anymore, huh?"

"So you coming or what?"

There was no way she could tell him no.

Like a dishrag used too long and left to dry, Janice looked worn out. It broke Sandy's heart to see her sitting at the bar, a Coke in front of her, everything about her desiccated. Sandy slid onto the empty stool beside her, snaked an arm around her shoulder. "Hey."

Janice's eyes shone like glass, tears seconds from falling. A heartbeat later, they did, two tiny drops racing down either side of her cheek. Sandy reached out and rubbed them away, drew her near. Pulled her from the bar, found a booth in the back. Ordered drinks, held one of Janice's hand. Asked softly, "Tell me."

"It's me. God, I know it's just me. I did this. Don't know how to fix it, only that I want to."

"Did what?"

Janice's head shook, her face, twisted. "Martha tried to tell me." Her eyes found Sandy's. "And for the first time ever, I listened to her. Heard everything she was saying, got it. Understood it. Was glad for it even, but by that time it was too late."

"For what?"

"Cliff."

"What about him?"

"We're not even speaking, Sandy. Living in the same damn apartment and we haven't shared twenty words since your party."

"What happened?"

This was the hard part of her. The part that was a gumbo covered in deep thickness, nothing exactness. "Rachel. Me. Cliff. I don't even know anymore."

Sandy did remember her brother and Rachel dancing a few minutes, but that was all. Decided then and there Janice was back to looking for monsters under her bed. Let her hand go, annoyed. "You're back to that, Janice?"

"I don't want to be, but it's like . . ." She couldn't finish. Dried her eyes with her fingers. Reached for the drink the barmaid arrived with. Took a long deep sip.

"How many times I got to tell you Cliff loves you?"

"I know he does, but I don't know it."

"That don't make sense."

"It does to me and that's the scary part."

"So what is Cliff saying?"

"Nothing."

"So what exactly happened?"

Janice plucked up her cocktail napkin. Blew her nose. Got herself together. "We were at the party and Junie was playing all that reggae mess." Sandy's eyebrow rose. "Song after song of lyrics I can't even understand and that nasty raunchy beat. Cliff wanted to dance. I didn't. Told him to go and enjoy himself."

"And he did."

"Yeah."

"So he did what you told him to do and you got mad."

"Yeah." Janice took another sip. "It wouldn't have been so bad if he hadn't danced with Rachel. But he did and then some slow song comes on and he's reaching for her." Her eyes drifted, thrust in memory. "His hands trying to slide around her waist, but Rachel tells him no. Walks away. Cliff comes back. Asking me if I was happy . . . don't remember what I said, but then he's gone again to get a drink. Rachel's there. They move close, laugh hard and deep." Her eyes found Sandy's, voice fading.

"So my brother dances with Rachel because you won't dance with him and he and Rachel laugh and the world is coming to an end." It wasn't a question. It was a statement, filled with all the animosity Sandy was feeling. Her head shook. "That's crazy, Janice." She had never used that word and her friend's name in the same sentence, but she had felt it often.

"Don't you think I know that? But it's like I don't know how to fix it."

"How about starting with an apology."

"To who?"

"Yourself number one for setting yourself up and then Cliff, for making him a part of your twisted plan." Sandy considered her. "Ever since I've known you, you've only wanted one thing—a man who treated you like you wanted to be treated. You got it now and you're blowing it."

"I know."

Sandy sat back, resisting sucking her teeth, shaking her head. The pity she had felt for Janice was gone. She was cutting off her nose to spite her face as far as Sandy could see. Sandy would not support that effort. She looked at her watch. "We better be going."

The announcement took Janice by surprise. She had thought they'd at least have another drink, but Sandy was downing hers, and standing. Janice took the hint. Stood too.

Rachel did not expect to see Cliff at her front door, but she was more than happy to see him. "This a surprise."

"Yeah, I know . . . got things on my mind. Can I come in?"

"Miss Cleef giving you da blues?"

Cliff smiled for the first time in days. "Blues ain't the word."

"Well, den, come on in." She opened her door wide for him, closed it, and locked it. Indicated her sofa, she taking a chair. Settled in it, waited for him to speak.

"Guess you're wondering why I'm unburdening on you," Cliff began.

"Thought did craws my mind."

"Can't talk to my mother about it, she'll know we're in trouble. Ditto Sandy. Wint's my boy but telling him will be just as good as telling Sandy . . . you, on the other hand . . ."

"Me what?"

Cliff looked away from her. "Got this wisdom about you."

Rachel chuckled, tickled. "Ya tink so?" She shrugged. "What everybody tink. Dem say, 'Ya see Ray-chell, she just smart and wise and dis and dat.' Know what me say? Me say me tired of bein' da marta. Me tired of just upholding dis one and dat one. Me want to live me life, just be Ray-chell."

Something moved into her eyes. It took a while for Cliff to realize what it was. Vulnerability. He had never witnessed it before, and the impact hit him hard. Too hard. So hard he just wanted to do what he swore he would never do again. He just wanted to hold her, touch her, kiss her like he used to.

They both looked away. She got up. "Getting sumting ta drink. Ya want?"

"No. I'm fine." But the truth was he wasn't. Truth was he wanted her. Truth was he was scared.

She came back, glass in hand. Took a sip, placed it on the table. Leaned forward, elbows to her knees, a hint of breast beneath the big shirt she wore. She gazed at him with sage eyes. Vulnerability vanished.

"So, tell me what going on wit Janice."

Cliff told her to the best of his ability, losing himself in what had become their life for the past few days. He sat back when he was finished, head shaking, still clueless. "It's like she wants me to do wrong. Like she's pushing me to do it."

"She insecure, dat's why. Whoever dat woman was that you first got togedder, she gone. Maybe dat woman just a front. Maybe dat woman just too powerful and it scares her." Rachel shrugged. "Who knows? But what me do know is ya got to make a choice. Ya got to decide if da woman she is now is da one ya want to spend da rest of ya life with. If ya can lub dat woman like you lubbed the one she was before."

Cliff nodded slow. "I know."

Rachel threw up her hands, lively. Brisk. "Well, den, if ya know, what are you picking my brain for?"

Cliff smiled, laughed a bit. "Sometimes we just need somebody to tell us out loud."

"Well, me told ya. So what are ya going to do?"

"Go home," he said, standing.

When Cliff came through the front door, Janice wasn't on the couch. She was standing at the door, her arms moving around him before he could speak.

Her arms went around him tight, holding fast, hard, never wanting to let him go. "I'm sorry, Cliff. I'm so sorry." The action caught him off guard, meshed against the slight self-betrayal he had been feeling all the way home from Rachel's place.

It took him a while to relax, a second or two to accept. Another to give in, return her embrace.

"I know you love me. I swear I do. I just got these issues with trust, you know? And it's not about you, it's about me."

He nodded, face pressed to her hair. He held her, remembering how good it felt. Held her, remembering how much he did love her. Held her, remembering Rachel's words. That flash of need that had speckled her eyes.

Cliff held Janice wondering if the woman she was would be the woman he, in the end, could be content with. If she was the one he would want forever.

Sandy lay across Winston's bed, head shaking. "Remember when you asked me why I had to meet Janice?"

"Yeah."

"Should have listened."

"So what was it about?"

"It was about looking gift horses in the mouth. About not thinking enough of yourself to accept the fact that, though life was shitty in the past, God has indeed blessed you this time around." Her eyes sought his. "That's what it was about."

"And I guess she needed you to tell her that."

Sandy grew peeved. "No. Girl knew it the whole time. Didn't need me to tell her jack."

"Maybe she did."

"Maybe she did what?"

"Needed someone to tell her. People know stuff all the time. But sometimes they don't *know* it until somebody else says it."

"I guess you're right, but still. Hell, we could have been getting our groove on at Pillards."

He slipped an arm around her. "There'll be other times."

"Who's your best bud?" she asked, curious.

"My what?"

"Best Bud. Buddy. Best friend. Hombre."

Winston looked away. Swallowed. "Adrian."

Sandy's voice grew soft. "Yeah, I remember. The two of you. Like twins."

"Poppa called us that. Said we were twins just that I chose to be born two years later for some reason or another."

"Maybe I was the reason. Maybe because before you were born you knew that Adrian wouldn't be here for me and I would need you."

Honey eyes slipped into hers. "Do you?"

"Do I what?" But she knew.

"Need me?"

"Haven't I always, even when I didn't know it?"

Winston nodded. Nuzzled her head with his nose. Was silent for a moment, deep in thought. "He doesn't visit me anymore, in my dreams, I mean."

Sandy nodded. "Yeah, doesn't visit me either." She shifted, laid her head against his fast-beating heart. "Maybe because we're both okay now. He knows we'll be alright."

"Maybe, but I miss him."

"Miss him too. Let's change the subject. I'm not in the mood for tears." But her words had come too late as she felt a drop hit her forehead. She looked up, surprised to see Winston's eyes chock full of wetness.

Understood. Allowed him his moment, the hurt still there, fresh as yesterday.

Randall knew what was in Britney's hand but he didn't understand why. "What's that for?"

Britney straightened her shoulders, head high, eyes off from him. "Part of what we owe."

"In two weeks, that's what we agreed to."

Randall was trying to be nice but Britney saw only a pity she did not want. There was no doubt she could have used that twenty-five dollars she was holding out to him, and the installments were supposed to begin when Maurice got paid again, but she could not let him go without giving him something now.

"Will you take it, Mr. Hoakes?"

Mr. Hoakes, since when? Since something changed in her life. Since the big old hug she had given him just the other day was becoming a fading memory. Britney was being so curt with him, he didn't even know how to begin to ask the one thing he had been dying to ask since he first walked through the door.

Randall took the money knowing that she needed it more than he did. Took it, trying to make his smile appear light and easy, trying to force the words off his tongue. He swallowed, goofy smile on his nervous face as he asked, "How's your friend doing?"

"Who?"

"Sandy . . . how's she?"

It took a second for Britney to connect the dots. Another four before everything became Kodak color clear. *How's Sandy?* Britney thought. *She's sleeping with her brother-in-law, that's how she's doing.*

She didn't speak that. Just smiled. Sandy may have been gone from Randall's life, but her memory sure wasn't. "You really want to know how Sandy's doing?"

Her question was a test, a validation of his interest. He had planned on being casual in his inquiry, but it was too late now. "I think that's why I asked."

"Give her a call and see for yourself."

Randall rewound Britney's words through his head on the drive home. He was trying to freeze frame how she looked when she said them. Felt all of fifteen again when Jessica Smiley had caught up with him after homeroom that day to tell him how much Paula had dug him. Knew he was trying to decipher the messenger from the message.

Drew blanks.

He had to be like Nike to find out—he had to just do it. Decided he would call her and see for himself.

# Chapter 15

They hadn't made it the previous night but Sandy and Winston made it to Pillards the next, a former bank building turned after-work club. Crowded with a five to one ratio of women to men, Sandy trailed behind Winston as they left the bar, drinks in hand. She took a moment to take it all in. Realized how nice it was to be out and about with someone she cared about, who cared about her.

Winston wasn't Adrian, no man ever would be. But what he did offer was more than enough to soothe, ease, give hope. That he was fine was icing on the cake, his presence drawing glances, whispers, and nudges. Women attempted eye lassos but that didn't bother Sandy. They could look till the cows came home. He was all hers.

They made their way toward the dance floor, bodies in motion a gravity they could not resist. Finishing their drinks, glasses were abandoned as they joined in the fun. They danced fast, slow, then fast again, Sandy doing what she enjoyed most, dancing like there was no tomorrow; dancing as if life itself depended upon it. While Winston, imbued with the woman before him, took all that the moment offered.

\* \* \*

Sandy dragged into her bedroom, shoes in hand, eyes sweeping the clock. It was a little after midnight and she was dog tired. There was once a time when hanging out during the week had been as easy as breathing, but she was no longer in her twenties. She had hit the mid-thirty mark and the partying had taken its toll.

But even in her weariness, she could see the light on her answering machine blinking red.

She hit the Play button. Heard:

"Hey . . . it's me."

Reached over and immediately pushed Stop. Randall. Calling. Doing the one thing she had needed him to do so long ago. Coming too late, when her life had settled, reconnected. Gone was the angry accusatory man who had stormed out her front door, in its place someone more forgiving.

But she would not play the message. Would not allow his voice, his words, his new reasons to reach her. One day she would; brace herself for the impact because she needed to know. Needed to hear him say it, speak aloud that she wasn't a leper, that maybe he wanted her.

The time just wasn't now.

Sweet love had entered their life again and Janice wallowed in it, holding tight to Cliff all night long, not wanting to let him go the next morning.

"You want me to be late?" he asked, smiling at her insistence to keep him in the warm soft drowsiness of her body and the comforter.

"No, I just want to make sure we'll be okay."

"I'm still here, you're still here. Together, right?"

It was not the response Janice had been looking for. She was in need of something a little more granite, hopeful. "That's not what I mean."

He nuzzled her nose, kissed the slope of her forehead. "We'll be okay . . . got to get to work."

He left the bed, taking the warmth with him, stealing the joy she had found last night. Old demons began to filter in the absence of his heat, the silence of his departure. Perched and taunting, they shifted through her eyes like a fire not quite spent, watching and waiting, expectant, near complete.

\* \* \*

The sun had not quite kissed the horizon but the royal blue settled at the edge said that it was on its way. Sandy stood at her bedroom window, blinds opens, looking into it; a crystal ball in which she was trying to glimpse the future.

Beyond her commute in forty minutes, the full workday she would put in, there was that message waiting to be heard. She had already gone for the Play button twice. Made herself stop before she could go for a third.

Not now, she told herself. Not now when life with Winston was good. But like a wolf baying at her door, she knew sooner or later she would have to face it. Play it. Know.

10:43 A.M.
It was just two minutes since the last time he looked at his watch and fifteen minutes since he checked home for his messages but all Randall wanted to do was put down the paint brush and ask Mr. Peterson if he could use his phone again.

Twelve hours and thirty-nine minutes since he had left that soul-baring message, Sandy had yet to call him. Constantly checking his machine wasn't going to change it, but he couldn't stop himself from hoping.

At lunch he tried three more times. Knew it was time to give up the ghost. Made a promise to himself that he would. But it became a promise he couldn't keep.

Sandy played the message.
She came home from work, went straight upstairs, and without taking the bag from her shoulder, the shoes from her feet, she sat, pushed Play. Closed her eyes and waited.

"Hey . . . it's me. I know you're not expecting this call and believe me last time I saw you, I never thought I'd be making it, but here I am." A sigh filled the air. "You scared me. Scared me damn near shit-less . . . AIDS? Just knew that was that, but that just goes to show you what I know—"

The machine clicked off. Sandy swallowed. Stared at the fake brown wood, silver dials. Heard the tape hiss. Let go her breath as it beeped.

"You need a longer message. But anyway"—more pauses—"I'm calling because I can't stop thinking about you, wondering about you . . .

missing you. I know . . . I was the one who did the walking. Well, that's it. Call me if I still matter."

*Beeeeep.*

Sandy played the message over four times before she had her fill. Played it until she knew every word, every nuance, all the hidden meanings. And when she had her vindication, that sweet validation, she picked up the phone and called Winston. "You know that little West Indian restaurant in Flatbush you took me to? Can we go there now? Just dying for some oxtail."

She had bypassed Winston once. Dismissed him for all the wrong reasons. She was experiencing the right ones now and wouldn't walk away from them, especially for someone who put fear before love.

Summer.

Randall could feel its mercurial arrival though it was still a month away. He could feel it in the warm breeze that moved past him as he stared into the darkness of his backyard. Could smell it in the earth releasing night scents like faraway secrets.

He brought the glass of wine to his lips, took a sip. Closed his eyes, massaged a temple. His head urged backward toward the pitch sky, the night brilliant with white stars. He felt small. Tiny. Alone.

He shifted his weight along the patio chair, reset the lay of his legs against the foot rest. Pursed his lips, whispered a name; a soft prayer that he hoped would reach its destination.

*What more can I do? I gave my heart in that message, upped all my secrets, and what? Nothing. Not a damn thing.* Like those stars above him, she was now a million miles away.

He hung his head, sighed a little. He'd waited too long. But even knowing that, feeling it, its density a bitter herb in the back of his throat, Randall looked back up into the late spring night sky and hoped.

"Just wine," Martha was saying as she poured herself half a second glass.

Though Calvin had not uttered a word, nor lifted a brow, she could feel his thoughts like a fever. Resisted the urge to down the drink in one long chug. He had been watching her, examining her closely when she came in from work, when they went out to eat. Even at home.

Wine was no stranger to their meals but suddenly the presence of the Chablis sitting on the table became some uninvited guest that Martha knew in her heart Calvin wished would go away.

On her job they called her Masterful Martha. But today she hadn't felt masterful at all. A guilty man had gone free on a technicality that she should have seen coming, but hadn't. All she wanted in that moment was to let the day go, leave it far behind her. The wine would do just that.

She took a sip, then another, picked up her fork, and resumed eating. Found herself studying the top of Calvin's head as he read a law journal. Wished she could crawl inside it and rearrange things, like his thinking.

Yes, they were back together but there remained a tiny crack in their foundation. It was a crack that would widen if they didn't take time to repair it. The problem was, neither seemed up to the task. No one seemed ready to revisit all the whys that had made the breech.

There was the issue with her drinking, the issue with killing off her dream to be with him, and though neither had reared its head in full view, both of them hovered like a storm cloud above them.

She had figured them safe. Figured her control on her drinking and not mentioning the "M" word had set them on a straight path. But in truth it was a tightrope they were walking, going forward and trying to kiss all that had happened a quick farewell.

But their determination had not dissipated what they were trying to leave behind. It was still like a void against their backs.

Beyond that, her day in court lay heavy on her shoulders and she wanted to do what she thought she'd never do—talk about it. But such conversations between her and Calvin had been halted with that nasty argument. Even if she got up the nerve to begin, he would not follow, partake, give her the chance to vent it, let it go.

Martha finished her wine. Stood taking up the plate that was still half full. She went to the kitchen, began cleaning and straightening. Hoped when Calvin came in later he would bear more than his dirty plate, his empty glass. Hoped that he would have words that would allow her what she needed most in that moment, a sharing of her day.

But her hopes were diminished when he came, set the dishes on the counter, and walked out. They were dashed as she heard the television click on, ESPN filling the air. Knew that they were far from healed, fixed. That she, the Masterful Martha, was not.

* * *

Before the flurry of relationships had happened, the four women would get together a couple times a month and have a soiree. Taking turns at each other's places, there would be food, drink, laughter, and sharing. But life had changed for them and such activities had all but disappeared.

Martha, in need of much, decided it was time to reconnect. She called everyone, setting aside the upcoming Saturday night. A god-send to all the women, they arrived eager and anxious to share.

The unwritten rule was that talk would remain light until everyone had settled with food and drink, but Sandy, burning with the latest incident in her life, jumped ship.

"Randall called me."

Heads turned, servings hovered, mouths opened. Eyes widened. A rush of movement sent everyone snapping up refreshments, finding that comfortable seat.

"No . . . he didn't," Martha said.

"Yes, he did."

"When?"

"A few days ago. Left this message. Talking about he's missing me, thinking about me."

Britney carefully brought a celery stick to her mouth. Bit, chewed, silent.

"Randall, the carpenter Randall?" Janice asked.

"Yeah, him."

"You never did tell us what happened between you two."

No time like the present. Sandy talked, leaving no stone unturned, down to the crotch rub against her dripping panties.

Janice was the first to speak. "No wonder he got scared. Body fluids and stuff." It was no surprise that Janice thought this, but it hurt to hear her say it out loud.

Martha's shackles raised. "Sandy doesn't have AIDS, remember?"

"Neither did Adrian until he did," Janice tossed back.

"Wrong," Martha snapped. "He had AIDS, just they weren't testing him for the right strains. Sandy's had every test. She's fine."

*They're talking about me,* Sandy realized. *Talking about me like I'm not here.* Her friends, one against her, one for her, and the other strangely mute, deciding what she was and wasn't.

But what hurt more was Janice's insinuation. *Body fluids and stuff.*

But that hurt quickly turned to anger, an anger that had been simmering since Janice revealed she was cutting off her nose to spite her face with Cliff.

Or maybe it came from that time that Janice chose that good-for-nothing Greg over her friends, or when she was thinking about marrying Brownie, who did nothing but dog her. Sandy wasn't sure, Janice's life was filled with too many faux-pas to count. All Sandy knew was Janice had not only hurt her feelings, she had pissed her off but good.

"And when's the last time you've been tested, Miss 'I'll sleep with any man if there's even a remote possibility he just might one day love me.' "

The room grew quiet, intense, tempered with a discernible edge that could cut.

Janice's eyes grew full of hurt. "That was low, Sandy."

"It was, wasn't it. Don't feel good, does it. Having somebody think something bad about you and then say it in your face . . . you, of all people. Shit stinking so high need a jet plane to get to the top . . . if my brother hadn't rescued your ass, lord knows where you would be, who you'd be with, or what you'd have."

"Sandy," Martha warned.

Sandy's head looped in her direction. "Sandy what? I ain't said nothing that none of us don't already know and has thought. She want to get low-down and dirty, hell I can get low down and dirty too." She saw Janice blink. "Hurts, right? Sitting there and people talking about you like you're not. All that crazy nonsense you went through with Brownie *and* Greg and you gonna try and tell me I'm not correct? Going all the way to Jersey for a man who didn't give two shits about you, but tried to have your ass arrested? Please."

It had been a moment in Janice's life that still stung, but didn't hurt nearly as much as when it occurred. Greg. Bringing out the worst in her during her rabid search for love. He had broken things off but she had not yet learned to take no for an answer.

Janice had thought she knew better and went to his apartment anyway. When he told her to go, she refused. When he said he would call the police, she refused again. She would have gone right on refusing to believe he didn't love her until the police officers came and took her away. Even then she had still held on to the hope.

"No man ever called the cops on me now, have they?" Janice looked away, a tear rolling. "Save the crocodiles. I'm not impressed." Sandy got up and went to the kitchen. Clutched the edge of the sink, head down, mind swarming, caught off guard.

She thought these moments were beyond her and her oldest friend. Thought they had both moved to a higher level of understanding. But obviously Janice hadn't and Sandy had gotten dragged down in the undertow.

Martha looked toward the doorway, back at Janice. "You set yourself up for that one."

"It still wasn't called for."

"Wasn't it? You were trying to insinuate Sandy has AIDS knowing damn well she doesn't, what do you call it?"

"All I was saying was I understand why Randall got scared."

"It's much more than that and the sad part is you don't even know it."

"What do you mean?"

"You know how hard Sandy struggled to believe she was good enough and you just told her in so many words she isn't."

"That wasn't my intention."

"Well, that's how it came out. Now you go in that kitchen and tell her you're sorry."

Janice started to protest, but got up from her chair anyway.

Sandy was standing, back turned, hugging herself, body trembled with quiet tears. It was such a bare-boned moment, so raw, so exposed Janice felt like a snoop just watching. It forced her to take a full accounting of her friend's life, what had happened, what hadn't. Janice wanted to kick herself.

She had forgotten the sorrow Sandy had gone through, the gut-wrenching last few months of her husband's life. Forgot how hard Sandy had struggled to regain herself, have hope. Live. In a heartbeat Janice had stripped that away.

Sorry didn't seem adequate. Sorry didn't seem to hold even a tiny bit of the remorse Janice was feeling now. They had had tangles in the past, but this particular one was the granddaddy of them all.

Janice swallowed, the name "Sandy" barely able to leave her tongue.

"Go away."

But there was no way Janice could. Since ninth grade they had been friends, Sandy her strongest ally in her weakest times. To leave now meant goodbye to that long history. Janice wasn't willing to do that.

"Sandy, please."

"Leave me the hell alone."

Janice swallowed, her throat choked. "Can't." She took a step toward her, another. Reached out and placed a hand on her shoulder. Was not surprised when it was shrugged off. She had no choice but to speak her heart. "I'm not that smart, okay? And I say things and do things wrong all the time. And I was wrong to say what I said, but I am sorry."

Sandy turned, faced her, cheeks streaked silver with tears. "But you thought that, about me right?"

Janice shook her head. "Yes, no . . . I mean. I don't know."

Sandy pushed past her. Went into the living room. Expectant eyes on her, awaiting a verdict. "I'm so tired of her. I swear I'm just through."

Martha's voice was calm, collected. "No, you're not. If you were, you'd be heading out the door putting as much distance between you and her as you can. Yes, you're mad but you aren't through. Besides, Janice is your girl."

"She was, but not anymore."

"Then why are you still sitting here, waiting for her to walk in? So you can tell her off some more? Ignore her ass? Hear her beg?" Martha sighed. "We're too old for this, Sandy. Life isn't a game to be played. If anybody knows that, it should be you."

She was talking about Adrian, referring to how quickly he had come and gone from her life and the futility of wasting precious moments. Sandy knew it. Everyone in the room knew it. It was up to her to concede to it.

"You can't see it, but I can," Martha continued. "It's the reason why you and Janice get to these asinine moments at all. You two care deeply about each other. It's just that thin line, that's all."

"Wrong."

Martha ignored Sandy's protest. "She's in the kitchen. You're in here. The both of you are mad as all get-out, but that's temporary. It won't last. What does last is love and I know you two love each other. So stop wasting time trying to prove you don't."

Sandy looked at her, anger still on her face, but something else moving in behind it. "You can be just too damn wise for your own good, you know that?"

"Yeah, but that doesn't change what is." Martha looked toward the kitchen doorway. "Janice? The coast is clear. You can come on out."

Janice appeared, tentative, uncertain, eyes fixed on Sandy. "You forgive my dumb ass?"

"Guess I got to, seeing as though we got this love connection."

"I do love you, Sandy, no matter what I do, don't do, or say. I love you like a sister."

"A bratty little sister," Sandy decided with a shake of her head. "And yeah, I'm sorry for saying those things too."

"So we gonna survive this?"

"Guess so."

"Good," Martha declared, changing the subject. "So Brit, how're things going?"

"The heater broke. Randall came to fix it. Nice guy. And . . . we're broke," Britney said, fast and quick before she could change her mind.

Martha's brow raised. "Who's broke?"

"Me. Maurice. Had to pawn my fur coat just to pay bills."

"You're kidding?"

"Why would I kid about something like that?"

"I guess you wouldn't . . . what happened?"

"Big ideas happened. Big old dreams my husband lays in bed at night talking out loud about. We had money, but not enough to support most of those dreams."

Martha considered her. "If things get too tight, you know you can always come to me."

"Me too," Sandy said, glad the conversation had been shifted to someone else, but mostly that she was in a position to help someone financially. She had had her own lean years.

"I'm getting married. I don't have much, but y'know," Janice added.

Britney smiled, shamed and relieved in the same breath. "Thanks a bunch, but we'll be all right. I already told Maurice that after the baby comes, I'm going back to work."

The three other working women in the room saw no reason why she shouldn't. She had been living the good life long enough.

Britney's financial update moved on to Janice's self-doubt, and lastly, Martha's woes. Nobody had a cure all for the next person, but there was a sweet release in the sharing.

Like the lawyer she was, Martha had successfully argued why Sandy and Janice weren't through. She had offered financial help if Britney found herself in a pinch again. Martha had handled her friends' problems with care and finesse. But she hadn't been able to do a thing for herself and Calvin.

She thought about who she was, the great performances she had always managed inside the courtroom, pretending the innocent were guilty and the guilty innocent. Martha thought about how she went outside of her own personal convictions and became whoever was needed in that moment.

Knew she had to do just that to save her life with Calvin. Decided there was no time like the present.

Calvin lived what Martha considered humbly. He could afford more than the six-hundred-square foot basement apartment he rented in South Jamaica. Could own a real place with lots of windows, sunlight, and a backyard he could access. But it wasn't his thing to live large, beyond, or even at his means. With the exception of his clothes and his car, it was hard to tell he made as much money as he did.

She didn't like the neighborhood that he lived in. Thought he could find better accommodations than the one-block strip of Gunter Lane. Parking was hard sometimes, and to get to his entry door, Martha had to navigate down a tight space along the side of the three-family house.

The other reason she did not like the neighborhood was that the very same drug dealers she had glimpsed in lockup could be found marketing their wares on Calvin's corner. No sooner were they booked, than they were back on the streets again engaging in their illegal twenty-four-hour enterprise.

Martha knew and Calvin had told her of the good honest hard-working people who lived there but it was hard telling to the casual passerby. But here she was, moving down the side of the house, careful not to brush her slacks against the waist-high rusted chained-link fence or snag her silk blouse against the sharp edges of the metal garbage cans.

She rang the bell, heard gunshots a block away. Held her breath waiting for the screams, the steps of people running. But the street went on as it had ten seconds ago. In that neighborhood the sound of gunfire wasn't anything new or different. Just was.

He looked sleepy and rumbled. Like he had rolled his skin up into an uncomplicated ball and left it in the bottom drawer. "Hey," he said, rubbing his face, stepping back, letting her in, knowing without knowing why she was there, mentally shrugging himself awake for The Talk.

Calvin knew it was coming, just hadn't been certain when. Their life together had been too sweet for it not to occur, too special to allow it not to go unsaid. He tromped down behind her on the thick wood stairs, held the fire door open as she stepped inside. Before her was the ten-by-eleven living space, holding a love seat, a director chair and a big TV. Beyond that was the wall full of books and beyond the wall his bedroom.

Martha took the love seat, Calvin took the director's chair.

She studied their choice, realized it revealed much. Patted the space beside her. "Over here."

But Calvin liked where he was, him and that chair, old allies. He had retrieved it many years ago from a garbage collection on the Upper East Side. The canvas seat had been broken and the name placed on the back, faded away, but he had it repaired, recognizing a good sturdy wood frame when he saw one.

"This'll do."

Martha agreed, mindful of the role she was now playing. "I know you love that chair, but I bet you a month's salary I love you more."

Calvin tried to duck the implication of her wager, but couldn't. He got up, shaking his head. "You know how to get to a man, don't you."

Martha's expression went soft, careful. "I thought I did. Now I don't know—"

"You still got to me, Martha."

"And you me, but it's not like it was and what it is, I hardly recognize." Calvin nodded, agreeing. She took up his hands. "Don't we deserve better? I know I do. I know we can have it because not long ago we did."

"I'm hearing you."

"Then hear this . . . I wanted to get married. You didn't. I decided it wasn't important, but now I know it is. I thought I could live without the dream, but it's there every time I look at you. It makes things tough. I don't want tough, Calvin."

"I don't want tough either."

She went in for the kill, giving him the one question that would at least force him to consider the ground she was standing on. "Now if you were me, what would you do?"

She was looking at him, into him, peeling back the layers that had overcome his heart in the last few weeks. She knew if she could still find herself inside him, there was hope, it was doable. "I was just telling Sandy and Janice about love," she found herself saying, hedging the bet, "about how temporary everything else is in life but." She looked away, deep into her mode. "Maybe it's not love. Maybe we just like each other a whole lot. Maybe that's why things are different for us now."

"Are you doubting that?"

"I can only go on what I see, and what I see is me and you being just fine together until I brought up the one thing true love leads to." She shrugged. "I have to wonder."

"How can you even entertain the idea that I don't. That we don't?"

"Like I said."

His head shook. For the first time Martha could ever recall, Calvin was getting flustered. "Of course I love you. Would have been long gone if I didn't. You ain't the easiest woman in the world to get along with and not everyone makes it to the altar. A lot of people love each other and never make it."

"But are we everybody? Or are we just us?" She sighed, stood. "I better go."

He stood too, perplexed, a little lost. "Go where?"

She looked at him deeply again, but it was with a realness that made her ache. Martha the performer was gone. "Away from you and what love isn't."

She turned, headed for the door. Kind of numb, but moving forward. She didn't realize Calvin was reaching for her, turning her around, kissing her as if he never wanted to let go until his tongue moved inside her mouth.

She pulled away, head shaking, tears in her eyes. "Either you do or you don't. Can't have in between. You either love me enough or not at all."

It felt like a lifetime before he spoke the word "All," but it wasn't.

# Chapter 16

A house was not a home unless you filled it with memories. In hers less than a year, Sandy's residence still held a transitory resonance, a just-moved-in feel. Like a blank canvas, the walls of her home awaited strokes of laughter, hues of conversation, the presence of loving family to give it life.

Sandy decided to have a Sunday dinner to do just that.

She called Mr. and Mrs. Burton. Called Rachel and Junie as well. Invited her mother, father, Cliff, and Janice over, set about making the day a success.

She and Winston went shopping that Saturday. Moved through the aisles of Walbaum's like a happily married couple. She picked up and he pushed the cart, a make-believe domestication taking hold.

"Think this will be enough?" she asked, hoisting a ten-pound roast beef his way.

"Never cooked it, but I've eaten enough of it." Winston shrugged. "Don't know."

She laughed because he really didn't. Laughed because the expression on his face was so open and honest. No, he didn't know everything. Wasn't trying to pretend that he did. It gave him a humbleness that made her chuckle. But his confused look brought it to a halt.

"Don't pay me any mind," she said with a wave of her hand. "Just being silly." Then she was on the move again, eyes fast to her list. She went right, then stopped and decided to go left.

*Just like a woman,* Winston thought.

There was nothing special about the loose jeans she wore, the white sneakers on her feet, or the scoop-necked cotton top. Not a drop of makeup adorned her face, her hair was combed back, but there was a glow in her near neon.

Winston watched the soft sway of her derriere, a hint of the long sleek chocolatey brown neck. He watched, affected. Felt like the luckiest person in the world.

"Soap," she announced with a snap of her fingers, heading into the aisle. She rose up on tippy toes. Struggled for three seconds before Winston came to her aid.

Reached with ease. "Got it."

"No, not the Tide . . . the Arm and Hammer."

"But you were going for the Tide."

She crooked her head. "Changed my mind."

"Fickle," he mumbled under his breath.

"I heard that, Mr. Burton."

"Glad you did, Mrs. Burton."

She stared into his eyes. The title—*Mrs. Burton*—drifting like a tender wound.

Sandy sucked up the last of her milkshake. Shook the cup for good measure and stuck it into the cup holder. "I forgot."

"Forgot what."

"That I was Mrs. Burton. Didn't remember until you told me."

"It was a joke."

"Yeah, I know." But she didn't, not really. "Past or present."

"Past or present what?"

"The name. How'd you mean?"

"Past, I guess."

Sandy nodded. Looked out the window, while Winston, various emotions moving through him, kept his eyes straight away on the road. It had passed through his mind a million times to ask her. Offer her the till death do us part. But his brother, her husband, was still early in the ground. Maybe sometime down the road.

Winston glanced at the traffic light. Saw just three cars ahead of them. It was a good sign. That particular mall exit that had a killer fast light, barely allowing five cars through before it turned red again.

Her hand landed on his wrist. "Wait."

"Wait what?"

"Home Depot. Pick up the burners. And a welcome mat. Towel rack . . . a fake ficus."

Winston made a left, and then a U-turn. "How come I've never seen this side of you before?"

"What side?"

"The indecisive side."

"Guess 'cause best behavior is over."

Winston didn't know if that was a good thing or bad.

Home Depot. A home improvement/want to fix up for the holidays/contractor's dream come true. Massive and as huge as an airport hangar, it was floor to ceiling with everything anyone would ever need to do a home from start to finish.

Two by fours rolled by on trolleys. Men in paint-splattered overalls and dusty caps gathered up packets of screws, measures of carpet. Middle-aged women held slips of fabric in search of the perfect wallpaper and trim. Ceiling fans whirled, enticing customers with their fast breeze on the too-warm day.

"I love this place," Sandy found herself gushing, taking in the fancy entry doors of wood and etched glass. "Don't you just love this place?" she needed confirming as she ran a finger over the smooth frosted pane.

"It's all right." But in truth, Winston felt like a poor man in a rich man's store, the fancy lettering on the price tags seemingly beyond his means.

He had never had the luxury of possessing half the items Home Depot stocked. The only house he lived in had been his parents' coming up. Old and dated, nothing was replaced until it could no longer be repaired. Even then it had been the basics. He could afford most of it now, but living in an apartment, he didn't have any need for it.

"What are we looking for again?"

"Burners, towel racks, a welcome mat, and a tree."

"You'll need a cart then."

"Guess so."

"I'll be back."

Sandy watched Winston slip from view. Started a slow stroll, taking in the magnificent doors. Feet taking her forward, eyes to the side, she was lost in a world of frosty etchings, shiny brass knobs, crafted stain glass in antique yellows and ocean greens.

It was a harmonious journey, filling her with envy and awe. Preoccupied, lost, she didn't realize the hazard until she banged into someone, hard.

She looked up, apology ready. Saw Randall. Her heart nearly stopped.

"Sandy." He breathed the word more so than spoke it. Said it as if he had been waiting a lifetime just to do so. His fingers touched her cheek. She stepped back as if they possessed fire. Stumbled over her own feet.

"What are you doing here?" a silly question. He *was* a contractor.

She didn't wait for one, just looked around her wildly. Winston would return soon. Couldn't have Randall here. Winston would smell their connection. Sense the need. Know. "You have to go," she decided quickly.

It took a second for him to realize she was afraid of something. Another second to understand that it was him. "This is Home Depot, right?"

But she didn't answer. Just turned and fast walked away.

"Sandy," he called, voice full of desperation. "Sandy, wait," he called again as she disappeared around the aisle. Randall felt stares but didn't care that he had became a spectacle. He was about to go after her when somebody who looked just like her dead husband appeared at the top of the aisle. He was looking for someone, his eyes scanning the half-dozen people milling about.

Looking for someone who should have been there. *For Sandy,* came the thought.

Randall swallowed, steeled his nerves. Tucked back his heart. Turned and headed in the opposite direction.

Was it enough? Sandy wasn't sure. Only that if she left the store, not get the burners, the mat, the plant, Winston would know something was wrong. She had no choice but to move through Home Depot with Randall about. Hoped her warning had hit home if they crossed paths again. That he would pretend like she planned to. Pretend she didn't know him. Pretend that nothing remained.

She saw Winston making a wide circle, the cart before him like an oversized box of orange wire. "Hey," she called, her heart beating so hard it hurt.

"Where'd you go?"

Her eyes danced around his. "Just went to check on some paint."

"Paint?"

"Yeah . . . pick up some color samples." She waved them for proof. Last-minute props to infuse her lie. A liar, who she had become.

"Burners, right?"

"Yeah."

Winston looked up at the signs hoisted from the ceiling. "I think they're that way," wanting to get out of the warehouse full of things that, even after he could afford them, still felt foreign and beyond his reach.


You have to go.

Like an old 45 record, stuck in a groove, her words corralled through Randall's head. *You have to go,* as if some part of her wanted him to stay, but the bigger part wouldn't allow it.

She had been afraid.

*Afraid of me. Afraid of what I would do? Say? Afraid to let me back in?*

It gave him comfort, but not enough to give him ease. Made the impossible possible, though. Gave him courage. No, it wasn't over.

But he has seen Adrian, or at least somebody who looked like him. Randall took a moment. Fought through the magma that became his brain and struggled to rethink it. Found himself back at Sandy's house, her wedding album in his hands.

He recalled the best man. The one who looked liked the groom's twin. The brother. There with Sandy. Randall's ease vanished.


She was quiet on the ride home. Having too much to think about, her head was a willing participant. Randall, appearing like magic. Touching her face, calling her back. Fear oozing through her like tree sap.

She snuck a look at Winston, a new tear in her soul. *I won't mess us up, I won't, not over some man who can't make up his mind.*

By the time they got home, she was emotionally weary, mentally spent. She told Winston she was going to take a nap while he installed the new towel rack. Lying in bed, curled on her side, she found herself wide awake and thinking, certain sleep would not claim her. But it did.

She came to with Winston's face inches from her own. Opened her eyes and whispered *Adrian.* Watched the smile vanish from Winston's face.

Sandy sat up, stunned at her own mistake. Saw the hurt in Winston's eyes. Whispered, "I didn't mean that." Latched her arms around him for good measure, but he refused her embrace. Said something about picking up clothes from the dry cleaners. How the shop was closing soon.

Sandy reached out and held him tighter. "No. Don't go. Get them tomorrow."

"Tomorrow's Sunday, Sandy," his voice wounded, tight.

"Well, get them Monday. Just don't leave me. Please, don't."

Her words turned to kisses, desperate pecks hitting the angles of his tense face, moving about it quick and fast until he yielded, loving her too much.

They clung to one another, holding on and holding fast. Something had entered their midst, something that could tear them asunder. They sensed this but would not surrender. Would go down fighting all the way.

They made love like the first time, fast, slow, and somewhere in between. Then they were off to the shower, got dressed, and talked about dinner. "Want to take a ride to Flatbush? Saturday. They're open until eight."

"Love to," Sandy answered, rescued, Randall's reappearance in her life shifting into memory.

The Pepper Pot was a family-type restaurant off the main strip that catered to the local community crowd. Ruby Martin, proprietor and sole worker, was looking forward to the end of her too-long day.

A tough business, a hard enterprise, she had managed to go from being just a kitchen cook to the full owner in five years' time. Native of Jamaica, West Indies, she had come to America ten years before with big dreams, one hundred American dollars, and determination to make a good life for herself, and eventually, her son.

She had left behind most of her family, a husband who preferred cruelty to kindness, and a baby boy not quite a year old. She had come with one suitcase, a purse full of personal mementos, and a need to make her life better.

Ruby cleaned offices, worked third shifts, and saved every penny she could get her hands on. When the owner of the Pepper Pot talked about going back home and selling the business, Ruby bought him out.

Sixteen-hour days and having only Sundays off had taken its toil on the thirty-five-year-old woman. But sacrifice had been a staple in her life much like bread fruit and salted cod. She had been raised on its steady diet.

She cooked and prepared all the foods. Cleaned the kitchen, rest rooms, and eating area. She stocked the soda cases and kept her own books. She arrived at five every morning. Ruby made her own deposits and kept the sidewalks outside her eatery clean. Not a booming business, but it was enough to keep her afloat.

She bought the one-story building wedged between the supermarkets and beauty salons. She owned the dwelling of brick and mortar, her own little piece of the pie. It was something she was able to put her mark on, claim as hers. A true measure of her success, it came with a heavy price. The business ate up all her time.

Half an hour to closing, the afternoon rush had all but become a memory. She sat behind her counter, the *Island Gazette* before her and the last of the curry goat at her side.

She read news of the various Caribbean Islands, looking for anything pertaining to home. Thought about the three hours she would put in after closing readying the place for Monday. Sighed. The fork had just left her mouth when the cowbell over the front door jangled. Holding back her grimace, she looked up.

Recognized the man, the woman at his side. "Me do'went 'ave much. Close to clowsing," she offered, getting off her stool, the long day settling a dull ache into the arch of her feet.

"Ya got Chicken Roti?" the man called.

Ruby nodded.

"Well, we take two orders, den. Ta stay."

Ruby turned and headed into her kitchen for clean plates, paper napkins, and plastic silverware. With the end of the day so near, her supply out front had dwindled to nothing and she had to go into her storage bins to retrieve them.

She came back, placed the napkins and forks before them. Asked if they wanted something to drink.

"Me have a ginga beer," the man with the honey eyes requested.
"Sprite?" the woman asked.

Ruby nodded and made her way to the soda case. She came back
with the drinks and went off to make the plates. Locking her front
door, it was back to the kitchen to start her cleaning.

Why do you want who you want, are attracted to who you are attracted to? Long for who you long for? Randall didn't know. It wasn't
even a real consideration. He was beyond the point of asking himself
why Sandy meant so much to him. Why every waking day held only
three certainties: he would stay black, die, and what he walked away
from had been the best something he had had in a very long time.

This Sunday morning Randall awoke determined.

Awoke, got out of bed, and got dressed. A warm day, he decided on
the antique Mercedes. Would let the top down. Hoped the fast breeze
would clear his head. Give him the right words to say.

He pulled out of his garage. Headed down Farmer's Boulevard,
Sandy's house his destination. A crazy plan, Randall was beyond ratio-
nal. He had seen it for himself just yesterday. They weren't done yet.

But the sight of the second Camry parked in her driveway gave him
doubt. The quiver of the front door opening made him drift a little
ways past her house. He pulled to the curb, enough to see the front
door but not who was standing in it. As long as Sandy didn't come
out, he wouldn't be spotted.

Spotted. Was he crazy? No, just in need.

Laughter reached him first. The back of a man, second. Standing
in her doorway, her soft arms draped around his neck, it was an inti-
mate heartbreaking moment, but Randall was beyond broken.

The man leaned in, a goodbye kiss? Stayed there awhile, those
hands, Sandy's hands, moving across the caramel neck like fronds in
a tradewind. *You sitting up here and she's back there with her hands all over
his neck, don't you get it yet?* Nope.

Randall waited until the man who looked like her dead husband
but wasn't opened his car door and closed it. Then as unassuming as
he could be, Randall eased away from the curb and headed up the
street. Took his time making his various U-turns until he was back on
Sandy's block, the second Camry gone from sight.

The way, clear.

*	*	*

The door quivered, opened, her voice "What you forget?" coming before her face did. A face that went from a chiding smile to sheer horror, Randall not the least bit expected.

Sandy stared, flimsy nightgown on her body that hinted at the aureoles of her nipples, the thick black down at the top of her thighs. She looked in his face and knew there was no ducking or running. That he was serious, about her.

Her whole body raised up in protest, everything in her, about her, rising out ready to force him away. But before she could speak, he was through the doorway. Closing the thick wood quickly.

"You have to hear me out," he insisted, hot, tempered, half crazed at the sight of her standing there immodestly dressed, infused with the man who had left not five minutes before.

"No," all she could manage, her face screwing up with indignation and anger. No. A one-syllable utterance that said he was intruding. But he dismissed her stunted protest and moved past her.

It took a hot second before Sandy could allow it. Follow.

"Let me get my robe," she said carefully, this new intense Randall surprising her, scaring her a little. She was half up the stairs when she saw it all fully. *What am I doing? Why did I let him bogard his way into my house, my life?*

But there was that other part of her, that part she had been pushing and pushing and pushing back. The part that was intensifying as she put on her terrycloth robe and tied it tightly about her body.

The part that snapped, crackled, and popped inside her as she made her way down the steps. The part that was waging a war against sensibilities, close to claiming victory. The part that said she'd been through enough struggles and wanting who she wanted should not be one of them.

He did not hear her coming. She found him sitting on the chair, head between his hands, a bit lost, bewildered. She rounded her coffee table, his eyes on her before her butt reached the sofa cushion. Felt his stare like a heat-seeking missile seconds from contact.

"You're with him for the wrong reasons."

"What are you talking about?"

"Talking about that guy . . . Adrian's brother?" He spit the word out and it felt like a slap to her face.

"What do you know about anything?" angry with him in the worst way.

"I know that I blew it big time and I've regretted it almost every moment since. I know that I was wrong . . . that I hurt you. That the love of your life is gone and you're trying to bring him back with his clone, I know that much."

She had not expected his arrogance, his steely exposé of her soul. Sandy was off the couch in a heartbeat. "Fuck you."

Randall nodded. "Yeah, fuck me." Calming, relaxed, his assumptions confirmed with her outburst. "But tell me I'm wrong."

She didn't. Spoke the different side of things. "You blew it. Not me. I wasn't the one who walked out. Got scared . . . me and Winston?" Her head shook, disgusted. "You don't know half of it."

"Then you tell me. Tell me why you're with him."

"Because I . . ." The rest of it would not come out.

He had her cornered. "Can you even say it?"

"What?"

"That you love him? I can say it, Sandy. I love you."

Her mouth fell open. She could not believe he had spoken those words. "You what? Love me? How could you? You weren't around long enough. I come to you with the truth and you curse me out and was gone. Love?" She laughed at his gall, something coursing through her—vindication.

She had been a leper, and now he was talking about love. He had dismissed her and now she was most important, all she really wanted. Not him, just those words. Not him, just the knowledge that someone else could love her, someone besides her dead husband and his living brother.

She had it now.

Ran with it. Came back swinging, uncaring. Venomous. "Now you trying to make a comeback? You wanted out of my life, well, mister, you got it. Now get the hell out of my house."

She meant it. That much Randall knew. But they were at a volatile point. Nothing was an absolute, even if she, in that moment, swore it was. So he didn't get out. Didn't move. Just sat there, staring, plaintive.

"You deaf? You got to go." But he must have been because he didn't budge.

Sandy marched to the front door. Opened it, breath heavy, near dizzy with rage. She stood there, waiting as two seconds became eight. Eight seconds became twelve. No Randall.

"Did you hear me?" she bellowed. "I said get out."

"No."

"I'm not playing with you. Get. Out."

She saw herself, front door wide open, a man who had no right to her, refusing to go. Saw the spectacle it presented. Wanted it over. Wanted Winston to come, save her. But he was on his way home.

She'd have to save herself.

She slammed her door, locked it for good measure. Marched into her living room, hands fast and furious on the tight tie of her belt. She slipped her robe from her arms, flung it in the corner. Planted her feet six feet from him and hoisted up her flimsy gown.

Stood naked and breathy before him, fired up and ready to maim. Flicked her hand at him, naked in all her glory. Nearly shouted, "Come on."

Randall was perplexed, mesmerized, fear settling in the back of his throat. It was what he wanted but not how he wanted it.

"Come on, damn it. You want me, then come the fuck and take me."

He could see her sex glistening, no doubt from the encounter she had what, ten, fifteen minutes ago? Could smell the scent of another man upon her body, a few love bites dotting a breast.

She seemed vulgar and loose, awash in some horrific sin. He looked away.

"Just what I thought," she snapped, grabbing her robe and fighting to get it on. "Now get out."

Randall stood, crushed, and slowly headed to her front door. When the sound of its closing reached her heart-beating-fast-filled ears, Sandy fell upon her couch and wept.

Janice didn't want to go.

She didn't want to go to Sandy's house and sit in the presence of Rachel. There was too much bad juju there, as her grandmother used to say. Still on the mend with Cliff, the last thing she wanted to encounter was bad juju.

Maybe that's why she had come down with the flu that Saturday night. Maybe that's why every bone she owned ached, she felt hot and cold and barely had enough strength to go to the bathroom.

It wasn't even flu season but the illness was upon her. She lay in bed that afternoon watching Cliff ready himself for the dinner and bit her tongue. She would not ask him to stay with her. Had to show that she was okay with him leaving her at home, sick as she was.

He had brought in a thermos of hot tea spiced with honey and lemon. Filled a microwavable bowl full of chicken noodle soup. Given her a cup of Thera-flu not five minutes ago. Placed a glass of ice and the liter of ginger ale by her bed.

Now he was readying himself to head out the door.

He picked up his keys, hoisted his wallet into his back pocket. Reached down and kissed her feverish forehead. "Want me to bring you back anything?"

Janice shook her head no, forced a smile, and closed her eyes as if exhaustion had overcome her. She watched him through slitted lids as he left their bedroom. Her heart aching with a start as the front door closed behind him.


Sandy knew where the time went to. Knew why she found herself, half hour before the dinner hour, not even showered. Sandy knew why the roast would not be done for another forty-five minutes and why she was taking the time she was supposed to be getting dressed to quickly dust the living room, remove the scum rings from the bath tub.

Randall had decimated her. Had pushed her so she had no choice but to come back swinging. And she had, stripping like that, bold, daring, half-mad. Daring him to take her, never thinking for a moment that he would.

It had taken that crazed performance to get him out of her house and that performance had come at a deep cost. Had left her weepy and sorrowed for over an hour. His words, "I love you," weighing on her. So much so she could do nothing but cling to the edge of her sofa as the tears faded and a migraine the size of Texas arrived.

It took an hour of just lying still to get the pounding down to a heavy throb. It took a trip to the bathroom to throw up and then lie still and quietly on her bed just to ready her stomach for the Tylenol. Then she had to return back to the bed for another hour until the nausea went away, before she could sit up without pain.

By the time she was able to get up, munch some dry toast, sip weak tea, it was past noon and dinner was supposed to be at two. The meat alone would take more time than she had just to cook properly.

There was the bag of apples she had bought to make a pie from scratch and fresh lemons which she was to boil to make her Grandma Tee's famous lemonade. She had wanted the dinner to be perfect, wanting her first outing to be flawless. But Randall had taken that all away from her. Left something devastating in its place.

The platters of cubed cheese, sesame crackers, and bread sticks went quickly as did the fruit punch and ginger ale concoction she had thrown together as well. Sandy knew her guests would come with empty bellies; that was why she had made a last-minute run to the store.

But she didn't expect the snacks to disappear so soon. Last check, the roast was a half hour from ready. "We're going to eat soon," she announced for the third time, and hurried off to the kitchen.

She was setting out sticks of butter on the little Wexford servers when Rachel popped in. "Anyting I can do?" she wanted to know.

Sandy looked at her, started to say no. Changed her mind. "Ever make gravy?"

"Gravy? Dat's my middle name," Rachel chided.

"Good. The pan's over there. The drippings are in that jar."

Rachel picked up the wooden spoon. Turned the burner to low. "Ya brudder, he coming?"

"Yeah. Cliff likes to run on CP time."

"Oh." Rachel began stirring. Lowered the flame. "Ya looking beat, San-dee. Everyting okay?" Rachel would be the one to notice. Sharp, keen, insightful Rachel.

"First time I'm cooking for all of y'all. Been running myself raggid all day."

More than that, Rachel was thinking, but let it go. The doorbell rang. Sandy went off to answer it. Rachel continued her stirring, careful not to let the rue burn.

Sandy opened the door, saw her brother all by his lonesome. "Where's Janice?"

"Bed with the flu," Cliff said, shaking his head.

Sandy was about to ask a second question, but her brother had disappeared into the living room. She was closing her front door when she heard his voice bellow, "Rude bwoy," and understood that she wasn't the only one Winston was close to. That for perhaps for the first time in his life, Cliff had found another male to bond with. Someone he could talk to and relate with. Someone who looked like him.

Extremely light-skinned, waves from neck to crown, eyes that would never be just plain brown. When looking into Winston's face, Cliff found his own, features Cliff's own sister and father lacked.

*"Reason why he teased you so much, Sandy. Why he called you those awful names,"* Janice had confessed to her.

*"You mean like Smokie and Blackie and Midnight."*

*"Exactly. Because he envied you. Envied the fact that you looked just like your father and he looked nothing like him. Made him feel different in a weird way."* Which had been an eye-opening moment.

Sandy had always envied her brother for the very things he had found a disdain for. Had always felt her mother and brother belonged to a select group of which she could never gain admittance. She understood the connection her brother felt with Winston. Saw the goodness Winston had brought into many people's lives. *Including mine.*

Guilt, which hadn't ventured too far, snuggled closer to her. It was hard to remember she had waged the battle and won it, a victory that was lessening hour by hour. Because Randall had changed the rules.

Rachel knew he would find her.

Like radar, she knew he would seek her out without even knowing he was doing it. Rachel stood at the stove, stirring the gravy. Waited for his arrival. Smiled soft and careful when it came.

"Hey," he called, surprised, delighted.

"Hey, ya self," Rachel answered, giving him a brief glance, expecting Janice's head, her voice to pop up behind him.

"Helping out?" he said, moving closer, looking into the pan of gravy she was stirring.

Rachel shrugged, calm. Cool. "Sumtim like dat." Looked around for the first time. "Where Janice?"

She heard him swallow. "Home with the flu." Did not move away as he moved closer until his hip was touching hers as he reached for the spoon, pulled up some gravy, blew. Took a taste.

Mr. Burton leaned back, napkin over the empty plate, eyes kind and warm on Sandy. "Fine fine meal, San-dee," he told her.

"Thank you, Mr. Burton."

"Have to agree with you there, Aldridge," Sandy's mother said. "That's the best roast I've had in a long time."

"Because I taught her how to cook," Sandy's father answered.

"I'm not much of a beef eater, but I did enjoy it," Junie's "friend" Julianna told her.

"Thank you, Julianna."

"Julie," she said shyly. "Everyone calls me Julie."

Winston laughed. "Junie and Julie. Ya sure you two don't get con-fewsed?"

"Watchit, bwoy," Junie told him, one eyebrow raised. "Ya may be de oldest but me still kick ya ar—"

"Junie," Mrs. Burton warned.

"Me jusa funning wit 'im."

"Not here and certainly not at the dinner table." Outside of a few hellos, it was the only words Sandy could recall Mrs. Burton saying. She had been quiet most of the visit, not even giving that Madonna smile.

Sandy had caught her staring. Was surprised to see not belliger-ence but sorrow in her eyes. It made Sandy uncomfortable but there wasn't much she could do. She couldn't defend her and Winston being together if she wanted to.

Randall saw to that.

If Sandy had any doubt, she didn't now. Called to the mat, she had not been able to say it. Had not been able to say out loud that she loved Winston, *because I don't, not that way, the way that counts.*

Sandy enjoyed Winston, appreciated Winston. Loved to be with him, but she did not love him. But she would not abandon him now. Would not leave him high and dry again. Sandy would remain with him for as long as she could.

After all he had done for her, she owed him that much.

After the meal they ventured into Sandy's backyard. Enjoyed the warm sun-kissed afternoon over punch and the apple pie that made it into the oven.

Sandy leaned into Winston. "Whatcha think?"

"About what?"

She urged her head across the yard. "Junie and Julie."

Winston's mouth turned down a bit. "Don't know."

"He ever do that before?"

"Do what?"

"Bring a girl to something."

"Not in a long time."

"He's getting older, you know."

"And?"

"They make a nice couple."

Winston turned, looked at her. "You got them married already?"

"Nothing wrong with marriage."

"Would you?"

"Would I what?"

"Get married again?"

It took a while for the answer to come. "Adrian wouldn't want me not to. Told me to live my life after he was gone."

"So is that a yes? a no, or what?"

She looked into his eyes. Saw the real question. Looked away. "Probably."

Winston nodded. "Going to go get a Stout. You want something?"

Sandy shook her head no. Watched him get up and disappear into the house.

Winston entered the back door, came into the kitchen, found his sister Rachel and Cliff in the kitchen. Though four feet separated them, there was a closeness to them that seemed touchable.

"He's taken," he told his sister, leaning into her.

"Whatcha say nuh? Git out of me face," she said, angry.

"Me teasing." But he wasn't. He knew it. Rachel knew it and Cliff knew it too.

Cliff picked up his beer. "Better go see where my sister's at." He headed out the door.

Winston stared at Rachel. Rachel stared back. Kept staring until Winston turned away, got his Stout. Left out too.

Afternoon became early evening. People huddled around Sandy's front door, bearing paper plates and plastic containers. She had just hugged her father good night when Winston came up behind her.

"Just going to go catch Cliff. Be back in a few." He made his way down the steps. Moved toward the gate. Brought his two fingers to his mouth, his whistle piercing the night air. "Eh, rude bwoy," he called, making his way toward Cliff's car.

"What's up?" Cliff asked, Winston coming abreast him.

"Got a minute?"

"Yeah, sure."

"Can we get in?" Winston asked, pointing to Cliff's car.

"Yeah, sure."

They did.

Winston did not look at him, but straight ahead. "You love her?"

"Who?"

"Janice."

"Yeah."

"So why you sniffing around Rachel?"

Silence. Thick and condemning. "I'm not sniffing round your sister. She's just a friend."

"A lonely friend who had her eyes set on you till she decided Janice loved you more, did you know that?"

In truth Cliff didn't. When Rachel had sent him away, he thought it was because she was done with him. It was easy to understand a woman as gorgeous as her getting tired of any man easy.

Winston went on. "You were the first man she ever had any interest in since her fiancé got killed. For six years Rachel refused to be involved with anyone. You were the first."

"Damn."

"Exactly. Now I know how attractive my sister is. Know there's something about the sharp West Indian tongue that can send any man into a daydream, but Bro, you can't be the one, not if you love Janice."

Cliff blinked.

" 'Cause see, the sister I know wouldn't be caught in the same room with you, not feeling about you the way she's feeling and you about to stroll down that aisle, but I saw it with my own eyes. You and her, in the kitchen. Don't know what's up with her, but it's not like her, not my sister."

"I hear you, Bro."

"You have to hear me and *feel* me. I'm a man. I know how it can go sometimes. You say to yourself, I'll just hit it and quit it. My girl won't know. Maybe she will, maybe she won't, but where will that leave Rachel on your wedding day? How you going to deal with you own self?"

"Guess you right."

Winston looked at him, waited for Cliff to do the same. "So we straight on this?"

Cliff held out his fist, Winston hit his against it. "We straight."

# Chapter 17

No more scrimping on food, pawning fur coats, getting loans against life insurance policies. Maurice took out a home equity loan.

It wasn't the way he wanted to go. Never thought on the day he closed that he would be getting additional mortgages on his house. But hard times called for hard measures, and when he started going to bed hungry every night because those extra helpings no longer existed, he went ahead and did just that.

Money in the account on a Monday, Tuesday Britney spent most of the morning writing checks. But what made her the happiest was having the money to pay Randall. Being late with a creditor was one thing. Being late with a friend of a friend was a whole different ball game.

She called and left a message that his money was ready. He called back within the half hour asking if he could come by later that afternoon. Britney told him around seven would be better, then made another phone call.

It didn't matter that Sandy was happy or not. She and Winston were just plain nasty. Sandy and Randall seemed so much better. Heck, she was doing her friend a favor.

* * *

Sandy held the phone to her ear, editing the letter as she talked. She didn't know why Britney wanted her to come over after work, only that she wasn't up to it. She had her evening mapped. There was that movie she had rented from Blockbuster and was due the next day and just wanted to curl up on her couch, pop some Pop Secret, and chill.

Going to Britney's after work would cut into the schedule, even if it would only be for "just a hot minute," as she insisted. "What's this about?" Sandy found herself asking. "You and Mo straight?"

In truth, Britney and Mo were fine. But judging from Sandy's voice, Britney knew that by saying she and Mo weren't, Sandy would come by.

"Don't know what's going on, Sandy," Britney said solemnly as she could.

"You call Martha?" Because in truth, Britney and Martha had the tighter connection.

"She's busy with Calvin."

*And I'm not?* "All right. Be over about seven, but I can't stay long." "That's fine."

Worry-free.

That's how Britney looked as she opened the door, let Sandy in. The expression on her face, beaming, delightful, uninflicted. Despite the pregnancy nearly five months in the making, offering a round punch bowl of belly beneath the terry cotton top, the stretchy pants, Britney looked as alive and as healthy as she had before the word "pregnancy" even existed in her vocabulary.

They made up, Sandy found herself thinking. Through some fate, whatever they were going through had been resolved. Didn't know whether to be mad or glad. Settled for somewhere in between.

"Better?"

"What?"

"Whatever was going on that you needed to talk to me about?"

A van pulled up. A car door opened, closed. Both women looked toward the curb. Only one smiled.

Sandy was naked in front of Randall again but this time she had on her clothes and was standing in Britney's kitchen.

She had turned away the moment he headed for the gate. Moved into the living room as he made his way up the steps. Vanished into the kitchen when Britney invited him in. Was considering a retreat through the side door by the stove when they came into the kitchen.

He didn't speak to her. Didn't look at her. Just waited patiently as Britney took a stack of bills from between the sugar and the flour canisters and handed it to him. Randall folded the roll and was tucking it into his pocket when Britney asked him to count it. "I make mistakes," she said with a weird little laugh.

No doubt she had just made a big one, that she had guessed wrong. Standing in the space between Randall and Sandy, the negative energy was so deep and raw Britney knew that something bad had happened between them. So bad, in fact, she was certain whatever they had had was long gone.

"All here," Randall said quickly, putting the money away. "Better be on my way."

Yes go, Britney was thinking, her good idea gone bad, Sandy like soured milk behind her.

He was barely out the door when Sandy's voice came. "You were trying to set me up, weren't you?" The disbelief in her voice resonated around the kitchen. "I'll be damned," she went on to say in awe. "I don't believe you."

Britney was right there with her. Because in that moment she didn't believe herself either. Had she ridden her high horse so long that she had lost contact with reality or had she bought into her own hype that she had mastered the art of what did and didn't make a relationship work?

Britney didn't want to turn around, face her friend. Didn't want to confess to how wrong she'd been, the trust she had misused. She didn't want to, but she did. "Thought wrong," all she could manage.

"Whoever said you could think?" Cruel words, but Sandy was on fire.

That hurt Britney, a way-below-the-belt hurt. Because in a heartbeat Sandy had cut her down to all Britney had been. Had pushed her back to the timid, lonely, unattractive woman, who less than two years ago, had agreed with the main consensus that she didn't know much about nothing.

"What gives you the right to mess with my life? Who do you think you are?" Sandy went on to say, fuming.

Britney didn't feel like she had the right. In that moment she felt like nobody. She just couldn't get her mouth to say it.

"Life's complicated enough without you putting your nose in my business." Sandy's head shook. "I don't believe you. Had me coming over there thinking something was wrong with you and Mo and wasn't nothing like that at all."

Britney had tried to help Sandy out, couldn't she see that? But it was obvious Sandy couldn't. Britney tried to explain herself but Sandy cut her off.

"Save it," Sandy told her, turning and leaving.

It wasn't so much that Britney did what she'd done. It was the fact that she had thought she was doing something good that stuck in Sandy's craw. That she knew a whole lot better than Sandy ever would. That Sandy needed intervention.

Yes, her life had gone through trauma and for a hot minute it didn't seem she would survive it. But she had. Couldn't Britney see she was just fine with Winston?

No, she hadn't.

So much so she had plotted and schemed to get Sandy and Randall in the same place at the same time, hoping they would no doubt have some magic moment. But there had been nothing magical about the moment at all. Embarrassing and profound, was all.

Embarrassing because of how things went with their last encounter and profound because even though Randall had not looked at her once, she felt his thoughts as if she had crawled up inside his head. Three words coming in the noncommunication: he was sorry.

It would have been better if he were mad at her. Better if he had thought vile viscous things about her, but he hadn't. In those few hot seconds they had been in Britney's kitchen, Sandy realized his feelings hadn't changed. He still wanted her even if he was still scared.

But there was a bonus to his fear. It slayed the demons of possibility. He still wasn't ready. And as long as he wasn't, he would leave her be. Still it did not excuse Britney, didn't excuse what she'd done.

Janice recognized the sound but it was coming too early. A little after seven in the evening, dinner was only halfway ready. But there was the sound of Cliff's keys in the door.

It was his last stand, though Janice didn't know it.

He had taken the words Winston had spoken to him and thought long and hard on them. Cliff had decided to give him and Janice one more go. Make a final attempt to heal the huge gaping rift behind them.

But Janice didn't know this as she grabbed a paper towel, wiped her hands free of tomato seeds, and headed toward the living room. Watched as Cliff came through the door.

"You're early."

"Figured I surprise you." She didn't notice the hand behind his back until a bouquet of flowers was before her.

"For me?"

Cliff looked around. "Nobody else here, right?"

"How come?"

"I bring you flowers and you're asking why?" Suddenly it became too much effort, too much work. He was trying to save them and she was cutting them down before he had a chance to try.

"Yes, I'm asking you why?" As far as Janice was concerned, her question was no big deal. She questioned everything Cliff did and didn't do these days. Because beneath his generosity, she smelled betrayal.

She had heard the stories, her own mother warning her. *If a man starts treating you real good out of the clear blue sky, watch out, because he most certainly is up to no good.* Janice's mother should know. Justine Duprey may have had only one child, but she had had four husbands. Janice considered her mother an expert.

He put the flowers on the table. "Forget it, Janice." Headed toward the bedroom.

Bad move, she realized. Sometimes she did get beyond herself. She picked them up, smelled them. Called down the hall. "I'll get a vase."

He came back to the kitchen, found her looking in a cabinet. "Got to go back out," he decided, last minute.

"Go where?"

"Run by Wint's." Because if he ever felt a need to talk to someone about all the things going through his head, his heart, it was now.

"In Brooklyn?"

Cliff held her gaze. He had tried. Tried to slay her demons. Tried to keep the peace. Cliff had tried to make a go, try to save their love, but in that moment he felt that maybe they were beyond saving. "Brooklyn is where he lives, right?"

He looked at the woman he had once loved enough to marry. Saw her trembling with a rage that seemed months in the making. The flowers left her hand and landed against his arm, thorns pricking him through his shirt.

"Don't lie to me," her voice low, intense. "I can take a lot of crap, have taken a lot of crap, but I won't take lies."

"You don't want lies, Janice? Fine. I won't tell you lies. I'm going to tell you the truth. I came in here tonight wanting to put us back together. I came in here tonight determined to give us one last go. And what do you do? What you've been doing—looking at me like I've been up to no good. Well, you know what? I'm sick of it and I'm not doing it anymore."

Her head shook. A strange chuckle leaving her lips. "Always the last to know. Why am I always the last to know?"

"Last to know? You're the one who's been doing this."

"Doing what, Cliff? Loving you? Because that's all I've been trying to do . . . love you."

It broke his heart that she believed those words. "That's not how love goes, Janice. Love isn't suspicion, it's about trust. And you stopped trusting me. I don't know why, but you did."

"Oh, and going to see Rachel behind my back says I should?"

"I went to see her once, to talk, about me and you," which finalized every vicious thought she'd ever had about Cliff.

"And I guess you were going back there tonight to talk about us again?"

"I wasn't going to see Rachel," Cliff answered, defeated. "I was going to see Winston."

But Janice wasn't hearing it. She had her proof now. Just needed a few more details. "You sleep with her yet?"

She wasn't hearing him. Did not believe. Never would again. No matter what he said, didn't. No matter what the truth was, wasn't, she would just go on accusing him and he could spend a lifetime trying to assure her fears but it would not change a thing or make it better.

It became the final nail on their coffin, their end flashing before him like a neon sign.

Cliff saw them then. Saw their future fading to dust. Thought about the wedding invitations that were printed, the catering hall they had rented. He thought about her wedding gown on order, the honeymoon already paid for.

He tried to find the love he felt when he asked her to be his wife. But it was in a void with no clear definitions.

Cliff let go of his truth. "It's so much more than that and you're standing here without a clue. I wanted to be with you. I wanted to marry you. The whole concept was foreign to me until we got together. But lately I can't even breathe right as far as you're concerned. One minute you're all in love and happy and then the next you're some angry crazy woman."

"I'm not crazy," she defended.

"No? Well, you could have fooled me." Cliff shook his head. "Every time I walk through that door, I don't even know which Janice is going to greet me. I'm putting in all these extra hours at the job but you think I'm messing around. I come home exhausted, just wanting some peace and quiet, and there you are, all hostile and shit.

"I come home, tired, exhausted, just wanting some rest, but I have to spend half the night convincing you that there's no one else." He took a breath, bewildered. "I can't do this anymore. It's not how things are supposed to work. Not how love's supposed to work."

"You don't love me."

"I do love you, Janice, but you've changed. You used to be so strong and assured. You never used to doubt my love. But now you act like I don't and I have to convince you over and over that I do. And things aren't getting a bit better between us for my effort. Just getting worse and I don't want to live life like that. Certainly not be in a marriage that way."

A bell rang in her head. Clear, precise, it faded as quickly as it came. *It's over. We're over. No wedding, no marriage. No happily ever after.* Janice found herself a little numb, but not nearly as surprised. It hadn't worked out for her own mother, how could she expect it to work out for herself?

Her eyes glazed as she looked his way. Cliff was before her, but it was Greg, Brownie, Fernando, Reginald, Mutakaber, every man she had wanted and could never keep. She felt a weird peace, a strange calming. The pain was too familiar to hurt, too old to surprise.

"Okay."

"I'm saying we're through and all you can say is okay?"

Janice blinked, blinked again, focusing. "If you want to go, nothing I can say will keep you here."

Cliff realized in that moment she wasn't going to fight to keep them together but she had pushed and pushed until there was no direction for him to go but away. So he gathered up his possessions in black garbage bags and left her apartment, his head telling his heart it was for the best.

Déjà vu.

That's how Cliff's mother and father felt as their son sat them down at their kitchen table and told them the wedding was off. Their daughter had called with the same message months before she was set to go down the aisle. They didn't expect their son to follow in those footsteps.

"She's sick?" his mother asked carefully.

It took a moment to understand the real question. "You mean like Adrian? No, Mom."

"So what is it, son?" his father wanted to know.

"She's changed."

His parent's brow went up. "Changed?"

"Yeah. She doesn't trust me. Hardly happy. We've been arguing a lot."

"And that's enough to call off a wedding?"

Cliff could see the annoyance in his father's face, the disappointment on his mother's. Wished he could explain it better. Couldn't.

"I thought you loved her, Cliff," his mother went on to say.

"I do . . . that's the crazy thing. But I can't get with the type of woman she's become."

His father fixed him with a stern eye. "You been straight with her?"

"All the way."

"So why is she suspicious?"

"Exactly. It's like she wants me to do something."

"Have you?"

"No, I haven't."

"Thought about it, though, right?"

Cliff looked away. "I'm still a man. Entitled to my thoughts, but no, I haven't done anything."

His father nodded, sat back. Sighed. Rubbed his forehead. His mother continued her study of her son. Wondered why the love that had sustained her and her husband had not transferred to him.

"You sure, Cliff? You sure? Sandy changed her mind a dozen times before she and Adrian made it down the aisle."

"I can marry Janice. Sure can. Put on that tux, speak those words, but at this point it wouldn't last a year." He looked around him. "I gave up my apartment. Would it be all right if I stay here a while?"

His father sat up in his chair. Fixed him with a steely eye. "We'll give you one month. Thirty days. If at the end of that time you aren't going back to your fiancée, then you find yourself another place."

With that his father stood. Left out.

As she sat around her quiet apartment, there wasn't much Janice was sure of. But the one thing she was absolutely certain was she wasn't up to a tribunal. She was in no mood for a powwow with her friends, circling around her, condemning her. Calling her foolish, crazy, in love with misery.

So she didn't pick up the phone to tell Sandy. Didn't tell anyone. They would hear about it soon enough. She didn't tell her mother. There would be time for that news later. For the moment Janice just wanted to experience all that the moment had to offer. Just wanted to lie down and lick her wounds, slow and adept.

"You sitting down?" was how Winston begun.

Sandy pressed the phone closer to her ear. "No, why?"

"Cliff and Janice . . . finished."

"What?"

"You heard right. Finished. Done, over. Wedding's off."

"When?"

"Few hours ago. He just left here."

"What's he saying?"

"He's saying that Janice has changed too much to marry. That he can't spend the rest of his life trying to convince her that he's being faithful. That Janice wasn't like that when they got together."

Janice had been looking for monsters under the bed. Looked like she'd found them.

Sandy sighed, her gut full of acid. Just when she thought her friend had it all together. Just when she was certain the God of Love had poured His blessings upon her fickle head. Just when the one thing Janice longed for was about to come true, it got cut off at the knees.

"He say where he was going?"

"He's back home with your folks."

Sandy was quiet for a minute. Trying to fit the pieces together. She had called off her own wedding because she was afraid. Knew in her heart Janice was walking on the same frightened ground.

"Stay out of it, Sandy," Winston warned. "I know she's your girl and all, but this is one time Janice has to find her way herself."

"And if she doesn't?"

"Then she doesn't."

"Easy for you to say. You don't know her like I know her."

"True, but Cliff didn't come and share his heart like he did with me. Things you don't know."

"Like?"

"You know I'm not telling."

"Can't or won't. He is my brother."

"And Janice is your girl. But what does and doesn't happen between them isn't our concern. You got to let them figure it out for themselves."

Janice was her best friend, Cliff, her brother. Sandy couldn't leave that alone if she wanted to.

It didn't surprise Janice that Sandy was standing at her front door. She had expected that. What she didn't expect was the worrisome tenderness full on her friend's face, the hug that engulfed her as if Sandy were trying to swallow her whole.

"I'm so sorry," Sandy found herself saying. "So sorry it's come to this."

"I'm sorry too," Janice managed back, pulling away. "Sorry I've messed up somebody else's life." She sighed, looked around her. "Cliff said I've changed. He's right, you know. I'm back to the old Janice, remember her? Thought she was dead and gone. Guess what."

"So what are you going to do?"

"Cancel."

Sandy swallowed, remembered her own tap dance across the perilous terrain, calling caterers and limousine services and everything in between. Remembered how every time she picked up the phone, her voice grew tight and tighter with each cancellation. That it had felt like the end of the world for her and she had never felt more alone. Wanted to save her friend from that fate, but knew she couldn't.

"You tell them?" Janice asked, closing her front door.

"Who?"

"Brit, Martha."

"No, not yet."

Janice nodded, affirmed in some quiet secretive place, "I'll do it tomorrow. Just can't deal with it now . . . so Cliff, he called you?"

"Wint."

Again that nod came, self-prophecies clicking into place. "He was going to see Rachel, did you know that? Came in here lying about having to see Wint, when the whole time he was scheming to see Rachel."

Sandy was careful with her words. "Actually, Janice, he went to see Wint." Sighed. "You were pushing him."

"Yes, I was. I've been spending the last few hours wondering why. Martha had it right. I just love misery. Like some kind of freaking vitamin, got to have it all the time."

"At least you realize that much. Cliff says you've changed. And from where I'm standing, you have to change again to make it work."

"I should, right? I should be right now this minute trying to get back to that woman I was, but a part of me doesn't want too. I feel this is the real me. I mean it was great while it lasted, but I don't think it's who I am."

"So you're throwing in the towel?"

"Feel like I never really had it."

"But you did, Janice. I saw it with my own eyes."

Janice's head shook. "For a hot minute, yeah, but you know the doubt was always there."

"Can't live your life in fear. Believe me I know. Fear will rob you of so much."

"But what if I like fear. What if it's all I've known? Has become a part of me like a finger or a toe?"

"Nobody really likes fear, not even you."

"You think so? Then why are my eyes dry, Sandy? Why have I not shed a single tear? Why am I not going to lose a drop of sleep over this? Going to sleep good tonight? I've sent the man I've wanted away forever. Why doesn't that hurt as much as it should?"

Sandy had no answer for that. Remembered Winston's words. Understood the meaning. "If you need me, I'll be here," the most she could offer.

"I know," Janice said softly. "And I appreciate it."

Sandy left Janice's apartment, waited for the elevator and got inside when it arrived. The car bounced and jingled as it made its way to

the lobby, each bump swelling her heart. She was blinking back wetness by the time she walked down the long corridor, had to use her
hand to wipe away tears as she navigated out of the complex. Was
near blurry-eyed by the time she hurried across Bedell Street, cars fast
and assiduous making the journey dangerous.

Behind the wheel of her car, she lowered her head to the steering
column, cried the tears her friend could not shed. Wept against the
injustice her friend could not feel. Wondered about the path her
friend had chosen, doubtful that she would ever see the right side of
things again.

Rachel hung up the phone, numb.

She stood in her kitchen, back against the refrigerator, shocked
and unmoving. She could not believe what her brother had told her,
her body running hot and cold with dread and hope. It was a bad feeling, coated in a sweetness, displeasure dipped in euphoria. When her
doorbell rang, she knew without glancing out the window that all of it
had arrived on her doorstep.

"It's over," Cliff's first words to her.

"Whatcha mean it over. What over?" Rachel refused to acknowledge what she already knew to be true. Grew tough and hardened as
she stared into his eyes.

"Me. Janice. The wedding. Can I come in?"

Rachel's face bunched up. "Come in? What for? Ya tink 'cause you
say goodbye to she, ya can just slide in here wit me?"

"Isn't that what you wanted?"

"Who say dat? Ya hear me speak dat? Ya ever hear me say me even
want ya again? Just 'cause ya tink ya through wit Janice don't mean me
gonna be all nice and open wit you." She stared at him, honey eyes
steely. "Ya cray-zee, ya know dat? Cray-zee if ya tink what we had is
wort a can of beans ta what ya just walked away from."

Cliff's face grew befuddled. His tone, soft. "Don't know what I think,
Rachel. Don't know what I think, feel, want . . . can I please come in?"

Didn't he see she was fighting for what he no longer could?
Couldn't he see that her words were just a front and there was no
place else she wanted him to be but there with her? That she was trying to do the right thing, even if sending him back to Janice was the
last thing she wanted. Couldn't he see that?

Either he didn't or cared not too. "Please, Rachel."

She looked away, a first for her. Tried to scurry up more defense from her cutting tongue but found her mouth was empty. That he was hurting. That she wanted him.

Rachel had sent him back to Janice once before and Janice had blown it. There'd be no second time. She let him in.

# Chapter 18

The world was going mad.

That was Martha's assessment when Janice called her to say she and Cliff had broken up; Sandy hot on her trail with what Britney had tried to do.

"Britney?"

"The one and only."

"You're lying, Sandy."

"If I'm lying, I'm flying."

"What was Brit thinking?"

"That she knew better than me. Be different if I wasn't with Winston, but I am and she doesn't want to recognize that."

"She has been under stress lately."

"Who hasn't?"

"Have you talked to Janice?"

"What another mess."

"I feel sorry for her."

"Me too."

"Do you think we should get together?"

In truth, Sandy didn't. She was sad for Janice and annoyed at Britney. She would rather spend her Friday or Saturday night with Winston. "Nah, not in the mood."

"She doesn't need to be alone."

"She's okay. Saw for myself. She's so fine, it's scary."

"Are we forgetting already?"

"Forgetting what?"

"How *fine* you were when the truth came out about Adrian and his wife. How *fine* you were to go on hiding in that little dark hole and would have been there still if I hadn't come and forced you out." Martha had come to her rescue and Sandy hadn't even known she needed saving. She never stopped to think Janice was in the very same place. "So which is it going to be, Friday night or Saturday?"

"Friday. Me and Wint have plans for Saturday."

"I'll let everyone know."

Martha hung up. She didn't see Calvin standing in the doorway watching her. Didn't know he was there until his voice came, awed, full. "Masterful Martha."

She turned, smiled weary. "Just trying to keep things together."

"Doing a good job from where I'm standing."

"I don't know about that."

"I do. I wouldn't even be standing here if you hadn't given me that ultimatum?"

"It wasn't an ultimatum."

" 'Either you do or you don't,' what do you call that?"

"I call it hard-hitting reality. The 'my back is to the wall and there is no place else to go but forward with or without you.' "

Calvin nodded, reflective. "I couldn't stand the thought of you gone from me."

"I didn't want to be gone."

"But you would have, right?"

Martha looked at him with earnest eyes. "Yes, I would."

"Which proves my point. Masterful Martha."

Bullshit. No man wanted a woman to take it. They wanted you to have free will, have the power to leave when the going got too bad. That's what Janice had, she had just lost it along the way.

Maybe Martha could help her find it.


Sandy waited.

Waited for the phone call, the reasons good or bad. Waited for that personal explanation from her brother as to why he no longer wanted to marry her best friend. Though she had heard it secondhand, she needed to have it direct. Needed to make sure nothing was lost in the translation; that Janice's self-doubt had undone so much.

But Sandy was the last thing on Cliff's mind and it never entered it that he should call her. He figured Janice would let her know and, however way she told it, would allow it to become the truth.

But Sandy got tired of waiting. She went to her parents' house to get an answer.

Sandy greeted her mother warmly. "Hey, Mom. Cliff here?" Her mother nodded and Sandy headed up the stairs. She rapped twice on his old bedroom door. Let herself in. It took him a hot second to look up from his magazine, but he remained spread across the full-size bed.

"You didn't call me," she began.

" 'Bout what?"

"You and Janice."

"She your girl. I'm sure she told you."

"She told me some things, yeah, and Winston told me some things, but I need to hear it from your mouth."

"Well, you take what Janice said and Winston said and leave it at that."

"Because she changed? People change all the time."

"I'm not having this conversation with you."

"You need to have it with somebody . . . she's my friend Cliff and she thinks she's fine but she's not. She thinks she's just in love with misery. I really need to know what happened."

Cliff risked his sister's eyes for the first time, a watery pain inside them. "She is, Sandy. She really is in love with misery. She pushed me and pushed me until I couldn't stay. If that's not loving misery, I don't know what is."

"So what are you going to do now?"

"Chill here for a while. Get my head together."

She reached out, touched his shoulder. "I'll be here if you need me."

When Sandy got home, she called Martha. "Forget it."

"Forget what?"

"About Janice and 'there's hope' talk. She caused the breakup to happen. So we'll just go over and keep her company."

"Britney's not coming."

"Somehow I'm not surprised."

"You hurt her feelings, Sandy."

"She had no right sticking her nose into my business."

"She thought she was doing something right."

"Well, she thought wrong."

"So you going to call her?"

"Who?"

"Brit."

"And say what?"

"What's she's waiting to hear—that you forgive her."

"I don't forgive her."

"You will sooner or later . . . yeah, she pissed you off, but everybody pisses everybody off at some point. We forgive each other and go on and get pissed off again, but that's what friendship is. Forgiving our flawed asses."

"Big flawed asses."

Martha chuckled. "Her ass is kind of big, isn't it?"

"And wide," Sandy offered with her own laugh.

"That's cold, Sandy."

"But true."

Martha was silent for a moment. "So you gonna call her."

"Yeah, I guess so."

"When we get off the phone?"

"Yeah, when we get off the phone."

"All right then. Catch you Friday."

Sandy pushed the dial tone button down. Moved her finger to the 5. Stopped. Wrong was wrong and Britney had been plain wrong; an idea that became stirred up in old envy. That envy that had been building from the moment she found out Britney was pregnant and Sandy never would be. Not with Adrian. *With what man?*

What man would ever enter her unsheathed? Spill his sperm into her life-giving womb? When was the last time a man had? It was so long ago Sandy couldn't even remember. Adrian never had and Winston never would. Negative or not, that part of her life would be on hold until she was in her middle forties. Her only option was artificial insemination at this point, but the idea of devices and tools entering her for conception was a bitterness she could not stand.

This was what Sandy found herself thinking on. She was supposed to call Britney, but in that moment, could find neither the guts, or the desire.

Rachel had reluctantly opened her front door to Cliff, inviting him to have a seat the first time. But when he returned days later and reached for her, she pushed away his attempted embrace. "Ya need some tinking time, Cleef. Ya need some time to settle all dat happened between you and Janice."

But Cliff wasn't hearing her or feeling her. "That's already settled."

"Ya tink?" Rachel asked disconcerted. "She was de only gal ya wanted to marry. Da only one and now you two are separated. Ya might tink ya ready for a go-round wit me, but me know better." She looked at him with earnest eyes. "One of da hardest tings me ever done was send you back to her. Me never stopped wanting ya, me never stopped missing ya, but me sent ya back anyway. I say dat to say, me gonna be right here for ya, but for right now we can't be more dan friends."

"But me and Janice is over."

"Yes, me know dat, but when you come to me, me want everything clean out, fresh. Nutten hanging over us." She gave a little smile. "Friends not a bad thing, ya know."

"Well, what's your definition of friends?"

"We talk on da phone. Visit. Maybe even party and ting, but das it."

"For how long?"

Rachel shrugged. "Who can say really, but when da time come, we'll both know."

"So it's okay if I call?"

"Sure."

"Drop by?"

"Every now and den."

It took a while for him to understand, a while to get the whole picture. He came to understand her decision, the wisdom of it. He looked at her in awe, full amazement. "You are one incredible woman, you know that."

"So me been told," she said with a wide smile.

"Winston wanted to know if I was going on the trip."

"Back home?"

"Yeah."

"What ya tell him?"

"I told him I'd get back to him. But I guess the real question is: Is it okay if I go, with us now being just friends and all? I mean I wouldn't want to tempt you running around in my Speedo."

She laughed, head back, full. "Oh, Misder Cleef, ya going to try and make dis tuff for me, aren't you?"

"Last thing I want to do, Rachel."

"Yes, come on to Trinidad. Me show ya the sights, its beauty."

But as far as Cliff was concerned, he was already looking at it.

He had been drawn to Rachel's strength, her no-nonsense approach to life; an attraction that had been halted when love become more important than like; when he was forced to face the fact that while he had liked Rachel, he loved Janice.

But that love had failed, and in Rachel he saw a new hope; the chance to take them where they hadn't had the chance to go before. A real ever-after.


Eating out became a luxury Sandy and Winston found themselves indulging in more and more. Bellies full, windows down, the dinner at Junior's became a sweet memory.

"Are you coming?" Winston wanted to know as they took the on-ramp to the Belt Parkway.

"Where?"

"Trinidad. Next month."

"Can't."

"How come?"

"Can't get the time, Wint. You know I took so much with Adrian, before and after. I have none left."

"Can't you take the leave without pay?"

"Yeah, I can, but that's two weeks with no money."

He considered. "You can afford it, can't you?"

She could, that and a couple of trips to Paris and a few cruises around the world with the money from Adrian's life insurance's policies, but that would diminish her nest egg. Sandy didn't plan on working until retirement. Had decided to quit while she was still young enough to enjoy it.

She had met with a financial planner and most of the money had been invested into a money management account, a place she planned to keep it, trade winds and blues waters or no.

"Have to be careful with it. Three grand ain't a drop in the bucket."

"You'll love it, Sandy. Get to meet the family."

"I know that. But I can't, not this trip."

She didn't so much see the hurt that found him as much as she felt it. It filled the Camry like hot air, thick full, oxygen stealing. "What?"

"Nothing."

"Don't tell me nothing. You're upset."

He swallowed, the swallow so deep she heard it over the hum of the wheels. "People you don't know, never met, are dying to meet you. My family, wanting to meet the woman who did so much, who gave so much of herself. They want to see the Yankee who made them take back every bad thing they thought about Americans." He paused. "And I want them to meet my heart."

It was the last part that touched her, that made her feel like a villain. The last part that made three thousand dollars incidental, gave her a change of heart. "Okay, uncle."

"You mean it?" his joy, returned.

"I'll ask my boss. See what he says. Let you know tomorrow."

"Tell him I said it would mean so much to everyone."

But unfortunately everyone did not include her boss.


Sandy stood by his desk, the exact middle, arms folded, peeved. "Just two weeks."

"At the height of the end of the fiscal year? You're joking, right?"

"No." She'd simply forgotten that June was the mad house season.

"Can't do it, Sandy. You want to take time in July, August, fine. But not next month."

"What about Cassandra? She filled in for me before."

"Yeah, she did and didn't do a good job either. Now I've been lenient with you about taking time before, but June is out of the question."


Winston didn't understand. "What do you mean he won't let you? You got the right to take the time, no pay."

"Sure, I got the right, but then what, come back to no job?"

"He can't fire you, Sandy."

"No, but he can make it so I'd want to quit. He's the boss, remember?"

"So many people wanted to meet you."

"I'm sure they did, but there's nothing I can do."

"Cliff's going."

That surprised her. "He is?"

"Yeah. Him and Rachel are talking again."

"Rachel?"

"Yeah. You didn't know?"

"No, I didn't."

"Before you start jumping to conclusions, Rachel didn't break them up."

"I know." But Sandy felt between a rock and a hard place. Janice was her girl, and in some ways so was Rachel. Still the idea that Cliff had left Janice and was now "talking" to Rachel was a surprise. "Did Rachel ever say anything about my brother?"

"Not a word. But I could always sense it whenever they were in the same room."

"How come I didn't see it?"

"Because you weren't looking."

"And you were?"

"Cliff was the first man my sister ever had any interest in since her fiancé died. I'm talking about years of just being by herself."

"But she sent him back to Janice anyway."

"You know what they say about love . . . set it free, if it comes back?"

"Meant to be," her voice barely a whisper.

But it was a truth Sandy wasn't feeling. She still adored Winston, still enjoyed being with him, but the love, the heart-stopping emotion that snatched away sleep, made his absence a tender wound, was not there for her.

Winston knew this.

He had known for a while. But she was still beside him and he would not send her away. That would be Sandy's decision.

# Chapter 19

A long work week, Maurice was glad to see it come to an end. Where once upon a time he looked forward to going out on Friday nights, those times had changed. This Friday night he would be home with his baby daughter, a couple of orders of hot wings, his favorite beer, his pal Calvin, and ESPN.

The fear that had visited him just a few weeks ago was long gone. The weight he had lost was becoming a fast memory too. Maurice was happy. Life had hit that balance again. He gave his daughter a hot wing, took up one for himself. Looked at the clock. Figured Calvin would be here soon.

He was opening his first beer when the doorbell rang. He greeted Calvin with open arms and an invite to park himself down. He was glad his wife was getting out of the house, going off to hang with her friends, but when he saw her come into the kitchen in her bathrobe, he understood something had changed.

"Brit?"

"Yeah."

"It's almost eight."

She didn't look up from her refrigerator search. "I know."

"Aren't you supposed to be somewhere?"

"Hey, Brit," Calvin called.

"Hey," she called back.

"Aren't you?" Maurice asked as the leftover macaroni and cheese hit the counter.

"Not going."

"What you mean you're not going?"

The jug of ice tea was next. "Just like I said, I'm not." She closed the refrigerator and took a glass from the cabinet.

"Why not?"

She looked at him for the first time, and for the first time in a while, he saw sadness in her eyes. The kind that was deep, wide, and endless. Maurice had not seen that look since they first met. "Because, all right?"

Maurice put his wing on a napkin. "Be back." Scooted off the couch. Went into the kitchen, stood before his wife, his back blocking Calvin's view. "What's going on, Brit?"

There were tears in her eyes. "Everything Mo. Everything."

He reached up, wiped one. "Everything like what?"

She had not told her husband of her great failed plan. Hadn't shared Sandy's harsh words that were still wounding her. She looked at him and for the first time saw not her prince in shining armor but a man who could stand to lose a hundred pounds. She walked out of the kitchen.

Maurice followed her with his eyes, caught Calvin staring. "Women," all he could mutter as he headed off behind his wife. She was on the bed crying, a Kleenex to her eyes. Maurice sat down beside her, took up a hand. "Something happened?"

Britney could only nod.

"What?"

She shook her head. "Something with your friends." She nodded emphatically. "Martha?" Her head shook no. "Janice?" Another evident no. "Sandy?" Britney didn't move her head, just leaned into her husband, feeling like a fraud.

In the days since Sandy had left her house in a huff, Britney had come to doubt everything good that had happened to her. Had come to doubt her own worth. She had none before Maurice and didn't feel like she had any now. Britney felt that she was just play acting and none of it was concrete or real.

Not the good loving man she'd married, the wonderful house. Not the nice clothes in her closet or the baby on the way. It was some mistake, some error of the universe. She wasn't supposed to have this life. Had done nothing to deserve it.

"You got to tell me, Brit."

She did, her story coming out in hiccupy dribbles, coated with sobs and tears. "I was trying to help her," was how she ended, her face slick.

"Yeah, I know, babe. I know. But you know how good intentions can go. Sandy's mad at you, but she won't be forever. And you can start the process now, by getting up, getting dressed, and getting over there."

"I can't, Mo."

"What you mean you can't. We didn't have a dime to our name, you went out and found it. Thought of things I never would, so don't try and tell me you can't do something as simple as get dressed and go be with your friends, 'cause I'm not going to accept that."

She had, hadn't she? She *had* found the ways and means to keep food on their table, without anybody's help. Britney had asked nobody, just went ahead and done it. Rescued her own self. Used her head.

Sandy had told her she had no right to think. Had cut her down with words and Britney had let her. But she never married a man with AIDS, never ended up with her husband's brother.

Between the two women, Britney had won, hands down.

Her life was good. She deserved it. How could she have doubted it for a minute? She felt foolish that she even entertained the idea.

"You right, Mo. I'm going."

"You believe in genetics?" Janice asked as Sandy sat across from her.

"What do you mean?"

"Genetics, certain predispositions. You know. Like your grandmother might like a certain food and you find yourself liking it too, how alcoholism seems to run in some families."

"Yeah, I guess."

"Well, I think my problem is genetics. My problem with men."

"Because of your mother?"

"Yeah."

"Well, maybe it's not genetics so much as learned behavior."

"Whatever it is, I never had a fair chance. Had three different daddies by the time I was eighteen. What does that say to a young girl?" Sandy didn't answer. Knew there was no need to. "Relationships are disposable. Not supposed to last long."

"So, what are you going to do about it?"

Janice sighed. "I made a great big leap with Cliff. Don't know if I can make another and stay there."

"Do you want to?"

"I don't know, Sandy. I don't know what I want. But being in this situation is familiar, y'know. Like keeping a pair of old worn-out shoes. You know you can't wear them nowhere, but they just feel so good on."

"So you're resigned to be alone then?"

"But I don't feel alone. I feel okay. Really."

"So did I, Janice," Sandy said carefully. "Just me and my heartache, me and my pain. Just stuffing myself full of it and liking it."

"That was different."

"How, how was it different?"

"Because you don't have my issues, Sandy. You didn't come up in a household where getting a new husband was like taking a trip to Macy's."

"True, but the bottom line is the same. The pain becomes like a drug. Becomes all you think you want until someone comes along and tells you it's not."

"I know that, but for right now in this moment, it's suiting me. Who knows, maybe one morning I'll wake up and won't want it, or need it. But for now, I just want to be by myself."

Sandy gave her a sideways glance. "Get ready."

"Ready for what?"

"Ready for the wake-up call. It's not going to be pretty or gentle. It's going to hit you like a sledgehammer. Turn your world upside down. I've known you a long time, Janice. And despite what you saying now, I know your heart won't allow you to stay happy by yourself."

Martha did a head count the moment she got to Janice's. She knew who was missing and why. "You didn't call her, did you?"

"No."

"Call who," Janice wanted to know.

"Brit. Sandy was supposed to call her."

Janice looked between the two women. "So she's not coming?"

Janice didn't know the story. Sandy wasn't about to tell it. "Guess not," she said.

Janice was about to ask more questions when the doorbell rang. She got up and answered. Let Britney in, Britney's eyes finding Sandy's. "I got something to say," she began. "I may not be the cutest, the sexiest, but you or no one else has a right to ever question my intelligence. I was trying to do you a favor and I was wrong and I apologize for that, but don't you ever imply that I'm less than anybody else, that I'm not important. Because I am."

Britney turned away. Went to the dinette table. Took a cup, the bottle of wine. Poured half a cup. Took the time to drink it staring at Sandy, daring her to rebuke her, tell her different. While Janice, mouth opened, eyes wide in surprise, could only stare.

The silence went on as eyes remained fixed on Britney, uncertain of what she would say next. But Britney was done and took a seat as if to say "So?" Settled back, refusing to meet anyone's gaze.

"Okay, let's get this party started," Janice decided, unsure of what it had been about, but mostly uncertain if what her friends had come to tell her would be worth the trip, or the listen.

"Didn't I tell you?" Sandy was saying hours later as the three women left the apartment building. "She is so fine, it's scary."

"Or maybe she really is okay," Britney's two cents.

"Maybe she is or maybe she isn't," Martha said. "All we can do is be there for her, either way." Martha's head scanned the parking lot. "Brit, where you parked?"

"Over there by the light post."

"Sandy, where are you parked?"

"Opposite side."

"I'm parked there too. We'll walk, Brit. Backtrack."

"I don't need nobody walking me. I'll be just fine." The attitude was still with her, became a fire that wouldn't go out. "I hurt your feelings, Sandy? Well, you hurt mine, but only one of us apologized, didn't they."

"Yeah, well."

"I'm not asking you, I'm just clarifying," Britney said quickly. "See y'all later." The disgust in her voice could not be missed. Britney walked away. Sandy and Martha watched her. The growing baby made her steps cumbersome, gave her an old tired look from behind.

Sandy couldn't hold on to her anger. Had to let it go. Called out. "Brit, Brit wait," hurried after her. She stood in front of her, back to Martha.

"It was more than what you did, Brit . . . I realized it was about what you got and I didn't."

"And?"

"And so I do apologize, from the bottom of my heart I do."

Britney blinked at her. Held the stern look.

"What else do you want me to say?"

"I want you to say the truth."

"I just did."

"No, you didn't. You just tapped danced around it."

Sandy got tense. "So what is the truth, since I don't seem to know."

"The truth is I wasn't supposed to have all I got. You, Martha, and Janice, but not me, and it pisses you off, makes you wonder why, turns you just green with envy, that's the truth. Well, you know what, Sandy? I ain't planned this life, but if God has seen fit to give it to me, I'm going to embrace it."

Sandy looked away.

"That's the truth. I know it and you know it. All you got to do is say it out loud and to my face."

Sandy swallowed, full of guilt. "You're right. From the moment Maurice bought you that house and you announced you were having a baby, I was jealous. Wanted to know why I couldn't have it for myself. And it was wrong and stupid. We've been friends too long. So I am sorry. Real sorry. Ask that you forgive me."

Martha couldn't hear the words but she saw the array of expressions until the right one came into the mix.

At that moment she knew that things were going to be okay.

# Chapter 20

"Boy, if you had been me, you'd never been born." In the last few months Randall had heard his father getting more vocal with his opinions, mostly about his state of heart, or lack of, but this was the closest Randall ever came to telling it. Telling it all.

He found himself wondering if his father would understand. Let go of some of it. "I tried, Pop. Went over and tried to talk to her."

"And?"

"And nothing. She's seeing somebody else, for the wrong reasons, if you ask me."

"I gather she's not asking you."

"Not even listening."

"Did she tell you to go away and never come back?"

"Close enough. Told me to get out."

His father considered him with a critical eye. "Was she piping mad, or all calm and cool like."

"Mad."

His father chuckled. "Then it's not over. When a woman still has feeling for a man, the emotions are like cream . . . they just rise to the top. Now, if she don't care two hoots, then she's not going to waste an extra breath on you."

"So what am I supposed to do?"

"Woo her. Woo her until she's crying uncle."

"How do you woo a woman who won't even let you in her front door?"

"FTD? UPS?"

Randall nodded. Understood.

It had been a hard case, a tough one, and the months that it took to bring it to a close had been long. But the jury had come in and found the defendant guilty and Martha's office was in high gear. Sometimes they tried a person where the guilt or innocence was in question, but there had been no doubt Anestio Perdina had killed his wife in cold blood.

Martha sat in her office, hearing the excited voices of her coworkers coming through the closed door. She knew what the plan was, but wasn't certain if she wanted to go. Celebration at Brendt's, her boss had announced, and even as she sat there, the office was readying themselves to go drink and celebrate.

Her battle with alcohol was still going strong; some days it seemed the next breath would send her toward the abyss she did not want to venture. Going and sitting in a place where indulging was expected didn't seem like a good choice. On the other hand, not going would cause suspicion.

She was still debating when two raps came on her door and a head popped in.

"Hey," Miles said.

"Hey back," Martha answered with a slow smile.

"You ready?"

"I was thinking about not going."

One of Mile's brows rose up. "How come?"

"Not a place I need to be."

"Brendt's?"

"Yeah."

"But we always go there."

"I know that. Just . . ." She looked into the face that at one time she had thought she wanted. Felt a deep need to share her secret. Understood the risk. Found some resolve. Shook her head. Locked her files and grabbed her purse. "I'll be out in a minute." She waited for Miles to leave. Picked up the phone and called Calvin, telling him she would be late and why.

She left her office, found Miles waiting for her, the two of them heading out.

It was not a long walk but Miles seemed in no rush to get there, his steps measured, slow. "So everything's cool?' he wanted to know.

"Everything's, everything," she answered.

"So I guess you don't need another hug."

There was something different to him now. Something that she had not felt since their ill-fated date. "You trying to rap to me, Mr. Miles?"

"Just been finding myself wondering what went wrong."

"Went wrong when?"

"That day you came to my place."

His place. Tiny, claustrophobic, smelly, she hadn't expected such a well-put-together black man, a man who read Garvey, who was into experimental theater and jazz, to live in such a hovel.

His pull-out couch had still been pulled out, revealing dingy linen and greasy pillow cases. The beauty of the bay window had been hidden under a couple of years' worth of dirt. There had been dust bunnies everywhere across the hardwood floors and the air smelled as if a fresh breeze hadn't entered it in a while.

Martha remembered how she had been willing to sleep with him and her last-minute change of mind. How not having anyone in her life at the time and Sandy's parents thinking she was a lesbian had her run after the first available man she'd seen—him.

Martha wasn't going to reveal any of that. Gave up an abbreviated version. "What happened, Miles, was I was in the wrong place at the wrong time for the wrong reasons."

"Thought there was something to us, Martha." He seemed a little hurt.

"I thought so too for a hot minute, but believe me, if I had stayed, we wouldn't even be having this conversation or speaking to each other, so let's just leave it at that."

"Think we would have made a great couple."

"Well, we're all entitled to our thoughts."

\* \* \*

Her first round she ordered a club soda, the plan being two club sodas and a white wine if pressed. But the smell of alcohol was in the air, bringing on a deep itch in the back of her throat, and Martha got up and went to the ladies' room to get herself together.

When she got back, there was a glass of Bacardi neat on the table in front of her chair. "Whose is that?" she asked Miles.

"Yours. Dominick ordered . . . what you drink, right?"

Yes, it was. Bacardi, no ice, no chaser, just four ounces of one hundred proof distilled in the hills of Puerto Rico. Bacardi, all golden amber and burning to the tongue, what she'd been longing for but refused to have.

Martha looked at the glass, looked over at Dominick, who was engaged in a loud conversation with Kelly. Knew she had two choices, was in need of a third. She could pick up the glass or pick herself up and go, but neither choice came easy, one prominent over the next.

*One drink, I can do it. One drink and I'll be fine.* It *was* a celebration. She *could* handle it. Martha's fingers clasped around the glass and brought it to her lips. Took a sip with the intention of putting the glass back down, but her lips refused to let go.

By the time the glass hit the table, half the drink was gone, mellowness easing through her like a long-awaited breath. Martha counted to ten in her head and downed the rest. Miles flagged the barmaid, ordered her another round.

Martha was reaching for the second drink when she caught herself, strung tight between want and common sense. She became aware of the noisy rush of conversation, of Miles beside her and the heady liquid in the glass.

Two choices—drink or leave now—weighed heavy in her heart. Deciding on the first, she reached for the glass. Miscalculating space and distance, Martha knocked it over. One hundred proof splashed her, formed a tiny pool across the scarred wooden tabletop. It took her a second to react, to get up, grab the flimsy cocktail napkins, dabbing her blouse and table furiously.

The barmaid appeared, a wet rag in hand. "Got it," she told Martha, wiping up the remnants, taking the soaked Bacardi napkins from her hands. "I'll bring you another."

"Don't bother." Martha got her purse off the edge of the chair. Rose, said good night. Left.

Her legs felt weak by the time she got outside. She wasn't certain they could carry her the four blocks to her car. Her whole body trembled, her heart beat wildly in her chest. She got as far as the corner and had to lean on the light pole. Knew the picture she presented but had no choice. She had to stay that way until her head cleared.

"You all right?"

The touch on her arm scared her, sending more adrenaline to the all ready thick rush. Martha felt faint, saw spots, weaved a little, Miles arms catching her. "Hey, you okay?"

She leaned against him, glad for the support. Stayed there as she waited for her world to right itself. A lifetime came and went before it did, she not refuting his insistence that he walk her to her car.

Martha let herself in, her heart heavy. She could smell alcohol on her clothes, no doubt from where she spilled the drink. She could smell Miles too, no doubt from when he held her up. No, she hadn't gotten drunk but it had cost her much.

No, she had not succumbed, but what would have happened if Miles hadn't followed her? Would she now be laid out on the streets in Brooklyn, people mistaking her for a drunkard, thieves seeing her as a perfect victim?

How many more times in her professional life would she have to play out that battle? Victories happened often enough and they always ended with rounds at Brendt's. She couldn't have another night like she'd had this night. Knew she had to do something.

Decided exactly what on the ride home.

She saw Calvin on the couch, fear and concern all over his face.

"Had a drink, but I'm not drunk," her first words as Calvin got up from the chair.

"I was worried."

She nodded. "I know you were, but I realized I can't go on like this . . . I'm joining AA."

It was what he needed to hear but hadn't been sure she would ever say it. "Good for you, babe, good for you."

Martha nodded, a bit bewildered. "Yeah, good for me." She put down her pocketbook, her briefcase, went to the closet and pulled out the Yellow Pages. Looked under the *A*'s and called the 800 number. She found a meeting place. Knew where she'd be tomorrow after work.

"I'm scared," she confessed to Calvin. "Scared to walk through that door, admit to strangers that I'm no superwoman. That I have issues and problems . . . on my way to being a drunk."

Calvin reached out his hand. Martha took it, appreciating the squeeze. "I don't know much about the twelve steps," he told her, "but I do believe the first is admitting something's wrong."

Martha chuckled, but there was no joy in it. "It seems from the moment I was born, something was wrong." She took her hand away. "I was supposed to get married. His name was Leon. We were in our last year of law school."

She had never told any man that story but Martha knew the time had come. "We had the date set, the caterer, the church and everything. Three weeks before the wedding, he called it off. Turned my heart to stone." Her head shook. "Looking back, I was always into some type of mind-altering substances. College? Not a day would go by without having some weed. A joint in the morning, a joint before I went to bed. When I got into law school, I forced myself to give it up."

She looked off, thrust in memory. "I became a social drinker. Me and a couple of classmates would go to the Raskellar after class, have a drink or two. Then when Leon left, I started drinking at home. Every now and then I'd just get wasted." Her eyes found his. "Then I met you and suddenly I didn't have to, want to, or anything. Felt God was giving me another chance, the one I lost with Leon. You came into my life and everything just got better, and then you were gone and I was back to wanting, but you're back and I'm still wanting."

"Guess it was time to face up to it all."

Martha nodded. "Guess it was."

St. Peter's of Moran, a stone buttress of thick stone and aged timber, sat like a faded jewel in the late afternoon sun within the affluent chasm of Forest Hills. Martha didn't know what to expect as she entered the side door but it was the closest AA meeting place to her, so this was where she came.

Raised Catholic, her brother an altar boy, the two of them had attended parochial school through sixth grade. But a point had come when she abandoned the faith, certain she would never again enter dwellings of timber and stone, fingering rosaries, confessions leaving her lips. Martha had been certain she would never whisper sins to the face behind the mesh, awaiting condemnation and absolution in the same breath.

But the church was surprisingly comforting, the atmosphere hushed; incense and burned candle wax, faint in the air. There was a reverence as ancient and prolific as God himself, and for the first time in a long time she felt a need to bare her soul.

She saw herself walking down the isle of polished stone, move off to the side to the dark wood confessional. Felt the lump that would find her as the little panel slid back, she readying her mouth to speak, *"Forgive me, Father, for I have sinned."*

Martha was contemplating doing all of just that when a gentle hand landed on her shoulder. "Can I help you, my child?" Martha turned, saw an old priest. Swallowed. "I'm here for the AA meeting," something pressing moving from her soul.

She begged off the free coffee. Took a seat in the back of the room. Did a quick study of the faces that surrounded her, wondered about their lives. As a newcomer, she was asked to stand, tell a little something about herself. Following the cues from the newcomers before her, she forced the words out when her turn arrived.

"My name is Martha and I'm an alcoholic. My mother is an alcoholic and I promised myself I would never grow up to be like her . . . guess I lied."

Sandy let herself in, the mail shifting gently with an air current from the opening door. Mid-month, she knew most of the mail would be junk, but there on the floor lay a lavender envelope. It was the first thing she picked up.

She didn't recognize the handwriting and searched back and front for a return address. Seeing none, she slit it open with a fingernail, pulled out a cranberry-washed card with gold letters. Read *Would you?*, the only words on the front.

She opened the flap, eyes searching the bottom for a signature. Was mildly surprised to see none. Found a seat before she read the words inside, knowing without knowing whom it was from.

*Believe me if I said we're not quite through*
*Believe me if I said I've been thinking of only you*

*Believe me if I said I was very wrong, and apologize for that*
*Believe me if I said all I want is to have you back . . .*

It wouldn't have been so hard to dismiss if the poem hadn't been scripted by hand. Would have been easier to toss if some card company had inked the tome. But it had been blank and Randall had taken the time to write those words.

The least she could do was keep it.

The next day when Sandy came home from work, she had a few things on her mind: a glass of ice water, a cold shower, and twenty minutes of cool-down with the air conditioner in her bedroom on high.

The temperature was an unseasonable eighty-nine, the late spring afternoon bringing in a heat wave that wasn't due until late June.

The commute home had been brutal, radiators giving out under the high temperatures, slowing traffic in some places to a standstill. Glad to be home, Sandy left her car, squinted against the blazing sun, and headed up her stoop. A rush of hot air came at her as she opened her front door and she knew it was time to pull out the standing fan.

She scooped up her mail, put it and her purse on the couch, and went about opening windows. Though the breeze was hot, at least it was moving air. No doubt they were in for a hot summer.

She snatched up the mail, her purse, and headed up the stairs. Turned on her unit and stood in front of its fast cool breeze. Sandy stripped, padded naked to her bathroom, and turned on the shower, wetting herself from head to toe.

Unlike her white counterparts, her hair wasn't wash and go and she hadn't had a drop of water on her scalp in over a week. Hair now wet, she would have to wash it, condition it, blow dry, and then curl it, but the cool delicious sensation was well worth that effort.

Twenty-five minutes later she was out of the shower, hair loose and wet. Later would come the blow drying and the curling, but for now she let the air half complete the job as she slipped on a sleeveless cotton gown, checked her phone for messages, and went through her mail.

The envelope was a soft burnt orange.

How she'd missed it when she first got the mail she didn't know, but there it was, no mystery like there had been just yesterday. Sandy knew the game. Knew more things would arrive on a daily basis. Had been victim to it once, wasn't in for a second go-round.

Brian, an ex-boyfriend, had played it so well he had taken her initial noninterest in him and spun it into a real-life, heartbreaking, "I-can't-live-without-him-no-matter-what-he-doesn't-do" affair. The end result had been three good months and twenty-one bad ones. Bad ones that would have gone on if she hadn't met Adrian.

She opened the card, saw more words, closed it. Went to her closet and got the old shoe box. The first card inside, she put in the second. Safekeeping, more items would be added as the days went by. Items that would both chain her and set her free.

The spring day moved through Janice's opened window, stirring up the sheer drapes along the edges. She had opened them when she got home and the fresh air was invigorating. Nothing else about her life was.

But that suited her.

No more waiting for the sound of the key in the door. No more snooping in the laundry basket. No more thoughts that made her head hurt, her heart ache.

It had been a while since she had been moved to do anything beyond sleep, eat, go to work, and watch television. The spring breeze changed that.

As old as time, the need to spring clean found her and she started in her living room. Old magazines were thrown away, furniture was dusted, and she gave her area rug a good vacuuming. Her bedroom was next.

She went through her dresser drawers, throwing out things she no longer wore and storing away items she would not use until fall. Janice went through her closet, finding two pairs of Cliff's dress pants. Debated about what to do with them.

They were tailored and expensive, and she could not bring herself to throw them out but could not bring herself to call him about them either. She called Sandy instead.

"Hi, it's me."

"Hey, Janice, what's been going on?"

"Nothing much. I was doing some spring cleaning and came across your brother's pants. I don't know if I should throw them out or try and get in contact with him."

"Knowing my brother, if he didn't grab them before he left, he doesn't want them."

"How is he?"

"He's okay."

"I guess him and Rachel are getting it on hot and heavy now."

"No, Janice. They're just friends."

Which Janice did not believe, but she moved on. "Well, it's the past now. My bedroom looks like a tornado hit it. I better get back to my spring cleaning. Take care, okay?"

"You too."

Calvin sat across from Martha, seeing on her face the battle she was waging. Between work and the hours she was putting in with her AA meetings, there was a weariness that hung in the corner of her eyes.

A week later she was still going, sometimes coming home with tears in her eyes, other times so unburdened it was like she was spanking brand new. He had done some reading up on the subject and understood that it would be a life-long journey for her. There was no cure, only maintenance.

Calvin asked the question that had been tooling around in his brain for a while. "How come you never talk about your family?"

"Nothing to talk about. My brother's off living his life, my father's off living his."

"What about your mother?"

"What about her?"

"I'd like to meet her."

"No, you don't."

"Yeah, Martha, I do."

"Why?"

"Because she's your mother and I'm in love with her daughter."

"I haven't introduced a boyfriend to her since college and I'm not about to start."

He reached out, touched her hand. "It's important . . . to me."

"Well, what about your folks? Haven't met them either."

"That's doable."

And she knew that they had taken that giant step.

They went that following weekend, Martha stepping into a home that had a time warp feel, from the plastic slip covers to the track trophies on top of the floor-model TV. She hadn't been certain what to expect, but was at total ease from the moment Calvin's mother opened the door.

"You're an assistant district attorney and I'm a garbage man. How could my parents not love you?" he confessed to her afterward. But they became words that haunted her as she made plans to give her mother the same fair look.

Calvin's Infiniti was a luxury car, and though Martha was nestled in the passenger seat, no luxury could she find. She found herself constantly trying to readjust her seat, get comfortable. But she knew it was futile. There'd be no comfort on this trip.

"That bad?" Calvin asked.

"She's the wickedest witch of the West . . . has so many issues all the good is just gone from her."

Seventeen minutes later they were pulling up to the curb, the two-story home simple, well kept. Calvin headed toward the front stoop but Martha called him back. "No, through the back, nobody goes through the front."

It was one of those idiosyncrasies Helen Alston had. Martha knew Calvin would not understand it. She herself had given up trying. Martha steeled herself as they made their way up the driveway, rounded the back of the house. Up the slight stairs, she rang the bell.

Martha was surprised to see how quickly the door opened. Her mother stood there, a wide smile on her face. "That's my Martha, always on time."

Helen Alston's eyes roamed over Calvin, the first man her daughter had brought home in nearly ten years. "Umh, ain't he something," she said, unabashed. "I'm Helen, Martha's mother. Never thought I'd see this day."

Calvin extended his hand, took up hers, shook it lightly. "Nice to meet you, Mrs. Alston."

"Naw, call me Helen. Come on in, dinner's ready. Been slaving over that stove all day."

Martha headed for the dining room, Calvin behind. They waited for Mrs. Alston to bring up the rear, point out assigned seats.

"Calvin, why don't you sit at the head, Martha over there, and I'll take this one." Then she was back in the kitchen banging pots. "Martha, you helping me or what. Only got two hands."

Martha looked at Calvin, one brow raised. He nodded, smiled soft, increments to get her through the visit.

"A million times better than that Leon," her mother said, making no attempt to keep her voice low or the conversation private.

Martha scooped small white potatoes and snap beans into the ceramic bowl, said nothing.

"That Leon was no good from the start. Knew it the moment I laid eyes on him. Course you wouldn't listen to me. You never do. Knew that boy wasn't going to marry you, that he was just telling lies."

Martha picked up the platter of lamb chops and headed for the dining room. Placed it on the table and moved back to the kitchen.

"Need spread for the rolls," her mother said. Martha opened the refrigerator, which was jammed with leftovers, dozens of Tupperware and foil-wrapped edifices filling the shelves. She began shifting through the clutter.

"What you doing? You blind? It's on the door, you know that's where I keep it." But Martha had been gone from her mother's house for so long she couldn't remember. Before she could even turn to search, her mother was pushing her out of the way and reaching for it.

"Something wrong with your nose? Don't you smell them rolls burning? Stop standing there and get them out that oven."

Martha grabbed the potholders, got the rolls. Waited for further instruction. "Put them on the platter."

Martha swallowed. Put the hot bread on the plate. She had no appetite by the time they sat down.

"Didn't think she'd ever find a man. Just knew she'd end up all alone," Mrs. Alston was confessing as she worked the lamb chop with her fingers and teeth. "That Leon just messed her up. Messed up her mind and her heart. Men will do it to you, I know. Martha's daddy just up and left me and I was a good wife.

"Didn't matter one bit though. He got it in his mind he was going and he was gone." She casted her eye toward Martha. "Her father left, just broke her heart. Me, I didn't hardly care. Good riddance I say. But Martha . . . sad all the time."

Which was not the truth at all. Martha understood her father's need to escape. Applauded him for it. "I wasn't sad all the time."

"Yeah, you were, I remember. Walked around here all moody and sullen, like it was something I did."

Martha bit her tongue. Pushed her plate away.

"You ain't hardly touched your food."

"Not hungry."

"Not hungry? What you mean you ain't hungry, as much time I spent cooking and now you talking about you ain't hungry."

Martha had had enough. She stood. "I'm not hungry and I'm not staying. Why? Because I am a grown ass woman and I don't have to. I tried to be nice. Tried to do right by you and all you can do is complain about what I'm not doing and won't do. Well, you know what, Mom, you enjoy yourself by yourself. I'm out of here." She looked at Calvin. "You ready?" He was only too happy to oblige.

"I'm sorry," Calvin said as they pulled from the curb.

"Tried to warn you."

"Yeah, but I had no idea."

"See what type of mother you could have gotten?"

"I'm proud of you. It took a lot of courage to sit there and it took even more courage to walk away."

"So how come I don't feel so hot."

"Because she's your mother and it hurts."

Tears filled her eyes. "Eighteen years of that, day in day out. Could never figure out why."

"She was drunk, wasn't she?"

Martha looked out the window, nodded. "Can't remember when she wasn't."

# Chapter 21

Rachel looked around the spacious two-bedroom apartment. Nodded her head. "It nice."

"Nice?" Cliff said emphatically. "This is more than nice. It's perfect. Close access to the freeway. Take me no time to get to your house."

Rachel gave him a careful look. They were still in the just-friends category but Cliff had the hope it would change soon. "Ya plan on making frequent trips?"

He placed his hands on her shoulders, the most contact she'd allowed. Waited for her eyes to find his, but they refused to. "You asked me to take some thinking time. Well, I have and I'm ready. I need to know if you are. I've been playing by your rules for weeks now, keeping my distance. I'm watching your eyes jump all over the place, Ms. Rough-and-Tough Rachel, afraid to look me in the eye, so don't tell me you're not."

"Me not afraid to look at you," she insisted.

"Then do it." She did, but it was a hard thing to do. "Now tell me 'not yet.'" Her mouth opened but the words would not come. "Now the way I see it, we can continue on this holding pattern or we can let down our wheels and land. We can go on acting like we don't want to really be in each other's life and spent the whole time in Trinidad trying not to, or we can start before we get there."

That brow raised. "Da way you figure it? What about me? Don't I get to do some figuring in dis equation?"

"Of course you do."

She stepped back from him. "Den give me some space so me can figure."

"I did that. Time's up." He reached for her, brought her close before she could react, back away again. Kissed her like he wanted to kiss her, like she, in truth, wanted to be kissed. It was then Cliff knew—she was ready too.

"Not often a man catch me in a lie," she admitted, pulling away, catching her breath, "but den again you aren't just any man."

"I hope not."

She turned away from him, eyes about her. "Me notice da two bedrooms. Ya getting a roommate?"

"Kids."

Rachel's brow went up. "Kids?"

He had never discussed the subject with Rachel but he had felt it often. "Yeah, you know, little people running around making noise."

"Sumbody pregnant?"

Cliff's hands moved across her stomach. "Could be."

"Fast mover, aren't we, Misder Cleef. We were just friends 'til two seconds ago."

"I'm not getting any younger, Rachel."

Her smile was kind. "Me know. An maybe somewhere down dat road we come to dat point, but for now, me just want to enjoy. Me want to be greedy wit the time I spend wit ya. Don't want to have no little ones to look after yet."

"So it's not out of the question?"

"One ting me learned is nutten is ever out of de question." Rachel stared at the secondary bedroom, nodded her head. "Time come, if it's a boy, we name him Adrian."

Cliff's voice grew thick. "Of course."

She chuckled softly. "Such a tender heart ya got, Misder Cleef. And me, all rough and ting. We make a nice balance, don't ya tink?"

"We sure do, Rachel."

"So, Junie and Wint gonna help ya move in, right?"

"Yeah. Early Saturday."

"I'll come make a nice cook-up. We invite San-dee and Julie. Have a celebration."

"How did I ever stay away from you for so long?"

"You were never gone from me. Me always felt ya"—she placed his palm across her heart—"in here."

"Like now?"

"Now so much better. Now me can allow meself to feel all I wouldn't let me self before."

"Which is?"

"Lub."

"You love me, Rachel?"

She didn't answer, just drew him near, planting the tenderest of kisses upon his forehead, the button on his nose. His lips. Her mouth, warm, soft, full of love.


Sandy hated to throw it away.

Pat Metheny's *Off Ramp* was a simple pleasure Randall had brought into her life. It was really good music, and he possibly had to special order it, but she knew she could not keep it.

She looked at the cover art, the gravelly road with the huge arrow, the words TURN LEFT hot-painted into the surface. Became a barometer in her life; a truth she could no longer ignore.

Swayed.

No doubt she was. Sandy was affected, influenced, altered; a pulling going on inside of her that went beyond cards and music. There was a shifting to her world, a perusing of other possibilities, and Randall was the nexus.

For two weeks he had sent her things; some Sandy kept, others she threw away. The Pat Metheny CD would be one of them.

She wondered how much longer would he keep it up? How much longer before he got discouraged and quit? Sandy wasn't certain, only that she would not hurt Winston. Would not abandon him for a possibility because, if nothing else, Winston was an absolute.


*Where did the time go?* was all Sandy could wonder as she and Winston sat in her backyard, the near summer night warm and humid, glasses of lemonade in their hands. Just yesterday it had been March. Now here it was the middle of June.

"Can't believe this time tomorrow I'll be back home," Winston said with a sigh.

"Me neither."

"I'm sorry you couldn't make it."

Sandy sat in the darkness, eyes off, envisioning the next two weeks without Winston. He was her anchor, her grounding, her foundation, and for the first time he would not be there for her. "I'm sorry too . . . it's late, let's go in."

They rose from the patio chairs and headed into the house. "Going to hop in the shower," she told him.

Winston sat on the edge of her bed, slipped off his sandals. He went to the closet. Placed them on the floor. Something fell on his head. He looked behind him and saw a shoe box, *full of cards?* Bent down and began picking them up.

Winston had no intention of reading them, but the hand-scripted words inside of one and the date in the corner drew his attention.

June seventh, nineteen ninety-four. Seven days ago.

*Every waking moment you're on my mind.* Winston closed it. Opened another. More words, more dates. More outpourings. Only one had been signed. The most recent one, dated three days ago.

Sandy had never spoken his name, and until that moment Winston had not known it, but he had no doubt it was the one who had run scared, breaking Sandy's heart in the process.

Winston had read them all by the time Sandy returned, the sight of him sitting on her bed with her cards before him stealing her breath.

"When were you going to tell me he wanted you back?"

She found her voice, moved past the fear, defensive. "You're going through my stuff now?"

"The box fell on my head. I went to put my shoes away and it just crashed on me. Cards everywhere. All those cards he sent you. Cards you kept," which was the part that hurt the most.

A man was entitled to his feelings, *even this Randall guy,* but the fact that she kept them, all fourteen, suggested that Sandy had feelings of her own. That she had use for his declarations and could not part with them.

Cornered like a mouse. Cornered and nailed to the wall, all Sandy could offer was her truth and hoped it was enough. Even though she was found out, even though her betrayal was clear, she still was not ready to leave Winston. Still felt a strong alliance with him. Was not willing to give Randall that second chance.

"Okay. He wants me back. Has for a while. But who am I with? I'm here, with you."

"Doesn't matter where you are and not, you kept those cards Sandy. If he really didn't matter and *I* did, you wouldn't have."

Silence, full and complete, entered the room; up ahead the corner waiting to turn. It had always been there, a doorway to their goodbye, but it had seemed far away until now.

Winston stared at Sandy, his brain was working overtime, trying to complete the picture, fill in the blanks. He was searching out a reason why Sandy was in fact still with him when it was obvious that she didn't love him. He was trying to determine why she had not gone back to Randall, the one who still owned some part of her.

A man who had come into her life with such a force it broke her heart all over again when he left. A man who stirred in her such an emotional hunger that she'd kept his outpourings of love up on the shelf like good housekeeping.

The answer came swift, startling. Clarified.

*Because she loves him, but she's afraid.*

Of what? Winston looked off, his eyes searching the final answer, the last link to the heartbreaking revelation. *Of committing.* She was afraid of giving her heart away because the last few times she had it had gotten broke. First by Adrian when he died and then by Randall when he walked away from her.

*So she stayed with me because I'm a safe bet.* Sandy didn't love Winston, never would. And without love, there could be no real commitment. Without commitment, her heart took little risk.

Winston saw it clearly now. "You love him?"

"Who?" But she knew.

"Randall. You do, don't you?"

Sandy looked away. Winston waited for her answer. Her eyes found his again, confusion and hurt strumming through. "I don't know."

"You love me?" He knew she didn't, but needed for her to admit it out loud.

Her confession came slowly. "Not that way, no."

Something in him had jarred, loosened itself, slipped away. It was Sandy. In that moment he let her go. "I knew that. I've known for a while. But being with you became more important than if you loved me, became more important if you ever would."

He was looking at her with keen eyes, knowing eyes. He was peering all the way down into her soul and glimpsing secrets she herself had never dared to consider. He was seeing the whole of her, studying every tendon, every marrow she possessed.

He had always tried to protect her, help her, and Winston knew that now would be no different. He would give her the truth, the one she had been hiding from, the one in that moment, she was still unaware of.

"You do love him, Sandy, or at least on your way to loving him, but you're afraid."

"Afraid? Afraid of what?"

"Afraid of that very thing that was snatched away from you when Adrian died . . . afraid of love."

"That's crazy."

"Is it?"

"Yes, it is."

"So why are you with me when you don't love me, and why are you keeping cards from a man who you profess you don't want?"

Her mouth opened, but no answer would come.

"He was the one who was afraid, wasn't he? The guy who got scared."

"Yes."

"And that hurt you, real bad, didn't it?"

"Yes, it did," her voice pain-filled.

"If you didn't care about him, it wouldn't have mattered. But truth is you did care about him, Sandy. Still do. But you're too afraid to give him a try. Too afraid to get your heart broken again, so you stay with me because you know I'll never break your heart."

Her surprised eyes flew to his, Winston's words speaking a truth that rocked her to her core. Winston *was* safe. Winston wouldn't break her heart, hurt her feelings, run away scared. Die. He was her "absolute," wasn't that what she called him?

"Oh God," she moaned, bringing her hands to her face. "Oh," she said again, realizing what she'd done and why. She had tried to be careful with Winston, had promised that she would be good, treat him kindly but she hadn't.

She had used him. Used him as a shield. Used him as a decoy.

Sandy had taken his concern for her, his love for her, to hide away in. She had used him, *like that first time.*

Tears sprinkled the corner of her eyes. "I'm sorry, Winston, I'm so sorry."

He had no doubt. "I know you are."

"You know I'd change it if I could. Take it all back."

"It doesn't hurt too much." But the truth was it did hurt. The truth was even though he knew Sandy didn't love him, he hadn't considered that she was just using him to keep herself safe, until now.

Still, it took two to tango and he had been a willing partner. Accepted some of the blame. "I was as willing as you, wasn't I? Guess we're both guilty." He patted the space next to him. Sandy went, sat by his side, allowed his arm to slide around her shoulder, the gentle press of his hand to move her head to his chest.

"Life's been real tough for you, Sandy, I know that. And all I wanted was for you to find some comfort. I won't regret giving it to you and I'll never regret the time we had together. You give and you get in this world. Remember that. It's always a two-way street."

Brave words uttered from a crushed heart, it was what was needed to set her free. Letting her go had been the last thing Winston wanted. But he understood now. There was no other option.

From the moment they'd met, Sandy had belonged to someone else. Once again they had come full circle.

Early the next morning Winston sat in his parents' kitchen sipping a cup of Café Buestello before their trip to the airport. From the open window came the sound of his father and brother's voices as they disagreed on how best to pack the luggage in the truck.

It gave him the chance to break the news to his mother.

He had tried to tell her as she prepared his strong coffee. Knew the opportunity was missed when she left off to check her flight bag one more time. She was heading toward the bathroom when he called out to her. "Me got sumtim to tell ya."

As far as Mrs. Burton was concerned, her son did not have to speak a word. It was all over his face. But she understood the importance of letting her son tell it, so she came, taking the chair on the opposite side of him. "What is it, Wint?"

"Me and San-dee, we through."

Mrs. Burton's expression softened as she witnessed her son's pain. She reached out a hand to soothe his, empathy full in her voice. "I knew it wouldn't work, Winston. And I think some part of you knew too . . . Always trying to walk in Adrian's footsteps. But you can't. You can't be anybody but who you are."

Winston shook his head. "Ya, me getting that part."

"She decided?"

Winston nodded.

"You know I wanted to go to her a dozen times and say: 'Sandy, what are you doing? Why are you with Wint?' . . . I knew she didn't love you, Winston, and as hard as it is for you to hear that, it's just as hard for me to say it. But it's true. Did Sandy care for you? Oh, absolutely, but love, the type that takes a couple through the good times and the bad."

"Like her and Adrian," Winston said.

"Yes, exactly, she didn't have it for you. I'm sure she thought maybe she would find it, but she never did." Mrs. Burton, pulling back, stood. "Well, today's the first day of the rest of your life, Winston. And you have two choices. You can try and hold on to what never really was, or you can open your heart to all the things that can be. Adrian is gone. You don't have to walk in his shadow anymore. It's time you made your own."

She moved around the table, leaned over, and kissed his forehead. "You're a good son and a fine, fine man. Don't you ever doubt it, or forget it."

Randall had sent the last gift two days ago. Financially and ego-wise, he was now bankrupt. Even if he wasn't, he couldn't see himself sending another thing. Besides, if it were working, she would have called by now.

Every time he had bought a card, every time he put heartfelt words onto the stiff squares of paper, he had felt like he was losing a little piece of himself. Became afraid that, in the end, he would have nothing left.

It took him a while to recognize it was just fear. Fear of rejection, fear of waging the war to win her back and losing. Fear that she was really gone forever and he would spend the rest of his days longing for what he could not have.

Fear was the thing that had sent him scurrying. He had to let it go. One more try, nothing else he'd go out with a bang. Take his losses and stay away forever.

Sandy's doorbell rang.

She looked at the clock, thought about who it could be. Understood that there was some fated destiny moving through her life, starting with that box of cards falling on Winston's head. The box had been pushed back on the shelf, wedged against the wall. Earthquake proof, but somehow it had come loose and fell on Winston, *because he needed to know. We both did.*

Sandy knew in her heart who was at her front door and readied herself as she opened it, before her the first man she had wanted since Adrian. The man who had lifted the curtain on her stunted life. The one who had made the possibility of loving, a reality.

"Can I come in?" his face humbled and unsure.

A soft smile filled her face. "I think at this point it's not even a question."

Winston had gathered up the scattered pieces of her life and had assembled them into a complete picture. Sandy had been studying it ever since. She knew now, and accepted it all. Randall was who she wanted.

He drifted past her, looking good, smelling better. Sandy found herself thrust back to the first time. Recalled her assessment, thirty-ish and kind of cute, plain brown.

Randall stood in her living room, waited to ask to have a seat. Sandy did with a swing of her hand. He eased into the overstuffed taupe chair, relaxing for the first time since he'd rung her bell. "This is my last stand, you know, except now that I'm here, I don't know what to say. I guess the cards said it all."

"I have to give you credit, you never stopped trying."

"I couldn't even if I wanted to."

"I'm glad you didn't."

His expression grew soft, tender, sensing the turn in the road for them, the possibilities that swayed like new leaves in the breeze. "Are you?"

"Yes, I am."

"You know I meant all those things I wrote."

"Yeah, I know."

"So do I get that second chance?"

"Are you still scared?"

"I wouldn't be here if I was, Sandy. I think you know that."

Yes, she did. She knew it when she asked. Knew it before he answered. Sandy had known it from the moment he had told her he loved her.

Because love *was* the ultimate power. Love conquered all. This Sandy had witnessed, this Sandy knew to be true. Love, the thing that had robbed her of so much, the one thing that had sent her fleeing, now welcomed her back with open arms.

Janice was indulging herself.

Even though the television was on, her mind was on Cliff and Rachel. Cliff and Rachel together. Cliff and Rachel laughing and having fun. Cliff and Rachel dancing the night away at some reggae club then making love till dawn.

She looked around her, the four walls that had been a comfort, now appearing to be closing in. She couldn't remember the last time she had ventured out besides to go to work and run some errands. Knew this night it was all going to change.

She got up and went through her closet. Pulled out clothes, high heels, and took a bath. With care, she scrubbed and rubbed until her whole body glowed. Dried herself, stood naked in front of her mirror applying makeup and fixing her hair.

She had never gone out alone, but this was a new chapter in her life. So she got in her car and drove to Le Club. She wasn't inside its walls five minutes before someone asked her to the dance floor, and by evening's end she was following him home.

"You awake?"

The light from the windows was muted, but not enough to hold back the brilliance of a new day. Janice squinted, saw a man hovering over her, blinked as she tried to remember his name.

"Got to get up. Got to get going." He turned away, showing the broad back she had clung to, the slim waist and meaty behind. He didn't have to turn around for her to remember that part of him, the memory of it filling her, rushing her with hot shame.

He left the bedroom and she took a hot second to get oriented. Tried to remember where she was at, even which borough. She had

had a few drinks last night, maybe too many to count, and all of it was covered in fog.

Carefully she swung her legs out of bed, felt cool air on her body. Tried to remember where her clothes were. She stood up slow, the contemporary wood bedroom furniture telling her at least he had some means of supporting himself.

But who was he? What was his name? Janice couldn't remember. She saw them dancing last night and his smile that seemed affixed to his face, especially when she said yes to his invitation home.

But where was home? She moved to the window looked out and saw a backyard. A play gym, Fisher Price toys in a sandbox. She looked around and noticed the family portrait for the first time on the dresser.

Him, a woman, and three kids he couldn't deny.

Her stomach churned. She just wanted to get away. Janice saw her skirt, the silk top on a heap on the floor. Could not find her panties, the matching bra. She was searching the confines of the king-size bed when he returned, his once-naked body now covered in a T-shirt and shorts.

"Really, you got to go," he said, with a point to the clock.

"Can't find my underwear."

"Well, you ain't got time to look. She and the kids due back soon."

She and the kids, connecting to him, for whom Janice had no name. She hurried into her skirt, slipped the silk shirt over her head. Looked around for her pocketbook, saw him sweep up two empty condom packs with his hand.

He showed her to the door, opened it, and gave her a gentle nudge out. Closed it with such force, a breeze ruffled her back. She stood on the top step for a hot minute, looking for her car. Spotted it up the street and quickly made her way.

Janice looked up at the street sign. Saw 162nd Street and 93th Avenue. Knew where she was, but not exactly how she got there. She opened her car door, put one leg in, the cool breeze reminding her she didn't have on any underwear.

It had been her favorite set.

The black lacy demibra and matching lace thong. She had bought them at Victoria's Secret and they had fit to a tee. That's what made her hang her head over her steering wheel and let loose fast hot tears.

Not Cliff, not Rachel, not the married man whose name she didn't know. It was her underwear, plain and simple, gone from her forever.

Sandy had found love, lost it, made a second attempt, failed. But now it had returned and it felt as if it could stay awhile.

Randall was back in her life, bringing a different energy to her world; her heart opening in a way it hadn't in a while—without restraint.

They were in his backyard, the afternoon sun sprinkles of light and shadow through the shade of the tall oak trees. Inside the tiny gazebo, Sandy leaned against the rail and sipped ice tea. She ran a finger along the smooth stained edge of the gazebo. "How long?" she asked.

"How long what?"

"To make this, how long?"

Randall shrugged. "Took my time so I took a couple of weeks. But this?" He grabbed the edge of a two by four. "Probably could knock it out in half a day."

"How much?"

"How much what?"

"To have one built? My backyard is so plain. Think one of these would make it better."

Randall smiled at her, still feeling the newness to them. "Wouldn't charge you."

"Of course you would. Time is money."

He took up her hand, kissed the back. "How could I charge you? Be like charging myself."

"Really."

"Oh, you don't believe me?" Randall shook his head. "You know, I'm looking at you in my tiny gazebo that most people laugh at it cause it's so small, but you see not only its purpose, but its beauty. Here you are, in my backyard, drinking my tea, here with me, and my heart wants to stop every time I think about how close I came to not having this. How could I possibly charge you for anything?"

"We did have some funky moments though."

"Yes, we did. When I showed up at your friend's to collect my money, I could have kept ice cream cold with the frosty reception you gave me."

"Can't blame me. You invaded my space not once, but twice."

"Yeah, you're right. But it's over and done now."

Sandy nodded. "Over and done."

Later that night Sandy called Martha and told her the news. Britney was the second to hear it, with a huge apology tossed in. Janice was the last on Sandy's list, but she got no answer. Decided to try again tomorrow and went to bed.

The next evening she called Janice again, but getting no answer, she tried her job the day after and was told Janice was out sick. Sandy immediately called Janice at home and the phone just kept on ringing. Something was wrong, and with her stuck on the job, responsibility fell to Britney.

Britney didn't know what to expect but she knew enough to drop her daughter over at her mother's house before she got there. Sandy hadn't elaborated. Just said she hadn't been able to reach Janice in a couple of days and she had called in sick, but not answering her phone.

She entered the Rochdale Village complex, went into the lobby, and rang the buzzer. Waited for Janice to answer. Janice didn't, which really worried her. Britney had seen Janice's car parked in her designated parking spot, so knew that she was inside. But there was no answering of the buzzer, which meant maybe she was unconscious or dead.

For a hot minute Britney thought to call the police, but decided that was a final option. An elderly man entered, glanced at her face, the swell of her belly. Held the inner lobby door open for her, for which she was grateful.

Britney moved to the elevator bank. Got inside when the car arrived. Worried and feeling periled, she hoped Janice was okay. She got off the elevator, went, and rang the doorbell. When she got no answer, she knocked on the door. She added her voice, calling, "Janice, are you in there?" nearly giving up hope before she heard Janice tell her to go away.

Relieved, then mad, Britney shouted back, "I've dropped my child at my momma's and came all this long way, pregnant as I am. I'm not going away and you're going to let me in."

Janice did. "Head cold."

It was evident in the tissues stuffed in Janice's hands, how red her nose looked, and how swollen her eyes were. "So why aren't you an-swering the phone?"

"Nobody important ever calls."

The head cold became something else, something deeper, some-thing emotionally unwell. Britney noticed the apartment for the first time. All the blinds drawn and there were a stack of dishes in the sink. Dirty clothes were strewn around, the garbage can was overflowing, and empty Chinese food containers were everywhere.

From the whiff Britney got, Janice hadn't showered in a while. "Since when you become so nasty?" Britney wanted to know.

"Like that record. I'm just a nasty girl."

Britney's face pinched. "You may be a little crazy, a whole lot lonely, and even a little funky, but you ain't never been no nasty girl."

A tear slid down Janice's eye. Then another. She opened her mouth and told her latest tale.

"And you don't even know his name?" Britney found it hard to be-lieve.

"No. And he's got my favorite bra and panties."

"Bra and panties? Girl, be glad you got your life. He could have been one of those crazies. Might not ever heard from you again."

But Janice couldn't let it go. It was the cause for her sadness. Everything else she could deal with but the loss of her most favorite lingerie had shot her world straight through. She tried to explain it to Britney, but Britney wasn't listening to that warped tale.

What Britney was paying close attention to was what wasn't being said. It took her time to digest it, her heart quaking when she got the full picture.

Janice, who had probably been dancing on the edge for a while, had taken the plunge.

Britney had known Janice's mother but had never cared for her much. Self-involved to the point of neglect, it was she who Britney called.

"There's nothing wrong with her. Her heart's a little sad, that's all," she told Britney.

"No, Mrs. Duprey, there is something very wrong with your daugh-ter. Depressed over a pair a thong panties and bra ain't normal."

"What do you mean?"

"Just like I said. She's sitting in the next room downright weepy be-

cause some man kept her bra and panties. She had not bathed, left
her house, or answered her phone in days because some man kept
her drawers. Now what do you call that?"

"What am I supposed to do?"

"You're supposed to act like a mother and get over here."

"And then what?"

"I don't have the slightest idea. But I do know I am six months
pregnant and your daughter has lost it. That maybe somehow, *we* can
help *her* together."

"On my way."

"Good." Britney hung up, rubbed the bottom of her belly. Picked
up the phone. Called Sandy then Martha.

People loved disturbances. Loved fires, car accidents, and out-of-
the-everyday dramas. This was the reason the pretty woman strapped
in a strait jacket and screaming about her underwear snatched the attention of the residents of Janice's building.

Janice was restrained but Sandy needed the same confinement.
She was fighting against the strong arms of Martha and Calvin as they
loaded Janice into the back of the ambulance.

"I got to go with her."

"You can't," Martha and Calvin insisted back, holding her until the
swirly lights moved out of the cul-de-sac, disappeared up the street.
Holding her until Sandy broke down in tears, the gathered crowd
slowed to move away, already missing the taste of thrill in their mouths.

They let her go as Sandy's sobs turned to sniffles. Sniffles lessened
and she was able to hold her head up, searching out Mrs. Duprey in
the crowd. She knew she would be the first to see Janice, felt a need to
pass a message. Hurried toward her, calling out her name.

"Tell her I love her, will you do that? Tell her, if nobody else does, I
do."

It was a tiny token Sandy wanted to give to her old best friend, but
it came off as an insult as Mrs. Duprey snapped, "Like I don't?" and
walked away.

They were inside Janice's apartment, the four of them. Clearing
out, cleaning out, and straightening up. "Should have seen it coming," Sandy said, hand to eyes occasionally, the sorrow still with her.

"There was nothing to see," Martha reminded. "Janice was being

Janice. How did we know? We didn't. Until now." She turned toward Britney. "Fast thinking, Britney."

Britney nodded. She had paused from the helping, taking the load off her feet. The bottom of her back had begun to hurt, and sitting lessened the pain. But the dull ache was still with her, and she rubbed it with her hand.

"You okay?" It was Calvin who noticed.

Britney nodded, face a bit pinched. "Just stress. Been on my feet for a good little while. Body's not used to it, that's all."

Calvin accepted her explanation, but kept his eye on her. Waited for the hand to stop the rubbing, for the slight grimace to leave her face.

"She's going to feel so alone," Sandy pondered out loud. "Thirty days, no contact. It's going to tear her up."

"Or maybe give her the breather she needs," were Martha's words as she gathered up dirty clothes from the floor.

"What about her bills? Her rent and stuff?"

"I guess her mother will have to handle it," Martha said. "You know I ain't got the best momma in the world either, but at least Helen wouldn't have had to be convinced that I needed help. Brit, I swear you were good, 'cause if it were me . . ."

A moan flew out of Britney's mouth, high-pitched and surprising, then she was clutching her stomach like it was trying to get away.

*What next?* the two women and one man were thinking as they sat in the waiting room at LaGuardia Hospital, waiting to hear the news about Britney. Maurice was pacing back and forth like a caged tiger. He hadn't been there to see it, but had heard—Britney had been bleeding badly from the womb.

He wasn't the smartest man but even he understood that, modern medicine or not, heavy bleeding wasn't good for Britney or the baby. That something had gone terribly wrong. He just wanted to know what.

They had kicked him out when he got loud and boisterous, insisting they were handling his wife too rough, just making her pain worse. Now he was out in the waiting room with everyone else, a security guard eyeing him for good measure.

The triage nurse stuck her head through the Plexiglas. "Maurice Campbell?"

"Present," Maurice answered, hand shooting up.

The nurse motioned him to the window, rose, her mouth close to his ear. No one could hear the conversation, only the motion of Maurice's head. One nod, another, followed by "I understand," the door opening to him like magic.

Maurice entered, was met by a doctor in a white coat. He tried to breathe as he took the hand extended, tried to quell his fears.

"Let's go to my office, shall we?" the doctor asked kindly.

But Maurice refused to take a step. Wanted to know and know now. "The baby? Is it okay?"

When the doctor faltered, insisting that they go where it was private, Maurice turned and headed toward the curtained cubicles, whipping back the hang of cotton. When he saw his wife's eyes filled with relief and sweet joy, he knew the doctors words weren't even warranted. They were going to be okay, his wife and his unborn child.

They crowded into the diner on Queens Boulevard across from Macy's. Sandy, Martha, Calvin, and Maurice. No one was really hungry, just weary, the long day coming to an end.

"Two lives saved," Calvin said as he put down his coffee cup.

"Three," Maurice corrected. "And sweet Jesus, I'm so damn happy, I could shit myself. If she'd lost that baby . . ." His voice faded, his head shook, tears springing into his eyes.

Calvin reached over, rubbed the tense spine. "But she hasn't, Mo, all that matters."

Sandy picked at the grain granules on her English muffin. She had ordered it but couldn't get herself to actually pick it up and take a bite. "Wondering how's she doing?"

"Janice?" Martha asked.

"Yeah. Wondering if she scared, still screaming."

"They'll keep her sedated until she's able to deal with things better." Martha looked off. "But you want to know the scariest thing about it? Could have been me, or you, all strapped up and out of our mind."

Sandy nodded. Had felt the same truth. Recalled the days she had danced on the edge. How close she came. Counted her blessings.

Maurice took up a napkin, blew his nose. His eyes swept between Sandy and Martha. "Doctor said she don't need any more stress, y'all understanding me? Whatever mess y'all going through or not, you keep my wife out of it. Don't be calling up and asking her to do jack, you got that?"

The women did and it hit them like a freight train on well-oiled tracks.

Once they had been four strong. Now they were two.

# Chapter 22

It had been a while since Sandy had been deemed the deliverer of bad news, but she knew that's what her parents were thinking as they took up space in her mother's kitchen.

She had gone over to see them. Had gone to share the news about both herself and Janice. She started with herself.

"Me and Winston are through," she began. "And please don't ask how or why, just that we are."

But her parents paid her no mind. Her father, beating her mother to the punch. "What happened?"

"Daddy, it's a long story, personal and I don't want to share it."

"But he was such a great guy, Sandy."

"And he still is," she responded, "but just not for me."

Her mother brought up the rear. "Is it someone else?"

"Is there someone else? Yes. It is because of this someone else? No. It was my choice and my choice alone."

"But you two were in love," her father stated.

Sandy bit her tongue. It was not to be their business. And responding would open a whole discussion she was not ready to have. She changed the conversation. "And," she took a deep breath. "Janice is in Creedmore."

"In where?"

"Creedmore." Sandy shook her head, sadness revisiting her with freshness. "She lost it. Last week. Tried to reach her. Couldn't. I was at work, so I sent Britney over. That's when we found out. Strait jacket, the whole nine yards."

"Oh dear," Jeanne Hutchinson murmured.

"Does Cliff know?"

"Haven't had a chance to tell him. But I will." She saw the look in her parents' eyes. Saw them trying to connect the dots. "It's not his fault. I've known Janice a long time, and believe me, she got to Creedmore all by herself."

"So how is she doing?"

"I don't know, Mom. No visitors or anything for thirty days. Her mother's not talking to me, so I can't find out."

If Janice was Jeanne Hutchinson's main concern, the new man in his daughter's life was Samuel Hutchinson's.

"So, tell me about this man you've met."

It was the first smile Sandy gave since she arrived. "His name is Randall Hoakes. He's the carpenter that came and repaired my basement."

"Carpenter." It was not a question.

"Yes, Daddy, a carpenter and a very good one."

"Do we get to meet him?" Sandy's mother asked.

"When the time is right, yeah," was all Sandy would commit to.

There had been no formal discussion, no set date, but when Randall came and picked up Sandy for a movie date, she knew that night would be the night.

He arrived at her house driving his Vintage Mercedes, top down. Asked her if she wanted to drive it.

It didn't take more than that for Sandy to slip behind the wheel, the afternoon sun brilliant in the sky above her. She glided her hands over the warm leather of the steering column. Adjusted the side and rearview mirrors, flipped the visor, smiled at herself and, with a deep breath, put the car in Drive.

Into the flow of traffic she moved, the wind in her hair, the stereo up, gathering stares from pedestrians as she moved the well-oiled machine down the street. The 1979 Mercedes 450 SL was a classic and it made her feel very classy driving it.

Randall didn't say anything, didn't flinch, press an invisible brake, or anything as she swung onto the Cross Island. He just took in the scene, bopped his head to the music, and allowed Sandy her moment.

At the movie theater, he held her hand for the whole picture, let her hand feed him popcorn, a different energy moving between them. He let her drive back, felt her joy as she pushed the button, the top gliding into place, and cut off the engine. "That was incredible," she said with a breathy sigh.

He reached over, smoothed down her windblown curls, his fingers lingering along her face, sending a rush through her as she got out of the car, into her front yard and up the steps.

They got as far as the foyer, the door barely closing before he was taking her into his arms. They began kissing, hardly separated enough to move upstairs to her bedroom.

"Condoms," Randall wangled proudly, dropping them on her nightstand and easing off his shirt. His chest, muscled, defined before her as she eased out of her jeans, her top. Bra straps were coming down when he stopped her. "No, leave it on."

Sandy was confused, uncertain, felt the beginnings of dread when she saw the look in his eyes. She knew enough to stand there, to allow a pause, letting him drink in the sight of her rich chocolate skin against the brilliant white satin bra and matching panties.

That she was doing something to him without effort, energy, or thought was an aphrodisiac that made her body pulse. He came up to her, his fingers cool against her shoulders, and planted a kiss on her neck. Slowly he moved, his breath warm along her collarbone, marking an invisible trail down to her cleavage.

She went to reach for him but he urged her hands down. "Be still," he whispered, making her shiver. With care, and finesse, he undid the front hook of her bra, using his mouth and his teeth and no hands. Only a skilled man could do that, that much Sandy knew. She had had trouble with the catch from time to time.

Cool air moved in where the hook came undone, followed by long warm breaths from Randall's mouth. She longed to touch him, reach out and hold him, but resisted as his lips shifted the cup of one bra, his tongue finding a hardened nipple.

She became lost to the world, lost to all things except for the feel of Randall's mouth and tongue on her body. Then he was leading her backward, her legs bumping the bed, desire sending her aback.

His kissed her stomach.

Nudged at the elastic waist of her panties with his nose, moving it down, deliberate and slow until they clung to her hips. Using his teeth, he urged them down to her thighs and then pulled them over her feet.

"Roll over," a command she could not refuse.

With joy she did so, the weight of him suddenly heavy against her spine. So heavy she nearly lost her breath. Then the pressure was easing, warm little kisses pleasing, hot little breaths playing tic-tac-toe along her spine. She reached back behind her, wanting to touch him anywhere, but again he forced her hands back.

The bed shifted, the weight and warmth of his body vanishing as she heard the sound of a zipper being unzipped. Then he was back on her, his weight light, yet full. Skin to skin, a delicious mix.

She felt his hardness, moved against it with slithery anticipating, kisses on her neck making her moan. Different, intense, it was a new journey he was taking her on and Sandy was ready for the ride.

He eased off her slow, wrapped strong arms around her until they were spooned, finger gliding her hips, the slope of her waist. They went on that way, a duet of motion, he touching, she refraining, trembling hard with need.

He moved from her, a second becoming five. In her mind's eye she knew what he was doing. Sandy rolled onto her back, eyes closed, breaths deep, her arms wrapping around him as he came back to her.

He guided himself in, moved slow, easy, his lips seeking hers, a deep explosion in the making.

Two empty condom wrappers.

It took a while for the sight to register, to feel the undercurrent in which their presence drifted. It took a second to find the wrong in the picture, its arrival jabbing her hard. They'd only made love once.

Sandy tried not to let it bother her but the more she stared at them, the more it did, the sound of her shower running full blast stirring up in the mix. She tried not to make it matter, unimportant, be unconcerned. But she couldn't as she waited for his return.

"I was just lying up here thinking about how I haven't even caught my breath yet and you already showered." Caught off guard, he didn't know what to say. Sandy didn't give him any time to answer. "And the two condoms? I can understand one, but two?"

"Sometimes they break," he managed, his voice plaintive. "Got caught out there one time like that . . . consequences weren't pretty."

"What does that mean?"

Randall looked at her, suddenly full of secrets. They swarmed about his face like locusts, buzzy, consistent. "Long time ago. I mean a real long time ago. Like when I was in my teenage years long time ago. Messed around with somebody I shouldn't have, but I was horny and she was willing. Word had been swirling around school that she had VD, but naked she looked fine to me."

Which explained a large part of Randall's hesitation if the story was leading to where Sandy thought it would lead. She looked fine too. And even though she wasn't positive, no doubt the idea that she had been exposed became mixed with Randall's long ago experience and had affected him.

Randall sighed, sat back, looked off. "So we did the do, next thing I know I got the burning. I was too ashamed to do anything about at first. Tried to ignore it. I was seeing somebody else at the time but she wasn't giving it up. Then one day we were alone and she says, "Okay," just like that. Now you have to understand I had been wanting her for, like, six months, and burn or no burn, I was going for the gold. I knew I needed protection, so I ran to the store, came back. Got in there and didn't want to come out."

It was a different Randall talking, a younger, juvenile Randall telling the story. His eyes were lit with memory, the moment long ago, moving through him.

"Condoms are only good for one time, I knew that, but I was being greedy and decided to go for two. But I only had one. I figured it was rubber, it was strong, it'll be okay . . . it wasn't. When I pulled out, the condom had broken. There was blood on it. She had been a virgin. First time out and she get's VD . . . from me."

He brought his hands to his face. Rubbed it a little. "She never forgave me, I couldn't see why she should. So I just started double bagging it, not because of you, but because of me. I've been doing it ever since."

It was a good story, but didn't explain it all. "What about the shower?"

"Some habits just die hard," he answered with a shake of his head. "I made the mistake of coming home unwashed. My mother smelled it on me and knew what I was up to. I didn't mind my father knowing, but my moms? So I just started taking showers whenever I could, that's all."

That's all. So little that, just a few seconds ago, was so much. "So you okay with me?" she needed confirming.

"After all this, all I went through to be here with you, you still asking?"

Sandy didn't back down. "Yeah."

Coast cleared, he moved toward the bed, sat near her. "So there won't be any misunderstanding, Two condoms? Habit. Showers right after? Habit, all right?"

Sandy smiled. Relief filled her. The boogeyman was finally gone from under her bed.

July 21st dawned bright and sunny, but inside Sandy was an ominous cloud of apprehension. She had wanted this moment from the moment she'd learned she'd wait to have it, but now that it was upon her, she was full of uncertainty.

Today was Janice's thirty-first day in Creedmore. Today Sandy would get a chance to visit. Middle of the week, Martha could not get off from work and Britney was on bed rest. Sandy took a personal day, got up early, got showered and dressed, and stopped off at the florist.

She didn't know if Janice could receive flowers but brought them anyway, wanting to bring some joy into her friend's life. She didn't know what to expect. Sandy had no idea what it would be like inside the infamous mental hospital. All she knew was she was going to see her oldest friend and that she loved her.

She entered the hospital and signed in. Took her pass and headed toward the elevator. Got off and went to the nurses' desk. Gave her name and was shown the waiting room. The sight depressed her.

People of every age, race, creed, and color filled it. Visitors uncomfortable with friends and loved ones who had not been able to maintain the balance of sanity, whose own minds had sent into a deep and dark despair, everywhere she looked.

A pity welled in her heart for them, then rebounded and claimed it as she realized she was one of them.

Sandy took a seat, waited, eyes quick on the door. She barely recognized the scrubbed face, clear-eyed, serene smiling woman that appeared. Something was gone from Janice, leaving her all brand new.

"Hey," all Sandy could say, rising and moving toward her, embracing her, surprised by the feel of skin and bones beneath the pajamas and robe.

"Hey, back."

Janice pulled away, eyes careful over Sandy. "I didn't know if you were coming or not."

Sandy shook her head. "How could I not come? So how are you doing?"

"I think it was the best thing that could have happened to me, believe it or not," Janice offered with a careful smile. "Are those for me?"

Sandy looked at the flowers in her hand. "Yeah, forgot I had them."

Janice took them, brought them to her nose. She inhaled, let the breath go. "Let's go over there and sit. Well, I'm not crazy, according to my doctor. I was just overwhelmed. Emotional breakdown, is what they call it. I had too much going on inside of me. It had to come out."

Sandy put her hand to her heart, relieved. "I'm so happy to hear that."

"I still can't believe I was screaming about underwear."

"It was horrible."

"But I'm much better now. I feel like somebody unstopped a sink in me. All sorts of things just let loose."

"How's the food?"

Janice smiled, tugged on her robe. "Can't you tell? I'm ready to storm the kitchen and show those folks how to really burn."

"So when are you coming home?"

"Tomorrow."

"You have a ride?"

"My mom." For the first time a hint of pain flashed in her eyes. "Think you and the girls would come over? Keep me company? Be like old times."

"Of course we will," Sandy answered quickly.

"Bed rest," Maurice was insisting over the phone. "At home, in bed."

"I know what it means, Maurice."

"Then good, so you know Britney won't be there."

"Can I at least speak to her?"

"She's resting."

"Maurice, let me speak to her."

"Whose phone you calling on? Mine? Whose wife you want to speak to? Mine. And if I say she ain't coming to the phone, then she ain't coming."

"Maurice, stop playing."

"Who's playing?"

Sandy sighed, a wall unmovable before her. "Will you tell her I called?"

"Oh yeah, I'll tell her." He hung up. Sandy stared at the phone, hating him for his ignorance but admiring his determination. Still one monkey wasn't going to stop her show. Sandy knew what she had to do and did it.

Maybe it was too much bed rest. Maybe Britney was gravely ill. Whatever the reason, she did look like death warmed over when she answered the door bright and early around seven the next morning.

"Hey," she said, rubbing her belly, pushing wild hair from her eyes.

"Hey. Now listen. I got to get to work, but I tried to call you and your husband wouldn't let me talk to you."

Britney nodded. "Yeah, he told me you called."

"He tell you why?"

"Janice is coming home today. You want me to go on over later."

So he had told her. "You need a ride?"

Britney's face screwed up. "A ride? I'm not going."

"Come on, Brit."

The hand on the belly shifted into a faster rub. "Uh-uh. Messing around with crazy-ass Janice almost cost me my baby. I ain't going nowhere till my baby gets here."

Sandy couldn't believe it. "So you are just going to be a prisoner to this house?"

"What prisoner, Sandy? I like my house and bed rest suits me fine. I don't cook, I don't clean, don't do nothing but lay around. Maurice and my momma do the rest. Shoot, girl, I'm living and will probably be the last time I get the chance." Her head shook. "No, I ain't coming. Count me out."

Anger found her and just as quick, let Sandy go. She understood. She had never raised a child herself but had heard stories, had witnessed Britney's weariness firsthand. And she had almost lost the baby.

Sandy smiled. "I hear you, girl." Reached over and gave Britney a hug. "You take all the bed rest you need."

"Tell Janice I said hi," Britney decided.

Sandy nodded, headed back toward her car.

It had only been a month but it seemed like a lifetime since Janice had been away as the three friends tried to find the comfort zone they once knew. Conversations started only to get stumped. Empty embarrassing silences came and went the whole time. By the time they were wrapping up dessert and saying goodbye at the door, everyone was relieved. They promised to get together soon but no one made any attempt to say when.

"Whew, that was sad," Martha said as they headed toward her car.

"Worst get-together we ever had."

"She lost so much weight."

"You noticed, huh. She said bad hospital food."

"It could be. You know how she liked to cook."

"Think she'll be okay?"

"I guess. They wouldn't have let her out if they thought she wasn't ready."

"It's like I don't even know her anymore."

"Yeah, I got that feeling too."

"Look at us," Sandy said with a shake of her head. "Britney on bed rest, Janice off in her own world. What happened to us?"

"Maybe that time we were tight has served its purpose, I don't know. But I do know that no matter what does and doesn't happen between us as friends, we have to take care of ours." Martha opened the car door. "So go on home, call up Randall, 'cause I'm sure going home and call up mine."

# *Chapter 23*

Sandy did not like the taste of rubber in her mouth, but she liked the feel of Randall inside it. Being with Adrian had made her a master of safe sex, and without barely a noticeable interruption, Sandy had slipped the condom between her teeth and in a heartbeat both it and Randall's penis was slipping past her lips.

He jumped up so quickly his hipbone banged her head, his penis bobbing *interruptus*. "What are you doing?"

"Trying to give you head," she answered, knowing her next words would rush him with guilt and something else, fault. "With a condom."

For the first time Randall noticed the condom midway his penis. He didn't know whether to laugh or cry. Found his head shaking in awe and utter surprise. "When?" he went to ask, some abrupt irony finding him, filling him with a grin.

"When do you think?"

It took a hot second for Randall to realize he was the only one seeing the humor, that Sandy was staring, peeved. "Did you really think I'd do that? Did you?"

It took a while for him to answer. "I'm sorry."

"That's not answering the question."

"I said I was sorry."

If it had been something trivial and unimportant, something that did not scrape at her heart, Sandy might have relinquished to his plea to forgive him, accepted that he was feeling remorse. But it was about who she was and how he perceived her.

"Better," he said softly.

"Better than what?"

"Than before. Give me credit for that much."

She took an accounting of where they had been, where they were now. A moment passed before she conceded, agreed. "Better."

"You got any other tricks I need to know about?"

She allowed the slight humor to push back the rest of her anger. Gave a barely willing smile. "Beyond some real freaky thing that involved Saran Wrap and lots of honey, no."

"Saran Wrap?"

"Kidding."

"It's a whole new world for me . . . got to realize that." His eyes did a low sweep. "I look at you sometimes and just want to put my mouth places."

"Quit it," because such a thing was a far-off dream.

"It's the truth."

"Don't be talking up things you can't follow through on."

"Maybe one day . . ."

"Give or take a decade."

"Not long."

"I'll be so old and funky by then, you wouldn't want to."

"I'd wait."

"Would you?"

"Yeah, I would."

"I'm going for another test soon," the words hurting her.

"Where?"

"My doctor in Hollis."

He looked at her for a long time, deciding things. "Want company?"

Fat.

It had always been a part of Britney's life but she was accumulating more and more of it every day. At five-six, she was tipping the scales at two hundred and fifty-seven. Baby or no baby, she was heading for scary limits.

Being on bed rest didn't help. Not having to lift more than her
body to go to the bathroom or head to the kitchen didn't help either. With three more months to go before she delivered, Britney
understood she could head quickly toward the three-hundred mark,
that doctor's orders or no doctor's orders, she had to be more ac-
tive.

She eased from the bed and found a pair of Maurice's sweat pants
and a T-shirt. Put them over her portly body and then took slow near
painful steps. She heard her mother in the kitchen readying an afternoon lunch. Looked around her for something she could do.

The carpets looked okay but she knew they hadn't been vacuumed
in a few days. It was a good way to get the blood pumping so she went
and retrieved the Hoover from the closet. She was rolling it toward
the living room when her mother appeared, dismayed and dead set
against what Britney was obviously going to do.

"You're supposed to be in bed," her mother warned, taking the vacuum away from her reach. "And you certainly aren't supposed to be
doing any cleaning. That's my job."

"Just tired of laying down all the time, Mom. I'm packing on
pounds by the hour. I need to do something."

Mrs. Weller looked at her only child. She knew her heart and soul
because she had raised her. "You need to worry about that baby you
carrying. Gaining weight is what happens when you're pregnant.
Can't be worried about it now."

Britney had always been chubby, as had her mother. Diet and exer-
cise had never existed in her household growing up. Being big was
just the way of life. But she didn't want that for herself anymore.

She wanted to go back to the gorgeous size twenty with an eye out
for the near-illusive eighteen. Pregnancy had pushed her up to a
twenty-six, and though she would lose some when the baby was born,
it wouldn't be nearly enough.

"I got to do something."

"Only thing you have to do, Britney, is take care of yourself and
make sure that baby comes here healthy." With that, her mother took
the vacuum cleaner back to the closet. Headed for the kitchen to finish her cooking.

Birds tweeting.

Britney hadn't noticed it when she first came into the room, but in
the silence of what she needed to do, it rode the hot breeze through

the open window. It drew her, making her part the sheer curtains and .
press her face to the dusty screen, breathing deeply. When was the last
time she had even been outdoors, felt sunshine on her face, fresh air
in her lungs?

For weeks the act of having to do absolutely nothing had lulled her
into a passivity where all she did was eat and sleep. But that wasn't getting it anymore. She needed to be outside, even if it was just to sit in
her own backyard.

Britney went to the kitchen and opened the side door.

"Where you going now?" her mother wanted to know.

"Outside. Get some fresh air." Britney closed the door behind her.

For the first twenty minutes it felt like some delicious guilty pleasure, being out of bed and outdoors. For the first twenty minutes the
world felt brand new. But the patio chair, while padded, wasn't that
comfortable and Britney found herself wanting more.

She wasn't certain what that "more" entailed, only that it would be
some nonstraining activity that did not dictate a lot of energy. A
movie popped into her head. A movie, some popcorn, and the shel-
tered darkness as pictures rolled across a giant screen sounded like a
plan.

Britney went back into the house and put on real clothes.

"I'm calling Maurice," her mother said as she watched her daughter kiss her grandbaby goodbye, pocketbook on her shoulder, car keys
in hand. "You supposed to be resting," her mother insisted as Britney
opened the front door to a new freedom. "I'll call him," her mother
insisted.

"Go right ahead," Britney tossed, waddling down the steps and
heading for her car. With a wave of her hand, she got behind the
wheel, made some adjustments on the seat and the steering column.
Eased out of the driveway.

It was late afternoon when she exited the darkened theater, the
bright sun making her squint. Britney stood there a moment on the
sidewalk, testing her endurance, the well-being of her body. Felt fine.

She thought to call home to assure her mother she was okay. Went
to the pay phone and did just that. When she headed for her car and
got behind the wheel, Britney realized she wasn't ready to go home
just yet.

She sat there thinking where it was she wanted to go, what other options she had. Realized that something important was gone from her, something that had been both filling and comforting.

Britney went off to reclaim it.

Britney didn't realize the walk was so long. She didn't know it until she was only halfway through it. She found herself leaning against a lamp post holding her breath, sweaty and panting. People moved past her, giving her looks, but no one stopped to see if she was all right or needed assistance. She saw herself as they no doubt saw her: She could have been pregnant or *just fat*. No doubt they had chosen fat. Fat and all alone.

Her mother was nowhere to be found. Maurice was nowhere to be found. No one she knew was around her and the thought made her heart race. She should have heeded her mother's words, the doctor's advice, Maurice's insistence. She should have just stayed home, in bed until the pregnancy was finished.

Britney never should have tempted fate like this, putting herself and her child at risk. But she had and there was only one choice now. She had to either head back toward her car or continue on her destination. Her heart made the choice.

Janice had not returned to work yet but had been seeing a therapist twice a week. While it was a painful journey, it was a needed one, she'd come to realize, as she let loose her demons with the comfort of a professional.

Sometimes the sessions sent her on incredible highs; other times they plunged her to despondent lows. Today's session left her somewhere in the middle, and as she made her way home, she knew before she made supper, turned on the television, or any of that, she would commit feelings into her journal.

Her journal had become her friend and ally, had become the comfort her friends used to give. Even though Sandy called her from time to time, she had not seen her in a while. Ditto Martha. Britney had other concerns, and while that had hurt a little bit, counseling had made her come to terms with it.

So she could not believe her eyes when she saw what looked like Britney lumbering slowly and painfully toward her apartment building. Janice thought maybe it was somebody else. She opened her mouth to call out her name, but it got caught on her tongue. Suppose she was wrong?

Being taken out of her apartment in a strait jacket, ranting and raving about her underwear, had caused public scrutiny to become a new issue. The idea that she could be wrong, could shout a name, get no response but furtive glances from her neighbors, stopped her.

She increased her footing, moving closer with deft and speed. When she reached the lobby steps, she saw that it was indeed her friend. "Britney, what are you doing here?"

Britney turned, relief filling her, her heart trying to find a more settling rhythm. "Coming to see you," she managed in between pants. "Feeling just about faint. Can we go upstairs?"

Feet up, air-conditioning on, ice water by her side, Britney felt better. She had phoned home, letting her mother and Maurice know where she was, that she was okay and would be there in a little while. As the cool air found the sweaty parts of her body, the cool water bringing comfort to her parched throat, she felt a hundred percent better.

"I wasn't coming back here, you know. Not until the baby was born. But an emptiness came into me today and I knew I couldn't stay away."

"Well, I'm glad you wanted to come but I don't think coming was a good idea."

"I thought I was going to pass out. People passing by me, looking but not even stopping to see if I was okay." Britney shook her head. "I'm thinking, what's wrong with these people, can't they see I need some help? But they didn't. They didn't know, didn't want to know . . . like me and how I felt after you came home. Your problems was your problems and I wasn't getting involved."

"But you did. You found me first. Got help."

"I meant after."

Janice leaned toward her, a secret she needed to share. "I would have decided the same thing, Brit, me and my scary ass."

"Sandy told you?"

"No, just that you were on bed rest. I figured the rest out for myself and I'm not blaming you."

A relaxation came into the room, settled along the edge of the sofa, the shiny flatness of the windows. "You heard about Sandy and Randall?" Janice asked.

"Sure did . . . we were right, or were we right?"

"As right as the white on rice," Janice decided as she held up her palm and Britney slapped her five.

Maurice had been pacing since he got home, torn between marching over to Janice's house and bringing his wife home or just staying put like his mother-in-law suggested. He had remained but he was about to wear a hole in the carpet when the lights of Britney's car swept the house. It was past dark.

He went to the door, flung it open, angry words ready on his tongue as he saw his wife ease her body out of the car. Except for that lumbering walk, she looked as fine as ever. In truth, she looked better, healthier, and more alive.

He bit his tongue as she took her time coming up the steps and into the house. Held it as she closed the door. She was heading for the comfort of the sofa when his voice came, full and hot with fire. "You trying to put *me* in the hospital?"

"Don't be crazy. Just went out for some fresh air."

"For six hours?"

"I got tired of the bed. Got tired of lying around all damn day. I wanted to get out. See my friends."

"Your friends? Your friends? They the ones that almost made you lose our baby."

Fear danced beneath her husband's anger. It became the part Britney claimed. Her face softened, her hand reached out, moved across the worry lines of her husband's face. "They didn't make me almost lose nothing, Mo. I did what friends supposed to do and it's done." She spread her arms. "I'm still here, baby, still here. You still here. Bereace. All of us, still alive and kicking. And this baby's gonna grow up big and loving like his daddy and you're going to teach him how to play basketball, take him to little league, have the chance to do all that stuff."

"Him?"

She reached out and took his hand. Lay it across the expanse of her stomach. "Can't you feel it? Can't you feel that it's a little you inside of me? That a boy's coming this time?"

In truth, Maurice couldn't. But he held his wife's words like magic stones in his pocket, pretty unexpected pebbles found along the way.

Britney woke up the next morning with swollen ankles and joints that ached, but that didn't stop her from getting up from the bed and going to take a shower. Her mother always arrived early and Britney could hear her in the kitchen. She just hoped her mother hadn't started breakfast just yet. This morning Britney wanted to do the cooking.

Lax and dependent were not characteristics Britney wanted to claim anymore. While she was not ready to run a marathon, she knew that she needed to slowly ease herself back into some kind of daily routine that went beyond sleeping and eating.

She was happy to find her mother down in the basement doing laundry and not a drop of hot anything waiting on the stove. It was early for Britney, she normally getting up around eleven, but this morning the clock was reading a little after nine. Perfect.

She took her time to lean over and search out the small pot. Ran water inside it and put it on the stove to boil. Her daughter Bereace came in, drawn by the sound of her mother's musings. Britney kissed her fingertips, told her daughter good morning.

She took two eggs from the refrigerator and two slices of bread out of the bag. Britney was laying out the butter when her mother came up the basement stairs.

"You're up early?"

"No more sleeping till noon for me, Mom."

"You want me to get that?" her mother asked, heading toward the stove.

"No, what I want is for you to sit right down there and keep me company while I make my own breakfast." She looked at her mother deeply. "That's what I really want."

Mrs. Weller looked upon her only child and understood. "Well, if you start to feel dizzy or faint or tired, you let me know, hear?"

"Yes, Mom, I'll let you know."

Sandy walked next to Randall, hands linked, the city rustling with late afternoon pedestrians and busy traffic. Before them stood the Arc de Triumph, beyond its stone structure, Washington Square Park.

"Man, those were the days," Randall said with awe.

"What were?"

"Washington Square . . . late seventies, it was the place to be."

"You hung out here?"

"Did I? I went to school right over there."

Sandy looked around. "Over where?"

Randall pointed to a set of buildings to his right. "Right there."

"NYU?"

"One and only."

"You went there?"

"Yep. Class of '79. Fifteen years ago."

"You graduated in '79?"

"One of the best years of my life."

"What was your major?"

He smiled. "Guess?"

"Architectural design," Sandy offered.

"I wish. No. I majored in what most people did when they weren't sure what they really wanted to be. I was a communications major."

"Really?"

"Yeah." He looked around him again. "Oh, the memories, the memories."

Sandy took a look at the sweet skillful man beside her. "Yeah, and I can just imagine what they were."

"If you only knew."

"Nope. Don't want to."

Randall spied a row of street artists. "How about a portrait?"

"Me and you together?"

"Sure, why not?"

"Well, who gets to keep it?"

He squeezed her hand. "We can take turns."

"What happens if we break up, who gets it then?"

He sought her eyes. "I'm not going anywhere, are you?"

"No," the word sweet on her tongue.

Janice knew she had become something of a curiosity with her neighbors. She knew that they still looked at her with leery eyes, pursed lips, like she had brought a terrible mark upon all of them. But life went on and she didn't have the luxury of hiding herself away. Understood the sooner she got back to the living, the better.

It was this reason she left her apartment, took the elevator down, the Saturday morning warm and sparkling sunshine bright. Her venture wouldn't be far, but it would be a major milestone. She felt a small comfort in the paisley-covered journal she totted in one hand.

The playground was around the corner from her building and about a hundred yards down, but as she spotted mothers parked on the benches, engaging one another and keeping a careful eye on their children, Janice felt as if it were a lifetime from her.

She steeled her nerves, determined to do what she had set out to do: sit out in the Saturday morning sunshine and give up emotions through paper and pen. The prolonged glances as she took a seat on an empty bench were no surprise. Janice understood why the conversation halted as parents took a study of her, making a quick determination of what she was doing there and why.

When she opened her journal and began writing a few lines, they decided she wasn't a threat to the half-dozen children who climbed the brightly colored apparatus with abandonment and squeals of joy. Their eyes left her and soon they were back into the flow of talking, their voices background to her thoughts.

Janice wrote a line, another, then another. Stopped and gazed up into the azure sky. She remembered how life used to be. But it wasn't like that now, and the thought sent her back to scribbling, her hand moving quickly to keep up with her thoughts.

On paper she wondered about Cliff and Rachel, about Sandy, Martha, and Britney, how often did she cross their mind. A tear came, plopping fat and swollen across the page. She closed her eyes and sighed, dabbed her eyes, and kept on writing.

*"It's really about choice,"* her therapist had told. *"Life is always about choice. You chose wisely or poorly, but it is always choice."* In truth she had chosen to dismantle the relationship between herself and Cliff. In truth she had chosen to go home with that married man. Now she had to make another choice: Accept what she had done and forgive herself for all that was wrong with it. Janice had to decide to hold fast to those lessons learned.

The cowbell over the doorway of the Pepper Pot jangled, causing Ruby to look up, seeing the same man she had seen for over a year coming into her establishment, but this afternoon his eyes were haunted, everything about him lost.

She had seen him come in quite a few times, sometimes alone, but as often as not, a pretty dark-skinned woman at his side. Ruby couldn't help but wonder where she was. If it were the reason for his dismalness.

There was no more goat, the last of it in her bowl of rice, growing cold as she got up from the stool, stood behind the counter, smiled politely, and asked what would he like.

"Ya got chicken roti?" he asked, kind of desperate, kind of hopeless as if he was certain he had just asked the impossible.

"Small, medium, or large?"

It took a moment for him to decide, to wage the depth of the emptiness of his belly. "Large an' a ginga beer."

"Salad?" she asked, turning to retrieve an aluminum container.

"Nah, just roti and da beer."

Ruby slipped into the back, came back with a large flat round bread that hung over the edge of the pan. She took the spoon, ladled up chunks of chicken, squares of potato, and laid in a thick helping of gravy.

She folded it up carefully, was slipping the white paper lid on top when his voice arrived. "No, me eat it here."

He ate like what he was, a man lost to personal demons, honey eyes glittery and faraway. It had been Ruby's intention of going back to her food, read the paper, but her gaze kept returning to him.

Back home in Jamaica they would call him a Coolie, his wavy hair, light skin, and light brown eyes a giveaway to European/Indian roots. She wondered which island he was from, though Trinidad seemed likely, where miscegenation had been in abundance.

"Trinidad?" she found herself saying.

His eyes found hers fast, kind of wild, and so uncertain. She realized he wasn't sure she had been speaking to him, so Ruby asked the question again.

"Me say are you frum Trinidad?"

He nodded twice and went back to his food.

"Live 'round 'ere?"

It took a second for him to realize that she was trying to engage him in conversation. Took a moment for him to accept the invitation to talk.

He picked up his napkin, cleaned his fingers, the width of his mouth, and shifted slightly in his chair so that he would get a better view of her.

Not as old as he had first suspected, it was the running of her business that had no doubt added years. Her hair was braided, big thick loppy braids falling from her crown like twists of licorice. Beneath the smock she wore a white cotton blouse, her wrist holding a fistful of gold bangle bracelets.

"East New York," he managed.

"I," Ruby said, nodding, calculating distance. "So 'ow you find dis place?" She was curious to know, her meal forgotten, the newspaper irrelevant.

"Just driving down da street one day. Me see da sign say HOME COOK-ING, da Jamaican flag in da corner, decided to try."

"Guess da cooking good den," Ruby said with a self-acclaimed smile.

He nodded. "Nice."

"Ruby," she said, the smile unwilling to leave her.

It took a second before he returned the greeting. "I, an I Wint."

Long after the last bit of roti gravy had been sopped up with an extra piece of flat bread and long after the ginger beer was gone, he remained.

Winston found himself requesting a chunk of black cake, taking coffee, reading through the *Island Gazette*, his eyes scanning the headline news from the over one-dozen islands spanning the Caribbean sea.

He had moved from the little table, took a seat at the counter, engaging Ruby in conversation as she served up the handful of customers that entered her shop.

Food had drawn him. A woman's comfort made him stay.

Group was a scary proposition.

It was one thing to express your darkness secrets to a therapist, but it was a whole different matter sharing it with a room full of strangers, but that's where Janice found herself on a Wednesday night, nursing a cup of herbal tea and feeling small.

She sat in the overstuffed chair listening to a forty-something-year-old ad exec talking about the anguish of no longer being the new kid on the block and how the world of sales was being taken over by the younger and smarter. "What was the point then?" she asked the gathering. "What was the point of putting a whole life on hold to achieve a status that I won't be able to keep?"

"The point is, life doesn't come with guarantees. That you have to take lemons and make lemonade," offered an older gray haired man whom Janice later learned was working through a deep guilt because his wife was going through Alzheimer's and he could no longer take care of her.

"Oh yeah, Martin? Where's your lemonade, huh? That why you come here every Wednesday like clockwork and weep all over the damn place because you've turned your lemons into lemonade?"

"Time, Gladys," Dr. McCarthy warned. His eyes looked around the group. "Anybody else?" Janice surprised herself when her hand shot up. A quick glance around the room told her hers was the only one. "We have a new member this evening and it appears that she is already braver than the rest of you. Her name is Janice Duprey. Let's all say hello."

"Hello, Janice."

It felt good hearing the chorus of voices welcoming her, letting her know that no, she wasn't alone.

Like a rowboat in a rough tide, Janice found herself being swept along as the group left the seventeenth floor of the doctor's office and crammed into the elevator. It was after eight in the evening and she had a long drive back from Manhattan to Queens. A bit hungry, Janice decided to stop in at the coffee shop across the street for a bite to eat.

She was waiting at the traffic light when Gladys came up to her. "Coffee, right? And maybe a burger on the side?"

Janice was about to ask her how did she know that when Gladys offered up an answer. "I'm in sales. Been in it most of my life. I peg people real easy."

"That or you're psychic," Janice said with a smile.

"Want some company?" Janice wasn't sure. Gladys was older, tough, and white. She had gray eyes that had the deadliness of a laser and obviously had no problem speaking her mind. "Group gets my hackles up, which is the point, but I promise I won't bite."

"Okay."

They took a booth by the window and ordered the same thing. Over their quick meal, they shared a little. "You were the type I've always hated," Gladys confessed. "You know, gorgeous, maybe not too bright, but men fall at your feet."

Janice laughed nervously. "I never had men falling at my feet."

"Oh, I think you did. Problem was they weren't the type you wanted. I was there tonight, remember. Know all about Cliff, what you did to both yourself and him."

"It wasn't about Cliff."

"Honey, it never is. It's always about you. Believe me, I know. Yeah, I sit up there and bitch about the women half my age running me out of town, but truth is that's only if I let them." Janice looked at her puzzled. "Why do I act like I don't know it's all on me? Because sometimes I don't believe I have the power to determine who I am, and coming to group allows me a chance to feel sorry for myself, even if it's detrimental. Some people drink, I come to group. It can be quite habit-forming."

"How long have you been coming?"

"What? Ten years now?"

Janice almost choked on her burger. "Ten?"

Gladys nodded. "Yeah, ten. Is it helping much? No. But I'm hooked. I've seen a lot of faces come and go, but I'm not the only old timer there. Brad's one and so is Sylvian."

"But isn't group supposed to help you?"

Gladys leaned in close. "Between you and me, honey? Heaven helps those who help themselves. If you got things half figured out, you're already farther ahead than most of us."

Janice took the thought and kept it.

They finished up their meal and split the check. Headed out of the restaurant. Hugged goodbye. Janice never saw Gladys again. Janice never returned to group. But Gladys remained a part of her. Her words, a keepsake.

Janice went home, got on the computer, and typed out a letter. She printed up three envelopes and took them to the mailbox the next day. Two days later she received three phone calls. Planned a special meal for Saturday, the day her friends would come together once again.

# Chapter 24

Martha hunched over her file from work, reading glasses on the tip of her nose, onyx eyes peering through the lenses to the stack of papers inside.

It had been a tough case, tougher than most and she had been working on it so hard and so long it felt like she was back in law school. But tough cases were just that and every now and then she got them. Martha knew she had to do what she always did—give it all she had then cut it loose.

Drained, she closed the file, standing for the first time in an hour. She yawned, scratched, went to the kitchen for a glass of water. Found Calvin inside straightening up, sparkling clean dishes lining the rack.

It was a simple moment for them, but swollen with completeness. They had battled for such tranquillity and gradually had won the war.

She poured herself some Evian, drank it leaning against the counter. Yawned again and handed the glass to Calvin. Headed for the bedroom.

It had become her drink of choice these days, the high pricey bottles stacked in the refrigerator, little miniatures in her purse. Martha kept a six-pack at the job, downing it when the urge hit.

Within her still lay the need for alcohol, for the different tingly rush down her throat. Bottled water helped ease the desire, AA and Calvin her backup.

Calvin had given up his tiny basement apartment for Martha's expansive one-bedroom on the twelfth floor in the middle of Jamaica Estates. It was a first step to the ultimate—marriage—but without the formality, and it suited her just fine.

Martha undressed, slipped on her nightgown. Wrapped the black silk scarf around her head. Tomorrow was Friday, Saturday would arrive fast and sweet. She was looking forward to gathering, the presence of old friends gone too long.

Maurice's loves were basic: He loved his wife, he loved his child, and he loved baseball. The New York Mets, having come off a spectacular previous season, were hot again. Getting tickets to home games was even hotter. But Maurice knew somebody who knew somebody and after a few phone calls and relinquishing two Benjamin Franklins, he had secured two seats for Saturday's game.

Calvin was his boy but preferred more literary pursuits, so Maurice had asked his brother to come along with him. He and Melvin weren't close, but they got along great when it came to the New York Mets, and his Saturday was well planned.

Until Britney told him different.

"You just have to go another time."

He took in his wife, standing there in a size double X T-shirt that hovered on her large belly and covered the just as big stretch shorts beneath. She had grown quite big over the last month, looking more like a beached whale than his wife, and every now and then the sight of her shocked him.

But there was more to her than the baby and the extra extra weight she was toting. More to her than the hair thick and full hanging off the end of a black scrungy. There was more to her than the ashy knees and ashy feet sprinkled white from her morning ritual of powdering the parts of her that stuck together in the summer heat.

There was a fire in her eyes, a steady uprising in her chest. She had become a warrior when he wasn't looking. It seemed that one day she was a wife easy to handle and the next she was not only running the roost but ruling it; orders popping out of her mouth like gum drops in the tangy flavors he did not eat.

It had started simple enough. "Honey, don't forget to take out the

garbage" shifting slowly into "Get them funky ass boots off my carpet." Maurice put it off to hormones and the responsibility of bearing
another life. Had bit his tongue so often he was certain it would be
permanently dented.

But this request was different and inconceivable. Long before
there had been a Britney in his life, there had been his Mets. First love
was first love.

"What other time?" he snapped back. "Do you know what I went
through just to get these tickets?"

"You don't really think I care, do you? Look, I've been cooped up
here like a hen in a chicken house. Haven't been anywhere to do anything in months."

"Maybe your mother can watch her."

"How? She's at Virginia Beach this weekend, remember?" Britney's
mother was the only person Britney trusted to watch her child, outside of Maurice. "Now I'm going to be with my friends and Bereace is
going to be with you. You going to that game, then be prepared to
take your child too."

Maurice had a comeback and it rushed up his throat hot and dry.
But Britney had already turned, and was waddling away, leaving only
the "B" word to filter into his mind for the first time ever.

They had stepped into the zone.

Maurice's own parents had ventured there and he was wise enough
to know he and Britney would not escape that fate. They were moving
into the second phase of marriage, where consideration went out the
window and you said exactly how you felt. The time had arrived when
doubting the viability of the marriage came often and some days you
became certain it might not last.

It was a testy, trying time that some couples never escaped from.
Years from now it would be just a memory, but in the moment it
loomed like a lifetime.

His parents had survived it, as had his grandparents. In the midst
of troubled waters, you always kept your eyes on the prize. It was his
grandfather's favorite saying, passed on to Maurice's daddy and then
to Maurice. Maurice had never fully understood the notion until he
found himself reaching out for that comfort.

He took a glance at his daughter, a month shy of being one-year-
old. Considered diaper bags, tiny jars of baby food, and his love for
his Mets. Decided there was always a first time for everything.

\* \* \*

Janice looked around her living room, her three friends gathered, the various changes in their lives about them like shawls of diverse textures and hues.

The peach of Martha's cap-sleeved cotton top suggested life had grown soft, comfortable; offering a hint of innocent wonder. The unassuming lines of Sandy's yellow sun dress seemed to speak of new parts of her gaining a simple freedom.

Tight and stretched to the limit, Britney's black oversize T-shirt and binding white stretch shorts edified restrictions; a temporary bondage of giving to get, homage to the requiem of new life on its way.

Therapy had widened Janice's horizon, had laid open her view on the world. What she had gone through had never been discussed, everyone attempting to sweep the dark chapter under the rug. But it was too important to forget, too pertinent not to go unexplored.

Her friends had been dancing lightly around the latest episode of her life and she needed them to join her in the circle of recovery, something that could not be done until she shared what it was for her.

"I need to tell you about it," she said, careful, soft. "Need to tell you what I went through."

"It's over. You're better. All that matters," Sandy said.

"But it's not," Janice resisted. "I went where nobody wants to go and it makes all of you uncomfortable and closed off from me. I need to speak about what it was like, so you can understand it fully. You all are here, but you're not here, not the way you used to be and I want you back in my life. I can't get you there unless I talk about it and you are willing to listen."

Britney shifted in her seat. Martha studied the light coming in the window. Sandy looked down into her Sprite. They didn't want to hear it. Didn't want to visit the scary place Janice had gone to. Her friends just wanted to make it a bad nightmare she'd awakened from; pretended and far far away.

But Janice could not give them that. Could not keep quiet or ignore its importance. She took a breath and opened her mouth, spoke, her words moving against the communal tide.

"Ever lay in bed at night with some problem that you just can't fix and all you can do is lay there, trying to find a solution but the more you try, the more hopeless and tense you feel? And your mind just goes on and on, spinning its wheels, and you feel like you're going to explode because there doesn't seem to be an answer, just the problem getting bigger and bigger?" A wave of nodding heads moved through the room. "Well, I exploded."

The magnitude of Janice's words hit them all—direct and with hot impact, each tasting the terror of a moment they had feared but gratefully never experienced.

"It was like my mind was trying to swallow me whole. Like I was being consumed by my thoughts and there was nothing or no one to latch on to. I was being eaten alive by my own brain and couldn't stop it . . . a living and breathing nightmare that I could not wake up from." Janice grew silent, the memory tingling her spine, rushing her with dread.

"All I could do was scream. Scream out to someone to help me, save me. Bring me back. It was never about my underwear." She wiped a tear from her eyes. "But in that moment my whole life seemed gone because of it and all I knew was if I could get them back I would be okay. But I knew I couldn't go and get them back and I wasn't okay. That I was locked up in my mind and could not get out."

Martha's voice came low, near whispery. ". . . damn."

"Everyone around me and nobody could help me. And all I could do was scream. Then they put that strait jacket on me and I couldn't move my arms or nothing and I wanted to die, but my heart kept on beating and my mind kept on consuming and all I had was my voice and my screams until my vocal cords abandoned me and I was riding in that ambulance, all strapped up and opening my mouth but nothing was coming out . . . next thing I knew I was coming to in a hospital strapped down and I didn't have any more will to scream. I could only lay there and wait for someone to come and find me."

"It was horrible, Janice," Sandy admitted. "One of the most horrible things I ever saw."

"Yes, it was. But as horrible as it was, as alone and scared and half crazed as I was, I know now that I needed it. I needed to scream it all away. I needed to be locked deep inside myself to free myself and that's what I've done." A fragile smile dusted her lips. "I feel better than I've ever been in my whole life, except everyone stayed away from me. And I tried to respect everyone's wishes, tried to say it was your right. But you all are my friends and I love you, need you, so that's why I wrote the letter, why I asked you to come. I knew you were afraid, that you didn't know who I was anymore and I needed to tell you what it was like for me."

"I had no idea," Martha declared. Sandy and Britney nodded. "I mean I had some idea, but I didn't know it was like that. I've been so busy with my meetings and work and Calvin . . ."

"Don't apologize for your life, Martha. That's not what I need. What I need is for you to understand that I am different, I have changed, but fundamentally I still need you in my life. Fundamentally I still want to consider you a friend. I don't want weeks and months to go by when I don't see you all and nobody calls me."

"Life has changed for all of us," Sandy said.

"Because that's what life does," Janice answered back. "But some things are worth saving, worth holding on to no matter how busy we get and I think our friendship is one of them."

Britney nodded her head. "You're right."

"I'd been dancing on that edge forever and I'm not sorry I took that plunge. Will it happen again? I hope not. Can I say it won't? No, I can't. It's almost like being born all over again. I have to discover who the new me is, but I want all of you there for my journey. I need your support."

That Janice had to ask caught each of the women individually by the throat, lumps forming that they swallowed back. It hurt to accept that such a thing had to be asked, spoken out loud. They had been friends forever.

"Can you give that to me? Can I depend on all of you to be there, even if it's just a phone call once a week to say 'hey'?"

Martha wiped a tear from her eye. "It shouldn't even be a question, Janice. Not with us, but yeah, I'm there for you."

"Me too," Sandy offered, eyes shiny.

Britney nodded. "Right here with you."

Janice let go a breath that she wasn't even aware she had been holding until it left her. A bittersweet smile flitted in her eyes. "You have no idea how much that means to me." But her friends did.

Martha stood. Opened her arms to Janice. Brought her to her close and tight, holding her until Sandy moved in. Sandy's arms moved around Janice as familiar as a homecoming, her tears wetting Janice's shoulder, her heart opened like a flower reborn.

Britney came last, her large belly making the connection awkward but even with the bulk between them, Janice could feel both her love and her concern. Janice broke away, dabbed her eyes, looked out among her friends. Smiled. "Anybody hungry?"

"Aren't we always?" Martha piped.

Janice went to her dining room table. Lit the tapers.

"Candles?" Martha asked, noticing for the first time the outlay of fine china, crystal glasses, gleaming silverware. Linen napkins

"Figured this time we'd have a real sit-down meal."

"What's on the menu?"

"We are starting with a grilled shrimp with a mango chutney sauce, then it's on to angel hair pasta with romano and fresh basil followed by my homemade raspberry sorbet."

"Homemade?"

Janice laughed. "Being home so much I've been heavily into my cooking shows." She went to the kitchen taking time to lay out each plate like a masterpiece. Her heart doubled as her friends oohed and ahhed over her delectable meal. Felt all the love she never thought was due her as request for seconds and the recipe came her way.

She knew she was well on her way to her better day as the four women crowded up in her kitchen, each helping with the cleanup, filling the tiny room with joy and loud talk.

They went back to her living room, sparkling cider in Martha and Britney's wineglass, Chardonnay in the others.

"I did love Cliff, y'know," Janice began. "Not the right way or the best way, but I did. And sometimes I find myself sitting on the couch waiting for the sound of the key in the door and it never comes. He will never walk through that door again and I have to accept that."

"I think you have," Sandy said softly.

"It's not easy, but you're right, I have."

"You know I was reading an article that says we have to clean out the clutter in our lives to let the good things in." Britney offered. "And I think that's what you're doing now."

"I hope so."

"That mind can be a cruel thing when it wants to," Sandy said. "Believe me I know. It had me holding on to Winston, a man I never loved, and saying no to Randall, the man I could."

"So you and Randall are going good?" Janice wanted to know.

"Now that I got my head on straight, yeah. In so many ways Winston was a godsend. And in some ways I do love him, but it's not the type of love that's true love."

"And Randall is?"

"Yeah, I think so."

Britney entered the conversation. "Well, Maurice is getting on my last nerve."

"Because you married to him, that's all. The honeymoon is long gone," Martha offered.

"Who are you telling? Take this time with Calvin and just enjoy it and him. You too, Sandy. 'Cause when that time is over, it's over. I can't remember that last time me and Maurice shared a joke."

"I hear children always change things."

Britney rubbed her belly. "They sure do. Remember when Maurice talked about having a whole tribe of children? Well, I do believe that notion has flown out the window. I've already made up my mind that this one is going to be the last one. I'm getting my tubes tied."

"Maurice know?"

"He will."

"Think he'll like it much?"

"What choice does he have? This is my body. I dictate it, he don't."

Martha laughed. "Well, listen to Miss Wicket Picket. Whatever happened to the mild meek Britney we used to know?"

"Gone," Britney said with intensity and a bit of flourish. "Mama San is large and in charge now. Like today. Maurice talking about he has a baseball game to go to and he can't watch Bereace. Well, didn't I tell him I was coming here and he could either go to the game with his child or stay home?"

Sandy laughed. "No, you didn't."

"Yes, I did."

"What he say?"

"I don't know. I didn't stay long enough to find out. He a parent just like I'm a parent. I have to have my time too." She took a breath. "If a man can make a baby, then a man can help take care of that child. Nobody gets a free ride."

"So you really going back to work after the baby comes?"

"Maybe part-time. I kind of like being home, but times are tight now, and when this little one comes, it will only get tighter. Maybe I'll do twenty hours a week or something." Britney shook her head. "One of the scariest moments in my life was when we had no money and checks was bouncing all over the place. I don't want to be in that position anymore."

Sandy nodded. "I hear that."

"I have some news myself," Martha said, a smile on her face.

"What?"

"Calvin has moved in."

"Really?"

"Sure has. We're not there yet, but we are on our way."

"Good for you, Martha."

"Yeah, good for me." She looked around. Smiled. Raised her glass. "A toast," she began. The other women raised their glasses high. "A toast to who we are"—they clinked them together—"and who we are yet to become."

"Here, here," Janice intoned, taking a long sip.

Company gone, apartment empty, and the hour moving to ten at night, Janice tied up the overflowing garbage can, slipped her key into her pocket, and headed toward the incinerator. Her joy was still with her, echos of her friends' voices and laughter still filtering through her heart. A peace she had been searching for had come to be.

She opened the heavy black door, pulled down the black handle, and forced the bag of garbage inside. Janice listened to the thirteen-story drop of her trash before she released the handle. Turned and left the incinerator room.

The elevator door opened. The sound of a leather sole hitting the hard shiny floor drew her head. The eyes looking back at her kept it hostage, barely two seconds passing before she blinked and looked away.

She headed for her door, slipped inside, the image of those eyes remaining, in no hurry to go away.

*Tap. Tap.*

Paced raps echoed against her door. She moved her eye to the peephole, saw the stranger fish-bowl view back at her. *Tap. Tap. Tap.* More raps requested her attention as she pulled back, lifted her hand to the knob.

She didn't know what he wanted but felt brave enough to find out. With a deep breath, she opened her door and fixed her face into something between indignation and fearlessness. "Yes?"

"I'm looking for Howard."

He was confused. It showed in the pupils of brown circled by white. He was also apologetic, somehow sensing that he was on the wrong floor, at the wrong door, even the wrong building.

"Howard?"

His head shook, eyes leaving her, taking full responsibility for his error. "This place always confuses me. Is this section B?"

It was a common enough mistake, the hollowed halls of Rochdale Village divvied up into sections, a wrong turn sending visitors to the wrong sections; he, just a victim to that quandary.

"No, it's A. B's on the other side. You took the wrong elevator."

"I'm sorry."

Yes, he was. She could feel it. Could sense the fragmented pieces of being caught wrong one time too many in life; of being on the wrong side often enough to tip the scales against him. Through his smile she could see the sadness lingering.

"Simple enough mistake," she answered, knowing he was sensing her too.

"Too bad," he offered, his smile widening.

"Too bad what?"

"Too bad Howard doesn't live here."

"Yeah." All she could offer.

He lifted his hand. "I'm Dennis."

She took the hand offered. "Janice." Felt the gentleness there as they shook, their hands slide to slow from each other.

"Warm hand," he offered.

"Cold heart," she said back.

He laughed, the moment shifting into second gear. "You? No way."

She laughed too, understanding that she was having a conversation with a stranger who had stumbled her way. "You're right."

"Do you know Howard? Howard Willis?"

Janice shook her head no.

He looked from her, some hope leaving him. "Yeah, probably not." He looked back up, his face lit like neon, bright and wondrous. "Married?"

"Close, but no cigar."

"Engaged then."

"Wrong again."

One brow raised. It was shiny and slick as seal skin. Beautiful. "Can't be single."

"Why can't I be?"

His voice came, filled with an awe Janice allowed herself to taste, take hold of. "You are the most beautiful woman I've seen in a while."

"Don't get out much, huh."

He laughed, shook his head. Scrunched his shoulders. Considered her. "Well, I guess I better go track down Howard."

"Probably waiting."

"Single, huh."

"Yes. And you?"

"No ring, no wife, no kids, nobody."

"How come?" Janice asked.

"Guess I was waiting."

"For?"

"To get on the wrong elevator."

It could have been a line but Janice knew it wasn't. She understood that the same finger of fate that had taken so much away from her was offering up a new bounty. That in closing one door, God was opening up another.

"Guess so."

"Can I give you my number?"

Janice hesitated, but only for a second. "Sure." Went off and got a pen and paper. He wrote it down for her, his handwriting neat, flowing. Like him, Janice realized, gentle and giving.

"You will call, won't you?"

"I wouldn't take your number if I wasn't."

"Well, I better head over to Howard's."

"Tell him I said hey." Simple words saying so much.

Britney hadn't been certain what she would see when she opened her front door. She wasn't certain if her husband would be standing there angry and outdone, or if he would be off and gone.

The last thing she expected was her husband fast asleep on the couch, his New York Mets cap on his head and her daughter just as fast asleep against his chest, a baseball banner tight in her little fist.

At his feet lay the baby bag, a baseball program slid into the outside

pocket. A big gulp with the orange and blue Mets insignia on the coffee table confirmed what she'd never expected. He had taken
Bereace to the baseball game.

Britney herself had attended a few games with Maurice. She recalled the long winded walk from the parking lot to the stadium, the
crush of people entering the tall structure of orange and blue. Britney remembered the uneasy downward slope of stairs to get to the
seats. The way it felt if you leaned too far forward that you would go
tumbling and could not fathom Maurice taking their eleven-month-
old there.

Eleven months old.

Soon Bereace would be one, gone from the baby stage and fast on
her way to toddlerhood. Once upon a time Britney had longed for
such a milestone, but the realization that it was coming so swift and
fast put an ache in her heart.

She found herself missing the days when Bereace was just a bundle
to be held and kissed. Missed the days when Bereace being mobile
meant a cradling in Britney's arms. Those days would never return
but would send her daughter toward more freedom until diaper
changes and newborn smells were just some vague memory.

That emotion sent her across the room. Made her reach down and
take up her child. It urged her nose to the silky curled lightly sweaty
scalp where Britney inhaled, and inhaled again. She kissed the button
nose, moved her cheek against the one still baby soft. She held her
against the mound of her belly, the fullness of her breast, tears filling
her eyes.

This is what Maurice came awake to, the sight of his very pregnant
wife cradling her child and shedding tears. He sat up from the sofa,
his face full of concern. "Brit?" all he could ask.

She shook her head, chockful of emotion and overcome with a love
so deep it could not be named or spoken.

"Everything okay?" Maurice asked, rising slowly, wondering what
new calamity had befallen his wife.

"Yes," she whispered. "Oh God, yes. Everything is just wonderful
and perfect."

"So why are you crying? Holding Bereace like that?"

"Because," the only answer she could find.

An intuitiveness Maurice had never known claimed him, the blanks being filled like Legos clicking into place. *Because she loves our daughter, because she's happy. Because we are going to be okay.*

"We didn't stay the whole game. Bereace got fussy. Guess baseball's not her thing. How was the party?"

Britney swallowed the lump in her throat. "Party was good and thank you."

"Thank me?"

"Yeah, you. Thank you for doing what you don't always want to do. For putting up with my demands and my mouth. Thank you for coming into my life and loving me like nobody ever has and no one else ever will. Thank you for making my life complete."

She had never spoken those words, and moments came when Maurice could feel them inside her, but there was no way Britney could not speak them. No way she could hold on to her gratitude. See all that she had and appreciate it all.

Wet eyes found his. "You've done so much for me, Mo, and I don't even think I ever told you so much as thank you."

"Ah, baby, you know I don't mind."

"That's not the point. I know this pregnancy hasn't been easy and I haven't been easy either, but I don't ever want you to doubt how much I love you and need you. I don't want you to think I'm taking you for granted."

"Never thought that." In truth he had. But Maurice was wise enough to know that you never told your wife everything and some things were best left unsaid.

"You eat?" she asked, easing her now-awake child onto the floor.

"Not since early."

"Got some leftovers. I can heat you up some."

"No, you come take a rest. I got it."

"You sure?"

"As sure as my name is Maurice."

"Well, I'll come on in the kitchen and keep you company, how's that?"

"That'll be just fine." He leaned over, kissed her forehead, the startled lids of her eyes. He kissed her nose, lingered over her mouth. Took up her hand, kissed that too. "You know how much I love you, girl?"

"As much as any man could ever love a woman," she relinquished, the words surrounding her like sunshine.

\* \* \*

"Straight Sandy, straight," Randall was saying a week later.

She lifted her safety goggles, her backyard warm and moist with the heat of summer. "I am." She never thought much about building until Randall introduced her to it. Now she was looking forward to making bookshelves and storage chests. She had a whole list of do-together projects.

"So why is the nail bent and those glasses are ridiculous."

"The nail is bent because it's defective, and even I know when you working with tools, you need to protect your eyes."

"To hammer a nail?"

"Right now I'm hammering. I'm going to be on the saw in a minute."

Randall looked at the saw, looked back at Sandy. "We'll see."

They were building the gazebo in her backyard, he teaching her basics about building and she an overzealous student. Scores of two by fours were laid to the side. The cement foundation had been poured and cured and was ready for its wooden dwelling. If Randall had been working by himself, he would have been finished by now. But with Sandy as his assistant, it would take another weekend.

"You said I could work the circular saw. I watch Bob Vila. I know how it's done."

His brow raised. "Oh yeah? Just because I watch a heart operation on The Learning Channel don't mean I ready to do surgery."

"Come on, Randall, you promised."

Randall considered her handiwork thus far. Made a safe bet. "Tell you what, get the next four nails in straight and you get to work the saw table." But even as he said it, he knew she wouldn't be able to. Her strokes were not strong and direct enough and she was too scared of hitting a finger to anchor the nail right.

It was sweet being outdoors with her, he showing off his abilities, she, her lack of them. But Sandy had enthusiasm, *about everything,* from working on the gazebo to spending every free moment with him.

He had gone with her when she went for the six-month checkup, taking the test as well. It was their way of showing their commitment to one another, their negative results drawing them close.

She had told him that it would be years before she knew for sure. A total of ten, she still had nine more to go. He told her that he would be with her all the way for the milestone and having babies past forty was no longer out of reach.

"For the long haul?" she'd asked then, her eyes wide and uncertain.

"That and a day," he had told her. "I let you get away once. Not doing that again."

Now as he watched her work the hammer against the nail, Randall found himself glad that he wasn't a serious betting man. He could not believe his eyes as the nail went in straight and smooth, followed by a second, a third, and then the final fourth.

"See, I told you I could do it," her smile bright and ready, eager to get to the circular saw.

As he readied the machine, taking time to mark the lumber, Sandy watched him. Gazed up into the God-given day and inhaled. Life had gotten offtrack with heartbreaking consequences, but she had survived the journey and was looking forward to new vistas.

Adrian still entered her mind and sometimes the loss felt overwhelming. He had been a love that would never come again, but she thanked God that she had someone in her life who was willing to make the attempt.

"Come on," Randall called, watching her make her way. Hands itchy, she reached for the handle on the blade, but he promptly swatted her away. "First things first," he said, easing the safety glasses from her forehead and adjusted the fit over her eyes. "Okay. Now. Check the toggle and make sure it's in the off position."

She did not ask, but it was all in her eyes. She didn't know what a toggle was.

"The on and off button in layman terms."

Layman. Sandy realized in many ways she was. What had been her life no longer was, a new one had come in its place. Like a newborn, she was off in a direction she had never treaded before, wide-eyed, curious, and eager to get there.

# SOME SUNDAY

## Margaret Johnson-Hodge

## ABOUT THIS GUIDE

The suggested questions are intended to enhance your
group's reading of Margaret Johnson-Hodge's SOME SUNDAY.
We hope you have enjoyed this story of finding inner strength and
the importance of having outside support from family and friends.

It is our hope that SOME SUNDAY will bring the issue of AIDS in the
African-American community to the forefront of discussions as we
continue on our quest to find a cure for the disease that claims the
lives of thousands within our community every year.

# DISCUSSION QUESTIONS

1. Sandy initially withdrew from the world after her husband Adrian's death. Do you think it benefited her or just added to her pain?

2. Some of Sandy's friends and family felt it was morally wrong for her to date Winston. Do you agree? Do you disagree? Why?

3. Did Randall have a real reason to pull away from Sandy when he found out about what Adrian died of?

4. If you could have chosen for Sandy, which man would it have been—Winston or Randall? Why?

5. Do you think Sandy was justified in saying to Britney, "Whoever said you could think?" when Britney arranged to have Sandy and Randall come to her home at the same time?

6. Do you think Cliff should have tried to make it work between himself and Janice?

7. What do you think happened between Winston and the restaurant owner Ruby?

8. Do you think Janice found happiness? If so, why?

9. What do you think became of Sandy and Randall?

10. Almost ten years have passed since the story's end and Sandy has just taken an AIDS test. Do you think the results came back positive or negative? Why?